Renfield Blues

A Grunt's First Grimoire

Jay Peterson

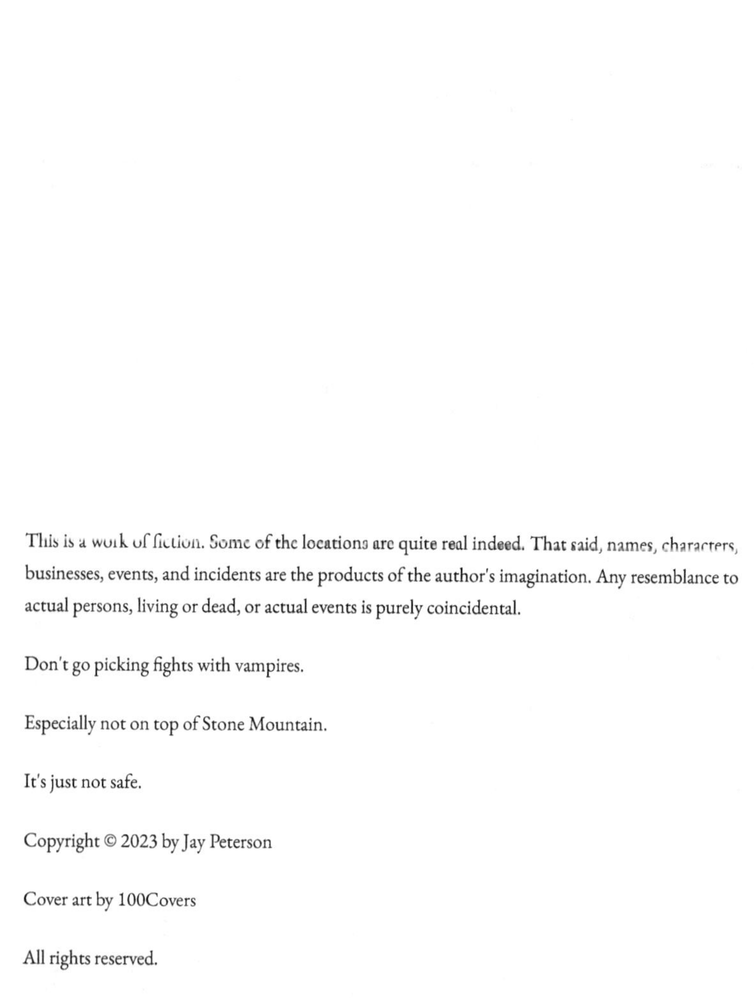

This is a work of fiction. Some of the locations are quite real indeed. That said, names, characters, businesses, events, and incidents are the products of the author's imagination. Any resemblance to actual persons, living or dead, or actual events is purely coincidental.

Don't go picking fights with vampires.

Especially not on top of Stone Mountain.

It's just not safe.

Copyright © 2023 by Jay Peterson

Cover art by 100Covers

All rights reserved.

No portion of this book may be reproduced in any form without written permission from the publisher or author, except as permitted by U.S. copyright law.

For Abby

Nobody makes one of these things alone.

I want to acknowledge my various alpha and beta readers,

who did everything from laugh at a snippet to checking out everything I had and wanting more.

Especially those who had the thankless job of telling me honestly where I wasn't measuring up.

I want to thank Sydney at True Edge Art,

for going through a learning experience with me.

I especially want to thank everyone I auditioned for from 2019-2022 who didn't cast me

for one reason or another.

The fact that I had time to write this at all is thanks to you.

Prologue

"Guideline Nine: Question everything you read.
Including, but not limited to, these guidelines."

The sooner you admit that you believe in magic, the sooner this is all going to make much more sense. I mean, it's not technically a requirement or anything. This book may be several chapters deep in the nuances of how the Otherworld works, but it's not going to burst into flames or anything just because it's being read by a nonbeliever. Of course, now that I think about it, putting a curse on distributors of bootleg copies may or may not be a legit practice these days, you never know.

But let's be honest with each other, shall we? You believe. You believe in just a little bit of magic, even if you won't admit it to anyone. Even if you won't admit it to yourself. Doesn't matter where you live, who you are, or what you do. I don't care how much of a skeptic you think you are. When push comes to shove and the sun has gone down? There are places you simply do not go. There are things you simply do not do. And there are things you simply accept, don't try to explain, and try not to point out too directly. These are the places where this world meets the Otherworld.

Which is where mages like myself come in. Most ordinary people can sense just enough magic to know what not to do. But ever since puberty hit them, mages have known for certain that magic is not only real, not only all around us, but can be manipulated by those who know the how and why. We've been learning those hows and whys ever since.

For the record, the Otherworld slang term for ordinary, not-explicitly-informed human being is "stander." As in "innocent bystander." Neither clever nor flattering, but that's the typical Otherworld way of being honest with you.

So how do you know when you have met a mage? Well, there's not a whole lot of hard and fast rules there. Even the traditional loose clothes and pointy hats are regional and seasonal affectations. We come from all around the world, go through all walks of life. Some of us may look a little odd, dress a little weird, and behave a little deviant. But these days, not so much of any of the above that you'd notice outside of a rather insular and homogeneous community. That said, there's two big clues that make us stick out of the crowd.

The first clue is the Otherworld Oath. It deserves the capitalization, trust me.

"Word of thy Oath make real, lest the Otherworld redeem thy failure."

This one isn't exclusive to mages, but it is a mark of someone who belongs in the Otherworld. There are quite a few flavors of supernatural and sentient people out there besides mages. A lot of them don't like each other much. And when I say that, I mean they leave behind bloodstains and bones instead of passive-aggressive little notes about your parking spot or your garbage cans. Which got just a tad embarrassing what with humanity going off and developing agriculture, metallurgy, and tax bases while the rest of us were off in the wilderness kicking each other in the head. So at one point, the world and the Otherworld got all the Otherworld folks together, sat them down, and pointed out they were going to need something to keep the bloodshed from interfering with business.

What the worlds came up with was the Otherworld Oaths. The coin of the Otherworld realms is the fulfilled word. Part medium of exchange, part assurance of good behavior. Ever since then, if you had even a bit of magic in you, an Oath was something you fulfilled or the whole Otherworld came down on your head. You back out, and life itself becomes the repo man until you pay up. Bad things happen to Oathbreakers.

And don't think empty pockets were going to get you a free ride either. Otherworld Oaths aren't sworn on balance sheets. They're sworn on any valued medium. A vampire may swear by their blood. A werewolf may swear by their claws. A mage might swear by their magic itself. In times past, even humans who didn't know of the Oaths might find themselves bound by them. By their head, by their heart, by their life.

So if you find someone willing to kill or die rather than break a promise they made? There's something magical about them. They might not be a mage themselves, but they're definitely walking in the same circles.

The second clue is the Law of the Magi. Also deserves the capitalization. It's a short law, but it's noticeable.

"We guide. We guard. We never rule."

Say you got someone in town who took the shortcut everyone knows you're not supposed to take, and they turn up missing? Everyone knows it was one of those places you simply do not go, and they went there, and now they're gone. No matter what the police or search parties or anyone else tries, they can't find hide nor hair of them. None of the traditional authorities can or will help.

But then you get to thinking. There's almost always one person in town who's, well, just kind of odd. Maybe they got some weird habits, maybe they give you the creeps, maybe there's just something off about them you can't quite put your finger on. But when an awful day like the one I just described comes? Somehow, someway, deep down, the same sense that told you never to take that shortcut tells you plain and indescribably simply that this one person can find the missing if anyone can. More often than not, they can, and they do.

Chances are, that's the mage.

That's the one side of the coin. Because we do know how to get around in the Otherworld, we got an obligation to help humanity when it suffers as a result of the Otherworld. Sometimes that means going off to find the missing kid. Sometimes that means going off to deal with what's waiting in the dark. Because we're the part of humanity that can.

Don't make the mistake of thinking we're all kindly or heroic about it. A lot of us are jerks, to be honest. Just because we'll do our best to not let you get eaten by a werewolf doesn't mean we won't spend an hour ranting about your stupidity of going into its territory on a full moon. We use what gets the job done, whether that's hot tea and kind words or fire and blood. Or, in my case, a multitool and duct tape.

So we guide, and so we guard. But you will never find a mage on a throne. This has been a hard and fast law throughout all history. Gaining power in the Otherworld means giving up our chance at ruling power in this world. That's the other side of the coin. You ever hear of a wizard king or a witch queen or a shaman chief? Doesn't happen anywhere. Not anymore. The one time it did happen, the nasty results spread worldwide. The Djinn fled to their own realm far off in the Otherworld, the Demons went deeper into the Underworld than they started in, and the rest of us have been hurting ever since. Thank you, Solomon, you arrogant jackass.

You could call me a wizard and be right, but it rubs me the wrong way. Yeah, I'm starting to see a gray hair or two in the beard, but I'm not even forty. That's why I prefer the term mage myself. I'm a Marine Corps veteran. Infantry, to be specific. Which means I'm predisposed to the monosyllabic when I can get it. Being a somewhat gender neutral term in English helps too. On top of that, there's an entire sub-branch of etiquette over who calls who a wizard, witch, conjurer, enchanter, sorcerer, or what have you. Mage fits my personal description and keeps things simple and less than immediately threatening. The weird looks from people who like obscure Christmas stories and play way too many video games are small prices to pay.

The Christmas magi were pretty useless, by the way. Great gifts for a deity, not so much for a traveling carpenter's family. Unless the gold bankrolled the trip to Egypt and everything else was used for the mother of all spa days for Mary, who probably needed it at that point. But a lot of the translations just make it more weird. If they were kings (which they weren't, see the law above), a little diplomatic pressure to ease off the targeted genocide would've been nice. If nothing else, a sit-down talk with some of the more judgy relatives who you know were giving Mary side eye from the moment she turned up pregnant would've been helpful. But no. They show up, drop the loot like a video game miniboss, then haul ass back to parts unknown. This is what you get when you let tea swilling protestants make a special edition re-release of your canonical texts.

But I digress. Get used to it.

Once a mage becomes established to a particular degree, they're encouraged to write a grimoire. A grimoire being a compendium of their magical knowledge and their contribution to the next generation to make their way in the Otherworld. Most don't need the encouragement. Some say it's because written language is one of the earliest known forms of magic to exist. Some say it's to pass on knowledge to younger generations. Personally, I think it's because getting this good comes with a streak of arrogance a mile wide. If you thought guys with a ruler in one hand and their zipper in the other were bad, you haven't hung around mages who lived long enough to get salty about it. While I'm at it, I'd also rather see any younger mages coming across this to avoid repeating my screwups. Making their own screwups is a much more effective use of their time.

Am I established enough of a mage to justify writing one of these things? Hell if I know. It's not like there's a gold standard. I've got some pretty good spots on my resume. I invented the Spartan Shotgun before I graduated high school, and made some refinements to the Strap Ball less than a year later. I survived the Blue River Massacre. I'm considered one of the brighter alchemists of my generation, and only slightly less notorious as a conductor. I've been around long enough to have learned some things the hard way, and here I am, passing the savings on to you.

That said, I don't like talking myself up even when I got an open forum to do it. There's not a lot of double-blind testing in the Otherworld, but there's a lot of quiet and powerful people out there waiting for some smartass to let their mouth write a bad check from the first national bank of their ass.

There are some who would fear this knowledge falling into the wrong hands. Most of 'em are the same some who thought Gutenberg was bringing about the apocalypse by letting all those unwashed peasants read. I've met wizards alive today who think that a grimoire should only be penned in blood-and-wine ink blends on vellum, bound in leather of questionable origins and chained to the shelves of some occult library somewhere.

Well, none of those old farts are training me these days, so the whole gaggle of them can pound sand for all I care. My library is better organized, I have more fun things to do with leather bonds, and I've grown accustomed to writing in a growing collection of pocket size rain resistant notebooks. Screw'em. They're lucky I haven't started blogging.

As a combo measure of pandering to the attention span of kids these days and making sure this is a properly educational grimoire, I've added a useful guideline for life in the Otherworld at the top of each chapter. Did my best to match a guideline by relevance to the chapter following it. So don't get wrapped around the wand if they're numbered differently from each other than you expected.

My name is Travis Wayland the Grunt. This is one of my stories.

Chapter One

The vampire blood hangover turned out to be the least of my problems.

Not that I appreciated it at the time. I'd definitely woken up in worse places than my own bed over the years. Soccer fields, strip club parking lots, and on one memorable occasion handcuffed to a gurney in sickbay aboard the USS *Ashland*. Let's just say I never made Sergeant for a reason. I still haven't returned to that part of France.

It was an unremarkable and partly cloudy midday in July when I brought to a finale my all-snoring revue of, "I'm alive, but everything hurts." You'd think a veteran of mundane and supernatural shooting wars would have their act together in a more coherent fashion. But no, there I was: an akimbo pile of drooling, unshaven meat. The ribs on my right side felt like someone had hit me with a baseball bat the other day, an act which I did not remember. Nor did I remember a jaw that hurt surprisingly bad for someone who still had the bulk of their teeth. Point of fact, I didn't know what the date was. It was warm enough that I had a ceiling fan swishing tirelessly away beneath the haint blue paint and stipple-textured plaster of the ceiling.

Unless you've lived in the South, you've probably never heard of haint blue. It's a pale shade somewhere between teal, sky, and robin's egg. The Gullah people of Georgia and South Carolina and the conjurers that lived among them would paint the underside of porch roofs with a special mixture, using indigo for the dye. The color would ward off unfriendly ghosts from the house. White southern mages, who understandably had problems with angry ghosts, stole the secret of haint blue during the zombie wars back in the 1870's. Along with any other supernatural life hacks they could get away with, if I'm gonna be completely honest. Now, in southern homes with mage occupants, the color is commonplace for ceilings indoors and out. Below the ongoing breezes of the air conditioning, I had only a thin sheet of questionable thread count to curl up with and occasionally drool on. The marginally thicker blanket had been banished to the floor among the dregs of my bachelor laundry. But I lived in Atlanta, where the hot and humid weather anywhere between April and October can easily justify such things.

I was woken up promptly at noon by my phone, which I've rigged to record and wake me up with the latest Otherworld Overlook podcast. Yes, the supernatural community has podcasts. What, did you think I was some sort of rebel iconoclast dead set on embarrassing the entire supernatural community? Bob the Night Owl has a voice like expensive whiskey, but hearing him go off about whatever act of stupidity poked humanity this past week never fails to wake me up. Thus my slumber was broken to the call of, "...*is on fire, along with the walls on multiple levels. Atlanta fire crews claim the blaze started in the early morning hours after closing. If you're a longtime listener, you know what this means. Two words: vampire hunters. Let's face it, a city starts having a bloodsucker problem, step one is to find the proprietor of the local late night watering hole and chuck a bulb of garlic right upside their head. I'm not saying it's inevitable, but I am saying that it saves a lot of time."*

My arm lurched out and turned off the phone alarm instinctively. Scraps of dream passed my mind as I came out of REM sleep: The chiming of small bells. The smell of old books and mint tea. A woman's sapphire eyes, lined with kohl. A thin blue scarf moving in a gentle breeze. A cheerful alto voice saying, *"follow yellow to know."*

As my brain started to boot up like a work computer riddled with unrestricted malware, I took inventory of the world as I knew it. Fingers were all present, accounted for, and appeared to be in working order. No new rings were currently being worn. Toes were in a similar state of affairs. Wedding tackle present and seemingly none the worse for wear, though I had no inclination of engaging a full function check. No new tattoos, scars, or piercings that I could see from my supine position. All of the old tattoos and scars were right where I'd left them. My dark brown hair was still long, and at that stage of the morning was not so much unkempt as had been used for a postmodern art project by a band of renegade hairdresser faeries. My full beard was still scraggly, with shorter stretches around the cheekbones and neck to show that I hadn't bothered to trim for some time.

I had a nasty headache that wouldn't let me fall back asleep if I tried. And yes, my tongue felt the tingling coppery sensation of vampire blood. It's a sickly-sweet narcotic taste; like rare steak, dark rum, the tingle of lingering Novocaine and the pheromones of an excited lover all at once. Once I realized that, my brain threw up a red flag. I'd never drank vampire blood before. How did I know what it tasted like? I filed the thought away for future reference.

Mercifully, there was a half-empty bottle of water on the nightstand, decorated with a battered sticker displaying the insignia of my old Marine unit. I managed to sit up, ignoring the creaks going throughout my muscles as I swung my feet over the edge of my California King-size bed. I could feel my pulse pounding against my temple, each heartbeat sending a hammer down on a spike of pain firmly lodged in my head. About half of my joints were demanding to speak to the manager, and some of the more colorfully bruised muscles were muttering about unionizing. I opened the wide, screw-on cap of the bottle and started sipping the relatively cool tap water. There were faded yellow-green bruises on my knuckles, and what looked like cuts healed just enough for the scabs to have fallen off. I didn't remember being in a fight last week.

Dehydration partially averted, I left the empty bottle on the nightstand. The pulse in my head hadn't abated, but at least it hadn't gotten worse. I stood up, ignoring the noises a body my age really shouldn't be making as I walked past my bed into the master bathroom and got a good look at myself in the mirror. Long hair, dad bod, old and broken-in tattoos and scars, those were all familiar in reflection as they were at first glance. My oldest tattoo, a barn owl on my left pec, sat impassively judging me. A massive green and yellow bruise on my right side still ached. From the look of it, I'd taken a solid hit in the chest with something heavy duty some days ago.

As I splashed some water on my face, something about the mirror made me get a closer look. A few moment's gazing led me to turn on the faucet again, cranking the hot water all the way up. Steam took its sweet time to rise. However, it rose in a pattern that grew more clear by the moment. I mimed the motion with my left hand, then nodded to myself. Yeah, I'm a southpaw. Sometime recently I had decided to write the words FOLLOW and YELLOW on the condensation on my bathroom mirror. Same thing the lady in my dream said. I didn't remember going to Oz either. Or sending anyone else there, for that matter. I really am a wizard. Sending someone to Oz would be a bit pointless. That was filed away in the mental notes before turning off the water.

As the wet heat dissipated into the house, the smell of fresh brewed coffee brushed past my nose. My eyebrow raised in curiosity. Coffee was new. I was not the sort of person to invest in a coffee pot that activated itself in time with an alarm clock. Nor was Shrapnel, my cat, likely to have begun brewing herself, talented and clever a feline as she was. Ergo, someone else was making coffee in my kitchen.

I spread open my hand on the bathroom wall, feeling the smooth old paint under my fingers. Closing my eyes, I began to breathe the drying, cooling air. In through the nose, out through the mouth, just as I'd been taught before I discovered magic existed. The skin on my fingertips began to tingle as I continued to actively breathe, extending my senses through the walls of my home. I could feel the walls, brick and sheetrock holding a sandwich of studs and insulation between them. Water pipes and electrical cables, paint and flooring and carpets. In the kitchen, I could feel the familiar feline energy of Shrapnel. And near her was a human form I didn't recognize. I didn't have regular human company. My theory of coffee was confirmed.

Along the doors and the windows, I could feel my wards. A home is a sanctuary from all manner of supernatural critters by virtue of being a home. But for those of us who deal in the Otherworld as a matter of course, some home defense upgrades are in order. Some wards just warn you when something ill intentioned arrives. Others make it harder for said ill intentioned to enter, one way or another. Mine were a combination package put together piecemeal for decades. The house itself had been in the family since my grandparents bought it during WWII. Nowadays, it officially belonged to my Uncle Mac. Mac, a wizard himself, lived a nomadic life these days and had left me the house in all but name. So long as I kept up with the maintenance, utilities, and property taxes, Mac was content to leave his own stuff in the Mother-in-Law suite in the basement and let me arrange the rest of the house as it suited me. Being a dutiful nephew, I'd kept up my end of the bargain.

Only you couldn't tell it from the feel of the wards. They felt weakened, worn, and faded. Which made no sense. It was early July, and I'd just done a warding ritual at Midsummer. I might be missing a day or two and gotten in a fight, but nothing I knew of would have degraded wards like this so fast. Worried, I gently withdrew my connection to the house and opened my eyes. I worked a lot of nights, so the blackout curtains prevented me from seeing the more-or-less accurate time of day.

I sat down on my bed again, opening my nightstand. I reached for the small gun safe inside before noticing a weird reflection in a drawer where I didn't remember putting anything reflective. After a moment I picked up a pair of what looked like test tubes. One was full of what looked like venous blood, only it had an odd shiny purple look to it you didn't normally see. The other tube had a few drips and dregs of the same stuff. I sniffed the stopper on the second tube, and the heavy scent of vampire blood filled my nostrils. I still didn't know how I knew, but I was convinced.

After a second, I focused my senses. Magic can be sensed intuitively, but focusing can tell you more than you'd expect. It feels weird the first couple of times you do it, like intentionally crossing your eyes. But after a while it's something you can do almost reflexively. It's kinda like closing your eyes to listen to music better, or smell something you're cooking. Only instead of blocking one sense to focus on another, you're focusing all of them.

Focusing on the blood in the tube, it was like looking at a lit cigarette with night vision goggles on. It couldn't just be seen, it glowed with raw power. There was only an ounce or so of blood in that tube, but it was saturated with magical energy. If it had been gasoline, it would have been enough to drive my SUV for weeks. No wonder vampires have some serious mojo in most of the known lore.

I caught myself staring at the tube for I don't know how long, then took a breath and unfocused. Another red flag came up in my mind. I'm as interested in a compact power source as much as any mad handyman, but

I'm not one to obsess over it. I was, however, well aware that a human who drank vampire blood became a renfield: a mind-controlled servant with dubious prospects for their future mental health. Me having a blood stash wasn't alarming, but it was concerning.

The tubes went back into the nightstand. I could deal with them later. First, there was the matter of the mystery coffee brewer. I punched in the code to the gun safe. A Beretta M9 lay in the bed of foam padding, the grip and slide both worn with use. A quick check found the magazine full and a round in the chamber. A sniff of said chamber told me I'd fired it recently. While it was possible that, for once in my life, I'd simply gone to the range and not cleaned everything when I came back, it was more likely that I'd been shooting in the relatively recent past.

Vampire blood, mysterious bruises, a recently fired weapon, cryptic notes in the mirror, and more mysterious coffee. Clearly, some excitement had been had the night before. A thought came to my mind, and to test it, I crouched over my bed, sniffing the pillow I had not visibly been sleeping on. No unfamiliar scents accompanied the familiar ones of laundry detergent and dozing cat. Whoever was making coffee at the moment, they had probably not been overly familiar company recently.

Stretching my fingers for a moment, I reached for the slim black cellphone next to the water bottle like it was a claymore mine emplaced by the new guy in the platoon you're not sure of yet. A light tap of the power button showed it was just after noon, and a long stack of missed calls, voicemails, and other mess was waiting. I ignored all of them to look at the date, then looked again with narrowed eyes.

It was July second. That couldn't be right. I'd left the house the evening of July second and it had to be late morning at least by now. Then I squinted at my phone, which still insisted it was July second. Specifically, July second of next year. As I thought about it, the more I was sure. It was still July, just a year later. That was another mental note made. The more my thoughts came into clear prominence in my mind, the more I noticed: a year of my life was effectively missing. Of course, it was possible that someone had mucked around with my phone, but given the state of the wards, something told me that wasn't the case. Even more disturbing was that last night, or rather, a year ago tonight, I'd reported to Chittenden. Chittenden was the vampire lord of Atlanta. I owed him a year and a day of service, per the terms of an Oath I'd sworn.

According to my phone, it was a full year later. I'd been in some sort of nasty fight, had samples of vampire blood in my nightstand, and my memories were missing. And if my phone was accurate, I still had until midnight tomorrow to fulfill my Oath. Something had definitely gone amiss. Time to make introductions.

Pistol in hand and pointed down at the floor, I padded heel-to-toe down the hallway of my home, towards the kitchen. The paneled wood floors thankfully still didn't squeak. The hallway to my bedroom was short, opening up to an open staircase that led down to my front door and further down to the basement. Past the staircase, there was an open L-shaped area that housed a dining room, kitchen, and living room. The end of the L in the living room sported a large fireplace with a modestly arranged mantle. Altars weren't quite my style, but if you can't put candles, incense, and various knickknacks on a mantle, where can you? On my left I passed the guest rooms and bath, glancing inside each as I moved from a combat glide into a more casual walk.

Standing in my kitchen was a woman I didn't recognize, but seemed annoyingly familiar. She was maybe five three, built like an athlete that didn't mind the occasional indulgence. Young enough that in other circumstances I'd ask to see ID. Black hair pulled back in a ponytail and a corvid cast to her pale features. Dark circles under her green eyes, but I couldn't tell if they were recent additions or old friends. She was wearing an oversized black tshirt advertising a band I didn't recognize, and a set of black yoga pants that flattered her previously mentioned indulgence. She gave me a demure smile and a little wave when she looked up from stirring some additives into a coffee mug. On her wrists were a distinct set of bruises. She'd been wearing leather restraints relatively recently, and she'd struggled in them hard.

I checked past her into the living room, gave the corners a quick eye scan, then let the gun down completely by my side in one hand. I have to work at smiling, after several decades of having resting war face. I gave what I hoped was a comfortable one now, saying, "I promise I'm not trying being a jackass when I say this, but I'm gonna assume we've already met. Who are you and how did you wind up being my guest? It feels like I've had a very full night."

She let a smile escape from what looked like a well-worn mask of stoicism and spoke in the mild southern accent that made a long-time Atlanta native, not too different from my own. "I'm Connie. I got kidnapped by a vampire last night. Then you killed her."

I blinked. That was new. And disturbing. Whether I'd killed at Chittenden's command or without his permission, it was not a good sign. And was this ridden hard and put away wet goth in my kitchen read in on the Otherworld? That would explain the lack of panic and heavy dose of polite apathy. She wouldn't be the first stander to wind up like that, but it's still a good idea to keep up appearances. I raised an eyebrow and cocked my head in true confused dog fashion.

"Vampire?"

She nodded, stirring her coffee with a spoon. "Mmhmm. It was a pretty big fight, but you killed her. A few others too. And then you set a bitchy-sounding little blonde on fire."

This morning was just piling up the surprises. The girl did look like she'd staggered out of a slumber party sponsored by Tim Burton, but that didn't mean she was completely clear about who and what I was. And I wasn't exactly clear how deep in the cesspool I'd landed. But there wasn't immediate danger, and rushing probably wouldn't help me.

"I see. There any more coffee? Looks like I'm gonna need it. And if you're offering breakfast, a big bowl of context, please."

She tilted her head towards the pot. "I made plenty. Sure you don't want to find some shorts or something first?"

I blinked. Then I blinked again. Then I looked down at myself. There's always something important that ends up being forgotten. I had managed to leave my own bedroom with my pistol, but hadn't bothered with clothes. I had just gotten up and it was shaping into a long day already. I looked back up. The sudden movement sent a newfound spike of pain into my head and I winced.

"Now that you mention it, shorts would be lovely. I'll grab a quick shower and be back in a moment. I take mine black, if you're pouring, please."

I turned and walked back to my room with my pistol and the remnants of my dignity.

*   *   *

Shower happened. Shorts happened. Coffee happened. Connie, in a lucky happenstance, had made a pot strong enough to throw a punch, just the way I like it. I was failing miserably as a host, but the unexpected company wasn't unwelcome. I'd even managed a fresh set of cargo pants and a clean shirt. Connie had waited before I was walking back down the hallway to pour me a cup, ensuring it was still hot when I got my paws on it. She'd even managed to feed Shrapnel, who had gone through her own breakfast and was headbutting her new benefactor's ankle in search of scritches. The furry little traitor. The pair of us sat at my dining room table, which was an enormous slab of oak big and sturdy enough for everything from feasts to surgery. My maternal grandparents had made it at some point, and they built it to last.

Connie brought me somewhat up to speed on the events of last night. Her mask of placid calm was only occasionally punctuated by emotion as she spoke. Either she kept a very cool head on her shoulders or believed in a philosophy of death before visibly flustered. I could relate to that. Both the Otherworld and the Marines are places where panicking gets you killed quicker than whatever you're panicking about. Still, even I'd find it hard to be nonchalant about being kidnapped by vampires. As it turned out, I had been considerably busy.

"Lemme sum it up: A vampire snatched you off your front porch, stripped you down, tied you up, and gave you to me as a present. Then I killed her, killed a few other people, set someone else on fire and turned you loose. We burned the bodies, and I took you home with me?"

"Well, you tried to take me home first, but that didn't work either."

I put down my cup. "I haven't had a Monday night like that since my twenties."

"So you really forgot all of last night?"

"All of last year."

She tilted her head in surprise. "Really?"

I shrugged. "Near as I can tell. What's today's date?"

There was a flash of pale midriff as she drew a phone from the waistband of her yoga pants and hit the button before rattling off the date. I nodded my head. "Yeah, July second. Sounds like a full year."

She nodded and put her phone away. "OK. You got a standard procedure for this or anything? You looked like you'd been hunting vampires for a while."

I shook my head. "I'm not a vampire hunter."

"So what, last night was amateur hour?"

I waved my hand in so-so motion. "Don't get me wrong, most vampires are pretty rotten people, all things considered. Even when they're not human trafficking for giggles. And the fact that I apparently killed three of em for involving me in said trafficking gives me a warm fuzzy. But making it a habit sounds like suicide for the complicated and crazy."

"So you just do gift exchanges with them?"

"I try not to have anything to do with them. Unfortunately, that's not a decision I have a lot of control over right now."

"So what exactly are you?"

So there it was. I took a deep breath with ambitions about how cleansing it really was. Coffee and context hadn't abated the headache or the bruises. It was confession time. I wasn't worried about not being believed. I wasn't worried about getting hassle from the SiS. But there really is no nonchalant way to say it. It's just a puddle of awkward you can't avoid stepping in with both feet.

"I'm a wizard."

The words hung in the air. I'd just admitted it.

"Really?"

"Yup."

Shrapnel, having gone five whole minutes without a personal display of affection, jumped onto the table and protested. I immediately went on scritch behind the ears duty. Connie cracked a smile.

"What's her name?"

"Shrapnel."

Shrapnel, hearing her name, fell over in a quiet yet eloquent demand for belly rubs. As I obliged her, Connie raised an eyebrow. "Dare I ask?"

"Still got some chunks of it in me from the war. Getting it out would be painful and not worth the effort."

"Is she your familiar?"

I shook my head. "No, most cats disregard personal space like that."

"What's a wizard need a gun for?"

"Quicker, more effective, and easier on the furniture than throwing fireballs."

"Can you show me some magic?"

I quirked an eyebrow at her. "I killed vampires, plural, in front of you, last night, but you need a show to believe in magic?"

"Yes, please."

Which is the second annoying thing about confession time. It's like saying you perform for a living. Everyone wants a free show. A show you spent years learning how to do, plus however much of your mojo you use doing it. If I wore the big floppy hat, I'd pass it around for tips.

I thought, for half a second, about parlor tricks. Then my brain reminded me of everything else that had filled the morning: missing memory, a day and a half left of service, vampire blood, whatever the hell following yellow meant. I needed info and I needed it fast. Fortunately, I had a major source of such sitting in my dining room. This was going to be all kinds of uncomfortable, but I really couldn't think of another option. I met Connie's eyes again.

"This probably won't sound as weird as it might have a day ago, but I gotta ask. Can I read your mind?"

She didn't miss a beat. "I dunno, can you?"

I rolled my eyes. "I deserved that. Yes, I am physically capable of reading your mind. What I'd like is your permission."

"What do you need my permission for?"

"My own ethical standards, among other things. You don't want to play with people who don't ask first. It's not a fun time."

That got me a nod of acknowledgment if not approval. "Makes sense. You just gonna read everything?"

I grimaced at the thought, shaking my head. "Oh, Gods, no. Even at the speed of thought, that would take me weeks. Human minds are... disorganized is a good word. Chaotic is better. It's a long story."

I barely noticed and didn't stop to think about the faint crack in her calm. "A lot of things are."

"Yeah, at the moment, I want to get a look at your memories from last night. Not sure how or why, but somehow, I'm missing a lot of my own recent memories. Looking at last night through your eyes can help me fill in some of the more immediate gaps, even ones you didn't notice or think were important, which is why I'm not just asking you questions and going from there."

She sat back down, then put down the remnants of her coffee. Her nails were trimmed short, but painted a dark crimson. "Is it going to hurt?"

"You? No."

She nodded. "OK."

There was a long silence until Connie broke it. "When do we start?"

"Use the bathroom if you need to. I'll set up here."

As Connie excused herself, I got up and headed for the fireplace at the back end of the living room. Along the way I stopped at my over-stuffed burgundy couch. The corners of the couch looked like someone had meticulously taken a shotgun to each one, which was entirely normal. Shrapnel was a very sweet cat with strong opinions that scratching posts were for other people and she'd have nothing to do with such silliness. The heap of body armor, on the other hand, was not typical of me. I'd done the odd security job since leaving active duty, but normally I was a handyman. In the pile was a black security shirt, torn and stained. Atop that was a vest pulled apart into sections by the Velcro. Picking up my vest, I found multiple tears in the fabric, along with a single hole in the upper right front. I opened the Velcro with a ripping sound and pulled out the pad. Sure enough, there was a flattened impact divot there. I frowned, looking at the bruise on my chest. By the look of things, I might have taken a hit to the vest. But my bruises looked over a week old. I'd presumably dumped the used vest last night. I filed that thought away and dropped the armor. I stepped over to the mantle, then shuffled through a few packs of incense until I found a stick of what I was looking for. Taking the stick and a burner, I headed back to the kitchen table.

Connie was back by the time I had the burner set up. I'd emptied the pockets of my pants, letting four knives, three disposable lighters, a box of matches, my wand, three ballpoint pens, two permanent markers, a flashlight, and a few bucks in loose change spill over my dining room table. And that wasn't counting the full size multitool and flashlight holstered on my belt, or the smaller multitool clipped to my keyring.

My parents' generation hoarded mason jars. I'm told my grandmother had a spice rack bigger than a footlocker. But mages my age? We hoard knives, pens, and lighters. An American educated mage with something to write with, cut with, and set things on fire with can improvise a hefty percentage of her magical repertoire. And hey, It's not as if we fly commercial if we can possibly avoid it. The only thing inherently, blatantly magical was my wand. It was disguised as yet another permanent marker, with the helpful label "not a wand" embossed into the side.

Wands aren't strictly necessary, but occasionally they come in handy. European wands are old school, long, and slim. Designed for an age where they could be tucked in a belt or down a bodice. In trained hands they can do some beautiful precision work. American wands are relatively new, half as long, but thicker. Easily fit in the pockets of jeans or jackets. Easily mistaken for small flashlights or permanent markers at a glance. It's not uncommon for them to be hidden inside canes, walking sticks, or staves. Done right, an amazing amount of power can be channeled through them. Plenty of ink has been spilled on snooty comparisons to small swords versus prison shanks. Heh. Eurosnob losers. If any of the authors knew mine fit nicely in the buttstock of an old school M-16, they'd probably have a fit.

I began with breath. Something we all do unconsciously day in and day out. Doing so intently is an easy step to paying attention to what we're doing right now. All the things our body does for us when we're not paying attention all comes from breath. So I breathed. Three times, then four. Now when I moved, I was moving and sensing at once. Suddenly I was present in the room in a way I hadn't been a moment ago. Magic, always flowing through me, began to swell and concentrate, like riverbanks swelling as the snow begins to melt further and further north.

Sweeping most of the gear to the center of the dining room table left the kitchen end free for the two of us and the incense burner. Connie, having left her cup in the sink, quietly watched. I opened my smaller multitool, where I kept the tiny knife blade razor sharp. I rubbed the blade with an alcohol wipe, then took the lighter and passed the flame back and forth across the edge. Putting the lighter down, I made a small cut on the back of my hand. Once I knew I was bleeding, I turned my hand palm up, letting a few drops of my blood fall on the short end of the incense stick, just before the coating of powder ended.

She raised an eyebrow. "What's the mutilation for?"

I set the incense stick in the holder, pushing it to the side. "A timer. If I'm not out of your head by the time it burns down to the bloodstain, it will pull me out."

"Well, it makes sense when you say it like that."

I cleaned and bandaged the back of my hand. "I try to be helpful. You ready?"

"Ready as I'll ever be. What do I do?"

"Get comfortable." I lit the incense, letting it catch before gently blowing out the flame. The end of the stick glowed, a small ember letting a tendril of smoke up into the room in a slow smolder. The scent of smoke and roses became more notable in the room. Taking up my wand, I drew a stylized raven on each of my palms. Setting the wand aside, I sat up straighter, holding my hands out across the table with my palms up. "Take my hands, please."

Without hesitating, her hands slid into mine, warm and not as small as I'd thought. I looked her in the eyes, a shade of green between seafoam and emeralds. Even her scent was comfortably familiar alongside the incense: leather and sandalwood. She met my gaze, a bit of a curious tilt to her head. I began to mirror her movements slowly, then led. After several moments, we were breathing in unison. I was not only sensing myself but her as well. She could sense an ache in my side. I could feel a bruise at her ankle. We were as connected as a long-time dance couple, invisible walls between us melting away. I gently began to speak, just enough for both of us to hear.

"We're going to look into your past. All we seek to do is witness. Keep thinking of last night. Beginning when you first encountered me. Continue until we parted ways. Follow it as it happened, and I will follow along with you. Let your eyelids fall as they will."

We continued to breathe together, make the slightest moves in time with each other. Our gazes settled comfortably with our eyes on each other. We closed our eyes together, and I disappeared into her memory.

*   *   *

Chapter Two

"Guideline Eighteen:
  Memory lane is full of traffic hazards."

I couldn't tell you how long I was floating in the void. A more comfortable void than you'd think. Instead of endless depths of space I could never reach if I lived a million years, I had the sense of soft, gentle boundaries just outside the reach of my senses. As I sank further, snatches of my own dreams came to the fore. Once again I heard the chiming of bells, going in a slow rhythm I couldn't place. A woman's eyes, lined in kohl and shaded in bright blue. A blue that complimented the fluttering scarf. The alto voice with the same phrase: *"Follow yellow to know."*

The fragments of dream faded as my senses began to come into focus. Our senses, as I could tell Connie was here with me. Or rather, I was here with her, passing through the outer limits of her mindscape. Our hearts beat slowly in a deep tone, reminding me of mighty, organic drums. Breath filled and emptied our lungs. The incense blended with the scents of each other, the distinction of me and her blending. I could neither sense my own body, nor hers. Just our presence, close enough for comfort. Our only separation was thoughts. I could feel her emotions and memories brushing past my mind, like fish swimming past me in a stream. The stronger ones

didn't feel like moving aside and just barreled through my mind, announc-
ing themselves as they went.

One moment, I was floating between currents of Connie's thoughts.
Then the next moment, I was behind the wheel of a moving Jeep. It
was dark, the streetlights flashed as we went by, doing at least thirty in a
residential neighborhood. I resisted the urge to seize control in the instant
it took me to remember it wouldn't work anyway. I was, in every sense,
just along for the ride. Connie was going through her recent memories,
and I was experiencing them the way she did. I did my best to be a quiet
passenger, even as I tried to get used to being in a new body. Connie was
half my weight and a good foot and more shorter than I was, which affected
everything from my reach to my vision to my stride.

I felt like a puppet strapped inside a puppeteer, controlled by someone I
was only somewhat communicating with. As I gently twitched and flexed,
thoughts I didn't remember thinking passed through my mind. My torso was too long. My boobs were asymmetrical. I had a stubborn fifteen
pounds that just wouldn't piss off and go away. Because I was getting used
to living in Connie's body, her thoughts that focused on self-image were
briefly becoming clear. I did my best to relax and ignore Connie's thoughts
that weren't on the job at hand. They eventually faded to the point I could
tell they weren't mine, but I sensed them as they brushed by my own
consciousness.

Connie was driving home after a long day at work. The thought of
flinging my bra across the room the instant I shut the front door behind
me was a slice of impending heaven. It had to be after 9 P.M. and the sun
had barely gone down. She drove on uninterrupted through the tree-lined
back roads of Atlanta's Decatur neighborhood. Nice area, Decatur. Still
affordable, if you're lucky. Connie pulled into the driveway of a cream
colored split level and parked the Jeep. Under the streetlight, I could see the
body of the Jeep was painted a deep metallic purple that looked really good.

If nothing else, I liked her taste in vehicles. Hell, most of us can't afford taste in anything outside of, "it runs and I can afford it," these days.

Connie grabbed a black messenger bag festooned with enough buttons and patches to let a goth scout earn a promotion to raven, then slid out from behind the driver's seat. As she stood up, a faint smell of fried, spicy meat passed through the air. She strode towards the front door of the split-level, more than ready for this day to be over. She slammed the door of the Jeep without looking back. Still walking, she held up the key fob to lock the Jeep doors remotely. Before clicking the fob, Connie vanished into the darkness, taking me with her.

*   *   *

Connie slowly opened her eyes, looking from the darkness into just more darkness. I was lying down on something soft but unyielding, like thin office carpet. I could feel it all the way down one side, which was because I was naked. Connie's instinctively trying to cover herself failed miserably, but did let me know my wrists were locked behind me with some sort of leather cuffs. Ditto my ankles. I was trying to scream. That wasn't working because I was also gagged. Pretty securely, too. I was going to start drooling in a bit, and it wasn't gonna be pretty. Connie's thoughts sped up rapidly. I was in a really well upholstered trunk of a car or something. It was getting hard to concentrate. I was getting more confused, already terrified, and exponentially more pissed off! Some dog-humping asswombat had stuck me tied up and naked in wherever here was!

Before I could try to focus on my own thoughts and look past Connie's rage, a crack opened up in the world and light stabbed Connie in the face. She blinked as her eyes adjusted, then tried not to scream. She was in some sort of box the size of a steamer trunk, lined in burgundy velvet. And looking down at Connie with a scary look on his face was... Me.

Damn, this me looked scary. I dubbed this one Past-me, just to keep everything making some sort of sense. Past-me was dressed in security blacks, with a blocky look in the chest that told me Past-me was wearing a vest under the shirt. Past-me's hair was tied back in a lazy ponytail, and a radio earpiece was in one ear. Past-me looked down at Connie like he wasn't quite sure if he was hungry, but definitely was interested in what was just presented.

That was just unsettling. I knew I had a bad case of resting war face, but was it always that bad? Probably. But it was still intense to feel on this end. Especially with Connie still being chained up. Connie's rage just kept building while Past-me stood there like an idiot. I wanted to scream into the night. I wanted to leap out of this box and eviscerate whoever put me here. What came out from around the gag was more of a muffled whimper. Great. A few sprinkles of humiliated was just what I needed on this naked and furious sundae. If I got out of this alive, someone was going to suffer.

Standing next to Past-me was a familiar face. Eva Marazzi was one of Atlanta's most prominent vampires. She had the kind of face and figure that Renaissance painters would've shanked each other with palette knives for the chance to immortalize in oils. And they'd want to paint pictures of her too. These days, she'd have the glitterati arguing for days on end over whether or not she was plus size. She was giving a lot of selfie-worthy smiles as she looked between Past-me and Connie. Everything about her cobra smile terrified me and enraged Connie more. Eva's eyes shone at Past-me, waving into the box presentationally. She purred, "I got her especially for you, Travis."

Wait, what? A vampire I'd barely interacted with decided to give me a bound, gagged, naked, and clearly unwilling gothlet as a present? I'd never been a renfield before, but that still sounded out of normal. I noted that with a huge question mark and filed it away. Past-me was still staring down at Connie with a dumbfounded look on his face. Was I really that big? That's what I looked like? Mirrors are really no substitute for someone else's eyes. Past-me was looking down more intently by the heartbeat. More fascinated than aroused, which was only scaring me worse. Eva laughed playfully, taking Past-me by the arm. "She's all yours. Of course, I hope you'll let me play with her too."

I tried not to vomit into Connie's memory. The creepy was strong with this one. Eva reached into the box after me. Before Connie could twist away, Eva grabbed one of Connie's nipples between elegant fingers, twisting viciously. Connie shrieked into the gag, digging her nails into the palms of her hands. Eva let go only when Past-me leaned down into the box, still with that dumb look on his face. He breathed, low and slow.

Then he whispered, "Thank you."

And then my eyes met, which felt twice as weird as it sounds. I've looked into someone else's soul before, but this was mirrors all the way down. Somewhere, and I'm not sure if I heard it in mind, memory, or something else, I heard a pair of voices whisper in stereo. "You?"

Past-me curled his hand in Connie's hair, spiking Connie's fear and rage faster and hotter. Past-me tightened his grip, sending an involuntary shudder down Connie's spine, reverberating through the fear and reheating rage I could barely think through.

Then something changed in Past-me's eyes. It was like a light bulb going off over the head of a student that truly understood the lesson on a fundamental level. I could feel, somewhere in the sea of angry and terrified, a tiny ribbon of comfort brush across Connie's terror.

All of a sudden, I recognized what I saw in Past-me's eyes.

I don't consider myself a very nice person. I've always been one of the biggest guys in the room. And I was taught early and often to know my own strength. To manage my own anger. Because while other people could leave bruises, maybe a broken bone, I could leave a corpse. Possibly multiple corpses. And that's before we even get into my love for guns and swords and explosives and all manner of fun ways to turn human beings into room temperature meat. Not to mention the possibilities that magic would add to the fun.

I have to bite back every aggressive impulse I've ever had. And while you get used to it after a while, it never really stops sucking. As you can imagine, that doesn't make me the most socially adept guy in the room. I've lived in and worked in enough hellholes to be convinced that a chunk of people in this world are crazy, stupid, evil, or some combo of the above. Unfortunately, one of the big trade-offs of civilization is that you're not allowed to treat said people with anywhere near the level of violence they deserved.

The look in Past-me's eyes was not the typical resting war face. It the look of a man who had, within his own ethical framework, just been given an enthusiastic green light to do as he pleased, regardless of how violent or sadistic. No safety catches. No safewords. His conscience had just signed a blank permission slip for anything about to happen in the room, then shot an azimuth due berserker on his moral compass. I could almost hear the opening bars of the first song on his 'Unrestrained Rampage' playlist.

Past-me let go of Connie's hair, and turned back to Eva, an awestruck smile across his face. I caught the shine of grateful tears in Past-me's eyes. Past-me whispered again, "Thank you."

Which was when Eva's face exploded. I caught a glimpse of Past-me unloading a holdout .357 revolver into Eva's head, black ichor splattering the walls. My world erupted in the gunfire roaring in a confined space. Eva let out a gurgling, inhuman shriek and backhanded Past-me, knocking him out of my line of sight. Eva shoved the box aside, knocking Connie ass over bondage gear out of the box and onto the tile floor.

I was in some sort of bedroom. The floor had a smooth black and white domino tile pattern, really easy to clean but uncomfortably cold to lie on. The walls were painted a deep burgundy. A wardrobe, armoire, and vanity along one wall were ornately carved and painted a gloss black with crimson accents. One end of the room opened into an anteroom, with the glimpse of double doors beyond that. Opposite the vanity was another set of black double doors. Behind me, past a poster bed that had to have been made strong enough to anchor a yacht to, was a single door. I mentally replaced the word bedroom with boudoir. I could feel a stray thought of Connie's that the place would be pretty awesome in other circumstances.

Eva's face was a bloody mess, her eyes shot out of her head. Her fingernails had darkened and curved into claws. The rest of her was still sheathed in an incredible black dress designed by someone whose name I couldn't pronounce two falls out of three. It clung to every curve and swell like it was the last chance it had to be a real dress.

Past-me had drawn my M9 and had it perfectly sighted in on Eva's center of mass, pulling the trigger repeatedly. The mystery of what I'd been shooting it for was now duly solved. A lot of people dislike the M9. People have bitched about it since before the U.S. made it the primary weapon across the military back in the 80's. But for my purposes, it had a lot to offer. The thick grip meant it felt good in the paws of a huge ape like me. I knew the weapon inside and out, which made things like swapping out the mag release to be used left-handed easy. It's heavy for a 9mm, which makes it easier to shoot one-handed than most. And since, unlike Uncle Sam, I have no issues whatsoever using hollowpoints, I also lack the issues of overpenetration at close ranges and lack of stopping power at far ones.

All of this helped in making the gaping holes Past-me was blowing open in Eva's chest. Ribs snapped and blood splashed with every hit. The smell of vampire blood filled the room. Unfortunately, she'd charged Past-me, aiming for where the pain was coming from. Like all vampires her age, she moved fast, hit hard, and could take a lot of punishment. Ordinarily, I'd be nothing but a snack to her. Going in my favor, Past-me had caught her by surprise. Past-me was doing much more damage than your usual human does. But if Past-me let her get close with fang and claw, then Past-me was nothing but a blood keg with ugly tattoos.

Absolutely none of this was realized by Connie, who saw an actual monster and a scary-looking lout fighting to the death, presumably over her. She whipped her head around, looking frantically for any sort of tool to break out of her bonds. Now that I had a half-second to think about them, I realized the bonds on Connie's wrists were really sturdy. I was pretty sure I'd made them myself.

Past-me tried to sidestep Eva, but one of her arms caught him. Even the glancing blow looked like it was from a sledgehammer. Past-me was sent flying several feet, smashed into a vanity mirror and rolled off the counter, landing on his ass just as Eva pounced. Past-me yanked an antique drawer full of lingerie free of the vanity, smashing the hand carved oak drawer into the side of her head. Thongs flew across the room in every direction.

Somewhere, somehow, Past-me had found a second wind. People don't expect big guys to be fast. I'm much, much faster than I look. But I've never seen myself this fast. Past-me rolled to avoid another swipe of Eva's claws, landing in front of a dresser. Leaning in a corner, Past-me grabbed, of all damned things, a baseball bat. I had no idea how Past-me was keeping up with a vampire like Eva. He wasn't casting any sort of magic I recognized. Some kind of talisman had been activated maybe? I stopped speculating and tried to pay attention. A swing for the fences caught Eva under the chin, splintering the wood and sending her sprawling. Past-me pounced on her and rammed the splintered end into her back, shoving open two of her ribs like a pry bar in a door frame. For a moment, I thought she was screaming in harmony with herself. Then I realized Connie, splattered with Eva's blood, was screaming into her gag on a similar level. Past-me rammed my fist onto the heel of the bat again and again, feeling rather than seeing the splintered bat rip through Eva's heart. Finally, the wood penetrated the cardiac muscle, and Eva's body went limp.

Past-me took a set of zip-ties from my belt, binding Eva's limp hands behind her back. Past-me came up to one knee and kicked Eva in the shoulder, rolling her onto her back. The heel of the bat stuck some inches out from her back, lifting her chest. The splintered end of the bat stuck up from between her breasts, covered in ichor. Her body sank a little with a wet wheezing sound.

"Eva, we need to see other people. Oh, and I quit."

Past-me moved fast, grabbing my M9 and changing the magazine. Connie was still on the floor, still terrified, still angry, and still naked. Past-me strode over to Connie, taking his sweet time. Past-me shook off whatever he was thinking, forcing myself to keep his gaze at Connie's face. Connie struggled backwards as Past-me prowled to her, until Past-me took a knee and put a finger to his lips.

"She's got other goons in the building. No way to get you out without taking care of them first. Understand?"

Connie nodded quickly. Past-me stood back up. I saw what looked like drumsticks in his boot at first glance but then realized they were prepared stakes Past-me had found somewhere. Then the outer doors of the boudoir opened, and two members of a security detail dressed identically to Past-me stepped inside the anteroom. And standing between them was five feet of high-heeled Russian prima donna. From Connie's vantage point, I recognized her.

Tasha had been turned into a vampire by Eva sometime in the last century. I have no idea why. She was petty, vindictive, sadistic, not terribly bright, and cute in a "works on it an hour daily" sort of way. And Past-me was standing there like an idiot, splattered with her dam's lifeblood. So Past-me improvised. Before the doors finished opening, Past-me strode up to them, barking orders like he had every right to. Along the way Past-me holstered the M9 and stuck his other hand in a pocket. Thank Gods for an NCO voice and bloodstripes you can't remove.

"She's dead! After them, dammit!"

In the half second they were processing that, Past-me drew a flare gun from his pocket and shot Tasha in the belly. Then he turned and ran back into the bedroom as a chemical hiss from the burning flare began to loudly fill the room. Tasha shrieked like a banshee as flames erupted rapidly from her abdomen, and the security guys recoiled, hissing like snakes. Past-me jumped over Eva's corpse, scooped up Connie-me and dove across the enormous bed. Seriously, I sleep on a California king, but this mattress was out of some sort of Sultan's playpen. Who even made sheets for this thing? A parachute company?

Somehow managing to not break our necks on the unyielding bedposts, we rolled onto the floor on the far side in a tumble. Connie squirmed, trying to get a look at something more than the floor. Past-me fired four shots high, ducking to catch a glimpse of the two still-hissing security guys taking positions outside the doorway.

"Kill him!" Tasha shrieked from somewhere up the stairs.

Past-me fired off two more rounds over their heads. Glass shattered as Past-me managed to hit one of the light fixtures. It looked like Past-me was trying to suppress rather than actually fight. Tasha's howling faded as she presumably fled. Past-me hollered, "Walk away and it won't get messier!"

Renewed hissing from beyond the bed was the only response. Past-me laid in the prone, blocking my view, and started shooting. Three shots in he was rewarded with a yowl and a thump of a body hitting the floor. Past-me pushed off the bed to go to a knee and bumped into Connie. She kneed Past-me in the side, getting a wince out of him.

"Shit, sorry!" Past-me muttered.

Past-me rose up into a crouch just in time to get himself tackled against the wall. Past-me fell back, landing half on Connie with a thump. Gunfire rang out as Past-me dumped a magazine into the hissing guard. Bracing his boot on the wall, Past-me shoved hard, sending himself and the guard tumbling over the bed. More gunshots, hissing, and a wet crunching noise happened. A magazine flew across the room, bouncing off a wall. Connie squirmed more frantically, her anger growing by the second, beating her own fear into submission. She peeked around the corner of the bed just as a shot rang out.

Past-me landed flat on his ass, yelping in pain before shooting anew at the one standing guard. Somewhere, Past-me had found what looked like a cross between a pirate cutlass and a machete. I vaguely recognized the design. He was staggering to his feet, still shooting with one hand before lashing out with the cutlass. I saw a pistol drop and severed fingers fly. Past-me kept driving the guard back, shooting and slashing in turn before dropping an empty pistol and drawing one of the stakes from his belt. One more slash sent the guard sprawling, his face torn open at the upper lip.

Past-me dropped to one knee and rammed the stake into the shredded meat that was the guard's chest. The guard shuddered and went limp as the wood squelched through his body. Past-me took two breaths, then rolled the guard over, zip-tying his hands behind his back. Groaning in pain, Past-me stood back up. Past-me switched the sword from his right to left hand, then slipped his right hand between his shirt and the ballistic vest. His jaw clenched, biting back a scream. But when Past-me slipped my hand out, there was no newfound blood, just sweat. The guard's shot hadn't penetrated Past-me's vest. Lucky me, I now had a partial explanation for my bruises.

Past-me walked out of Connie's line of sight. A wet thump and the sound of zip-ties told me what he was doing to the other guard. Past-me walked back into the center of the room, dropping the cutlass, then picking up and reloading the Beretta from where he'd left it. Past-me turned and walked back over to the bed, crouching beside Connie with a wince.

"I'm gonna get you out of these. Hold still."

Connie nodded. Past-me grabbed the chain between the wrist cuffs and whispered, "*red light, red light, red light.*"

The wrist and ankle cuffs unbuckled themselves, dropping to the floor. Connie yanked her wrists apart, then grabbed at the buckle of her gag. The cuffs were enchanted, a magical set I'd first helped make years ago, unimaginatively called a Strap Ball. As they fell, the cuffs coiled around themselves in a neat ball, easily secured to a belt. Past-me waved towards the wardrobe, which had somehow survived with only a stray bullet hole.

"There's clothes in the wardrobe. Help yourself, but make it quick."

Connie unbuckled the gag, gently sliding it past her teeth before throwing it across the room. She staggered to her feet, finally having a good look at the carnage. Eva and the two guards were all staked, bound, and torn open with multiple wounds. One had lost three fingers to a cut from the sword. Sprays of blood, shards of mirror, and shell casings were everywhere. The air stank of blood and smoke.

Tiptoeing past the mess, Connie opened drawer after drawer. Lingerie, lingerie, an impressive toy collection, more lingerie, an even more impressive toy collection... this was getting ridiculous. Did femme fatale vampires just give up the chance to lounge around in yoga pants for a slow night? Horrifying to contemplate. The next drawer was full of security blacks, all in my size. Screw it. Connie threw on a black tshirt with SECURITY printed across the front. On her, it went down to the knees and billowed like a sundress. A pair of cargo pants were ridiculously oversized on her, but a belt stolen from one of Eva's bathrobes let it somehow not fall off of Connie's hips. Shoes her size were nowhere to be found, but wearing two pairs of my socks together gave her at least some protection.

While Connie had dressed, Past-me was cleaning up fast. He opened some sort of medical pouch with a syringe setup I'd never seen before. Taking a small light, he turned it on and held it between his teeth. Using the syringe setup, he drew two tubes of blood from Eva, pocketing the tubes. I didn't know Past-me had learned to do that. I had nothing against needles, I just didn't like to look when I had injections and the like. Watching someone stab me gave me an urge to stab back, and doing that to the docs is just plain rude. Past-me pulled the last of the sheets off the bed when Connie asked, "What's your name?"

Past-me stopped, but didn't answer. After a long moment, he finally looked over at Connie. In the back of my mind, I realized he was trying not to stare.

"I said, what's your name?"

"Travis. You?"

"Connie."

Past-me didn't have a response to that one, just averting his eyes and looking back at the flames.

"What... were they?"

Past-me shrugged. "Vampires."

"Oh. So what happens now?"

Past-me shrugged again. "I grab the last of my gear and we run."

With that, he wrapped the bodies in the sheets, secured with duct tape. Connie looked around and spotted her messenger bag in a corner. Tiptoeing through the carnage, she began rummaging through it. Wallet, keys, phone, nothing looked like it had been tampered with. Not as good as finding, oh, clothes, but under the circumstances Connie wasn't complaining.

Past-me spoke up. "How much do you remember about who took you?"

"I walked up to my front door and woke up in a box."

"Good."

"Why?"

"Because your head was messed with. Which means Eva probably snatched you herself. Hopefully, that also means she found you on her own. Which means there's no record you were ever here. Even if Tasha's alive, she probably didn't notice you were even in the room. With luck, anyone who comes sniffing after Eva or myself will have no idea you exist. We get you out of here clean, you're free and clear."

"What about you?"

Past-me had a duffel bag open on the bed and was throwing anything that was actually mine inside. He paused before grabbing another pair of cargo pants. "Not free and clear. But that was going to be the case either way. Hopefully I won't be your problem anymore either."

Connie didn't have a response for that one. Past-me opened the toy cabinet inside the wardrobe. Eva had apparently been an enthusiastic collector. Past-me carefully took a half-dozen floggers in various sizes and colors, along with two sets of restraints. I recognized all of them as pieces I'd made myself. He also picked up the Strap Ball, then tossed it in the pile. That got Past-me a raised eyebrow from Connie.

"They're the only things in the cabinet that are mine. The rest is hers."

The look didn't stop. Past-me looked annoyed for a split second, then calmed down. "Look, yeah, I enjoy that kind of thing. But only with people who also enjoy it, not with people who're forced into it, all right?"

"Okay."

Connie was nowhere near completely convinced. But then again, Past-me wasn't trying too hard. Past-me picked up one of my drop pistols, a Ladysmith in 9mm with a chrome slide. Slim enough to fit in a pocket, small enough to look like a toy in my meaty paws. It still shot straight, though, and that's all that mattered. He looked up at Connie.

"Can you shoot?"

"Absolutely."

Past-me handed it to her without question, butt first.

"Keep it in your pocket. Don't start anything until I do."

She nodded, making a press check before putting the piece away in a pocket. Connie had a flash of annoyance, seeing how my borrowed pants fit her hand and the pistol easily. "What's the plan?"

Past-me had reloaded the flare and was aiming it down at Eva's twitching body. "Run."

He pulled the trigger and the world burst into flames.

*   *   *

We stepped outside into the twilight. The world was tinted in that blue color the early morning gets before the sun rises. I realized we were in the parking lot of the Cotillion, one of Atlanta's bigger nightclubs. Because of course we were. Nightclubs, vampires, I swear; there must be some kind of zoning code.

Past-me tossed his bag into my Yukon, hopping into the driver's seat. Connie took shotgun, barely closing the door before Past-me peeled out of the lot, heading East on North Avenue. My Yukon was a beast, but she barely needed maintenance. And I took a small amount of pride in the fact that I drove an SUV that occasionally saw dirt roads. In Atlanta, that was a rarity.

As we passed Highland Avenue, I heard sirens in the distance. In the rearview, I could see smoke billowing from the horizon in a single, lonely column.

The drive to Connie's was mostly silent, on winding back roads through Decatur. The thick trees giving us mottled shade nearly the entire drive. We eventually pulled up to a cream colored split level on a decent-looking street. No garbage or junked cars in view. Not even kid's toys strewn around the nearby lawns. Most of the locals had already been off to work and gone about their day.

She rummaged through her bag before finding a ring of keys, a small figurine of a cat hanging from the chain. She hesitated at the door, like a date wondering how to turn me down gently. Past-me had several visible claw marks and a black eye. His shirt and pants were torn and stained. His left shoulder had bleeding scratches and there was a bullet hole in his shirt just under his right nipple. Past-me smelled like cheap cigar and burned meat. When the awkward got palpable, Past-me gave Connie an out.

"Easier if the neighbors don't see you giving my gun back. I got my own mess to deal with anyway."

She jumped on it with a too-quick nod. I could feel her mind racing between survivor's arousal and the serious desire to be nowhere near me. If the concept of that sounds crazy, congratulations, you haven't lived a dangerous life. Surviving life-and-death situations makes most healthy humans hungry, horny, and exhausted, in no particular order. I'd been through it enough to know Past-me was going to have to get some food, rub one out, take a shower, and hit the sack for a few hours. Connie was facing bits and pieces of that combined with a heavy load of fury at what Eva had done to her and a bucket full of fear of what I was capable of. The fact that I was feeling this in more or less real time, from inside her head, should have made it less awkward. It was rapidly becoming the opposite. I kept my thoughts as quiet as I could make them.

She turned the deadbolt and opened the door. Her living room looked more like a library at first glance, which I heartily approved of. The bookshelves were all the pressed fiberboard kind designed to last one apartment or one degree program, whichever finished first. One held a number of psychology texts. Not my field, though I noticed one set of volumes that made me roll my eyes. The next shelf over was devoted to paperbacks, popular fiction mixing in with enough classics to round out a humanities section. Most of them looked read instead of displayed. An older but serviceable entertainment center was set up optimally. Art on the walls was framed nicely and not from artists I recognized. One was a depiction of a tarot card: the eight of swords. It hung above a small but practical fireplace. Something about the smell of the place was incredibly familiar, a combo of leather and roses.

We stepped inside to find two guys in security uniforms loafing on her couch.

"Oh, shit!"

We all went for our weapons and all held our fire at once. Past-me grabbed Connie's shoulder at the same moment. Past-me had to grip it tight before she'd lower the Ladysmith. Past-me holstered his own weapon, and gestured for both of the guys to do the same. Intuition took over, and both holstered their sidearms. Past-me seized the initiative.

"What the hell are you two doing here?"

One was a lanky guy with a Minnesotan accent and dirty blonde hair too long for most security firms. Not that Past-me apparently gave two shits, what with my own mane. The other was one of the bigger guys I'd ever met. Not to mention ugly. I'm nobody's idea of pretty, but this guy's face looked like a fist with a week's worth of stubble. The lanky guy spoke up.

"Boss lady sent us, Wayland. This house, stay until after sundown tonight. What brought you here?"

"Just you and Josh?"

"Yeah."

That weird spicy meat smell was back. And not welcome, given that I'd recently been getting a whiff of roast vampire. Past-me held up a finger in the "stand by" signal before leaning in to Connie's ear. He murmured. "Pack a bag. Clothes for a day or two, and any keepsakes you can't live without. We'll need to be quick."

Connie gave a nervous little nod and darted into a hallway on our right. Past-me remained in the living room as Connie strode down the hall into the bedroom at the far end. The sight of the bedroom blurred as I strained to hear the conversation in the living room. Connie shucked off her borrowed clothes, throwing them in a corner heap before opening a drawer. I let my own sight blur deeper as I tried to listen in. All I could hear was the front door opening and closing.

As I was listening, Connie had changed into worn black jeans and a black peasant blouse. As I refocused on seeing through her eyes, I watched her pack a gym bag quick with what looked like some clothes, a toiletry kit, a journal, and a small wad of cash. Opening a small lockbox in her nightstand, she drew a single stack pistol. She did a quick press check, then tucked it into an IWB holster. I was moderately jealous. The civilian weight I'd gained left me unable to carry at the appendix. I could hear the front door open and close again. She dropped two more magazines and a box of ammo into the gym bag, taking it and her regular bag with her. Now I was impressed. This girl had her act way together than most I knew. No wonder she was so chill. Connie picked up the Ladysmith and headed down the hallway. I could hear the deadbolt slamming home just before Connie turned a corner and ran head-to-chest into Past-me.

Past-me was sweating freely and looked like he was just catching his breath. He gently stepped back and glanced down.

"Got everything?"

"Yeah, are they...?"

"Gone. For the moment. We need to be the same thing. Ready to move?"

"Yeah."

She offered my Ladysmith back. Past-me took it, press checked and tucked it into a pocket. I could feel a hint of jealousy from Connie.

"You sure? They could be waiting for us at the end of the block."

She drew the single stack, fast and practiced enough to convince me, muzzle pointed nowhere that raised my hackles. Past-me flashed a goofy smile.

"Fair enough. Got your car here?"

"Yeah."

"Follow me. And by that I mean stay on my ass. I'm not far."

*   *   *

Another blur and I was back behind the wheel of Connie's Jeep, reversing into my driveway. I lived at a far corner lot just outside the perimeter, maybe fifteen minutes drive from the Cotillion. The backyard was enclosed with a ten-foot privacy fence, but the front was open. My front door led to an old-fashioned footpath to the street, where it might have met a sidewalk decades ago. A pair of regularly trimmed oaks shared space on the far side of the footpath from the driveway.

Past-me grabbed the bag of weapons and toys from my Yukon, letting us both into the garage. The house was surprisingly dark for a morning. Just after coming through the garage, Past-me raised his left hand, bringing us both to a stop. Past-me opened his right hand, laying it on the wall from fingertips to palm. Several breaths went by as I recognized he was doing a ward check. He eventually nodded, then led us up the stairs and into the dining room.

Past-me dumped his gear bag in front of the entertainment center, then waved a hand around. "Help yourself to a seat wherever."

Connie sat at the dining room table, not dropping her overnight bag. Shrapnel trotted up, looking suspicious at Connie, then turned promptly to Past-me and let out a long and indignant meow. I'd found Shrapnel in the parking lot of a Waffle Crossroads one morning. One thing led to another, and she'd wound up ruling my house. She wasn't a familiar so much as the one roommate everyone liked. Past-me threw up his hands in mock indignity. "You're not my mom. You don't get to complain when I bring a lady home."

Shrapnel meowed again, causing a judicious nod from Past-me as he opened the pantry and brought forth a scoop of kibble. "Tardy breakfast, on the other hand, I deserve the ass-chewing there."

Past-me returned the scoop, changed the water in Shrapnel's other dish, then rolled his head around on a thick excuse for a neck. Past-me looked like hammered shit: claw marks and bruises from his fight with Eva and the guards, solid dark circles under his eyes, and a ten thousand yard stare. Past-me looked ten times worse than I had when I woke up this, or rather the next, screw it, IN the morning.

"Well," Past-me told my new house guest, "We weren't followed and there's no gunmen hiding in my closet. Want a drink?"

She nodded. "Water, please."

Past-me fetched a pair of bottles from the fridge, then claimed the far end of the sofa. Connie moved from the dining room and took the comfier armchair, letting her overnight bag hit the floor. Past-me shucked his shirt and played with the hole in his vest. Wincing at what was probably cracked ribs, Past-me started pulling Velcro.

Connie grimaced, "You need a hand?"

Past-me waved her off, peeling away Velcro straps until the front of the vest came off, leaving him in a sweaty and torn undershirt. Turning the panel to get a closer look, Past-me pulled out my multitool and levered the round out of the panel. He turned it back and forth, the flattened slug clenched in the jaws of the multitool, then smiled.

"Glad I went with the ounce of preparation instead of the pound of cure."

She made a face. "How bad did that hurt?"

Past-me shrugged a little. "Knocked me on my ass, cracked some ribs, maybe broke one. I'll have a bruise from tit to hip in the morning. Beats having a collapsed lung and more blood loss."

Past-me dropped the panel on the floor and looked half ready to nod off on the admittedly-comfy couch right then when Connie murmured, "What's next?"

"What was that?"

"I said what's next?"

He shrugged, which must have moved something painful because he soon winced. "Shit, I don't know. I've been making it up as I go along."

"So we're going on the run?"

"That's one possibility. I liked your outfit, but our first date kinda sucked. You sure you're ready for a road trip level of commitment?"

We both laughed at that. Then stopped and laughed again. The kind of hard, sincere, but pathetic laugh of people in the middle of the shit but somehow found something funny about it. Past-me got a thoughtful look on his face and shrugged, then winced before taking another sip.

"I'd say you were in the clear. But then I didn't expect to find those two in your house. But even so, If you can ditch your place and leave town, start over, you might make it free and clear."

Connie tilted her head. "Why do you say that?"

Past-me folded and holstered my multitool. "Everyone who knows what really happened besides us is dead. Except for Tasha, and she didn't get much of a look before I set her on fire. Nobody else on my team has any clue. Any other vampire shouldn't find out what's going on until tonight. Sometime between dusk tonight and dawn tomorrow, all hell breaks loose."

She nodded in loose acceptance.

"What kind of hell are we talking about?"

Past-me started to rub his chin in thought, then winced at touching growing bruises.

"Figure a dozen vamps, plus another dozen people more or less as good with a gun as I am. Assuming one of them doesn't just have the cops roll me up and arrange an accident."

"Why not run?"

"I got a big debt to pay here. The kind you don't run from if you have any other option."

"So now what?"

He grimaced. "Why are you so interested?'"

A flare of annoyance flashed across Connie's mind, pushing back the comfort of rescue and adrenaline drop. "I'm along for the ride, aren't I? I mean, if I go run to my parents, won't I just be waiting for some bloodsucker to drop the hammer on me?"

Past-me didn't have an answer for that. He tapped a finger against his other hand for several seconds. Finally Past-me downed the last of the water in the glass. I started to smell smoke.

"Maybe? I dunno. The adrenaline drop's hitting hard and I'm not thinking so good. Shit. I'm sorry."

"What for?"

"You wouldn't be in this shit if Eva hadn't decided you'd make a new toy for me to play with."

"You're blaming yourself for your psychotic vampire ex kidnapping me?"

"I'm blaming myself because she chose exactly what she thought I wanted."

"What the hell is that supposed to mean?"

Past-me folded his arms at that one. The staredown went longer than I thought it would. After a moment, Past-me pulled myself off of the couch. It took effort that I could see from all the way back in Connie's eyes. Past-me moved like I'd aged twenty years in as many minutes.

"I'm getting some sleep. Spare room's second door down the hall to your right. Bathroom's the first door down on the same side. I'm at the end of the hall. Help yourself to whatever. The wards will stop anything short of an Abrams, but wake me up before trying to leave so I can let you through them."

Past-me lurched down the hall to my bedroom. Connie got up and followed him. The smell of smoke grew heavier, and the back of my hand started to itch. I resisted trying to make Connie scratch her hand as she spoke.

"Travis?"

"What?"

"Thank you."

Past-me shut the door, and acrid smoke filled my senses as the room vanished.

*   *   *

Chapter Three

"Guideline Six:

If you have to swallow your pride,

wash it down with whatever you please."

When I opened my eyes, we were back at my dining room table. The incense had burned down to the bloodstain. I gently took my hands from Connie's, and a wave of anger fell from my mind. Her face was back in a stoic mask, but I reminded myself not to dismiss her. For a human thrown into what she'd experienced in the last twelve hours, she was holding herself together better than some Marines I'd known. I stubbed out the stick in the holder, and the pain in my hand vanished. My headache came back in a throbbing wave, making me wince. I could feel sweat in my hair, which was sticking as much as my shirt. I rolled my neck and shoulders, then did some gentle stretching. Several of my joints, annoyed at the interruption, began popping and cracking at the indignity of it all. The jerk supervisor of my consciousness told them to shut up and get back to work.

Connie blinked, looked around the room, then linked her fingers and pushed her palms out, rolling her back like a cat before relaxing. She closed her eyes and rolled her own neck slowly, moving through what looked like a familiar stretching routine. "So that's what it's like to have a wizard in me."

I bit my tongue before commenting on that one, then started to shake my head before my headache cranked up at the motion. "I did my best. Sorry if rerunning any of that was uncomfortable."

Her hand curled around the handle of her mug as she tilted her head. "Weirdly, it was kinda reassuring that it actually happened. Knowing you were in there was a little funky. I could kinda hear you thinking, like someone on their phone at the next table in a restaurant."

I nodded. "It's like that a lot. One of the signs someone else is in there, anyway."

"You find out what you needed to?"

"Yeah, some."

Connie went to take a shower. I found a notebook and my phone before pouring an ice water and setting about deconstructing my recent life. Fortunately, it looked like vampire work hadn't turned me into a social butterfly. The news mentioned a fire at the Cotillion.

What surprised me further was who I'd been talking to and who I hadn't. From what I remember, Lord Chittenden was the one who held my Oath and had summoned me last night, or rather last year, to start paying it back. But going back a few weeks in my phone, I hadn't corresponded with him directly at all. Most of my communication had been with Eva Marazzi, who apparently had owned the Cotillion herself. Go figure, a hot vampire chick runs a club. And if I was reading my email right, I'd been working as her chief of security. That explained the clothes and casual armor. Odd, but not out of the question. Normally I was a handyman, doing small repairs, making custom furniture, that kind of thing. That said, I'd stood enough post in my active duty days to be able to run a security setup easily enough. That I could deal with.

Much more unsettling was the fact that I'd apparently been her renfield. Vampire blood had some really wonky capabilities, and no mage I'd heard of had managed to do a comprehensive study. But what I'd looked up in the last few years had taught me a few things. A human drinking a vampire's blood got some pretty intense physical benefits. Enhanced strength, speed, and accelerated healing, for a start. Everything from promoting muscle density to preventing lactic acid buildup. The kind of thing that would put every athletic supplement company out of business. A mage had it even better. Vampire blood was like drinking raw magical energy.

The downside was in two flavors: one was a heavy addiction to vampire blood. The other was some sort of mental sympathetic magic that put the drinker under the influence of the donor. Serious influence. On the plus side, I'd managed to kill Eva. Which meant said influence wasn't unbreakable. And with Eva herself reduced to a carbon footprint, her further influence shouldn't be an issue. I also had answers for the tubes in my nightstand. It looked like I'd drank the one of them before falling asleep. Which explained why I'd woken up with a nasty headache and some old-looking bruises, instead of unable to sit up. And I had another one for a rainy day.

Looking deeper through my phone, I scrolled through my texts with Eva. My stomach lurched and my headache returned as I saw how she'd influenced me. It was like reading someone else's phone. Or maybe I was trying to convince myself of something. Besides the head of her security team, we had definitely been in a physical relationship. A very active physical relationship. If the texts hadn't made that blatantly clear, the pictures did. I'd been not only in bed with my boss but in every room of both house and office.

In hindsight, I'm amazed I didn't throw up. My Oath to Chittenden and being a renfield made my consent to the whole thing feel questionable at best. I had never had much luck with romantic relationships for a laundry list of reasons, but this string of sexts had all the passion of a porn site playlist. I couldn't call us lovers, even in my mind. Implying that there was anything loving about it felt depressing as well as delusional. Add in the fact that the relationship had culminated in kidnapping a stranger for the Gods knew what. Looking away from that thread almost made it worse. I'd barely texted or emailed anyone in months for anything besides work or booty calls. I felt a surge of gratitude that Connie was still in the shower. I put the phone down and took a deep breath.

I was alive, I was home, and still had my brain and my magic. Having my magic meant that I hadn't violated my Oath. Yet. I could do a lot with that. On the downside, I'd spent the last year ditching every friend I had to spend my time working for and frequently banging a vampire. I may or may not be wanted dead or alive for killing said vampire. I felt like I'd spent the last week getting my ass kicked. And I had a house guest or possibly kidnapping victim, who was good company if a massive wild card in the deck. If I wanted to move on, I needed to stay alive.

Noting that and putting it aside, I decided to take stock of the house. I went down the stairs, buttonhooked at the entrance and headed further down to the ground floor. In the leather and textiles room, boxes of stock and my embroidery machine were still packed up from where I'd put them last year. I had a side hustle selling morale patches that I'd shut down to focus on repaying my debt. Everything seemed normal. Nothing unusual in the laundry room. Apparently being a renfield still let me clean my clothes on the regular. I paused at the heavy oak door to Uncle Mac's suite. Those wards, at least, were strong and steady. Then again, Uncle Mac was a much better mage than I was.

Turning the other way, I took a pair of keys from my ring and unlocked my garage workshop. Opening the door felt like opening a crypt, with the hinges giving an old school creaking as the reinforced door opened. The track fluorescent lights overhead hummed and flickered to life, giving the workshop the feel of a morgue. The shop was set up just the way I'd left it, in that organized cleanliness rare in shops that saw regular use. Tools were in their places. Pieces for half-done projects were tucked away. The floor was clear. The vault was locked and barred. It felt haunted, like another me was at the workbench, sketching out a design or altering a piece to fit. On a hunch, I touched the steel housing of my belt sander. I took away a fingerful of dust, revealing the blue paint beneath. Nothing in the room had been touched in months, other than a walkway between the house and the carport outside. My mood sank a little further. It was like standing in a room full of more friends I'd left behind. I was tempted to step outside and take a look at the small forge I had set up in the backyard. But a part of me thought that if I went out, I couldn't bear to come back. I couldn't remember the last year of my life, but I could see what I'd given up during it.

Back upstairs, I checked my nightstand gun safe, steamer trunk, and gun cases. Apparently, being a renfield to a nightclub owner paid well. I'd upgraded some of my gear over the past year, and the cash stashes I kept in two places had grown by a zero in each. On a hunch, I checked the banking app on my phone. Confirmed: being a renfield paid very well. I hoped I'd remembered a good accountant, or my taxes were going to get exciting next year. Assuming I survived.

Beside the gun safe was a silver picture frame, closed like a cigarette case. I slowly reached down and flipped it open. It said something about my life that keeping a boudoir pic of my long-dead girlfriend was one of the least weird but most embarrassing parts of my life, but there it was. I had taken it before digital photography had been much of a thing. The original print stayed mounted under the glass of the frame. Years later, I still wondered what Heather McKay ever saw in a guy like me. If I'd flown a bomber in the war instead of carried demo and a rocket launcher, I'd have painted her on the side of my cockpit. She was what my grandparents would have called a big girl but a big hourglass. Skin pale enough to almost glow in the dark, with a mass of bottle-red hair that went down to her waist. In the picture, she was lounging on a sofa covered with one of those Celtic patterned blankets. A peasant skirt the color of autumn leaves hung low on her hips, and a chemise top cropped just under her breasts had teamed up with a weapons-grade bra to keep her contained. Silver gleamed at her ears, navel, and ankle. But it was her smile that drew me in that picture. Especially after the rest of her had drawn the eye, she was there with a smile that asked if you liked what you saw, even when she clearly already knew. The Mona Lisa could play poker with her smile, but Heather's smile could get you to try a drink that changed colors with the last ingredient. Kindness blended with mischief all the way down in those deep green eyes.

I want to be remembered like this for a thousand years.

That's what she'd said when she started to pose. I remembered shooting that picture, downstairs from where I sat, on a warm spring night. We had come home early from a date when a power outage shut down the movie theater. She'd gotten it into her head to play dress-up and pose for me. I had been a self-taught photographer, back in the film days, where you wanted to make every shot count. I'd just started to get good at it. Then that night I made my masterpiece in that discipline. Everything I'd shot since was more documentation than art, there to record something else. But this one made a moment I could return to. I managed to smile a little before closing the cover of the frame and putting it back.

I reloaded my battered and almost empty leather wallet from a cash stash just as the doorbell rang. I headed down to the front door, hearing the shower turn off as I passed the bathroom. On my generic doormat stood an old friend who looked to be in his mid-20's. A mane of dreadlocks were tied back and high, letting the breeze cool his neck. Dark eyes shone with a look of smooth mischief. His skin was a warm brown, and his smile was a warm sunrise. He was not quite six feet tall, with the muscles of someone who used them. He wore cargo trousers in gunmetal gray, with a polo shirt to match over sturdy boots. All of this topped off with a rich burgundy waistcoat straight out of the 1800's. Byron Hunter even made tactical chic look good.

Before he could open his mouth, I held up a finger. "Before you say a word or cross my threshold, you should know this: last night I killed Eva Marazzi, set the Cotillion on fire, lost my night job, and took a stoic yet cranky woman home with me. You sure you want in on this?"

Maybe I was being paranoid, but it's only polite to warn your frequent wingman about possible open warfare and other workday hazards.

His teeth flashed in a broad smile. "Finally! It's about time you got off your ass about it."

He patted me on the shoulder and stepped inside my home, letting me close the door behind him. I watched him stroll up the stairs and head for my kitchen, then shrugged. "That answers that question."

He waved my concern away like it was a hovering waiter. "It was all over the news at breakfast: The Cotillion on fire. Fortunately, the damage was supposedly minimal. Otherwise, we'd have suburbanite goth kids crying into their journals until Halloween decorations went up."

I locked the door and ascended the stairs to find Byron at the dining room table in his usual spot, having made himself an ice water. Shrapnel made a series of running leaps from chair to table to his arms, before crawling up and around his neck to lay across his shoulders like a mink stole. He laughed heartily and scritched her behind the ears. "Good day to you, mistress. Are you taking good care of your pet stoic? He looks like something you dragged in." Within seconds, Shrapnel's head lolled dramatically under the effects of Byron's affections, purring for more. He chuckled quietly, keeping up with the cat's demands as he took a drink with his free hand. Shrapnel and Byron understood each other. Probably an apex predator thing I didn't understand. That said, Byron was a hetero lifemate if ever I could claim one, and the closest thing I had to a best friend.

Byron was... Byron. Young for an elf, only in his 220's. He'd been as-signed as my warden after I made an Otherworld Oath that was probably unwise. Not the one I'd signed with Chittenden, another one. Yeah, I know. For a bright young man, I was pretty dense in some ways. Anyway, that particular oath had left me with a friend. He wound up joining the Marines on a buddy pass with me. Sounds like a bad joke, I know. An elf and a wizard step onto the yellow footprints. You'd think that joining the Marine Corps right in the middle of both Don't Ask, Don't Tell, and a two-front war in the Middle East would be a considerable challenge for someone who seemed about as fruity as the menu at a smoothie bar.

You. Have. No. Idea.

First off, he was a complete PT stud. Medium height and medium build guys usually were. But Byron was a child of the Hunt. Capital H definitely deserved. He'd hunted down prey beasts on every continent since the days when you could hit Canada from Louisiana. He'd also been dancing the night away at least since before Prohibition. And he partied just as hard playing beer pong every night in an infantry barracks.

That didn't even touch his impeccable fashion sense. He'd rather be dead at the bottom of the New River than wear moto shirts or shower shoes in town. If he'd been a little older, he'd probably have tried to assassinate Beau Brummel for crimes against fabulous. As it is, I'm glad we both left active duty before he became a squad leader. I can only imagine what unholy terrors he would've unleashed upon the world doing a uniform inspection.

Connie emerged from the bathroom, once more in her band shirt and yoga pants, hair in a towel. Byron turned to me with a raised eyebrow and a smile I was half-sure Connie could see. "You bastard! When were you going to tell me you'd brought home a night-blooming rose?"

I nodded in her direction. "Byron, this is Connie. Connie, Byron. Byron is..."

"Enchanted." He rose from the table with a winning smile, smooth as Grandma's homemade cake frosting. He took her offered hand and bowed halfway towards it. Byron had heard vague rumors about men shaking a lady's hand instead of kissing it these days, but he wasn't convinced of their reality.

Connie quirked a smile that I couldn't tell was more charmed or amused. "Where were you hiding him?"

I shrugged, peeling the banana I'd left behind. "I've given up trying to keep track of Byron."

Byron released both her hand and her gaze, grinning like a fool in my direction. "As if you could track me if I didn't want to be found."

I swallowed a hunk of banana before answering. I'm classy like that. "Fair nuff. What brought you round this early?"

He prowled back to his chair. "As I said, the flaming Cotillion, which I'm not sure would be a better name for a band or a cocktail, was all over the news at breakfast." he took a drink before continuing, "But you were hale and hearty. I figured on letting both of us sleep it off first."

Connie took one of the empty seats at the table as I devoured the remaining banana and tossed the peel into the trash can. "Does he know?" she asked.

Shrapnel came to me for her tribute, succumbing to my petting power as I answered Connie. "About me in general, yes. About last night, enough to know better, but he's sticking around anyway."

"He a wizard too?"

Byron snorted. I raised my eyebrow at him before answering. "He's a long story."

She shrugged at that. "Aren't we all? How did he know you were alive?"

Byron dug into his shirt to pull out a small amulet hanging from around his neck, which I waved at. "Byron's an excellent tracker. And he's got a big enough piece of me to let sympathetic magic find me just about anywhere."

The amulet disappeared back into his shirt. "So what did I miss from the last exciting episode?"

I drank more water. "I was totally Eva's renfield. And her security chief. And at least her side boy."

"Vegas odds said that, but it's nice to have confirmation."

I quickly filled Byron in on the story of last night and this morning. Mercifully, Byron's seen enough in his time that none of it really phased him. After capping off the debrief, I shrugged. "Not how I expected to spend a Tuesday afternoon, but here we are."

Byron shook his head in deadpan mock disappointment. "Not even the holiday weekend yet and you're already making a mess. At least you brought home a cute one this time."

I shrugged. "Double-G, Byron. The law's pretty clear."

Connie raised an eyebrow, which Byron answered. "Guide and Guard, honey. You're a human who stumbled into the Otherworld. A wizard like Travis here is bound by law to see you safely out of the mess you're in. So make yourself comfortable, nobody's throwing you to the winds anytime soon."

I waved my glass in Connie's direction. "And for Gods know why, Eva decided to kidnap Connie, strip her down, tie her up with one of my strap balls, and give her to me as a present."

"That's-" Byron's brain rewrote his thoughts into something more diplomatic. "-not something you'd enjoy with unwilling strangers."

Connie quipped, "Comforting to hear, says the unwilling stranger in question."

Byron shook his head in puzzlement. "I guess even someone playing the game as long as Eva steps in it completely sometimes. Not to stereotype a species, but let's face it, vamps ain't exactly the type for open and healthy communication."

I nodded. "It's creepy, but if we're talking about a world where I was a willing renfield, then a goth in a box as an attaboy present might make sense somehow too."

A faint pink tinge that might grow up to be a blush someday swept across Connie's pale features. I kept going, wagging a finger in a vague direction. "And then something happened. No idea what it was, but it happened. Our eyes met, I pulled your hair, I thanked you, and then I emptied a revolver into her face."

Byron looked impressed. "Now that, I've never seen happen, across a crowded room or otherwise."

Connie cracked a hint of a smile. "I'll admit I didn't expect that reaction. I don't know what I expected. If I did. There was a lot going on."

"And you were rather cranky, I remember. Secondhand, anyway. My guess is that something about you broke the renfield... curse? Connection? Mind control? Whatever it is Eva had on me."

She gave half a shrug. "No idea what I did, though."

"Me neither. You're really familiar for some reason, but I can't put my finger on it." I sighed, sitting back in the chair. "But now I've got a lot more questions."

"Like?"

I ticked off on my fingers. "One, why did Chittenden have me serving Eva instead of himself in the first place? Two, how did I kill not only her, but a pair of country vamps too? I took an ass-kicking doing it, but I still managed to do it. I'm not as fast or as strong as a vampire her age. So how? Three, why didn't I visibly use magic the entire stress-riddled time? Four, why are country vamps taking marching orders from a bratty city vamp like Tasha? Five, why you? Too much makes no sense."

Byron raised an eyebrow. "Wait. You killed Eva by yourself without magic?"

"Yup. And here's what's weirder."

I took off my shirt, to raised eyebrows from the two of them. Byron, of course, opened his mouth. "Not that I'm not tempted, Trav, but this is hardly the time."

"Shut up, Byron." I dropped the shirt and pointed to my side. "This happened yesterday."

Connie's eyes widened a bit. "Shit, you're right."

"I took a round in the vest and got my ass kicked by three vampires maybe twelve hours ago. I should be black and blue and barely able to walk. These bruises look at least a week old. And I don't remember casting a spell for that or anything else. I took two tubes of blood off of Eva before killing her. Looks like I drank one last night, there's just one left. Looks like renfields heal fast, too."

Byron frowned, then shook his head. "I got nothing. So what's the plan, Trav?"

I took a sip and contemplated. "I have 36 hours or so to report to Chittenden. I need to stay alive that long, get my memories back, get Eva's children to back off, and figure out how to make sure Connie gets out of this mess."

Connie half smirked. "Appreciated."

I remembered something. "While I'm at it, do the words 'follow' and 'yellow' mean anything to you two?"

Connie tilted her head. "Just the obvious. But you're already a wizard. What would you need to go to Oz for?"

Byron shrugged. "A heart, a brain, courage... his shopping list gets weird sometimes."

I rolled my eyes. "You're so helpful."

I lost myself in thought for a moment. My headache hadn't gone away. I was hungry and thirsty and a little nauseous all at once. I needed more information across the board.

Shrapnel headbutted my hand, having gone unpetted for at least two minutes, and I obediently scritched her behind the ears. "Any ideas what I've been up to in the past year, Byron?"

Byron raised a finger as he finished off his water, then set the glass down. He kept the finger up and started using others to count. "A year exactly? A year approximately? Or a year and a day?"

I tried to repress a shudder. A year and a day is a significant timeframe, magically speaking. And particularly significant in my own personal sense. My Oath, as sworn, was to serve for a year and a day. And something wiped my entire memory of it thus far. And I had a day and a half of it left, or thereabouts.

I finally shrugged. "All of the above. I was asleep for the transition."

Byron didn't let up. "Because a year and a day would make a lot of…"

"I know it makes sense. But it didn't take that long. I reported to Chittenden on the night of the second last year, which means my service ends tomorrow night at midnight. Besides which, I can still check wards and cast a cognimancy spell, so whatever else is going on, I haven't broken my Oath."

I could feel Connie's unspoken question hanging in the air in front of my head, which I shook in the negative. "Byron, broad strokes, what the hell have I been doing for the last year?"

Byron gave a quiet smile, then shrugged. "About a year ago, you said Lord Chittenden had called in your Oath, and you'd be busy for a year and a day. Inside of a week, you were working for Eva Marazzi. By Samhain, you weren't talking to anyone any more than absolutely necessary. We still went shooting at Warwell's once a month, but didn't talk much. I backed off as much as I dared. I saw you were balls deep in vampires, but once you fell, you stayed stable, if that makes any sense."

I went over that in my head. "So I never fell deep enough for you to have to take your obligation physically. This just keeps getting more interesting."

Connie frowned "His obligation?"

The doorbell rang before Byron could open his mouth.

*   *   *

Standing in my doorway when I opened it was an athletically built black woman in a cheap but well-tailored suit. Very well tailored, given that it hid the lines of all the weapons I knew the wearer carried on a daily basis. A deep purple shirt was open one button at the top with no tie. Her hair was bound back in neat, wide cornrows, and simple gold studs adorned her ears. She was a head shorter than me even in duty boots, but had no problems looking me in the eyes.

Standing next to her was a burly fellow dressed like a truck driver. Long hair crammed under a black ball cap, worn flannel over a shirt and jeans, comfortable hiking boots. His thumbs were tucked into his pockets in a gesture that screamed either military, law, or both.

I raised an eyebrow at both of them. "I didn't know the reboot was filming in town. Which one's Smokey and which is the Bandit?"

The woman's smile flashed shining teeth at me. That smile was not on my to-do list. But neither was rebuffing an old friend either.

"You look like hammered shit, Trav."

"Hey Babs. Social call?"

The smile didn't waver. "Can be."

I let them in and latched the door behind us. I holstered the pistol I'd held behind my leg as I checked her out. Babs would turn heads if she'd wanted to dress the part, but she was on duty, and intimidation was more effective than seduction in her line of work. She gave a half-handed wave at Byron as we climbed the stairs and headed to the kitchen. Her companion followed behind, apparently unconcerned about turning his back on me. Byron strutted an advance in our direction and gave Babs a smile that oozed charm but was completely wasted on her. Byron loved a challenge, and Babs was a walking one.

"Good morning, Deputy."

Byron got a smile for that. "Sup, Byron. Good to see you still hanging out with my favorite knucklehead."

"Wouldn't miss it for less than the world, sugar."

She smirked. "You've swung and missed this already, boytoy."

Babs gently pushed him out of her way and nodded to Connie, who offered a hand. "Connie Chandler."

Babs shook it. "Barbara Ward."

Byron nodded at the trucker with a lazy salute. "Marshal."

The Marshal, to his credit, tipped his hat respectfully. "Your grace."

Connie tilted her head at Babs. "Deputy, is it?"

I took my time sitting down, answering for her. "Deputy U.S. Marshal Ward. SiS division. The gentleman would be Marshal Sims, her supervisor."

Babs frowned. Connie pondered a moment. "Special Investigative Service?"

Byron winked. "Sisters in Spellwork, Soldiers in Sorcery..."

Connie took this in. "Didn't know there were magic feds."

I gave a dry chuckle as I sipped my water. "Oh, there's feds for everything."

Babs rolled her eyes. We all took our seats, Babs and Sims facing me. I sat back, trying to be polite. "So what's on your mind, Babs?"

Her look didn't change. "What the actual fuck, Trav?"

I squinted. "You're gonna have to be more specific. Work handed me my ass last night. Connie here came home with me, and I just woke up a bit ago. Feeling better than I was, but I ain't getting any younger."

Every word that came out of my mouth was true. It was also slippery, and Babs knew it. She opened her hands and sighed. "OK. I'll start with federal and work my way down to local."

I sighed. "And just like that, the call got less social."

Her gaze didn't waver. "Iron Council has you under investigation."

Byron and I answered in stereo. "Again?"

I shook my head. "What's the excuse this time?"

"Before last night's adventure? You're too good."

My eyebrow didn't come down. "And that's bad?"

She didn't take the bait. "That's suspicious."

"People should learn to mind their own business."

"You haven't been studying with any of the other barn owls, I know that much."

I threw up my hands. "Of course I haven't. They're all under investigation too." I started counting on my fingers. "Cyrus was questioned for active necromancy..."

Babs sighed. "Which was bullshit..."

Byron held up a finger. "Don't forget racist."

I kept counting. "Becky Sue was blamed for mountain lion sightings in the Carolinas..."

Babs kept her gaze at me. "There's plausible and there's showing off."

I kept counting. "Seb, for living in Florida, which I can kinda understand. Bubba, for harboring illegal wildlife that turned out to be Becky Sue. Lori, because they didn't like her homeschooling her kids. Thumper, for the high crimes and misdemeanors of struggling to live with brain damage..."

Babs held up her hand. "I get it, Trav."

I reloaded my counting hand and started firing fingers again. "Then there's my investigations. One for studying with Lady Sina instead of a proper grounding, which none of us got. Then I had the audacity to enlist..."

"Breaking the Treaty of Rhodes."

Sims spoke up. "Which was there specifically to keep mages from being slaughtered..."

I tried not to sneer at him. "... and look how good that turned out for us. I had Byron for a battle buddy. Much safer than when I was under council supervision. I don't recall any bitching when you decided to pick up a badge, Babs. Or are you just used to having your life messed with?"

I struck a nerve, but she didn't let it show. "Look at it from the Council's side. Half our class was killed and the council's response was bullshit. What we did to fight back was desperate enough. You don't think it's possible that one of us would go even farther to make sure it never happened again?"

My silence was enough of a response for her to go on. "Seb and Becky Sue join family trades. Respectable and normal. Bubba apprentices to a healer upstate. Lori, Cyrus, and myself are active members of the local Nimuen. And yeah, I said yes when they offered me a badge. But after you muster out of the Corps, you lock yourself up in here and go completely Frankenstein. And you're wondering why they look at you just a little bit harder?"

She had a point, but I'm stubborn enough to not want to admit it. "Yeah, well, maybe I went out on my own and worked my ass off."

"And maybe you're screwing around with things you shouldn't."

I knew exactly what she implied. And it pissed me off. "You saying I took that road?"

She sat back and folded her arms. "I'm saying you've made some Oaths that weren't very wise."

"When we were young and trying to stay alive, and future time was all I was willing to risk. Those Oaths are old enough to grow hair in funny places and start touching themselves at night. One of them I've spent the last year making good on, thank you very much."

"None of which explains how powerful you apparently became in the meantime. Unless Byron's been hooking you up?"

Byron had been looking oddly amused at us, but at his name he just held up his hands. "Don't look at me. I'm just an innocent stander."

I shook my head. "This is some serious bullshit, Babs. Because I rode off the end of their precious little bell curve and they don't know how I did it, so I must be in tight with the fallen?"

Magical society, at least under the Iron Council, wasn't much for law and order. Most of what a mage could do wrong could be solved by mortal justice, and often was. But SiS was brought in for things mortal justice couldn't handle. Demonic influence, for example. In that case, it was more like the Wild West. As in wanted posters with dead or alive being the viable options.

Connie stage whispered to Byron. "What's going on again?"

He whispered back. "Travis is a billy badass and didn't save the receipt. Wizard feds think he got it from the devil."

Connie's eyes got sarcastically wide and hopeful. "Can I get out of defending my thesis that way?"

Babs ignored them. "It's suspicious, Trav."

I let out a long sigh. Bad enough I just got out of bed with one devil, now I was all but accused of being tutored by another. "What do they want from me?"

She took a breath before letting it out. "Soul scans. You, your tools, your sanctum, any familiar, artifact, or magical object in your possession."

"No."

"Just to reassure the council there's no latent infernal presence."

"Fuck the Council and fuck you too if you're their hatchet woman, Babs. I'm apolitical. I'm a Blue River Survivor. I'm too strong for their liking and they're uncomfortable not knowing how. Tough shit. They should be leaving me alone."

She raised an eyebrow at that one. "The way they left Ethan alone? The way they left Doug alone?"

I shook my head. "I'm amazed you, of all people, are even trying. They left you and Lily twitching on the floor. Now they gave you a job, a badge, and a pat on the ass and it's all good?"

Sims raised an eyebrow. "She give you the impression that it was all good when, exactly?"

I sneered. "You got a point?"

Sims shrugged. "Deputy Ward said it herself, grunt. The council fucked you over. Your entire class. My predecessor screwed the pooch. And they did so because it was encouraged to leave people be to handle things themselves. One of the biggest disasters since the study hall system was created. And they don't want it ever happening again."

"Still waiting on a point."

Sims lit a cigarette without asking and ignoring the dirty looks he got from everyone in the room. After his first drag, he looked me in the eye. "Demons are undisputed champions in exactly two things: corruption and deception. Closest thing we have to a warning sign is mages getting too skilled in ways that ain't documented. You're a master alchemist and conductor, grunt, and you're not yet forty. You're not from one of the noted families. You studied under MacGregor and Sina for less than six months combined. You ain't Daedeli, you ain't Nimuen, and you sure ain't Right Hand. You're a hundred percent Celtic Nordic flavored and Americana filtered white boy. Which means there's nobody in the Conjurers, the First Tribes, or the Councils of Jade, Ivory, Obsidian, or Brass who would give you the time of day. That eliminates human teachers."

I sighed. "Go on, Marshal. You will anyway."

He took another drag, then nodded. "Yup. You ain't been learning from the Fae. Because there's only so much they can mess with you without damaging the Hunt's toy. And there's few who'd mess with that one's daddy."

Sims pointed at Byron, who waved. "I'll tell him you said hi. He loves men in uniform."

Sims rolled his eyes. "You ain't a shaman or a necromancer, which means you ain't learning from spirits or the dead. A Djinn's never been seen on this continent, thank the Gods. Which leaves demons as one of the very few beings capable of teaching what you know as fast as you've learned. There's other possibilities, from stolen texts to honest hardworking genius. But you can see where the process of elimination whittles down rapidly."

Damn him, he had a point. "Answer's still no. I know I'm not working with demons. And I don't trust the council not to fabricate whatever it wants to get rid of an inconvenience."

Sims turned to Babs. "Man's got a point." He stubbed out the cigarette in his palm and tucked the butt into a pocket of his jeans.

Babs closed her eyes, sighed, then held up her hands. "Fine, screw it. If you get yourself killed by the weekend, it'll all be moot anyway."

She'd lost me. I squinted in confusion. "What?"

Babs sighed, then met my eyes again. "There was a fire at the Cotillion early this morning. AFD found three dead in the boiler room. Looks like something jacked up with the furnace."

"Shit." I muttered. I opened my eyes, and Babs had her damned cop poker face staring right into mine. I made a judgment call and prayed I was right. "Eva Marazzi and two of her goons. That's who's in the basement."

I got a raised eyebrow from that. "Courtesy of you or Ms. Chandler?"

"Me. She was tied up at the time."

Byron snorted. Connie smirked. "You know, breaking a renfield bond ain't exactly helping your too good for comfort case."

"That's the least of my problems at the moment."

I turned back to see Marshal and Deputy trading looks. Babs didn't even try to keep a poker face. "You broke a renfield bond?"

I nodded, then shrugged. "Yeah."

Sims looked impressed. "Well, that's new."

Somewhere behind those eyes, Babs made a decision. "What can I do to help?"

Not about to look a gift horse of information in the mouth, I shrugged. "I've been up to my ass in vampires from months. I could use a fresh perspective. What's the city look like from your end?"

Her frown deepened. "Chittenden gets a very messy werewolf attack and loses his son last year. Rumor has it the only reason he's not a pile of ash is Eva Marazzi's son Victor. Chittenden lets Victor become a resident of Atlanta. An understandable reward, but it means Marazzi now has two children living in the same city. That's a sizable power bloc for a vampire. Especially for Chittenden's chief rival. Chittenden calls in your Oath to serve him. A year and a day for a night, that was what you owed. But you've spent most of the last year shacked up with Marazzi. That makes sense too, using an owed Oath to cover a favor. Now this morning, Marazzi's business is on fire, and she's dead in the basement with her bodyguards. SiS would be very interested in getting an official statement from you. But something, can't imagine what, tells me that Chittenden won't appreciate you being incommunicado. Am I right so far?"

I nodded. It was the simplest thing to do in the moment.

She shook her head, smelling the bullshit but unable to step out of it. "Can you at least tell me how many bodies are going to end up on the floor?"

I tilted my head in apology. "As few as I can manage."

She couldn't keep the disappointment out of her voice. "If you wanted to play in this kind of sandbox, you should've joined us."

I snorted. "Me? Join SiS?"

"You enlisted."

"Which drove SiS crazy. Speaking of suspicious, how far up your soul did they scan you when you signed up? I mean, you still had bits of half the Council's asses stuck in your teeth."

Her eyes softened. "You're an asshole, Travis, but you're good. You were a jarhead, so I know you can work with a chain of command if you need to. And after Blue River and the fallout I know you can handle a fight better than most. We could use you."

I shook my head, then winced as the ache told me not to do that. "Sorry, can't pass the credit check. Got some debts hanging over my head, you know?"

She frowned. "You're not the only one who paid a price to wear the barn owl, Travis."

"Yeah, but here I am, years later, still paying for it. Not interested in a badge, Babs."

Connie turned to Byron. "Are they always like this?"

He nodded, rolling his eyes. "I keep telling him to just put a ring on it if they're going to go at it like this." He caught Babs and I both scowling at him, then gave a beatific smile. "Oh don't mind me."

Babs took a deep breath, then let her voice drop.

I met her eyes. "My Oath is almost fulfilled. Just give me…" I checked my phone. "36 hours. By midnight tomorrow, it'll be over one way or another."

She slowly nodded.

I sighed. "Anything else I need to know before I get back to the unlicensed flesh golems I got out in the tool shed?"

"Not unless you go wandering around in the woods a lot, smartass."

I shrugged. "Not outside of making sure Byron gets his exercise, but go on."

Byron stuck his tongue out at me as Babs continued. "Been finding some weird-looking bodies out in the sticks lately. Human and animal. From a couple states up the Appalachians to as far South as Dahlonega."

Byron rose an eyebrow. "Weird as in how?"

Babs went on. "Not sure what's leaving them. At first we were thinking werewolves. They're torn up enough. But the fresher ones have way too much meat left for scavengers. No always-missing organs, no markings. Just something big enough to take down anything between a dog and a horse, then not eat much, then leave chunks lying around. Barney Warwell, our fish and wildlife guy for the region, is stumped."

I shrugged. "You got me there. Tried asking Bubba if it's some critter we're not used to? Or Becky Sue? She's-"

"- If you say, 'a cougar who can turn into a mountain lion too,' I'll punch you in the junk."

I bit my tongue before continuing. "I was gonna say a primal who knows the shapeshifting crowd. Maybe someone's turning into something too big for them to handle?"

Babs shrugged. "Already called them both. They're stumped too."

"Add me to the stumped list then."

She looked over at Byron. "What about you, Hunter? Sound like anything you play with?"

Byron shook his head. "Not that I can think of. You're right, that's a weird combination. I'd be more than happy to brief you about the Otherworld fauna of the American Southeast over dinner."

"Nice try, but I'll pass."

Byron sighed languidly. "One day you'll find my charms worthwhile."

She got up, shaking her head with a smile. "You watch his ass, Hunter. And your own."

Byron nodded in a way that looked almost like a formal bow. "Always, my lady."

Sims got up and tipped his hat. "Afternoon, all. I'll see myself out."

We all nodded in his direction. He closed the front door behind him.

Babs stood up, nodding at Connie. "Good luck, Ma'am."

She gave a small salute with her coffee mug. "Thank you, Deputy."

Her eyes, a touch softer than they had been before, met mine. "Take care of yourself, Trav. If it's humanly possible, just hunker down in this split-level fortress of yours until the clock runs out."

I blinked. "Why?"

Her look turned incredulous. "You mean you still haven't connected those dots?"

I frowned. "Explain it like I'm stupid."

"Marazzi is dead, you somehow found a magical way of breaking the renfield bond, and there's still a day and a half to go before your Oath is fulfilled."

I knew all of that. "Yeah?"

The look in her eyes softened again. "Trav, most of the region knows Chittenden holds your Oath until midnight tomorrow. That includes any other rivals for his throne, anyone who's insulted him, anyone who owes him money, anyone who even thinks they've aggravated him. And now they all know you as his pet gunslinging wizard. How many are finding out about Marazzi and thinking they're next on your hit list? How many are gonna get proactive about it?" She took a breath, wanting to say more but giving up. "Watch your ass out there."

Babs followed the path her boss took, gently closing the oak front door behind her.

Byron, with his typical sense of tact and decorum, waited until he'd heard Babs drive off to start snarking at me. "Shit. She's right."

Connie raised a hand. I stopped myself from taking a drink before tilting my head at her. "We're not in class, Connie. Ask whatever you like."

She pointed to the door Babs just left. "Pass the context on the watchlist, please?"

I sipped my water, then breathed. "The study hall system doesn't teach much beyond the rudiments of magic and how to get around in the Otherworld without getting yourself killed or humiliated. And there's not a lot of postgraduate magic education around out there. Studying on your own takes a lot of time. Not to mention more time finding the right books and still more time double-checking to make sure you're doing it right. So most people with magical ambitions find like-minded friends or find someone willing to teach them. Everything from apprenticeships to political factions."

Byron chimed in. "And when that doesn't work, the dull and dim try finding something else to teach them."

I tapped my nose with my finger and pointed to Byron. "Which doesn't end well. For anyone within several miles, in some cases. From what I hear, there are only two kinds of beings that can teach magic that mages can use. There's the Djinn. Vast majority of them fled to their home realm after the war, far away from humanity."

That got me a raised eyebrow from Connie. "War?"

I nodded. "King Solomon's War. He was the last mage to rule on earth, breaking the Law of the Magi. He tried to come up with new methods of magic to fight demons. Kick them off our plane of existence and back into hell. What he actually discovered was how to enslave Djinn. Body, mind, and soul. And yes, it's about as morally disgusting as it sounds. Most of the Djinn fled to their realm in the Otherworld before Solomon died. The few left are trapped in bottles and such in odd corners of the Middle East. Really powerful and got an understandable hate-on for mages."

"Gotcha."

I took another drink before continuing. "Fortunately for us, Solomon did eventually manage to banish the bulk of demons into their own realm.

By the time Rome fell, there were no mass demon incursions. Just onesies and twosies. But one of the big ways they can wind up on earth and gain power quick is to educate a mage and work through them. Especially solitary, ambitious mages who don't want to play with others."

"And this council is suspecting you?"

"Apparently." I shrugged and sighed. "Not that I'd ever do it. Swearing Otherworld Oaths is bad enough. Demonic education is like loanshark money. Only the dense, desperate, or both even try. Unfortunately I've got a teacher and former schoolmates who did just that. Which is one reason they're suspecting me. And I'm a solitary, which bothers them. Solitary mages my age are supposed to be too weak to do much beyond parlor tricks."

Connie looked a little puzzled. "But, it's magic, isn't it? I mean, once you know the basics in school, can't you just... Do it yourself?"

I shook my head. "Magic isn't a substitute for anything. Not work, not energy, not processing information. It just shuffles the work around. The real world substitutes much better than magic."

She frowned at that. I noticed the bruises on her wrist, then went for a different track. "Remember the cuffs you wore last night?"

Her frown deepened. "Yeah."

"They're magical. I made them and I helped refine the design."

"How?"

"How isn't important. What's important is everything that had to be accounted for in the end. It sounds like a simple effect. Leather cuffs that put themselves on someone and take themselves off on command. But I had to program those cuffs like a computer. They needed to know what on someone and off someone meant. They needed to know how bodies moved so they didn't dislocate someone's joints trying to restrain them. They needed to know what were acceptable combinations of tie downs were desired. And they had to let go on a safeword command. Yeah, I could have just made leather do what I told it, but I had to account for all of that first."

Byron rolled his eyes. "Keep asking questions and he's gonna use the cheeseburger paradox."

I got indignant. "Hey, the cheeseburger paradox works."

Connie smirked, folding her hands like the girl in the front of the class. "Well, now I have to hear about the cheeseburger paradox."

I downed the last of my water before beginning. "Theoretically, a mage can do anything with magic. Practically, it's much harder. You have to know exactly what you want and what needs to be done to make it happen. Say you want a cheeseburger. Easy enough. There's over a thousand restaurants in the metro Atlanta area that would be happy to serve you a variety of them. With me so far?"

Nods all around. I continued. "Now go back in time a thousand years. Theoretically, there's nothing physically stopping me from having a cheeseburger right then and there. But practically, it's a stone cold bitch. Assuming from the beginning that I even know what a cheeseburger is in the first place, I have to hunt down all the components. A thousand years ago, the closest cow to where we're standing was probably owned by a Viking somewhere in Newfoundland, so that's the first hurdle. The closest wheat is in Spain, the closest tomatoes are in Mexico, I'd have to look up to see if lettuce in Spain or Siberia is closer, but you get the point.

"Then, even if you do have everything you need in one spot, you still have to build it from the ground up. Assume for a moment you've got the baking skill to make a bun, the butcher skills to cut, grind, form, and grill the patty, the skills to find and slice the appropriate bits of produce, the cheesemaking knowledge, and the sauce making skills to make tomato ketchup, yellow mustard, and mayonnaise. We'll even be generous and say you have the preserving skill to make a pickle. You'll still have to assemble everything, tools and materials, to make all of the above. That's a lot of research and a lot of work even if you technically know how."

Connie nodded. "So this Council doesn't see you showing your work, so they're assuming you're cheating somehow."

"Exactly. Magic doesn't have the logistics tail or knowledge dissemination the Industrial Revolution gave to practically everything else. You can't find eye of newt at Walmart. And even most farmer's markets will look at you funny."

"So where do you get your eye of newt?"

I pointed my thumb vaguely northwest. "That flea market with a billboard of a cow. About an hour north on 85. Section nine is run by goblins. Anyway, there's only about ten thousand mages in North America, total. So they're looking at me coming up with things like the Strap Ball and wondering how I'm doing it. They've got a point, but they're drowning in so much paranoia that they're ignoring that I'm mostly an alchemist and a conductor. My magic study runs heavy to making things and directing energy. They're also ignoring the possibility that I'm that damn good, have no life, and I'm working my ass off."

I stood up and got a soda out of the fridge, cracked open the can, and crumpled back in my chair, ignoring the renewed aches from half of my body. Connie kept watching me like a patient crow.

Byron shrugged. "OK, deadline man walking. What next?"

I watched bits of dust play in the sunlight for a moment. "Cyrus still holds office hours on Tuesday afternoons, doesn't he?"

Byron raised an eyebrow. "You and he ain't exactly on friendly speaking terms."

I shook my head, "No, but I'm counting on his professionalism being deep enough to look past that."

Connie chimed in. "Should I ask?"

I shrugged. "You already did. Dr. Cyrus Dowdell. Professor of Philosophy at Emory. He's also a brilliant cognimancer and one of the best research mages I've ever met. We went to study hall together. And I'm hoping he knows enough about vampire blood and memory spells to help me unfuck my head and get the vampires off my ass."

Byron nodded. "Trouble is, Travis and Cyrus got into a drunken fight over politics years ago and haven't talked since. Seriously, bro, there's got to be another specialist you can call on. How about Seb? The man's forgotten more lore than you've ever learned."

"If I needed to know folklore, yeah. Memory magic and blood isn't his thing. Besides, he's on the road, probably in Bristol by now."

"Bubba?"

"He's a veterinarian, not a researcher."

"Becky Sue?"

"The last thing I need is hillbilly divination from an oracle in daisy dukes."

"Lori Homestead?"

"I still have both balls and an opinion. She's never gotten over that."

Connie raised an eyebrow. "Pity. So much charm she's missing out on."

Byron nodded smugly. "She really is."

I sneered. "You're both helpful."

The doorbell rang. I finished my glass and stood up.

"For someone who's been a blood-addled recluse for the last year, I'm popular today."

*   *   *

Chapter Four

"Guideline Two:

Magic is not a substitute for anything.

However, it can be used to find a substitute for almost everything."

Standing on my front porch was a slender, middle-aged black man in a tailored navy blue suit. Not as well tailored as Bab's, even if it was much more expensive. Then again, Babs was curvy and carried enough ordnance to share with a fire team. Oswald was built like a tall glass of water and only carried a single pistol, if the bulge I was looking for just under his left armpit was any indication. A quick glance around told me he was alone. I holstered my own pistol, stepped forward and closed the door behind me, then nodded politely at him. "Oswald."

He answered me with all the warmth of a collections rep. "Mr. Wayland."

I gave a warm smile in return, just because I knew it annoyed him. "What can I do for you?"

"Answering your phone would be a good start."

For Oswald, this was a zinger for his stand-up act at the Punchline. I shrugged. "Sorry, I've been busy."

That got me a raised eyebrow of judgment. "Apparently. I'm assuming that Ms. Marazzi is among the vampire corpses discovered at the Cotillion fire?"

"You assume correctly."

"Lord Chittenden will be expecting a full report."

"He'll have it. Tomorrow night."

The eyebrow raised higher in annoyance. "No updates for today?"

I shrugged casually. "You know me, Oswald. I'd rather be late than wrong."

Oswald really did fascinate me. I had no idea what led him to be the renfield of a Confederate vampire like Chittenden. Thinking about it raised uncomfortable questions about just how long Oswald had been his renfield. Despite his severe anal retention and my teasing, I actually liked the guy. When you're surrounded by conspiracy-addled vampires who are all playing their own games, it's kind of nice knowing someone is being straightforward with you. I just tried not to think too hard about why he was being straightforward.

Before he could comment, I heard brakes squealing at the end of the block like blue-collar banshees. A green four-door sedan with big patches of paint peeled off and all the windows rolled down turned the corner nearly hard enough to lift one side. The sedan came gunning down the road straight for the end of the block, a path that would take the ton of rusting Detroit steel right past my house.

Obeying instincts that I'd forgotten had been left on standby, I dove for the deck. I may or may not have told Oswald to duck, but he was not far behind me. I slammed my open hand against the front door and triggered a ward with a single word. Magical power rushed over me in a wave as I took a single breath. The ward thickened the air over my entire yard. The sunlight seemed to dim as the now viscous air bent the light in odd ways. I saw a bullet, going slow as a foam football gently tossed to a child but red-hot with friction, pass over my head and splatter into a small mushroom shape against the railing of my porch.

Still prone on the porch, I bit my tongue trying not to scream as the reality of what I'd done checked in. I'd activated the first ward I could think of to use against a ballistic attack. But the one I used was designed to be used while the defenders were indoors. The air that slowed down the bullets was also too thick for Oswald or I to breathe. If I kept the ward up too long, we would both suffocate.

I saw muzzle flashes from inside the sedan. The car was still going well over the speed limit past my house. But when bullets passed over the gutter, they slowed down instantly, the friction making them burn visibly even in the hot summer day. What would have been the cracking whip sound of the rounds breaking the sound barrier instead were muffled, low, and drawn out as the thickened air all around the house slowed everything down. The fired rounds curved in slow arcs from the guns that fired them, glowing like fireflies on kamikaze runs, landing in tufts of dirt on the lawn several yards before they got near us. The kicked-up grass floated like dandelion seeds in a slow wind before coming back to the ground. I only got one look at the shooter in the passenger side: it was the big and ugly guy from Connie's house, out of security blacks and wearing a dirty tank top.

I strained to hold my breath. I'd need it in a moment. I heard a gasp from Oswald as he found out the nature of the ward the hard way. If the shooters stopped to make sure of their work, we'd be sitting ducks. Twitching, gasping, and sitting ducks.

The sedan squealed around the corner, going past the gutter, into a neighbor's yard, and missing a fire hydrant by inches. I could feel the air pushing in on my nostrils, straining to push the thin old air out of my lungs and fill them anew, like pouring thick syrup into a glass bottle. Grass flew as one of the back tires ripped into the turf. My head throbbed and chest burned as I stretched out my arm towards the front door. At the corner of my eye, my vision blurred as the sedan hauled ass out of the neighborhood.

My hand pushed through the viscous air to make contact with the smooth wood of the door. I gasped a single word, then began to gag on the thick air flowing too slow to reach my desperate lungs.

The ward instantly went passive again. A gust of warm, humid, but wonderfully breathable air blew past us. Another gust filled my lungs, only for me to cough repeatedly. Several breaths later, my body convinced itself that it was breathing good old fashioned normal air. Only the distant barking of dogs remained to say anything exciting had happened recently.

I glanced at Oswald, who was catching his breath on his own and holstering a pistol I hadn't seen him draw. It took me several breaths before I grabbed the railing and stood up. I felt miserably out of shape. The headache was no help either. Nor were the bruises. Trying not to lean on the railing too hard, I waved at the road the shooters had taken. "Those guys after you or me?"

Oswald's eyes narrowed as his gaze followed my hand. "I'm not sure." He turned back and met my gaze for several long moments. Uncomfortable moments. Before it got truly weird, he quietly said, "You realize there's no substitute, right?"

"For being wrong?"

His face never wavered. "For blood, Mr. Wayland. There is no substitute. Not food, not showers, not caffeine, not alcohol, not red meat. Nothing."

"Dunno what you're insinuating, Oswald."

I was unimportant enough that he could let his annoyance show, and he took full advantage. "You're not the first renfield I've seen in withdrawal, Mr. Wayland, and you won't be the last. It would behoove you to make finding a new sponsor a high priority."

I nodded politely from a lack of anything better to do. "Anyone you'd recommend?"

"No. I will, however, point out that Victor Marazzi is often hiring."

On the bulletin board of my mind, I put a red pushpin in that. Oswald wasn't someone I'd go out of my way to have a beer with, but the only scheming he did was in Chittenden's name. If he was pointing me at Victor, there was a reason for it. I nodded again without additional sass. I'd poked him enough for one day and he still seemed to be giving what he thought was honest advice. "Thanks for the heads up, man."

"Until tomorrow, Mr. Wayland."

*   *   *

Connie had dried off her hair and hung up the towel somewhere. She sat back and watched me close the front door and make my way up the stairs. Byron's own eyebrow raised as he opened his mouth. "Dare I ask?"

I waved at the door as I made my way back to the table. "Oswald." A half-second later, I remembered Connie was there and filled in the details. "Lord Chittenden's renfield."

Connie almost looked concerned. "Well, he's not having you taken to the dungeon, is he?"

Byron shook his head. "Ozzy knows Trav has plenty of dungeon right here at home."

I dropped into the stuffed armchair, then immediately regretted it as something in my body objected. I winced and shook my head. "He's not. But I got to report to the man himself tomorrow night. Which I was going to do anyway, so no worries there."

Byron's eyebrow stayed up as he counted on his fingers. "After killing one if not three of his subjects, assaulting another of his subjects, and still having no idea what you're actually supposed to be doing to work off your debt. Did I get it all?"

I nodded, swishing the ice remnants around in my glass. "Yeah, more or less. Think he'll be upset?"

He stopped counting and shrugged. "Only a lot."

I pointed my thumb at the front windows. "Oh, yeah, and we just had a drive-by shooting."

Connie dropped a spoon. Byron's eyebrow raised, more in indignation at missing the fun than concern over anything. "Wait, that was gunfire?"

"Yeah, I set off a ballistic ward when they started shooting. There's a round in the front porch, a couple others in the front yard. I'll dig 'em up in a bit and see if I can make a connection. Shooter was one of Eva's old security goons. Couple of slack-jawed yokels managed to get a sedan running long enough to leave the family junkyard and throw some lead in my direction."

Connie threw her retrieved spoon in the sink. "You really are popular."

I sighed. "I need more information. And Cyrus is the best cognimancer I can probably get to talk to me. Ergo, I'm gonna have a heaping helping of crow and talk to him."

There was silence as I double-checked the ceiling again, as if the ghost-banishing paint had a bonus divination feature. I finally looked over at my companions, settling on Connie. "You look like a question's burning a hole in your head."

She smiled nervously. "So, you gonna wipe my memory when this is over?"

I blinked, then grimaced. "What the hell for?"

She gave an awkward shrug. "Well, I know about magic and vampires and whatever Byron is and, well, you. Isn't there some sort of law about keeping humans ignorant?"

I shook my head and dropped into lecture mode like a fighting stance. "OK, first off, I'm not a jack of all magic, I'm a handyman. You want something to last longer, go faster, explode bigger, or all of the above, I'm your huckleberry. Just gimme a roll of duct tape and my multitool. But mind magic isn't my specialty."

"Weren't you just running around in my memories a while ago?"

"Yeah. I had a preplanned spell, your consent, your active participation, and I knew what I was looking for. I still had to concentrate hard enough to make my headache worse. Hiding and rearranging every memory you've had since last night? Way more difficult. The odds of me forgetting something and the entire charm unraveling are just too high. I'm sure there's mages out there who can break through the homefield advantage and do it, but I'm not one of them."

She nodded at that. "You sound like you had a list. Don't let me stop you."

I took the invitation and ran with it. "Secondly, no, there isn't a law about it. There's not much point. Most of humanity hides from the Otherworld and hides harder when it gets scary. They try not to think about what ordinary people are capable of doing to each other, let alone anything supernatural. It's not like anyone believes any evidence anymore. I mean, go ahead, put video online of me calling down thunderbolts and riding flying carpets all you want. Your responses are going to be spam links, complaints about bad special effects, and asking you for nudes. And I haven't even mentioned Florida."

Byron lowered his head and shuddered. Even Byron had issues with Florida.

Connie smirked and conceded. "OK, you're probably right there."

I nodded. "The world thinks Blue River was a school shooting for a reason. Trying to keep myself and the other survivors from being considered suspects took more effort than convincing anyone that nothing supernatural had happened. Hell, the only good thing to come out of Blue River is that coercive mind magic was declared a serious crime in and of itself. More than one duel's gone down because someone got caught screwing around in someone else's head. So no, depending on how this goes down, I might get you killed, but I'm not going to wipe your memory."

The smirk made itself comfortable. "How comforting. What do I do now?"

I sat up. "That's pretty much up to you. I'm obligated to pull you out of the Otherworld and back to a normal life to the best of my ability. If you want to run and hide somewhere? I can follow you to your hideout to make sure you're not jumped along the way. If you want to just leave and take your chances? You're a grown woman, I'm not gonna stop you. Though I'd appreciate it if you'd leave me a number so I can tell you when or if the coast is clear, assuming I survive. Or you can stick close to me, trust that I'm lawbound to jack up anyone who tries to finish what Eva started, and check my progress as I go."

She shrugged. "Staying with you for the moment sounds better than waiting for a phone call or another attack. But I got a question."

I shrugged. "If it's someone else's secret, I ain't telling. Otherwise, fire away."

"How did you wind up owing an IOU to a vampire lord?"

*　*　*

Chapter Five

We all stepped out of the garage. I'd taken the time to gear up for a negotiation that might turn hostile. My standard cargo pants, this time in navy blue. Button down work shirt with short sleeves. A few pouches on the belt, smallest being the multitool over my right hip. I wasn't that heavily armed, what with only four blades on me. A holdout pistol was holstered in my left front pocket. I had a pair of extended magazines in the Yukon's glove compartment, but I figured they'd gather dust before I'd ever use them in a fight. My wand was in my other pocket next to my phone, and the pouches held other tools that had come in handy over the years. I could handle a fight if needs be, and looking more like an overweight grad student would help me talk my way out of one, which was preferable.

Connie looked me up and down. "I didn't expect to see a wizard in cargo pants."

"What did you expect?"

"I dunno. Robes and a pointy hat?"

I grimaced. "In a Georgia summer? No way."

Byron shook his head. "Oh no, honey. This is the South. Last time a paunchy white boy calling himself a wizard dressed like that, he was not good company." Byron's fangs flashed in a smile I recognized as his reliving a fond memory of being as vicious as he wanted to someone who completely deserved it. "Made for a fun night's hunting, though."

Connie had kept her band shirt, but traded the yoga pants for some cargo shorts and a pair of boots that looked like they spent the weekends cracking skulls. I approved. She also had found some oversized sunglasses that only made her poker face more impassive. Byron was still in the ensemble he'd worn making an appearance on my doorstep.

We all climbed into the Yukon. I'd poured the last cup of coffee from the pot into a travel mug, which was loaded into the holder as I got behind the wheel. Ever the gallant, Byron slid into the back to allow Connie to ride shotgun. The effect was only partly spoiled by the sheer volume of stuff I had to clear off the seat to make room for it. When I started the engine, Bob the nite owl began to lecture us from the speakers.

"...round of mermaid abductions on the gulf coast is the latest attack on the domestic oil industry. America thrives on the efforts of these wrench-turning roughnecks, and their heightened risk of being absconded with by some tarted up manatee is nothing less than..."

I clicked off the stereo, then took a breath. I didn't want to discuss it. I don't want to write it now. But I really didn't want to discuss it then. However, I said I'd tell her if it wasn't someone else's secret.

Byron gave me a look from the backseat. "You sure you want to be doing this while driving?"

I let out another breath. "No, but I promised I would."

I opened up a picture on my phone, then left it in a holster before putting the Yukon in drive and heading out of the driveway. After several moments, I finally spoke.

"I don't owe Lord Chittenden an IOU. I owe him an Oath. Big difference. And I owe him an Oath because in high school I made some very stupid choices while trying to stay alive."

Connie's expression didn't change. "How cryptic."

Byron raised an eyebrow, but still looked concerned. "Trav, I know you're in guide and guard mode, but she's a little past the keep her in the dark and tell her what not to do stage."

"I'm getting there, Byron."

"Byron's right, you know." I glanced back at Connie. Her hands were held tight around her empty water bottle, kept there for something to hold onto. Only the road turned my gaze from her. Her jaw was tight, and for the first time I could feel tension in her voice. "I've been in the dark for hours. Ever since I was snatched by people working with you. Given to you like a gift card for the employee of the month. Watching you butcher three people in front of me. Since you brought me home to people you knew and I didn't in my living room. Since you had a drive-by shooting while I was finishing breakfast. If your duty is guiding and guarding, lemme know when you're gonna start."

There was a low whistle from behind me. I looked in the backseat to see Byron fanning himself. I sighed, turned back to Connie, and nodded to acknowledge the rebuke. "How long you lived in Atlanta?"

"Since I was five or six."

"Ever heard of Blue River?"

"The suburb or the school shooting?"

I let out a long breath. "I wish it was a school shooting."

Her look said, "Get on with it." I sighed, then held up my hand a bit.

"I'm getting there. But to get there, I have to talk about study hall. And to talk about study hall, I have to talk about Magic. The ability to use Magic, capital M, makes itself known in humans at the age of twelve. Don't ask why, there's several arguments about it. We call it the Epiphany. The moment you know down to the bottom of your soul that it's real. Everyone can sense magic a little. And anyone could manipulate it a bit if they tried and knew how. But after the Epiphany, you sense it everywhere. Learn how to use it and control it, and you can probably live a decent life with it. Don't learn to control it, you usually go insane, get yourself killed, or both. So, how do you learn to control it?"

She followed her line deadpan but amused. "I dunno, Travis. How do you learn to control it?"

I snapped my fingers and smiled in true carny barker fashion. "I'm glad you asked. Gold standard going back to cavepeople has been apprentice-ships. One on one. Usually, no matter how backwards your tribe was, there was a wise woman or a shaman or someone who knew how to get you functional, maybe even impressive. If nothing else, they taught you what you could do and what your community needed. And when they passed on, you took over the job. Then when we stated living in cities, secret societies cropped up. Small groups that knew what to look for and took in who they could. Made mages useful and life better for everyone. Or at least for them and theirs. Between the apprenticeships and the secret societies, mages lived more or less comfortably among the rest of humanity. Sometimes more openly than others. Which worked, more or less, for centuries."

"Then it stopped working?"

I nodded. "Yup. Weird thing, Magic isn't exclusively hereditary. It's a tiny percentage of the population. But it's more or less the same tiny percentage of the population. We've had entire magical families and tribes wiped out before. But somehow there always seems to be enough mages to go around."

Connie glanced in the back at Byron, who raised his hands. "Don't look at me, honey. I'm still amazed the wizards ever finish trying to understand the universe long enough to mate, let alone breed. And when they do, it's like visiting the zoo at just the right time." He flashed a smile that should have had an adults only rating on it.

I resisted the urge to roll my eyes and kept them on the road instead before continuing. "Then the world population doubled between 1800 and 1900. Then doubled again by 1950. And that's even with two world wars and the Spanish flu epidemic."

Connie caught on. "So suddenly there were a lot more witches running around."

"Exactly. After World War II, the Iron Council decided to upscale and sort of standardize magical education in North America. Seventh grade through the end of high school, you go to study hall. One period a day to learn how to deal with magic when everyone else thinks you're being babysat."

"In every school? Bullshit."

Byron chuckled. I nodded. "You're right, that would be bullshit. Which is why it's not every school. Just twenty-four in the continental U.S., six per region. Divided by the Mississippi river for East and West, I-64, I-70 and I-80 for North and South, respectively. You turn twelve and start talking to ghosts, throwing lightning bolts, or lifting cars one-handed, someone finds you. And if you're in melting pot America and one of the other societies doesn't snatch you up, your parents wind up needing to move and you end up in study hall."

"Other societies?"

I shrugged. "Dunno much about 'em, but they're out there. Apprenticeships and small family groups, mostly. Some of the Native American tribes out west prefer to train their own. And given the Dawes Act, which is a great read if you don't feel like sleeping right for days, there's no way to blame 'em. Southeast, especially on the coast, families with hoodoo in their history prefer to do the same thing. I've heard rumors of a group called the Right Hand. They supposedly take in anyone with parents in old money or the Fortune 500 and train 'em to be kingmakers or whatever. There's probably more out there, but I don't know the details." I shrugged. "Anyway, study hall is what I wound up in. You ever draw that funny-looking 'S' on your notebook in school?"

She looked at me incredulously. "The one that looks like two diamonds stacked on top of each other? Yeah, everyone did."

"That came from us. It's a sigil. It was originally used to mark the door of a study hall. The base for a spell that kept looky-loos from seeing anything they didn't need to."

"No shit?"

"No shit." I wove my hand in dismissal. "They're everywhere now, of course. Mostly as just little bits of normal graffiti instead of a spell sigil. Anyways, every year, you get a new study hall instructor. We call them monitors. Primus through Sextus. The system's supposed to give a well-rounded education and keep any one teacher from building their own private power base or cult. Because that was so effective with us."

"You're getting sarcasm all over your steering wheel."

I shrugged. "I'll mop it up later." I let the light turn green and went through the intersection before continuing. "The Blue River Massacre was the result of my study hall class stopping our Monitor Sextus from sacrificing most of our graduating class in a huge, nasty, necromantic ritual."

Connie frowned. "I kinda remember the news at the time, but I don't remember seeing anything occultish. The news was all something about a meth gang and dogs attacking students?"

I nodded. "Hellhounds. Think saber-toothed rottweilers with bad attitudes and you've got the idea. She summoned packs of hellhounds to attack a graduation party. The meth gang was actually on our side."

"How'd that happen?"

I almost growled at the memory. "Iron Council let us twist in the wind."

Byron spoke up. "Wizards are more territorial than some animals. And students are prime territory."

I nodded, pushing myself. This was like pulling my own teeth with a bottle of whiskey and a multitool: sounds badass, but it sucks in the moment. "In a lot of ways, the Iron Council, wizard government, another long story, is ridiculously old fashioned. Making the study hall system was really progressive for a lot of them. In the apprentice and society models, students means allies, it means people who owe you favors, it means prestige, like fraternities or alumni groups. And one of the oldest faux pas out there is messing with someone else's students. Duels have been fought over it."

I sipped my coffee again before continuing. "Anyways, asking to teach as a Monitor was a trade-off. You had access to a lot of students, but for much less time than they'd usually study under you. Until they became an adult. A lot of people wanting to learn magic further went on to apprentice under one of their former Monitors. So they kept a lot of the old traditions. Big one being, a Monitor has almost unlimited authority to go with the responsibility. Takes damn near a unanimous council vote to get an American mage to act against a Monitor, no matter how badly their students are being treated."

I took another breath that was more of a sigh. "We knew she was sleeping with two of my classmates. We suspected a lot more. But we couldn't prove she was plotting mass murder or necromancy. And a lot of the established mages really don't give a shit about Monitors sleeping with students. So any adult mage we could contact was forced to back off and couldn't help us until we were already in deep shit."

Connie looked appalled. "That's... disgusting"

"Yup. Anyway, we couldn't get help there, so we looked elsewhere."

"The vampire lord."

"Yup. Gave us all the weapons and ammo we needed, plus the meth gang as a screening element. They shot any hellhounds that got past us before they could get into a neighborhood or something."

"And this was your study hall class?"

Keeping my eyes on the road, I offered her my phone. Turned on, it opened a picture I'd kept saved: A group shot of twenty teenagers, all mugging for the camera in a goofy yearbook way. I pointed in the picture's general direction. "My study hall class. We lost one of us to a car crash when we were juniors. Nineteen of us kicked off senior year. Swipe it."

The next picture was a scan of a color photo taken by a news photographer. I had pestered the photographer for a print after seeing the headline. Ten people emerging from a treeline, filthy and exhausted. Only seven of the ten were walking under their own power. I recognized the younger version of myself, carrying a smaller classmate. Next to me was a younger version of Babs, sporting a thousand-yard stare. "Ten of us survived the night."

She frowned a bit. "I thought thirteen people were killed?"

I nodded. "Our graduating class had three hundred people, nineteen of us mages. Maybe half of the class came to party in the park. Our Sextus tried to kill them all. We managed to save all but four. And nine of us were killed in the process. My best friend, my girlfriend, half the friends I ever had."

I sighed, trying not to let my thoughts wander anywhere that would really let me break down in traffic. Or in front of a near stranger.

I want to be remembered like this for a thousand years.

After a second, I spoke up again. "We got patched up. The ones who lived, that is. Me, Babs, Cyrus, Seb Hardy, Thumper Ross, Bubba Nolen, Lori Homestead, and Becky Sue Jackson. Then we all got drunk. Then got tattooed." I tapped my chest more or less where the barn owl was. "There was an investigation. And a trial. Nobody in the Iron Council's employ faced punishment for allowing our monitor free reign. But active necromancy was outlawed throughout North America. Not that the Conjurers give a single damn there. What the Iron Council did demand was the right to read the minds of students and Monitors at will. They didn't quite get it, but there's all manner of drama about just cause. There's still an occasional duel fought over it. A day late and a dollar short to help us."

There was a quiet moment before she asked, "And the others?"

"What others?"

"You said ten survived. You only mentioned eight."

I took another breath before answering. "They made it through the night, but not the summer. None of us reacted well to the outcome of the trial. Babs and Lily almost threw hands on the Council floor and had to be sedated before they got into a bigger fight. About a month after the trial, Andy Bennett decided to sleep off a bender and never woke up. A month after that, Lily Dawson jumped from a bridge into the Savannah river. That's what finally got the active necromancy ban passed. Useless council idiots."

She quietly asked, "Is there a passive necromancy?"

I had to think for a second there. "Shit, probably. I never studied it. Listening to the dead, talking to the dead, trading favors, that's probably cool. Hell, I kissed a ghost once. Like hanging with anyone else. But compelling the dead? Controlling them? Even if there was a definite answer whether they have a nature or free will, that's creepifying. And given what a resurrection looked like?" I shuddered. "Fuck that. I watched her just touch one of my classmates and they went from human to rotting alive and screaming human to dust and bones in moments. I don't know when they actually died but it wasn't nearly soon enough."

I took a breath and cursed the fact that I couldn't drink. After a sip of coffee and a few more breaths I quietly said, "That didn't answer your question."

She shook her head negatively. I nodded and let out my latest breath. "To be honest, I wouldn't even know who to ask. The few openly practicing in the country got quiet about it quick. Rumor has it that the hoodoo families still practice what they want, to hell with the Iron Council. But I don't know anyone doing it personally. And to be honest, I don't want to. I'm too young to have this much death from fucking with the dead in my life. I'd just as soon leave any more alone, given the choice."

I took another turn when traffic let me. "Which leads me to Otherworld Oaths. There are a lot of sentient species out there, none of which are particularly loved by humanity. No police. Babs and her cohorts can barely manage mages, let alone anyone else. Nothing resembling common law. And a lot of people capable of doing a lot of damage. So one day, long ago, the Oaths were created. Enforced by the world itself."

"So, your word really is your bond?"

"Exactly. At least it can be. You can hear pieces of it in old stories, fairy tales, that kind of thing. The vows people made and the terrible things that happened when they broke their word. Break an Oath, and the world punishes you for it."

She murmured. "What did you swear?"

"By my magic. For one night of men and materials, I owed Lord Chittenden a year and a day of service. I'm coming down to the end of that time. So I need to know what I was doing for him last year. And how I need to finish it. Here's hoping Cyrus pulls that off for me."

*　*　*

Chapter Six

"Guideline Seven:

Be specific.

Know exactly what you want and make sure exactly what you're being told.

And that's before stopping to wonder if you're being lied to."

Samuel's was a bar and grill just outside of the Emory campus. The exterior was original brick, the interior carefully stained hardwood. Generations ago, a place like Samuel's would have been patronized by a steady stream of blue-collar men expecting hot food and cold beer with a minimum of difficulty. These days, it was more of an assurance to each year's incoming crop of undergrads that they were grownups as well.

Even without my blathering, it was a short trip northwest through the thick forests that Atlanta's suburbia planted itself in between, like small villages with driveways. Until the 1990's, builders in Atlanta only cut down the bare minimum of trees needed to build on any given lot, and simply worked their way around any others. It's hard to describe how truly green Atlanta is, but the trees everywhere but the most recently developed or deeply urban are the first clues. Stand on top of Stone Mountain and look to the west, you'll see a handful of skyscrapers poking up from a thick forest that keeps rolling out all the way to the horizon and beyond.

I pulled the Yukon into Samuel's true treasure in an urban college town: a free parking lot with spaces open. Parking hood out in case we needed to leave in a hurry, I shut down and climbed out. I was fairly sure we weren't being followed, but evasion wasn't something I specialized in. A couple quick looks around the parking lot showed me nothing I didn't expect to see in the area, but that did nothing to dial down my hackles. As we got to the door, Byron shook his head. He hadn't noticed anything either. That settled me down a bit. Tracking someone like Byron without him knowing about it was far more difficult than it looked.

It was late afternoon, with children home from school but office workers not quite ready to clock out. A few students were scattered about the main floor in singles and small groups. Most of them were buried in their books and laptops as the few servers kept them loaded with caffeine and appetizers. The bartender, a doe-eyed young lady with more jewelry than orifices in the face, gave a charming smile as we entered.

I pointed to the back of the room. "We're here to see the doc."

The Bartender gave me a thumbs-up in return and traded flirtatious smiles with Byron before going back to wiping down mugs. Connie stashed her shades in her bag as we walked.

At the far wall was a thick velvet curtain that spanned all the way up the wall, possibly reclaimed from a small theater. Next to the curtain was a carved wooden sign hanging on the wall made from a thick slab of oak. Into the sign had been carved and burned the phrase "The philosopher is IN. 25c." On a small table below the sign was a coffee can wrapped in black gaffer's tape. A small slot had been carved into the plastic lid.

Byron's hand slid into his pocket and Connie started rummaging around in her bag as I took a handful of quarters from one of my smaller pouches. I deliberately dropped three into the slot, one at a time. After a moment, a slider on the sign moved, covering the word IN and exposing the words AT WORK. A tenor voice from behind the curtain said, "Enter."

I took a breath, then held up a hand. If Cyrus was going to take a shot at me, it would be now. Byron nodded in acknowledgment, having already put himself between Connie and the curtain.

Making sure my right hand was open and empty, I took the curtain in my left hand, pushing it open all the way to my left. Beyond the curtain was a room just big enough for a private round table. Another door stood in the corner to my far right. At first glance, the table was empty. The slight creak of a spinning ceiling fan was the only notable movement for several moments. My eyes flickered to my left, seeing Cyrus leaning against the far wall. His eyes grew a touch wider in surprise behind a pair of horn rimmed glasses.

My hands up and open, I couldn't help cocking a half smile. "You still sit the way I showed you."

The surprise vanished in his eyes as his gaze met mine, replaced with mild contempt. "It's done well by me. Which is more than I can say for the one who showed me how to do it."

Cyrus Dowdell was a dark skinned black man standing right at six feet tall. His slender build leaned more to wiry than skinny, short sleeves of his burgundy shirt showing defined muscles in his forearms. The sleeves were a concession to the weather, complimenting his matching gray slacks and waistcoat. His rounded goatee was neatly trimmed, as was his hair, carved into a Mohawk some two inches wide and an inch high. His look wavered somewhere between professional courtesy and a poker face. I'm sure I wasn't helping the tension in the room. I took a shot at defusing it.

"Don't tell me you're still that cranky with me, Cyrus."

His gaze didn't change. "Depends. Did Chittenden send you to kill me?"

I shook my head. "Nope. What'd you do to piss him off?"

"We're in the wrong century for slavery to be a nightly occurrence. Yet Chittenden still keeps his chattels. I've objected to that on multiple occasions. In the process, I may have said unkind things about other facets of his being."

"You? That uncouth?"

"Only about his physical fitness, applied intellect, and probable ancestry."

"That would do it. For what it's worth, you're not a target as far as I know." I glanced down for a second and noticed something. "Hands under the table? Cyrus, are you finally holding me at gunpoint?"

He sneered, slowly holding up his ring-bedecked hands. He twirled a pen between his fingers. "I never developed a need nor a taste for pistols. If I need to reach out and touch someone, I'll close the distance instead of risk bystanders. And once I'm up close and personal, if I've a need for offense, I prefer something more precise."

The pen he was spinning became a Bowie knife. His fingers didn't miss a turn as the blade flipped, landing tip-first into the wood of the table.

It annoyed me more than it should have. I've heard a lot of the same sneering at guns from blade fetishists who could barely chop vegetables for soup on a good day. If he'd been an ordinary mortal, Cyrus' attitude would have made him a bullet sponge. But as it stood, Cyrus was good enough at illusions that keeping him in your sights was a pain in the ass even if you knew he could do it. On top of that, he was good enough with his chicken slayer to hold his own in a fight. The jerk.

Byron ignored said tension and nodded to Cyrus in a way that suggested a more flirtatious sort of bow. "Hello, tall, doctor, and handsome."

Cyrus returned it just as casually with none of the flirtation. "Hunter."

Connie extended her hand with a quiet smile. "Connie Chandler."

Instead of shaking her hand, he stood up and wrapped his fingers around hers, turning her palm down. I snickered. We had been trained with old world manners, which included kissing a lady's hand. Not the sort of thing his mundane circles would approve of. He kept the awkward to a minimum by lifting her hand about an inch and nodding politely, meeting her eyes. I never said the man wasn't smooth.

"Doctor Cyrus Dowdell, Ma'am."

She cracked a smile and even bent her knees in the shadow of a curtsy. "Charmed, Doctor."

"Quite so." He let her hand go and faced me again with professional neutrality. "Since you're not here to kill me, dare I ask the occasion?"

Emotions churned, but I forced myself to return the professional courtesy. "Office hours, assuming you're still holding them. Needing a bit of a consultation."

He looked me over for just a moment longer than was comfortable, then slowly nodded. "Have some seats."

We sat, the wooden chairs comfortable enough for college students to occupy for hours on end, yet sturdy enough to withstand the punishment of student shenanigans. I was opposite Cyrus. Byron near the curtain and Connie near the kitchen door. A waiter appeared from the door with barely a word but a quiet smile, taking our drink orders and disappearing back into the kitchen. Cyrus kept his hands on the table, folded like a poker player.

"I heard about the Cotillion this morning. Glad to hear you weren't one of the bodies they found."

I shrugged a little. "Wasn't for lack of effort on the other guy's part, but the thought's appreciated."

He nodded. "You still look like hammered shit."

Byron snickered. "Babs told him the same thing. Great minds..."

That let me tilt my head agreement. "It was a rough night."

"You're coming to me for advice. I can only imagine how rough. Unless Byron here nagged you into seeing sense."

Byron held up a finger to his lips and almost blushed. I ignored him and waved my hand back and forth. "Six of one, half a dozen of the other."

Cyrus kept his gaze on me. "You're still a dick."

"Guilty as charged."

"And another-" Cyrus stuttered as his ears caught up with his rant. "What?"

"I've been a jerk for a while now, looks like." I shrugged a little. "To you, among others."

"So what, you're kicking off step nine?" Cyrus lowered his glasses so he could look at me over the top of the rims. I waved negatively.

"Don't be dense. You know I'm not the type to say, 'Hi, I'm Travis, and I'm a stubborn asshole' for the free coffee. But I've recently had some disturbing personal revelations that are making me want to start some lifestyle changes. I'm not deluding myself into thinking I can just waltz back into people's lives without putting in the work. That said, I'm also both on the clock and under the gun, hence coming as a customer instead of an old friend."

Whatever Cyrus had planned to retort was interrupted as the waiter emerged with drinks. They also came by with a small loaf of fresh rye bread before disappearing into the kitchen again. I cut off a quarter of it with the provided knife, spread fresh butter from a small cup in the inside, and sprinkled salt from the shaker. Keeping a small plate for myself, I passed the bread tray to Byron. While he cut and prepared a piece for himself, I took three deliberate bites from mine. Byron finished, his bread buttered and salted. I passed the tray over to Connie while Byron began to eat. Connie shrugged, cut the remaining loaf in half, and buttered a slice. She passed the tray over to Cyrus after I nodded in his direction. Then she got her slice halfway to her mouth before I opened my hand, palm down. She stopped.

I murmured, "Salt, too."

She gave me a look for a moment, shrugged, and shook the shaker on it once. Satisfied, I nodded and sat back. When Connie swallowed her third bite, a tension barely noticed before came loose, and a sense of relaxation came over us all. Cyrus buttered, salted, and ate the remaining bread in silence.

Why the dance of the appetizers? The first and most important things taught about the Otherworld aren't about magic, they're about manners. Old school rules about what guests and hosts are supposed to do are the norm here because they still follow their original purpose: keeping the involved parties from killing each other. Breaking them should be reserved for making sure the posthumous stories told about you are impressive ones.

Now, Cyrus may or may not have a ward under the table set to put anyone showing him active hostility to sleep. I sure as hell wouldn't put it past him. But by sitting at his table and eating his bread, butter, and salt, we'd made it clear that we had come as guests and would conduct ourselves accordingly.

Cyrus nodded in satisfaction, customer service standoff face well in place as he spoke. "So what can I help you ponder today, Travis?"

I counted off two fingers. "Blood and memory, in no particular order."

He nodded, "Any context you'd care to fill me in on?"

"I do. But in the interest of finding what I haven't noticed yet, I'll go from a magical generalist stance for a start."

Cyrus nodded, took a sip from his ice water, and leaned back. His lecture voice, strong and steady, was aimed more at the ceiling than at me. "Blood. Most easily recognized of the four humors. Stands for life, extended family, and instinctual truth. Men can only provide it by means of a wound. Standard medium of sympathetic magic, personal sacrifice, and judgment by combat."

I put my drink down. "And vampires?"

Cyrus raised an eyebrow at me, then shrugged. "Thought you'd out-knowledge me there, but here goes: Homo sapiens hemovorous, the European city vampire. Considered a form of undead, using humans as both food sources and breeding stock. Ageless and unaffected by known diseases, but vulnerable to sunlight, fire, decapitation and aggravated dismemberment. A stake through the heart causes paralysis, accounts differ as to whether those affected are aware of their surroundings. Obligatory hemovores, though whether that's from gaining energy and nutrients from blood itself as opposed to it merely being a vector to consume life energy, that's an argument I stand in the middle of."

I pondered that for a moment. "Anyone done work on the properties of vampire blood?"

"As a stand alone? Once or twice. The Daedeli might have more that they're not telling about. Vampires aren't any more eager to have their strengths and weaknesses on record than we are. It's notably different than human blood. It's thicker, more viscous, and doesn't seem to utilize what we think of as red blood cells. My educated guess is their version of plasma is either alcohol based or some sort of oxygen saturated peroxide. Would explain the strength, the resistance to damage, and the aversion to flames, at least to a degree."

"That makes sense as far as the chemistry goes. What about renfields?"

He opened his hands in a mild shrug. "Some kind of instinctual mind magic. The master uses their own blood as a sympathetic link. Probably some sort of euphoriant in the blood too."

I nodded, then dropped the big one. "Any accounts of a renfield being cured?"

It was the million-dollar question and everyone at the table knew it. Cyrus shook his head.

"None. If I had to guess? Killing the master, surviving a truly noxious hangover and staying off the blood forever should do it."

I sighed in annoyance. "Well, I'm two out of three there."

For the first time, I saw sympathy in Cyrus' eyes. And I hated it. Everything we said and did on leaving speaking terms came back to my thoughts and slammed right into his insulting pity. A wall in the back of my mind came crashing down, blocking me off from him. I needed his brains but I'd kill myself before I'd take his sympathy.

Finally, he said, "I was hoping it was just rumors."

I shook my head. "Me and Eva Marazzi? Most of the last year. I killed her this morning at the Cotillion."

He sighed. "Well, that explains your last visit."

All of us looked surprised there. Byron spoke up. "Last visit?"

Cyrus nodded. "You came by office hours six months ago, alone, sometime around twelfth night-." His eyes grew bright as a puzzle solved itself in his mind. "-which explains why you're interested in memory. You're missing a chunk at the very least."

I thought about giving him shit, but in the end I just opened my arms. "Got it in one, Doc."

"Current? Past life? Universal?"

"Current. Personal. Missing."

He tilted his head like a raven. "You don't look like you've taken a shot to the head. Must be under that scruff."

"Very funny."

He sat back and steepled his hands. "How much you got missing?"

"A year."

"A year. Exactly a year?"

"I woke up this morning and it was the same day, the next year."

"Any reconstruction?"

"Only secondhand." I pointed a thumb at Connie. "The young lady was around for the excitement last night and was kind enough to give me a look at her memory."

He nodded thoughtfully. "Explains why you've been more of a prick than usual these last couple months."

I could feel my jaw tighten. "You of all people know exactly why I started serving vampires, Cyrus. Forgive me if I don't apologize until I know what for."

He paused for a moment, then nodded. "That's fair. So, a more or less exact year of your life gone."

"Sometime between racking out this morning and waking up this afternoon."

"Mmhmm. Any head trauma I'm not seeing?"

"Eva had a bitchslap that sent me across the room, it's the only one I noticed."

"Then we can probably rule out trauma. Any geas, curse, or hex that you know about?"

"Not really."

"Are you sure?"

I looked him in the eyes. "If I'd violated my Oath, I've done enough magic since that I'd notice if something weakened or backfired, so that's a no. If there's anything else, I don't know about it."

After a moment, he nodded. "Are you certain that the vampire you killed is the one that renfielded you?"

Now that I hadn't thought of. "...No."

"Does this have anything to do with Blue River?"

"I'm not sure... wait, maybe?"

"Go on."

"When I woke up this morning, I saw the words 'follow yellow' written on my bathroom mirror in the condensation. In my handwriting. And I've heard a woman saying the same phrase in a dream twice now."

Cyrus looked like a fisherman, patiently watching dinner for the family nibbling on a lure, waiting for it to be well and truly hooked before making too much of a motion. "Intriguing. Does the phrase mean anything to you?"

"Besides vaguely the wizard of Oz? Nope."

Byron spoke up. "Dibs on the tin man."

Connie raised an eyebrow. "You don't have a heart?"

Byron smirked. "Left a trail of broken ones."

I turned to him. "Byron, we've got the doctor on the clock."

Byron pouted playfully. "Pay attention to the man behind the curtain, says the man who wouldn't surrender Dorothy."

"Hush."

Cyrus had his eyebrow up. "Oz, the river, or something else entirely, that sounds an awful lot like a code phrase."

I frowned. "But it didn't do anything when I said it."

Cyrus shrugged, his hands open. "Maybe it's not supposed to. When you think about it, memory is just information storage. You can destroy it. But it's usually much easier to make sure it can't be found."

"You're saying my memories aren't gone, they're just locked up?"

"Entirely possible."

"Who would do that? And why now? Why wipe a year of my memory? And why wipe the year I spent serving vampires?"

Connie quietly asked. "Another vampire?"

Cyrus shook his head. "A vampire wouldn't have a reason to give him a code phrase."

I frowned as the math added up in my head. "You're telling me I wiped my own memories?"

Cyrus nodded. "Or someone you trusted to do it did."

"Did you do it?"

Cyrus tilted his head in that corvid way again. "I said someone you trusted."

I shrugged. "Fair. But as long as I'm here, I might as well ask. Which is why I'm asking everything. You're the best mind practitioner I know personally."

"Thanks."

"You earned it. And follow yellow is a code phrase?"

"No, it's a clue. If it was a code phrase, saying it would have taken the blocks off your memories."

"So it's a clue to the code phrase?"

"A clue to whatever unlocks your memories. Could be a phrase, a picture, a tune, just about anything, really. Did this woman say or do anything else?"

I frowned. "No. I saw... Blue eyes. Big blue eyes, lined. A blue scarf. And I heard bells."

"What kind of bells?"

I thought for a moment, trying to find a description that worked. "Like jingle bells or something. Slow, but kinda rhythmic."

"They all could be clues then. Or bits of your memory getting in the way, but since they're showing up repeatedly, I'm guessing you left yourself clues when you had your memories wiped."

"Why would I do that?"

"Not sure why you did it. But I know why I'd do it, if I were you."

We all listened like good little pupils. Cyrus settled comfortably into lecture mode.

"You knew you were going to serve vampires to pay off your debt to Chittenden. And everybody knows vampires can use forms of mind magic. So you needed to lock up parts of your mind, specifically memory storage. But you couldn't keep the key on you. You couldn't even know where the key is. Because anything you knew, vampires could find. So you made up a riddle that would lead you to the key, but be nonsense to anyone looking in your mind for it."

I shook my head. "This is why I hate cognimancy. My brain hurts just from hearing that. But it makes sense."

"Find follow yellow, you find your key."

I thought for a long time, then nodded. "Thanks, Cyrus."

He opened his hands. "Convincing myself the rumors were bullshit is worth the extra work."

I stopped short. "Wait, which rumors? The ones that I'm a renfield are real."

Cyrus sighed. "Well, at least I'm reminded of what my foot tastes like."

My eyes narrowed as something fell into place. "You mean the rumors about..."

"You're too good, Travis."

Byron frowned. "Babs said that too."

Cyrus nodded. "Babs is right. Someone with your record shouldn't be nearly as good as you are."

I could feel my jaw get tighter. "So demons is the answer?"

Cyrus held up a pedantic finger. "It's an easy answer. One you make easier."

"Because I won't join a faction? Screw 'em. The Daedeli are stuffy old assholes, the Nimuen are sniveling bullies, both of them think the world owes them. Oh, yeah, not to mention I got Oaths to a vampire lord and the fucking Hunt."

Byron raised a hand. "Present."

I almost snarled. "Can't imagine why I'm not a catch for any coven looking for an alchemist."

"It's still an easy answer. And a bullshit one."

My brain stumbled over my mouth. "And a... What?"

Cyrus shrugged. "If you had a deal with the fallen, I'd know. I don't know how you've gotten this rep, but I know it's not demonic." He folded his arms. "But what do I know? I'm a sniveling bully."

I looked around the room and mentally redesigned it. "The curtain, the table, or the bread?"

He smiled in pride. "The good don't give away their secrets."

I dropped my head, took a breath of relief, and cracked a smile. "Thanks again, Cyrus." I held up a hand before he could speak. "I got a lot of not being an asshole to do, I know that. If I live, I'll get to it. But for now, thank you is the best I got."

Cyrus smiled at that, opening his arms expansively. "All part of the service."

I took the thicker of two blank envelopes from the cargo pocket of my pants and slid it across the table. Before I lifted my hand from it, I raised my other finger.

"One last thing. What was I doing here six months ago?"

"Looking for a spellbook. An original copy of Cronesfoil."

I frowned. "Cronesfoil?"

"Yeah. You were all business. I lost a bet with myself that you'd say 'just the facts' before going."

"I ever find the book?"

"I sent you to a good dealer I know, so probably."

"Did I say what it was for?"

Cyrus shook his head. "Not really. All you said was that you'd been asked about a virgin sacrifice."

*   *   *

Outside the restaurant, shadows were starting to grow longer as we headed for the truck. From inside the parking lot, I heard an inquisitive whistle. We all turned our heads to see a pixielike bohemian redneck emerge from between the cars. A shock of mussed strawberry blonde hair hung like a halo over bright eyes and a smile full of mischief. I cracked a smile from the sheer good luck at seeing another old friend.

"Hi, Thumper."

Thumper opened their arms and tilted their head in a question. I nodded, and they immediately launched into my arms. Thumper was barely four foot ten and hadn't grown an inch since I met them in Sixth grade. We spun around for a moment before I let them down. Thumper waved to the others.

Byron smiled. "Hello, cutie."

Thumper batted their eyelashes and held a hand to their heart.

Byron winked, then turned to Connie. "Connie, this little fireball Trav is too rude to introduce is Thumper."

I didn't even bother defending myself as Thumper looked Connie up and down. Thumper's whistle turned decidedly wolflike for two notes, which made Connie crack a smile. Thumper looked back to me, hooted like an owl, and pointed a thumb back at the restaurant.

"Yeah, we just saw Cyrus."

Thumper smiled, then kissed their open palm, looking up at me in a question.

"Here on business today, Thump. We haven't kissed and made up quite yet."

They huffed in disappointment, then pointed to themselves and then the rest of us, giving a questioning whistle.

"You want to come along?"

They nodded.

"I've been in a bit of a rough spot lately. You might not want to get on this train."

Thumper gave me a stubborn look, hooted again, then held up their hand, all the fingers and thumb spread open. I sighed, shaking my head.

"All right, but we got to be quick."

I held up my hand, lacing my fingers together with Thumper's. Our palms met, and the world disappeared.

*   *   *

I was alone in the woods. The pines were lush and green, but everything else was bare and brown, thick enough to block every view further than a few yards. A stream I could jump across in most places wound through the area, banks having eroded into shallow beaches in some spots, knee-high cliffs in others. It was cool, the remnants of a breeze just managing to make their way through the pines. The sun was hidden by the treetops and plenty of cloud cover, but promised hours of light to see by. Up against a tree, a familiar pair of backpacks had been laid down. One was a battered old army surplus pack I'd had, the other a patched bookbag.

A rhythmic clicking sound approached from one of the trees. From the shadows between the pines, Thumper appeared. They wore a sequined evening gown of bright crimson, which clung to their athletic figure and was slit up to the thigh on one side. Their sling-back stiletto heels crunched on the scattered leaves as they sauntered towards me in a glide worthy of a red carpet. They clicked a bright red lighter in one hand, touching the fuse of a cherry bomb in the other. With a practiced turn of the wrist, they tossed the bomb across the stream. It burst in a small but satisfying explosion, leaving a small crater in the sand on the far bank.

Thumper had been raised a girl, which was how I'd met them when we were both in Primus year of study hall. A very tomboyish girl. The only classmate I ever had who liked blowing shit up in the woods more than I did. At the time, my concept of genderfluid was limited to a badly made documentary we watched one day in sex ed. But by the time I'd graduated high school, I'd met people who could fly, change into animals and converse with the dead. Getting the pronouns right wasn't exactly a stretch for us. Thumper leaned on both ends of the spectrum depending on their mood.

"What you get yourself into this time, Trav?"

In the real world, Thumper couldn't speak anymore. At Blue River, they'd gotten caught in one of their own explosions and had been thrown into a tree. When they came out of the coma, they couldn't form sentences, having ended up with a form of what the docs called Aphasia. Thumper could hear and comprehend fine and dandy, but somewhere between their brain and mouth, responses became word salad. They could make simple noises and whistle, which served them well enough. They'd spent the time ever since learning mind magic.

And mentally, where a powerful cognimancer like Thumper was in their element, they could speak easily. Of course, Thumper kept their natural Mississippi bayou accent, which was thick enough to cut with a chainsaw. Sounded more like, "whutchoo git yersel intuh dis thyme, Trahv?"

I held out what looked like a smartphone with a pair of earbuds. It was all I knew about what had happened lately, in one big information dump. "long story. Fill yourself in."

Thumper took the phone, put in the buds, and pressed play. After a few moments, their eyes got wide. "Sheeeit! You weren't lyin about being in a tight spot, Trav."

"Nope. Still want in?"

"Hell yeah!"

"Then let's get a move on, eh?"

"Gotcha."

Thumper lit another cherry bomb and tossed it. The spot in the woods vanished moments later in the explosion.

The last thing I heard was the chime of small bells.

*   *   *

In the real world, only a second or two had passed. Thumper was grinning like a fiend. Byron was snickering patiently and Connie was watching with her usual mild curiosity. I was used to having stoic goths in my life, but Connie was the type to watch a tanker truck catch fire, then do the math in her head to time how soon each of the tires would explode.

I gave everyone a smile I hoped was encouraging. "OK, Thumper's coming with us."

Connie tilted her head. "Looking for a brain or courage?"

Thumper grinned, then curled their hands into mock-claws and made a snarly face. Connie nodded in approval, then turned to me. "Where we off to, Scarecrow?"

As I answered, Byron touched the outside corner of his eye with two fingers. To anyone else, it would look like like he was messing with a contact lens. Between him and me it was a signal: we were being watched.

"Well, I haven't found a brain here. But we're not that far from Warwells. I think I could use a second opinion."

I unlocked the Yukon and we started climbing in. Connie looked a bit wary as she fastened her seatbelt. "First a professor, now a restaurant and gun range? Hell of a way to get a second opinion."

I shrugged as I started the truck. "Nobody grows opinions fresh daily like the porchmen."

*   *   *

Chapter Seven

"Guideline Twenty-One:
Cleverness is the duct tape of wisdom:
Gets a lot of jobs done,
but only weirdos rely on it exclusively."

Warwell's is a shooting range and restaurant just southeast of Stone Mountain. It's been family-owned for over a century, and just about every member of the extended clan has been magically inclined. The restaurant looks like a three-story antebellum plantation house in the middle of nowhere. A sign at the main road told you where you were, letting you turn down a winding, tree-lined road before emerging onto the main parking lot. On the east side, a berm covered with pine trees separated the parking lot from the range area.

The lunch crowd was thinning out, so we managed to park in the middle of the lot. I gave Byron a small gesture, at which he shook his head negatively. Whoever had been following us had fallen behind.

The front porch was framed by four Corinthian columns, bigger around than the width of my shoulders, supporting the porch roof all the way up on the second story. The wraparound porch roof was only half that height, held up by unadorned stanchions every couple of feet. The porch roofs, combined with the eggshell white paint on the outside and high ceilings on the inside, helped keep the rooms cool in a time before central air was a thing. Given that southern summers had probably been every bit as hot and sticky a century ago, every little bit helped. The porch itself was painted a deep forest green that matched the shutters on the windows and frame of the big oak double doors that made the main entrance. Looking up would let you see the ceilings of the porches were all in familiar haint blue.

A number of heavy duty Adirondack chairs painted the same eggshell white as the walls were neatly arrayed around the porch. Each and every chair was heavily weathered from years out in the heat, the seats polished with a multitude of backsides over the years. On the eastern side of the entrance, four of them were under perpetual occupation by a quartet of men. Although they appeared to be more middle-aged than old, each looking somewhere between forty and sixty, they all looked like they had been middle-aged for quite a long time. More than age was the seasoning. They looked like the human version of quality tools: well made to start with, used a long time on hard work, then well maintained and put back with care. I remembered that they hadn't notably aged since the first time my Uncle Mac brought me to Warwell's back in the mid-90's.

Living in the South all my life, I was intimately familiar with the breed of human known for being old, self-important, and outrageous liars. Those who decided they'd seen and done it all by their forties, and were content to sit on their ass and pour out their wisdom upon any they could get to stand still long enough to listen. And if today's young people didn't want to pay heed, well, they could suffer accordingly for not giving the old fart oracle their due. They could have been made at the same factory: Codger, old, bullshitting, one each.

And the ones who hung around places of, well, call it applied conflict, were even worse. Shooting ranges, boxing gyms, and off-base bars seemed to spawn old guys who couldn't run to the end of a driveway or throw punches for longer than a minute at a time. But they sure could fill hours of the same old bumper sticker slogans. Old age and treachery this and old where men die young that. Whatever.

The porchmen, on the other hand, were different. You didn't get the thick feeling of ego and pride rolling off of them. Oh, they still would bend your ear all day about this weapon instead of that or what would have changed this other battle. But none of them seemed to have anything to prove with it. You got the sense they were more interested in discovering something new than being right from the start. Which was part of why the locals enjoyed rather than tolerated their presence. However old they truly were, and whatever adventures they had in the past, now they contented themselves with relaxing on the Warwell's front porch, commenting on the state of the world and bickering with each other. All of the staff and clientele had fun with them, but the Otherworlders knew all four of them were also infamous and powerful mages.

They belonged to no faction but themselves, with the possible exception of the Warwell family. Rumors abounded as to their exploits in younger days. The one I personally believe claimed they had run in a cabal with old man Warwell himself. Which old man Warwell would be the active question there, which I had never managed to answer.

All four of them wore the core elements of the tactical chic fashion trend: sturdy boots, cargo pants in neutral colors, and polo shirts in the same palette. Hardly a pocket was seen without a knife clip hanging from it. They were only a few ball caps and ballistic sunglasses away from looking like the executives of a private military contractor.

The Otherworld called them the four porchmen of the apocalypse.

I approached them slowly, with my hands as open and away from any pockets as I could get without being obvious about it. That was the other thing about the porchmen. They never talked about how sneaky and dangerous they were. You could feel it in the way they looked at you. It was like they were filling the downtime in polite conversation with deciding exactly which of your major joints they had to shatter to make you into someone else's problem.

I was holding out hope that neither the Warwells nor the porchmen considered me a danger, given the morning's gossip. If they did, I was probably going to be dead before I stepped off the parking lot. I felt the comfortable blanket of combat stoicism gently wrap around my shoulders. Somewhere out there was a deathblow with my name on it. There were also plenty without such helpful labels. Nothing to do about it but go about my business as best I could. It would have been even more helpful if I could convince my heart that was the case.

Jim looked up as we approached. "Hey gents, it's Crockett and Tubbs." Jim was the smallest and second oldest. He eschewed cargo pants for a black kilt, his skinny legs tanned between knee and boot. His rapidly graying ponytail was barely held in place, preferring to be in a mane to match the intensity of his thoughts. A lot of people talked with their hands, but Jim ranted with them.

The other porchmen looked up from their distractions to take note of us. My companions and I stopped in the grass before the porch, out of the way of any diners coming in or out of the restaurant. The shadow of the building showed mercy in keeping the sun off us. The grass was freshly mowed, but thin on the ground, bearing memories of countless seekers of knowledge that came for the porchmen.

I shook my head in mock disappointment. "And here I thought we'd at least get Murtagh and Riggs?"

Byron nodded. "I am getting too old for this shit."

"You're not even three hundred yet."

"Hush, infant."

Lars looked us over. "Two mages, a ranger, and a daughter of the night. Anybody else hear dice rolling?"

Jim snickered. "I thought they were all supposed to meet inside?"

Matt shook his head. "Nah. There's probably a meetup app. Single fighter seeks party."

Lars chuckled. "That's not an app. That was my freshman year of college."

Byron smiled. "No such app, gentlemen, but if you have any cute ones within, we're flexible about class."

Jim said it before I could. "So we noticed."

"Ma'am." Keith nodded in Connie's direction. For one of the porchmen, that was a sweeping bow. "I trust these two reprobates are behaving themselves in your company?" Keith was the oldest looking and tallest of the four, his lanky frame looking like an understuffed scarecrow. A khaki range vest held most of what he'd ever need to use in the course of the day, and hung on his frame comfortably. A shock of white hair was still on his head, and a thick mustache that would've looked well on an old west sheriff hid his upper lip.

Connie tucked one combat boot behind the other and gave an actual curtsy. "As much as one can reasonably expect, sir."

He looked at us like we were a suspicious pair of horses someone was trying to sell to him cheap. "Well, I don't expect much. But they look more or less housebroken, so I suppose they can stay." That got a snort and a smile out of me despite myself. I looked over at Thumper. "They've gotten wise to us, Thump. Expecting us to clean up our own mess. Did you bring the broom along with the dynamite?"

Thumper gave me a look of wide-eyed despair, turning out suspiciously empty pants pockets. I shook my head in mock disappointment. "Curses, foiled again."

When I looked back up, Lars was looking me in the eye. "Did your insurance cover it?"

I raised an eyebrow but played along. "Cover what?"

"You made a joke, Grunt. The stick had to have been surgically removed from your ass. I was just wondering if insurance covered it."

The porchmen broke into the chuckles and snickers. Connie gave a mischievous smile of her own as she faced Lars. "Oh, come on, sir. Have some sympathy. We all know that was a preexisting condition."

After a deep and abiding pause, Jim turned to Matt, deadpan. "I like this one. Can we keep her?"

Byron huffed in mock indignation. "When we're done with her, please do. She's stealing my good lines."

Connie stuck out her tongue at Byron's words. Matt shook his head negatively with a deadpan expression, causing Jim to sigh and snap his fingers in disappointment. Matt was only a touch taller than Jim, but had twice the muscle, looking like a barrel with scarred knuckles. His hair and goatee were marginally less graying than the others. He had a tasteful navy blue waistcoat worn open over his gray shirt. He was the second-most laid back and the one most likely to look for a middle ground.

Lars spoke up again. "You come to eat, shoot, or both, Grunt?" Lars was the largest and quite possibly the youngest of the four. His shoulders were broad enough to nearly hide the back of his chair, and his forearms looked like he worked in a forge for fun. He had musclebound fingers, which I normally only saw on dwarves and people who spent all day in a metal shop. He was the only man of leisure I ever saw with them. He was balding, and the hair he had left was salt and pepper as his bushy goatee.

I shook my head. "Came to ask, actually. Got me a bit of a bloodsucker problem."

Lars nodded. "Dealing with something called a bloodsucker is a good indication of a problem."

Keith drawled. "You didn't marry her already, did you?"

I shuddered. "No, sir. But my ribs are still bruised from the breakup."

Jim squinted at me. "Is it your own lawyer or someone else's?"

I shook my head. "Vampires."

That set all four to nodding knowingly. For a while they all kept silent, as if mentally arranging their forces around the problem they had set to attack. Matt stroked his goatee in thought, then held up a questioning finger. "City or country?"

I shrugged. "Both, now that I think about it."

He nodded. "They working together?"

"Country vamps working for a city vamp."

He pondered that one. "Now that's unusual."

Jim nodded, "Yeah, I've never heard of them being chummy."

Neither had I, which is why I was there. I asked, "Are they natural competitors or something?"

Matt waved his hand in a so-so gesture. "Sometimes. The big difference outside of territory is hunting style. City vamps are deception predators. They offer something a human wants, whether that's money, sex, or whatever. They get someplace private, it sucks up what it wants, heals the prey up and sends it on its way. Some of them get a routine going, have the same prey coming back every week."

Jim twitched. "Sounds like my first wife."

Lars chuckled at that one while Keith shook his head. Matt continued. "Country vamps are much more simple. They're good old fashioned pursuit predators. Wake up hungry, find something, chase it down, drink up, move on. By the morning, what's one more dead animal in the woods? They don't play the games that city vamps do. I don't know what they'd be working for a city vamp for."

I remembered what Babs had said about carcasses in the woods, then shrugged. "Well, they were working for one as of last night."

Matt stroked his goatee again. "Is that a fact?"

I nodded. "At least two were in Tasha Marazzi's entourage."

Matt pondered this. "Interesting." After a moment, he nodded to his companions in approval, then turned back to me. "Have we solved your problem?"

"You've definitely gotten me closer to it." Something crossed my mind and I took a shot in the dark. "Ever heard of a renfield being shared between vampires?"

That got me a raised eyebrow from Keith. The others looked equally incredulous before turning to Matt, who shook his head. "Never. The whole point of a renfield is ensuring loyalty through the blood. I can see one being given away as a gift, or traded permanently in a deal, but never shared."

I nodded. "Ever hear of a renfield being cured?"

That got me looks between them followed by all four shaking their heads negatively. Matt was the first to speak up. "Most of them eventually end up dead."

Jim nodded. "Or bug-eating crazy, then dead."

Matt held up a notional finger. "Bug-eating crazy, tortured to prove a point, then dead."

Keith waved a hand back and forth. "It's technically possible. If said renfield managed to kill their master. Then successfully turned down any offers to get a new master."

Matt nodded. "And those new offers would be getting made right when the withdrawal is at the absolute worst. And let's not forget, most vampires think consent is a character from a Victor Hugo novel. They're not above anything from dosing drinks to just holding one down and dumping blood down the throat."

Keith nodded. "I wouldn't put bloodboarding past some of them...."

Matt sneered. "Now that's just wasteful."

Byron shook his head. "Now y'all just making me hungry." Thumper elbowed him.

Keith gave them a look and continued. "But what I said stands. With the master dead, it's like any other addiction. Which means your mileage varies." Matt snickered. Keith carried on. "Anything else you want to know?"

Since I had plenty of ammo, I took another shot in the dark. "Does the phrase 'follow yellow' mean anything? Specifically along with bells, blue eyes, and a scarf to match?"

Jim snorted. "You looking for a brain, a heart, or courage?"

Matt nodded. "It's gotta be a brain."

Byron nodded helpfully. "I called dibs on the heart."

Thumper made a growly face and held out their hands like claws.

Keith shrugged. "Only bells I hear these days are when Elaine's students come in. Sounds like a Christmas reindeer stampede."

Lars nodded. "Get a bard drunk enough and you can probably get a nice ballad out of it."

I nodded to each of the porchmen in turn. "I figured it was worth a shot. Thank you, gentlemen. The help's appreciated."

Something that gets beaten into your heads in study hall is a fundamental law of the Otherworld: Everything has a cost, even if that cost isn't paid immediately or by the recipient. I'd come to both Cyrus and the porchmen looking for information. Cyrus I'd paid in cash, the porchmen with current news. Everyone went away happy.

All power may come at a price, but you don't have to bankrupt yourself to keep going.

*   *   *

"So now what?"

"I keep thinking there's something to do with Blue River. We're not that far, and it's still light out. Maybe checking it out will tell me something."

Byron shrugged. "It's either that or get some food and wait for Elaine Warwell to get out of class so we can hear some bells."

My brain connected two unlabeled wires and a light went off. I looked back up into the rearview mirror at Byron.

"How many belly dancing weavers do I know?"

Connie frowned. "Weavers?"

"Divination, not textiles."

Byron and Thumper turned to look at each other, then bust out laughing. Byron recovered soon enough to wave a hand excitedly. "Try half the women you've ever met, Trav! Seriously. I mean, Lori Homestead, all of the Sues, and every female Warwell, just to start. Then there's Seb's wife, whatshername, the one from Minnesota? I'd lay Vegas odds on Babs. Hell, I'd bet even money on Connie."

Connie managed what on someone else would be a blush. "What brought that on?"

"The bells I heard in my mind. They weren't on a sleigh, they were on anklets. The chiming I heard was someone wearing them as they were walking."

"But that doesn't narrow it down, does it?"

"Nope. We'll see if there's anything at the river."

*   *   *

On the way, I had to stop for gas. Byron, Thumper, and Connie went inside the Quiktrip to use the facilities while I fed the Yukon. Cyrus had helped me fill in the blanks and the porchmen had given me a look at the bigger picture, but specifics were still eluding me. I was deep in thought while watching the numbers flash by on the pump and stopped paying attention to what was going on. That is, until I heard the death threat.

"You're a dead man, Wayland."

I blinked, then glanced. At the opposite end of the pumps from the station was a skinny teenage kid. His face seemed locked into a sneer, with brown hair long from not bothering rather than anything resembling a style. Raggedy jeans, a belt that was more frays than canvas, and a shirt that a thrift store wouldn't buy or sell. Right hand in a front pocket.

I looked him up and down, then shrugged and looked back at the pump, quietly looking for any backup the kid had. My left hand was still on the gas pump. My right slid my wand out of my pocket.

"Threatening people's not nice, kid."

"Neither was taking our chance at a steady gig, bloodlicker."

I checked my corners again, not caring if someone noticed. There was nobody near me. The closest parked car was an old Honda over by the air pump. This kid was alone. But my hackles were well and duly raised. It felt like Iraq, in those moments where innocent bystanders vanish just before someone tries to kill you. Then the wind shifted and I got a noseful of spicy meat in the air among the gasoline and summer pollen. It was coming from behind me.

I managed to say the first syllable of *"Skjoldur!"* before I heard the gunshot. The shield erupted from my wand, gripped in my fist like a hammer. I finished turning just in time to see the first round ricochet off the shield. Stepping off from the gas station sidewalk was the lanky guy from Connie's house, pistol in hand. He was shooting one-handed with lousy technique, but his rounds kept hitting the shield. He was stronger than he looked. The one driver in the lot dropped the air pump, dove into the Honda, and peeled out.

I turned away from the shooter, feeling the shield flex under more gunshots. I let go of the gas pump, leaving it on my truck and drawing a knife. A tiny bit of my thoughts somehow weren't being kept busy. I assigned them to pray to any Gods that were listening. I did not want to have to shoot a kid. Nor did I want anything energetic to happen to the gas pump I was standing next to. One shot ricocheted off the shield and took a chunk out of the numbered sign above the pump.

Crazy as it sounds, I was suddenly relaxed. All of my doubts and questions about blood and memory and Oaths all just faded into the background. Someone was trying to kill me. That was nice and simple. I just had to stop him, not get killed, and not make too big a mess. Nice and simple.

The kid hadn't moved except to give a smug smile. He took his hand out of his pocket, empty, and gave me a wave. Behind the kid, a familiar green sedan pulled up, brakes squealing. The kid bolted, diving into the open backseat. Looking back, the lanky guy had lowered his weapon and ran behind my truck. I turned again, running to the sedan with my wand out.

The lanky guy had sprinted past the last row of pumps, jumping into the sedan's open backseat door after the kid. I dropped my shield and aimed a bolt of pure kinetic energy in the sedan's direction. The driver's window shattered, but I couldn't get a good look at the driver. I didn't want to start throwing lightning bolts around a gas station, of all damn things. But I was tired of screwing around and having no answers.

The second the lanky guy was inside, the door slammed shut and the sedan roared off, coming inches from hitting a woman walking down the sidewalk and nearly T-boning a minivan coming around the pump islands. The minivan's driver laid down on the horn, screaming gracious Southern obscenities as the sedan pulled a right out of the parking lot, disappearing into westbound traffic. The woman who'd almost been hit shook her head and went back to lighting her cigarette.

I turned back to see Byron, Thumper, and Connie stepping out of the station, all of them looking wary. Byron and Thumper both had their hands out, ready to go for weapons. I pocketed my wand and knife, then gave them a thumb's up. Byron nodded and they all approached at a trot. The pump had stopped in the confusion. I said a quick thanks to whatever

Gods had hooked me up, replaced the nozzle, and closed up the Yukon's gas cap as my friends walked up. Byron pointed his thumb down the road. "What was that all about?"

I shrugged. "Dumbass kids. Dressing like morons, trying to kill you, shooting near gas pumps, you know how it is."

He let out a low exhale. "Dread Millie. Anything important get hit?"

I glanced around. "No dents, flats, or flames. I'm gonna go with no."

Byron nodded. "Small favors. Now let's get out of here. The clerk called the cops."

We all piled in and I pulled out of the lot before speaking again.

"It gets weirder. They got in the same car the drive-by shooters used. And they smelled exactly like whoever kidnapped Connie."

*　　*　　*

Chapter Eight

"Guideline Fifteen:

Honesty is like water.

You need plenty to live, but too much can kill."

We were headed east on 78, past Stone Mountain on our way to blue river. I was keeping my eyes on the road and checking my flanks instinctively. The shooting at the pumps had made me properly paranoid again. I let Bob the nite owl play through the Yukon's stereo.

"..U.S. Fish and wildlife service in conjunction with the DoD have put no less than three active werewolf packs on the civilian contractor payroll at Ft. Benning, North Carolina. Supposedly the werewolves were relocated in an effort to protect remaining members of the Carolinas' red wolf population, by herding them away from impact ranges and other hazardous zones in the land surrounding the base. This is yet another encroachment of the federal..."

"What was all that Cyrus said about a book and virgin sacrifice?"

I turned off the podcast and shrugged at Connie's question. "Not sure. I know the book he was talking about, maybe even the spell, but it doesn't make sense to me."

"Why not?" Connie asked from the shotgun seat. Thumper had taken the backseat with Byron, who they were currently using as a lounge. Both were playing games on their phones.

"Well, there's two schools of magical thought."

Byron spoke up. "For all-American mom and apple pie mages like Trav here."

I stuck out my thumb in Byron's direction. "What he said. Anyway, first up is the Daedeli. They're old school. Grumpy ass old guys would be more accurate. And not fun ones, like the porchmen, I mean professional sticks in the mud. Individually, they're more powerful than most and they usually live longer. But they're kind of set in their ways and suspicious of anything new."

Connie batted her eyes, which was oddly enhanced with the eyeliner swoop. "Conservative old people?" Her hand went to her heart in mock shock. "I'm from Georgia, I don't know anything about that."

I snorted. "Smartass. You'd get a little conservative too, if grad school taught you how to blow someone's head off with a lightning bolt by reciting the right sonnet. Anyways, Daedeli think there's two major reasons for a virgin sacrifice to be included in a magic ritual. One is innocence, the other is potential."

"Potential?"

"A virgin that reaches maturity has the potential to be anything. It's one of the two states of humanity that are irreversible once changed."

"What's the other one?"

"Taking a life."

"How symbolic." In two words, she'd managed a level of sarcasm thick enough to cut with a chainsaw. I didn't blame her.

I shrugged. "You're a virgin, and then you're not. You're not a killer, and then you are. And there ain't no going back either way. It's pretty me-Tarzan and I personally think people take it way too damn seriously, but I can see where they're coming from."

"Uh huh. What's the other school of thought?"

"The Nimuen. They trend younger and less powerful individually. But they've got a lot of explorers and innovators in them. First person to find a new sub-branch of magic is almost always a Nimuen. Unfortunately, a lot of them get blown up, eaten by something they pissed off, or otherwise broken in the attempt of doing something new. According to them, there's never been a virgin sacrifice that was magically necessary. They've found powerful creatures that demanded one for reasons of their own: demons, demigods, dragons, what have you. But magic itself? Totally unnecessary. No ritual or spell they've documented makes a magical difference involving a virgin."

"No shit?"

"No shit. Cyrus was on one of the teams that investigated it."

"And what do you think?"

My jaw clenched. "I think the last person I met willing to sacrifice human beings for magical power killed half the friends I had in the world. Including the only woman I've ever truly been in love with. I don't give a damn about the social lives of her victims. I should've shot her in the head when I had the chance."

She took a beat to think, then nodded. "Comforting to know."

Byron tilted his head, then turned to Connie. His look turned from a smirk into a delighted fascination. "Really?"

Connie met his gaze and instantly flushed, then frowned. "What?"

Byron didn't look away, he just smiled bigger, which just made Connie flush further.

Thumper gave a low, suggestive whistle, which made Connie flush deeper before clenching her fists and growling. "Yes! I am! Really! OK?"

She waved them back. Byron leaned back in his seat, looking smug. Thumper lounged against him, leering suggestively. I managed to keep my eyes on the road instead of rolling them. After a couple of awkward moments, I broke the silence. "I apologize for their antics, but thanks for letting me know."

"Why?"

"Because that might be why Eva grabbed you in the first place. I've been wondering about that since breakfast. But if I came to Cyrus six months ago, asking for the Cronesfoil and reading up on virgin sacrifice, there's a good chance I was acting on Eva's orders. Hopefully, there's an original in my house."

"Why original? Did the paperback have typos in it or something?"

As the road dipped gently south, I caught the first glimpse of Stone Mountain. This deep in the summer, it was easier to see the trees growing on the western slopes. One more line of thick conifers among a multitude. Then you realized that it wasn't a gently rolling hill of dark earth, but a single huge hunk of granite bigger than the shell of a kaiju turtle. "Yes. Cronesfoil is one of the first anvil spellbooks, one of the first to be printed instead of handwritten. Some alchemists turned to printing in onesies and twosies. Let you store a lot of knowledge someplace besides your own head."

She frowned, a bit puzzled. "Well, yeah, that's kind of what books do."

"And if you're an apprentice or a lower member of a secret society..."

She nodded. "... then you only learn what they feel like telling you."

"Unless you go off and can learn it for yourself."

"So what, they just print and leave 'em lying around?"

"Nope. They printed half the spells."

"What?"

"Imagine printing a cookbook with just the ingredient lists and the mixtures, but nothing about cooking time or preparations."

"What good would that be?"

"Pretty decent, if you already had a good idea of how your oven worked with what. Hell, you can find reprints of some of these books online. It'll tell you all about making some sort of wacky concoction naked by the light of the full moon. But then it won't tell you whether to drink it, smear it on yourself, or whatever."

As the highway kept going, we passed the mountain and it disappeared in my rearview as we went down another hill. The open highway turned into a commercial zone, and the coniferous forests gave way to long lines of strip malls. Connie continued. "Sounds dangerous even if you know magic."

"It is. That's why you buy one of the originals if at all possible. The first part of the spell was printed. The second was handwritten in invisible ink. They called it nexttext."

"So you'd need to know it was there and how to make it visible again."

"Yep. Some were written in milk or lemon juice. You could heat the page to show the second half of the spell. If you were really paranoid, you wrote it in semen. These days, you can see it with a black light. But back in the day, you had to cast a spell that let your eyes see in that spectrum."

"Clever. Grody, but clever."

"So yeah. Whatever I was looking for is in the Cronesfoil, which doesn't make sense."

"Why not?"

"The Cronesfoil is a joke book. A French witch wrote it in the 1490's after getting her hands on the Malleus Maleficarum. Filled it full of really vicious sounding spells and wrote elaborate punchlines in the nexttext. Figured anyone in the know would have a good laugh and any clueless idiot vile enough to try the first half deserved an Inquisition."

"Sounds like someone I wouldn't want to mess with."

"A lot of witches are like that."

*   *   *

Chapter Nine

"Guideline Twenty-Four:

   Living in the past is one thing,

   staying there is unhealthy."

Even in the more developed areas, Georgia is full of parks. Usually they can't be seen when you're just passing by. You have to turn into the park and beyond a screen or two of trees before they'll reveal themselves. Blue river finally showed itself when I turned off the main road, the sign declaring the park existed all but overgrown by a weeping willow.

Early evening on what had been a sunny and hot day, and the parking lot only had a few spaces occupied. The temperature was gently dropping, but the air was humid as it could get. A breeze from the north, following the river and carrying the scent of cut grass, offered a touch of respite from the constant summer heat.

To even get to the park proper involved taking a path from the parking lot through the trees. After a few minutes' walk, we emerged into an expansive oval-shaped meadow. Runners, dog walkers, and small families all were scattered about the playground; with the giant, shaded pavilion just south of it looking like an old plantation house. Beyond the pavilion was another treeline, concealing the river further east.

I turned to Connie, "You ever come here?"

She gave a bit of a shrug. "Once or twice."

"This was where they held the party. The loudest parts, anyway. The playground wasn't there yet, and a band was set up on a stage over there by the pavilion. Couples who wanted to be alone, well, there's a lot of woods to be alone in."

Byron took in the view. "Pretty. Which way, scarecrow?"

I thought about it for a second. "Going down memory lane, widdershins is as good a direction as any," I said, turning right and heading for the southern walking trail. After a long walk, the trail left the meadow and disappeared further into the woods.

*   *   *

We emerged in a clearing maybe half the size of a football field when the trail split. One end kept going south, into the dense pine forest where we could just see the shape of a wooden bridge a few dozen yards away. The other fork in the trail buttonhooked north, heading closer to the river itself. I hadn't seen it in daylight for years, but I recognized it.

"The end of the line for us."

Byron looked around critically. "A natural choke point."

I nodded, "This is around where you and yours would've come from, if it had turned out different."

Connie tilted her head. "Byron was here?"

I shook my head. "Fortunately, no. If my Sextus had gotten her way, he would have. She needed over a hundred souls for the ritual to be successful. So she tried to catch us between a rock and a hard place. Hellhounds coming from the north, and the Hunt from the south."

Connie looked skeptical. "The Hunt as in..?" She held her hands up by her head and made a pair of fake antlers out of them. The rest of us nodded. I pointed North.

"Hellhounds go for the kill on sight. The Hunt prefers to capture rather than kill immediately. When they're on the move, at least. Both of them are relatively easy to summon, but a stone bitch to try and banish. With the road and the river providing natural boundaries, anyone escaping the Hellhounds would have met the Hunt coming up from the south. Once she got her sacrifices, the Hunt could take any stragglers they pleased."

"You never said the Hunt came here."

"They didn't. Ethan told the rest of us what Sextus was planning. And we knew we couldn't fight Hellhounds and The Hunt at the same time. We couldn't stop her from summoning them, either. But banishing Hellhounds requires either the faith of a saint, or..."

Connie cut me off. "... Or a deal with a devil. And you couldn't do that."

I shook my head. "Nope. A friend and I managed to claim a favor."

"How?"

Byron smiled. "Faced one of my cousins in single combat. And mopped the floor with him."

Connie frowned at Byron, folding her arms in annoyance. "Alright, quit beating around the bush. What are you?"

Byron, like a lot of humanoid fey that spent most of their time around humans, kept up a glamour whenever he left his own house. A glamour is a mild illusion that doesn't hide anything so much as convince observing humans that what they expect to be there is what's really there. This isn't as hard as you'd imagine. Modern human senses are easy to overload. So the mind filters out what isn't considered important. Now, back in the day, a human considered things like extra-long fangs in a human-looking mouth important. A well-done glamour put such things into the unimportant category.

Thing is, glamours normally go on and off like a light switch. It only takes a tiny bit of concentration to keep them going. But once in a while, they slowly fade. Usually when the one behind the glamour is really getting their bloodlust up. I've known Byron for years, and the only time I've ever seen his glamour fade is just before someone walked into an ambush we set up.

Ever heard of the uncanny valley? When you see a movie special effect or something that looks almost human but just off enough to be creepifying? We, and by we I mean humans, react like that for a reason. Statistically speaking, each and every one of us alive today is descended from a human who saw a glamour fail, then saw blood hit the walls, then somehow survived. A part of us remembers that. It damn well should. Because the people behind those glamours are still out there.

Byron's glamour dropped in the blink of an eye. He was still a handsome young black man. It would take an awful lot of effort to make him other than handsome. But now there was no hiding his pointed ears. His eyes had gone from soulful all the way to easy to be lost in forever. And when he smiled, it revealed that all of his teeth were as sharp as his canines, which gave vampires a run for their money.

He winked, "All the better to eat you with, my dear."

Connie nodded, seeming unimpressed. "That's why Cyrus called you a hunter." She turned to me, "So what, is he bound to serve you now?"

Byron snorted a laugh. I shook my head, annoyed. "Don't be ridiculous. You think the vampires are the only IOU I wrote out trying to keep my friends alive? And it's not hunter, it's Hunter. It deserves the capital letter, and so does he." She didn't move, only her glare speaking for her. I went on. "Once Chittenden's satisfied, I owe the Hunt some time too. Byron's around to make sure I don't run off."

She nodded, moderately embarrassed. "Got it. Just so I know for sure, Thumper's not a dwarf, are they?"

Thumper widened their stance in a squat, puffed out their cheeks and swung an imaginary ax. Byron gave his snarky grin, his glamour back in place. I shook my head. "No, Thump's a mage just like me. Just prettier."

Thumper dropped the farce, whistled, pointed to each branch of the trail, then shrugged in a question. The fork that crossed the bridge was labeled with a blue circle. The fork that turned to follow the river upstream had a yellow circle. I nodded to the upstream fork.

"If I'm gonna follow yellow until further notice, that's not a bad one to start."

*   *   *

The river flowed gently on our right as we walked, heading South on ever-important river business. After a while we stopped seeing other people, the tree canopy keeping us in shade growing in the late afternoon. Up on our left, the clearing where we began slowly revealed itself, the backside of the pavilion resting on the slight hill. Old memories started filling in blanks. Looking both ways, I nodded to myself, convinced.

"It looks more like the killing fields, coming up this way."

Connie queried. "Yeah?"

I nodded, trying not to shudder. The faces of long dead friends started flashing to the forefront of my mind. "We made our first stand here. Some of us herded classmates all the way back to that fork, some fought hellhounds here.

Thumper whistled low, standing at the base of a giant oak. They touched the trunk with all the reverence of visiting a tomb. I tilted my head. "Is this the one I'm thinking about, Thump?"

Thumper nodded. I stepped a little further into the clearing, stroked my goatee, and nodded myself. "Yeah."

"What is it?"

I looked, then pointed to a depression in the ground the size of a garbage can. Years of erosion had kept the grass away. It looked like it easily flooded during rainstorms. "See that shallow spot a few dozen yards out? Thumper was caught in an explosion there. They got blown all the way to this tree. Thump hasn't really been able to talk since."

Connie quietly asked. "Not even with magic?"

I shook my head. "Not a lot of witches become neurosurgeons. Or psychologists, for that reason. Thump can hear and understand people fine, and they're a really talented cognimancer. But the connection between their brain and their mouth is screwy."

"How about ASL?"

"Similar. They can play charades. But anything beyond that gets garbled just as bad as speech."

Thumper nodded in agreement, shrugged nonchalantly, then spun a finger next to their temple and whistled. I cracked a smile myself. "You do enough science and people start admitting they only got the most basic maps of the brain, only have vague directions in the mind, and no clue about the soul." I picked out a bit of pinestraw that had somehow wound up in Thumper's hair, dropping it on the trail. "Thumper's seen a lot of docs over the years, and just about as many healers on the magic side. Every last one of them can only diagnose so far. Going any further is a guessing game. And nobody's willing to use Thumper as a guinea pig."

Thumper nodded, then slipped under my arm and hugged me. I gripped their shoulder for a moment, smiling again.

Byron clapped me on the back and shook his head. "You know, you've told me about this more than once, but I've never been here. Seventeen trying to save two hundred against however many hellhound packs on ground like this? To a hunting party like the one I grew up in, this is just a target rich environment."

I nodded, tousling Thumper's hair before letting them go and starting to walk along the treeline again. "Bubba and I treated it like one once we got the chance." I pointed north, where the field disappeared into the treeline. A single path marked a hole in the ranks of the evergreens. "We got on either side of the trees, made sure nobody human was north of us. Then we lit the place up."

Byron tapped me with his finger three times in a row when he'd touched me, a sign of danger. His eyes flickered for an instant to the northwest. We were being watched again. No point in letting whoever it was know they'd been made, but something to keep paying attention to.

Connie asked. "Rifles?"

I shook my head. "Shotguns. I didn't have enough trigger time on machine guns to be good with them back then. But I could do a lot with shotguns."

"You enchanted your guns?"

"Enchanted my guns? Don't be ridiculous. I enchanted the magazines. Scraped some metal shavings off the inside of the tube, wove it into a patch on the bottom of my backpack. Then wove thread from the patch into the magazine tube spring. A little sympathetic link and three cases of twelve gauge later and I didn't have to reload the entire night. My shoulder didn't stop hurting until Midsummer, but it got the job done. Bubba and I physically destroyed probably more hellhounds ourselves than everyone else combined." I sighed. "Still wasn't enough."

I started walking again. Connie managed to break the silence. "You know, you're the only one I've ever met who wanted more firepower for humanitarian reasons."

I cracked a smile. "Stranger things have happened."

I stopped. I'd wandered right up to the tree I was looking for. A magnificent oak bigger around than I could span with my arms. The oak we were standing under.

I want to be remembered like this for a thousand years.

I don't know how long I stood there.

Byron broke the silence. "Trav? You good?"

I managed to breathe, then nod. I stretched out my hand, letting it run along the bark.

Connie quietly spoke up. "Where is this?"

I didn't turn away from the tree. "Last place I saw my girlfriend alive."

Saying it, I felt like a jackass. Like I was turning Heather into my own damn lost Lenore. I loved her. A part of me always will. But we were high school lovers and it's been years. But... I still miss her. Thumper pushed past Byron, wrapping their arms around me. I let them, my free arm dropping on their shoulders, pulling them in close.

Connie quietly asked. "What was she like?"

It took me a while to find the words. Any words. My chin resting on top of Thumper's head, I finally let them out. "Kind. Heather was always kind unless she didn't have a choice. Funny. Sexy. Kinda shy. Really clever. She was one of the first of us to come up with her own spell. I dunno if we would've lasted. High school romance, you know? But she was good to me. I hope I was good to her."

*   *   *

"Still creepy after all these years."

The upstream pavillion's parks department basic style was nothing spectacular. But the varnished wood beams had, after twenty-odd years of weathering, acquired the feeling of something sinister. The multiple knee braces where the columns met the roof made them look like thick pitchforks. The floor had been stripped, sanded, and repainted over the years. But I could still see where the blood splashed. The feel of the place somehow managed to, even in the afternoon, give the impression of some sort of Gothic ruin. No picnickers were out this far, nobody enjoying the day. Even hikers stopping to see the view over the river didn't stay long.

It didn't help that whoever had been following us was still around. They'd stayed in the woods west of us, but hadn't come close enough to be seen from the trail. Thumper had figured it out. I wasn't sure if Connie had. On the walk up the trail from the clearing I'd double-checked all my gear as I went. Being nonchalant and ready was all I could do.

Byron looked the place over with a professional's eye. "Last stand."

I nodded, brushing some leaves off the cement floor with my foot. "Yeah. We finally managed to stop them here. Just before the cavalry came: my uncle Mac, some of our other monitors, the SiS Marshal, a few others. They took away the Sextus, hid our weapons, and got rid of anything that suggested magic. The gangs fell back and escaped by car. Most of 'em were arrested later, but none of the witnesses saw them attack anyone, so nobody was charged." I turned back, looking south. We could just see the beginning of the field through the treeline from where I stood. "We swept the field. Noted our dead. Picked up our wounded as we went. Then we crossed the river just north of the bridge. Came back a while later, where the news and the cops were waiting. That's when the newspaper picture on my phone got taken."

I leaned against the pavilion railing, watching the river go by below. There was a large sandbar and a lot of shallows near the pavilion, letting the rush of the water turn into a slow whisper several feet below me. After a long time, I finally spoke up. "Byron?"

'Yeah?"

"How do you guys sense demons? Elves, I mean."

The others had the quiet of those who were paying close attention. I was looking out on the water, but I could almost see Byron shrug. "The simple answer is magics, same as you. But I don't think that's the question you're asking yourself."

I bit my lip, watching more of the river go by. "Coming here made me think about how we fought this. And how I'd fight it today. And there's so many things I'd do differently."

"That's hindsight, man."

"No, it ain't. There's so much more I can do now. I made those Oaths because I didn't know enough magic. None of us did. We all knew theory. And we all had one or two spells we could count on. But it wasn't enough. Not for what we were up against."

I finally caught his eyes. He shook his head, making his dreadlocks sway. "Travis, you were kids. Amazing kids. Going up against your own teacher? Two of your own friends? Only idiots blame you and the others for that."

I sneered. "Didn't they? It's not like they listened to us. But now I know so much more. I could have made armored clothes for everyone. I could have made better weapons and smoke and pyro and healing potions and things that could have made a difference."

"It's called growing up, man. It's been over a decade since the massacre. We all grow and learn."

I could barely say it. "But I don't know how I know."

Thumper almost stepped towards me, but convinced themselves otherwise at the last moment. I took a breath and went on. "I don't remember how or where I learned how to make all these things. If you asked me to enchant a smoke grenade right now I could write down the recipe and instructions without thinking. But I couldn't tell you where I learned to do that or why I know it will work."

None of them knew what to say. I kept going. "Byron, I'm not just missing last year. I'm missing how I learned almost all the magic I've picked up since we left active duty. Even pieces of that deployment. I remember truck three getting hit in an ambush in some kind of fucked up way we had no clue about. And I remember we found out what happened eventually. But I don't know exactly how and I don't know how I found out. We've already seen what I was willing to do back then. I swore an oath to serve a scumbag like Chittenden, of all people. What if I made a bargain with something even worse and don't know it? What if the Iron Council is right and I don't even know it?"

Byron waited a moment, then spoke as smooth as I've ever heard him. "Trav, I'm not gonna say I'm sure. I'm not an expert. I do know demons and their influence are really hard to discover. They are the champion liars of the Otherworld, and I'm a Fae saying that. But I'll also say that I don't see someone who followed his moral compass hard enough to break a renfield bond being dense or desperate enough to make a bargain with a no-shit demon, either."

Connie gave an awkward look I was starting to recognize as a blush trying it's best. Thumper decided to bodycheck me right there, refusing to let go. I caught a breath, blinking tears away and nodding a thanks at Byron. He gave me a smile without even any sass.

I turned to look out at the river when the scent of spiced meat went past my nose. I resisted the urge to turn fast, gently slipping my wand out of my pocket. Byron caught my eyes and nodded, a dagger already in his hand. Connie looked about to ask something when the first growl came. There were at least one each from the north and west. Finally Connie hissed, "Coyotes?"

I shook my head. "Coyotes aren't this big."

The first one had stepped out of the brush. On all fours, it stood taller than my belt. It was still wolf-shaped, but scaled up. Its dirty blonde fur was the same shade as the kid's hair from the gas station. Myself, Byron, and Thumper had formed up with Connie in our center. Thumper didn't carry a wand, but their hands were out. I counted on Byron to watch my flank while I looked down at the wolf in a slight crouch, wand out.

"All right, look. I know what you are and I know you speak English. I have no idea what I've done to piss you guys off, but I apologize. It's been a screwed up couple of months for me. If I owe you guys, let me know, and I'll do my best to make it right. That said, if you won't take an apology or reparations, the options go downhill from there."

A growl from my flank came, deeper and louder than the one in front of me. My eyes flickered towards it and off the one staring at me for half a second. Even as it happened, I knew we were already in the thick of it. The kid charged, eating ground in a huge loping stride. I gripped my wand and lashed my fist out, gripping it like a roll of quarters and whispering a word of power. The kid stumbled in mid-stride like I'd punched him in the head with a mallet from several yards away. I heard a slicing sound and a yelp of pain followed by another body hitting the ground.

Something the size of a hockey puck flew past my head, then hit another wolf coming up from behind. The puck exploded on contact, bowling the wolf over. I turned to see Thumper holding another one of those pucks, ready to throw.

I yelled. "Head for the truck!" Thumper took the lead as we all made a run for it. "Don't kill unless you gotta!"

I could hear Byron snort even over the blood rushing in my ears. "Four of us against a werewolf pack and you're pulling punches?"

"I like keeping my options open!"

I ran past a bigger werewolf with darker fur that staggered drunkenly beside the trail, which must have been handled by Byron. Two others burst from the brush behind and to my right, running fast. I spoke another word of power and lashed out again with my wand. The wave of kinetic energy caught one in mid-stride and let it stumble hard. Another one of Thumper's firecrackers flew by and hit the other one, making it fall with a painful sounding yelp. I turned and sprinted, seeing Thumper and the others burst from the treeline and sprint for the truck.

I'm faster than I look, but I was not built for distance running. I had seconds to think of something or start doing serious damage. Fortunately,

I remembered one of my toys that should do the job. With the treeline coming up, I pulled a green cardboard cylinder the size of a prescription bottle out of my pack. There was no wind, but I couldn't light the fuse and run at the same time. I got to the treeline and halted, looking back.

All four were back up, gathered a couple dozen yards from the treeline. The biggest one had a bloody wound, and they all looked pissed.

I snapped my fingers, which let a flame erupt from my thumb. The thumb lit the fuse, which sparked to life.

"I said I was sorry."

I dropped the bomb and ran. The families and joggers had disappeared. Which I was thankful for, because I was going to have to start shooting if my last trick didn't work. Behind me I heard a crackle, a hiss, and multiple canine yelps. I didn't look back, pulling out my key fob and pushing the unlock button repeatedly. I saw my lights flash as Thumper reached the Yukon first, diving into the backseat. Connie slid in after them, while Byron ran around the hood to take shotgun. Angry howling followed me until I got to the Yukon, jumping into the driver's seat and gunning the engine.

Looking out, I could barely see movement in the treeline. Pulling out of the space, I took a hard right and headed for the road. Connie's eyes were wide as I pulled out of the lot.

"What did you do?"

"Pepper spray grenade. I hate littering, but given the alternatives..."

"And you just had that in your pockets?"

I shrugged, checking the mirrors to make sure we weren't followed. "I believe in being prepared. And I hang out with a hunter, I'm used to thinking about scents."

Byron's teeth flashed in a smile. "You learned well, dumpling."

I turned onto the road and gunned the engine, putting some distance between us and the wolves. Shaking my head, I glanced in the rearview. "Thump, you never told me you upgraded those toys of yours."

In the backseat, Thumper shrugged.

I shook my head. "I know I didn't ask. How'd you light them?"

Thumper held up a flat palm, then punched it with their other fist. Then both hands pulled apart from each other, wiggling fingers.

I nodded. "Contact fuses. Got it. You've gotten stingy with your explosions over the years."

Thumper held up three fingers, counted them down, then shrugged.

I changed lanes while glancing in the mirror. "You only brought three. Makes sense."

Connie wasn't impressed. "You irritate wolves often?"

I shook my head, making my next turn. "Wolves don't live in Georgia and don't come up to my waist. Werewolves can and do."

"Noted. You irritate werewolves often?"

I managed to catch my breath. I was really out of shape. "Lately? Just these guys. No idea why. But they're the ones that did the drive-by, and the kid that threatened me when we stopped for gas."

Connie frowned. "The drive-by hillbillies are werewolves?"

"Yep. They're also the ones who kidnapped you. And two of them are the guys who were waiting in your house. I could smell them in your dream."

"The drive-by hillbilly werewolves kidnapped me for a vampire?"

"Sounds like a bad movie when you say it like that."

"Is there a way to say it that makes sense?"

I turned off onto 78 and headed west back towards the city. "Good question. Maybe Eva needed work done before dark and contracted them out. They look like they need the money."

"That doesn't make sense either. That sounds like the movies, where all the vampires dress like runway models and the werewolves are always blue collar stiffs at best."

"I know, sounds really cliché. But you've met Eva and seen these guys, so here we are."

Byron shrugged. "History turned cruel that way, man. Before the Renaissance, there were a lot of knights that got hairy under the moon. Back in the day when all you had to do was fuck up anyone who messed with your peasants? A lot of 'em were good at it. But to retain power these days, you need to know who to smile at while stabbing them in the back, how to look good in clothes designed by someone whose name you can't pronounce, and know random shit about wine even though you never drink it. Werewolves are natural warlords, vampires are natural slumlords. Civilization sucks sometimes."

I cracked a smile. "Does that mean burning down the Cotillion was striking a blow for equality?"

He shrugged again. "Shit, call it that if you want. I never liked the place."

Connie relaxed enough for a smile of her own. "Well, we followed yellow. Now what?"

Byron and I spoke in stereo. "Food."

*   *   *

Chapter Ten

"Guideline Five:

Eat, sleep, clean, and reload whenever you can.

Sometimes you won't have the chance."

The unofficial boundary of Atlanta is I-285, which encircles the city, the airport, and several of the closer suburbs. The locals just call it the perimeter. It was full dark by the time we crossed back inside the perimeter, stopping at a Wacross for dinner. Waffle Crossroad is an ubiquitous southern diner chain open 24-7. Every location is built the same way, and every location is built on a current or former crossroad. Wacross is the slang term. Sounds like lacrosse.

The difference between a Wacross and a place like Warwell's is mostly a question of scale. The Warwell family have a century-old reputation for hospitality, power, and lack of ambition outside their own territory. Wacross, on the other hand, was founded by those who saw a need for consistently enforced neutral territories. In every location, at least half of any given shift are either from the Otherworld or read in on it. They work there because the jobs are relatively simple, the pay is decent enough, and the violent bullshit is aggressively kept outside the doors. The food is decent and filling, but it's the peace of mind that draws both the clientele and the staff.

Loretta saw me the moment I came in through the doors, shaking her head in a manner so world-weary I last saw it onstage from a comedian. "The prodigal son returns!"

I touched my forehead in a lazy salute, which got me a winning smile. "Good timing, Trav. Yer usual's open."

I returned the grin with the relief of seeing a friendly face. "It's good to be back, Loretta."

Loretta's always on third shift at this particular location. She looks like a friendly, short, middle-aged black woman with the shoulders of a linebacker, forearms of a blacksmith, and a bosom that would triple your chances of surviving a car crash if you landed in it. She looked like that twenty years ago when she taught my barely teenaged self how to properly tip. She'll most likely look like that in another twenty years. Under her glamour, her beard goes down to her apron strings.

Working the grill behind her was Grover, who was a distant relation to Loretta somewhere, but I'm not sure exactly how. Shorter than Loretta and a touch lighter-skinned, he was still built like a beer keg with fists. He gave us a wave in passing before turning his attention back to the grill.

Byron and I went to the far end of the area and took the side of the booth with our backs to the wall. Connie and Thumper graciously took the opposite side, Thumper with a knowing grin and a small shaking of their head. Loretta made her appearance at the head of the table before we'd even sat down. "Thank the hammer, y'all! I done heard about the Cotillion this morning, Trav. Worried myself sick you were a goner, but here you are, not a scratch on ya. Good to see you and your hunting buddy finally found some nice company to spend time with. No wonder you two ain't darkened my door for a while."

She slid her ticket book out of her apron, innocently letting the seax dagger she kept sheathed under it become visible and at hand. Behind her, I could see Grover casually check a throwing axe hanging just under the grill. Loretta's smile didn't dampen one bit as she raised an eyebrow. "Y'all ain't got no business to attend to while under my roof now, do ya?"

I found myself slowly putting my hands in view on top of the table while shaking my head negatively. "No ma'am."

The others made it clear in various gestures that assassinating supernatural creatures were the farthest thing from their minds. Naught but weary travelers in search of 24 hour breakfast food.

Whatever dwarvish sincerity test Loretta put us under, we apparently passed. The dagger disappeared under the apron as she nodded in approval. "Just making sure. Do an old woman a favor and don't go frying any leeches while you're here. But I'll be merciful and not tell tales in church. What y'all drinkin?"

Byron smiled flirtatiously, "My usual for tonight, Loretta, please. I'll need my strength when I carry you off later."

Loretta snickered. "Don't tempt me, handsome. My fourth husband's already getting on my nerves. I'd wear you out in a season and get no end of grief from your daddy about it. How's about you, Trav?"

I nodded, "My usual, hon. Hold the ravishment."

Connie looked up. "Coffee and a water, please?"

Thumper whistled, pointed to Connie and then themselves, following it with a thumbs up. Loretta nodded. "Forge in the snow, compass rose, you got it, darlings."

The South gets picked on a lot for the way we talk, but I guarantee you, you can't miss a linguistic experience like picking up dwarvish diner lingo.

When Loretta vanished behind the counter, Connie leaned in. "The sun's down already. Do we need to be out with Eva's people and the werewolves after you?"

I shook my head, then winced. The last of the adrenaline from the werewolf attack was wearing off, and all my aches were coming back in force. "On the road, I'll watch out, but not in a Wacross. Even if someone is plotting to jump us, they'll stay back until we're out of the parking lot."

Byron chimed in as Thumper picked up a menu. "Nobody picks a fight here. Not unless they want an ass kicking with a side of banishment."

That got him a raised eyebrow from Connie. "The crew of a diner chain is scary enough to make the Otherworld behave?"

Byron and I answered in stereo. "Yes."

Byron played with a toothpick, walking it across his fingers. "Loretta and Grover are enough by themselves. She keeps a battle hatchet under the counter by the register, and can choose which eye socket to split open with it at fifty feet. And I once saw Grover knock a werewolf on its ass by throwing a dinner plate."

Loretta reappeared, laden tray in hand. She distributed glasses and mugs with the sure hand of a blackjack dealer. "That's hot coffee and ice water all around, loves. Y'all know what you're wanting to eat?"

I gave her a smile. "Yeah, Loretta. I'll have a medium steak covered in hash browns with cheese."

She turned to Byron, who nodded. "Hash bowl with sausage, cheese, and ham."

Connie smiled quietly. "Just a short stack for me, please."

Thumper pointed to the blueberry pie on the menu.

Loretta nodded, scrawling on her ticket book. "All right then." She gave us a winning smile, turned her head, and bellowed like a drill instructor. "Hey Grover! I got a king under the mountain, a hack and slash with gold, a hockey game and a sapphire mine!"

Grover didn't look up from his work, spooning another measured ladle of melted butter on the griddle as he spouted a stream of rapid-fire dwarvish into the opposite wall. It didn't sound too insulting, for Grover. Then again the only word I understood was, "Behov Pathelm," which was just the dwarvish word for humans. It literally means, "must pad their knees indoors." Under the glamour, he tucked his waist-length goatee into the neckline of his apron. His arms were covered in intricate tattoos that looked like they had come from ancient cookbooks. I was too far away to tell for sure, but I saw multiple knives, a cauldron, and a whisk depicted in there. Loretta, apparently satisfied, wandered off to her next customer, leaving our table alone.

Byron picked up where he left off. "And it's not just the staff. People like having places they can go to eat in peace. Especially powerful people with long lists of enemies. And everyone answers to someone. Start something in a Wacross, and every friend, mentor, and ally you ever had will jack you up, just to make sure they don't catch your banishment like a cold." He picked up his mug by the rim and pointed it at me. "We are gonna need a plan of action once we get to your place."

I shrugged, curling a single finger around the handle of my own mug. The smell of short-order cooking dulled my headache into something almost comfortable. Meanwhile, my stomach was reminding me that I hadn't eaten in hours. I made a mental note to order seconds, maybe another steak. I could use the protein. I switched the tracks on my train of thought to answer Byron. "I was gonna go with hunker down, get what rest we can and fight off what we need to. Better off sheltering in place than running. My wards aren't what they used to be, but the house is stronger than it looks. I've got a copy of the Cronesfoil in my library. I'll start studying it in the morning."

After a sip, Byron set down the cup and opened a vial of creamer. "A part of me would rather you went on the offensive. I mean, you already gave Tasha a navel piercing with a flare gun. What's a good old fashioned rampage going to hurt?"

I shrugged again, then stopped when my shoulder protested. "If I knew that's what I needed to do to wrap this up, I'd be more than happy to. But I don't see where that helps. With Eva dead, way too many people think I'm gunning for them next. I'd rather not kill anyone for just being understandably paranoid. Besides, I promised Babs I'd keep the body count to a minimum."

Loretta reappeared, her tray laden with steaming plates. "All right, y'all, sapphire mine, hack n slash, hockey game, king under the mountain. Y'all need any condiments? Refills?" There were smiles and shaking heads all around, which she nodded in satisfaction. "All right, loves, enjoy." Her tray slid out of everyone's way with the grace of a dancer before she headed off to her other charges.

A tenor voice with a frat boy twist opened up. "You're a big ol' busy beaver, aren't you?"

The chill running down my spine got in the way of my poker face. We looked up. The stool on the near end of the counter, just before the wall, had somehow become occupied while I wasn't looking. He had a swimmer's build and dirty blonde hair that had been gelled into submission. As we watched, he spun on the stool.   His presence made me suddenly want a shower.

I took a breath, trying not to let it out as a world-weary sigh. "Hello, Victor."

Acid washed jeans, a white tank top tucked into them, and an open canary yellow Hawaiian shirt over that. Scuffed brown slip-on loafers on his feet. Aviator shades straight out of an action movie. He had been maybe twenty-four the day he had stopped breathing. The man looked the spitting image of an exchange student who hadn't gotten comfortable with the idea of shorts or sneakers. He grinned around the toothpick clenched in his teeth like a cigar. "Travis! My man with the battle plan! Hunter, pleasant as always."

Byron nodded, giving a small gesture with the spoon he drew from his coffee. "Victor."

I managed to catch my manners and indicated the others. "Victor, this is Connie and Thumper."

He nodded dismissively fast, "Thumper, sounds like a fun story there. Connie..." He slid his sunglasses down his nose and looked over the top of them hungrily. "Travis finally found some taste."

Connie didn't touch her own shades or miss a beat. "I'd call that accurate. Given that he abruptly stopped banging your mom to be with me and all."

I could just barely see the rage in Victor's eyes before his mask of calm settled back into place. Neither Byron nor Thumper had their hands in sight, both were waiting to follow my lead. I was halfway through opening my mouth to apologize when Victor laughed out loud. Heads were already starting to turn our way as Victor slapped his leg. "Damn, Travis! You are one lucky sumbitch, ain't you? Woman with a tongue that quick has got to feel amazing everywhere else. Congratulations."

My brain completely vapor locked. A part of me imagined exactly what he implied and wanted to blush. Another part of me wanted to shudder at how creepy he was being. A third was happy I had one hand resting on a knife, and the fourth was wondering if I was about to have yet another price put on my head. I wasn't good with this. Machines, energy, materials, tools, that I was good with. Put me in the middle of a system I understand and I'll play with its limits like an orchestra conductor. But with people and emotions, I needed clues badly.

He waved off whatever I would've managed to say. "Anyways, Trav, I heard about last night, and it's no problem on my end. We can still move forward easy enough if you can deliver the goods."

I blinked, confused. "What the who now?"

The others were as confused as I was, but Victor kept on going. "Absolutely. I know my claim ain't as strong as mom's would have been. But let's face facts. Chitty ain't getting along with the times. I'm fond of the fat old bastard myself, but he's been top dog too long and he's getting in the way of change we need. Nobody's going to take our notion of progress seriously if a chubby old confederate is still calling the shots, am I right?"

"I can see that." Every meditation technique I could think of was going through my head. Eva was toast, but Victor was planning on overthrowing Chittenden either by himself or with Tasha. I wasn't sure if Victor had a pair of solid brass ones or if he was just committed and desperate. Even money either way, but getting proof was suddenly my top priority. If nothing else, I needed to show Chittenden something more than guesswork, a trail of bodies, and holes in my memory. I almost missed Victor continuing his pitch. The leech was more pushy than a time-share presenter.

"So what you say? You up for it? That heir presumptive spell you talked up sounds like it would hit the spot just fine for our purposes. You ready to finally get that monkey of an Oath off your back and get in good with the incoming administration?"

I shrugged in what I hoped was a noncommittal way. "Did I have any reservations about doing it for Eva?"

"Not that I saw, man."

A thousand noncommittal conversations with clients over the years saved me by running on autopilot as I nodded. "You're right. Chittenden's a lot of things, but forward thinking ain't one of them."

He took what looked like a glass test tube from his front pocket, full of a crimson liquid so dark it was nearly black. "If you're good, I'm good, man. This should be all you need."

I took it, somehow keeping my hand from shaking. I could feel the power radiating out of the tube, same as I did the one I'd taken from Eva. I could almost smell it even with the stopper sealed. I resisted the urge to openly sniff it like a fine cigar. My mouth went dry. An uncomfortable number of seconds went by before I reminded myself where I was. Nodding to myself, I tucked it into a pocket. "This probably wasn't easy to come by."

"Old school KGB trick, man. A human wouldn't have moved fast enough to find the vein. But I was already there pulling him out of the fight. If I accidentally poked him with a pen, easy mistake. Been holding onto that for a year, now."

Connie stopped with a forkful of pancake section in midair. "You don't have a Russian accent."

All of a sudden, he did. "Says who? Is just not only one I have. I keep a bit of it handy, for when I cruise the colleges. I sound like exchange student. It really impresses the undergrads. And I love undergrads. No matter how old I get, they still taste the same."

Byron rolled his eyes but mercifully didn't comment. I suppressed a shudder. "Where and when do you need me?"

Victor shrugged, left a pair of twenties on the counter and stepped off his stool. His accent was mercifully put away. "Long as your work is done by the witching hour on the fourth, we're good to go and I'll text ya." He tilted his head in curiosity. "You don't look so good, Trav. Sure you don't need to be topped off or something?"

I couldn't move. He was offering power, there for the taking. Power to fix every battered inch of my body. Power enough to try and bust open the lock on my enemies. Power as a bonus, now that he'd handed me proof of his own plot against Chittenden. Then something out of the back of my mind reminded me: it was power under his control.

As neutrally as I could manage, I mumbled. "No thanks."

He shrugged. "Later, folks."

He gave us a two-finger salute he thought looked cool and headed out without another word. Every diner in the place watched him go. Several of said diners had their hands out of view, even with half-eaten meals in front of them. Once he was out the door, everyone turned back to their meals and companions. The prospect of an actual fight in a Wacross had vanished.

Connie put down her fork. "Well, I had an appetite."

I downed the rest of my coffee. "I don't blame you. Fortunately, Wacross believes in to-go boxes."

* * *

Chapter Eleven

"Guideline Eight:

Sometimes, the answer is right in front of you the whole time.

Find it before it explodes in your face. Embarrassment heals faster than burns."

We were back in the truck and headed home in minutes. Victor was nowhere to be seen in the parking lot, but all of us had heads on swivels by then. The hash and coffee I'd managed to throw down my throat took the edge off the hunger, but it took some effort to not drive and eat my steak at the same time. I'm classy like that. Connie rode shotgun again, to-go boxes balanced on her lap. Thumper lounged in the backseat, amusing themselves with their phone.

Byron kicked off the commentary. "That was unexpected. Change of plans any?"

I shook my head, pulling into traffic. "Not with Victor wanting me to work for him instead of kill me."

Connie lifted her hand palm up, showing off the nothing resting in it. "But your memories aren't intact yet. And we still have no idea what following yellow means."

"No, but now I know for sure that Eva and her children were plotting to overthrow and kill Chittenden. Which explains why he had me in Eva's household to begin with. And now I have proof of it in my pocket."

Byron nodded. "So hole up at your place until tomorrow night?"

"Yup. There's not much that can breach my house that isn't measured in kilotons. We start hitting the books tonight. If we don't have a line on follow yellow by midday, I'll ask the Sues for a reading."

Thumper nodded emphatically. Connie looked confused. "The Sues?"

The light turned green and I made a turn into the neighborhood. "One of the best divination teams in the South. Bobbi Sue, Becky Sue, and Betty Sue are the current triptych. I won't get a straight answer out of them, but if I need another clue, they'll find me one."

We pulled up to my house without being followed, near as Byron or I could tell. I backed up into the driveway, giving a good length and a half between my SUV and Connie's jeep. While everyone was climbing out, I scanned the neighborhood. It was around ten-ish on a weeknight, relatively quiet for the area. And by relatively quiet I mean the frogs and crickets were outdoing each other in making a racket that for southerners is damn near tranquil. In the distance, someone was shooting off fireworks already. The temperature had dropped a bit but the humidity stayed, giving the streetlights a hazy halo around their burning bulbs.

I sensed movement out of the corner of my eye. As I turned to look, a petite blonde stepped out of a shadow. As in physically stepped out of it, as she wasn't in the leftover illumination from the streetlamp on the corner. Flanking her were a pair of guys in security blacks. No visible weapons, but game faces on and locked into place. They were either country vamps or renfields with really good discipline.

The blonde was Tasha, dressed in an internet age answer to Daisy Duke. Cutoffs tight enough to hug every curve and low enough to show a whale tail of dark-colored thong. Combat boots tied right. Gunbelt holding up a full size pistol on one side and a pair of magazines on the other, for symmetry. Tank top tied off in a knot under her breasts, which were lifted and displayed prominently as modern textile engineering could manage, showing off an impressive set of abs in the process. Doubly impressive, given that I'd shot her with a flare last night. I wondered how many flunkies she'd had to drink to pull off that kind of healing. Topping it all off was a high ponytail and an immaculately painted resting bitch face.

Years in the Marine Corps left me with a habit of tucking my thumbs into my front pants pockets, a habit that kept my hands in easy reach of both a knife and my holdout pistol. I casually tucked my thumbs as I nodded to her politely. "Hello, Tasha."

She smiled and let out an accent so Southern it almost poured us a mint julep. "Hey, y'all! Sorry I'm late. Had me a photoshoot earlier and this hair just doesn't behave itself at sundown."

I could almost hear Connie's eyebrow raise behind me. "Photoshoot?"

Tasha's teeth flashed. "Hell yeah. I'm an online model for the firearms industry. Strike a pose with a gun and I make bank. In sponsored products alone I got me enough firepower to conquer Latvia."

Byron shrugged, smiling. "I guess you found a need and filled it, gorgeous."

Tasha gave him a knowing smile. "You guess right, honey. Back where I come from, they'd expect me to run a bad farm good enough to keep everyone from starving. Here I just need perky tits, a flat belly, and the knowhow to keep a booger hook off a bang switch and the world's at my fingertips. Merica really is the land of opportunity."

Connie spoke up again. "I thought you were Russian."

Tasha's smile melted into a mean girl sneer. "It's called assimilation, sugar. I've lived here thirty years, plenty of time to lay it on thick as that pancake syrup y'all insult by calling it tea."

I held up a hand for peace. "She actually grew up here. You might not want to insult the tea."

Tasha waved me off. "It's all good, Trav. Victor done tole me y'all kissed and made up. I just wanted to let you know there ain't no hard feelings."

That was a surprise. "There's not?"

She laughed. "Oh hell naw. I'll admit ya done pissed me off something fierce. A flare gun is fighting dirty and you know it, ya bigass lugnut. But I know it was just to keep up appearances. It ain't like you could go ahead and and play kissy face with me while ya got momma staked out on her own boudoir floor. You knew I'd gone to all that trouble of having you find that spell. Not to mention all the ingredients. Do you have any idea how hard it is to find a virgin these days?"

Byron sighed, rolling his eyes. "Preach, girlfriend."

Tasha gave him a winning smile before reboarding her train of thought. "Then somehow Eva figures out who I'd pegged to throw on the altar, and she goes and snatches her up for herself. Selfish old bitch. I was coming to punch her ticket myself, but there you were, taking care of business before I even got in the door. All that and I didn't even get to take out momma myself? Now that bunched my undies something vicious. But I got over it. The old hag having you for a renfield is out of the way, and you all set to deal with Chitty for us. Water under the bridge, honey."

"What about the country vamps?" I asked incredulously. "I took two of them down too. Last thing I need is more people gunning for me."

"What part of water under the bridge is hard for you, Travie? I gotta paint you a picture?" Tasha rolled her eyes in exasperation. "Country vamps are very straightforward. If they wanted to spend time thinking about complicated stuff like revenge, they'd be city people. The two I set on you died trying. I don't want you dead no more, so the others ain't thinking about killing you no more. If I wanted complicated, I'd have kept that pack of white trash werewolves momma used to have hanging around the place.

They can get shit done in the daylight, but so can renfields, and they don't ask all the stupid questions all the damn time."

That somewhat explained the werewolf pack. They'd been the ones to kidnap Connie and wait at her house. Which means they must have been working for Eva. But if Tasha wasn't lying, then Eva had planned to fire them afterwards and replace them with country vamps. I must have screwed over the werewolves while Connie was changing in her room. No wonder they were pissed at me.

Of course, I'd already apologized and still had to hit them with anything short of shooting them. Not that I minded shooting people who repeatedly tried to kill me because I happened to be the working stiff that gave them their pink slip, but it was one more hassle on the stack of hassles I didn't need. If I lived to see the sunrise after next, I was gonna have to arrange some kinda weregild for that wolfpack.

While I was pondering and without me noticing, Connie had slowly stepped between Tasha and myself, moving with an oddly light step in her combat boots. Connie slowly looked the Russian vampire up and down with a thousand yard stare, like an old drunk reminded of a long-ago catastrophe. Tasha, who to be fair was not very swift on the uptake as far as I knew, looked very confused at the shapely goth stepping up to her like an old west gunfighter. Tasha tilted her head like a confused dog, sniffed the air, and her eyes went wide right along with her smile.

"Oh, Travis!" She cooed. "You stole her back and didn't even soil her for me? You paladin, you!"

Byron nodded in solidarity. "He really is."

I nearly hissed. "Shut up, Byron."

Connie's stare didn't waver. Her voice escaped purple-black painted lips just a hint stronger than a whisper. "You're the one? The one who decided to... use me?"

Tasha's smile was so sickeningly condescending I wanted to shoot her again with something bigger that burned longer. "Oh, I did, darling. I picked you out special." She lifted her arms with a ballerina's grace and cradled Connie's face between her immaculately manicured hands, like a society lady stroking a favorite pet. "You are the most exquisite virgin I've seen in decades. Even a foolish demigod wouldn't reject a scrumptious little morsel like you as a tribute."

My hackles raised instantly, and I worked hard to keep my poker face on. My thumbs twitched in my pockets, my hands ready to draw one weapon or another. If Connie had backed away, I'd have drawn on Tasha. But Connie didn't flinch from Tasha's touch. Rather, she breathed a sigh that was nigh-orgasmic, eyelids fluttering closed, her lips parting in a smile I'd never seen on her. Her body shuddered in near ecstasy as her hands came up, fingertips with their glossy black nails gliding along the skin of Tasha's toned arms. Tasha beamed like a proud stage mom watching her daughter wow the judges. The rest of us were dumbstruck at the sight, barely able to move.

Quick as a snake, Connie's hands clamped down on Tasha's wrists, muscles clenching tight. Her eyelids shot open, her eyes glowing a bright green. I could feel the power radiate off of her, the way you can feel a huge thunderstorm coming in the air. Her voice took on newfound power as she spoke, "*Putro!*"

Connie's hands, gripping tight on Tasha's arms, glowed as green as her eyes. Tasha screamed as her own arms began to swiftly rot. Toned skin shriveled and blackened as flesh melted into pus and putrid drippings. Tasha managed to shove away from Connie, snapping both of her fragile wrists in the process. Her hands disintegrated as they fell off, disappearing into plumes of dust and two handfuls of press-on nails as they hit the ground. I couldn't hear it over Tasha's screaming, but I could see Connie laughing as the vampire continued to fester at her touch.

Chapter Twelve

"Guideline Twenty-Three:

Your need to sit down is an opportunity

for those waiting to bite you in the ass."

There's a lot of argument about whether or not time can slow down in a crisis. Magically, the jury's still out. If there are magical ways of actually altering the flow of time, I've never heard about them. Personally, I think your brain just overclocks to the point where you're processing input faster than you can respond to it. Which is why the fastest magazine reload in the world to other people feels like it takes a lifetime to the poor bastard downrange in the middle of it.

At that moment, I was processing the fact that the comfy little gothlet I'd rescued from a vampire's virgin sacrifice last night and taken along for the ride ever since was One, a skilled mage in her own right, and Two, a necromancer powerful enough to make a centuries old vampire rot on cue. Tasha, on the other hand, was both a galloping bitch and didn't care if her own retainers lived or died, let alone me. Three, the country vamps may have been solid, blood-of-the-earth people, but they were still Tasha's retainers, and none too pleased about what Connie was doing to their mistress. The decision about who to shoot first took a fraction of a second, a smaller fraction than it normally took me to draw my holdout pistol.

I had said *pistol* halfway out of my pocket before Connie thrust a hand at the rest of us and yelled, "*Recumbo!*"

A wave of kinetic energy knocked all three of us off our feet. Out of the corner of my eye, I could see my Yukon rocking back on its tires. I thought a silent thanks to the Marines for weapons rule three, as I had no idea where my head was pointed, let alone the muzzle of my weapon. Tasha was still screaming as her arms crumbled from the wrists inward. The country vamps had been knocked down as hard as the rest of us.

I scrabbled to one knee and finished my draw, whispering, "*Hollywood Hollywood Hollywood,*" as I let my pistol sights line up on a country vampire's center of mass.

A normal suppressor turns the sound of a gunshot into something more like dropping a college textbook from waist height. It also makes something like my Glock 26 too uncomfortable to holster in a pants pocket. The Hollywood Silencer spell was laid into engravings on the barrel and slide a long time ago. Activating it with the incantation made the air surrounding the weapon spin for about a foot in every direction. While the bullet went on it's merry way, the gunshot sound, which was just air vibration, traveled several miles in the space of twelve inches before dissipating. As I found out during testing, it looks really neat when there's a fog machine working next to you. Here I had to settle for not waking up the neighbors.

Power surged down my arm and into the gun as I sighted in on the country vamp. Pulling the trigger twice, the shots sounded no louder than a cat sneezing. A part of me wasn't sure why I bothered, what with Tasha screeching like banshee karaoke, but every little bit helped. Out of the corner of my eye I saw the other country vamp take a pair of throwing knives in the eyes, stumbling. The vamp I'd shot, on the other hand, burst into flames from the chest out.

There might have been a time in my life when I thought thermite hollowpoints were hazardously ridiculous. That time was before I had to deal with jackass vampires on a regular basis. As it was, I was mostly worrying about missing and hitting someone's house. Don't let the humidity fool you, it's depressingly easy to start a brushfire in Georgia in July. Safety first, after all.

The flaming vampire ran across the street and into the shadows, but the one with knives in their eyes lunged for Connie again, so I fired at their center of mass. This one took four rounds before visibly igniting, running off in the same panic that afflicted their companion. Throughout the entire mess, Connie hadn't paid attention, grabbing Tasha's hair at the base of her neck, holding the screaming, handless vampire steady.

At this point, I would have expected to see her pull a wand out of her bag. A Bowie knife wouldn't have phased me. Even a Khukri would be understandable now. Instead, Connie pulled a folding entrenching tool out of that bag. It unfolded in mid-draw, blade and handle locking into place with a flick of her wrist and a clacking sound. The shovel blade was painted a matte black, which had worn away with use into bare shining metal all along the edge. The handle was wrapped in pink and black paracord. Tasha, her arms completely rotted away, hissed like a snake the size of a coed, her fangs bared and her eyes deep red. Before I could say a word, Connie's right hand came down in a circular arc. The blade sliced through Tasha's neck in one chop, like a kitchen knife through a water bottle on the home shopping channel. Ichor splattered my lawn and the street as Tasha's body landed with a wet squelching noise. Connie dropped Tasha's head immediately afterwards, Tasha's ponytail fluttering like a tassel as it bounced once, then started to crumple. Connie pulled a white, lace-trimmed hanky from her back pocket and wiped down the blade of the entrenching tool.

Dropping my muzzle, coming up to my feet, and somehow remembering to breathe, I screamed. "Connie, what the fuck?!"

Not my most eloquent, I'll admit. You try and be locquatious when your new friend turns out to be an angry necromancer and butchers a vampire on your lawn.

Any reply she might have made was interrupted by the squealing of tires. A crimson pickup truck framed by flailing, flaming vampires in the bed came roaring up to the corner. I raised a forearm and yelled, *"Skjoldur!"*

Energy surged through my body and shot out in a concave shape before me. Blue light crackled in two places as bullets impacted, ricocheting into the dirt. I could hear the sounds of the shooting as the truck came around the corner fast enough to almost be on two wheels. There were at least four people in the bed, two of whom were trying to put out the two shrieking, flaming vampires with blankets. The driver was firing a pistol with a number 4 somewhere in its caliber out the window at all of us. Connie ran past the driveway and dove out of sight. Something the size of a screwdriver landed point-first in the driver's side door, then crumbled to dust. I looked over at Byron, who was lifting another throwing knife. "No! Let them go!"

There wasn't anything to be gained by butchering a truck full of renfields and country vamps. And if we were lucky, the neighbors hadn't called the cops yet. Byron nodded as the truck sped off, turning at the end of the block at full speed and vanishing out of sight. I dropped my shield and turned to see Byron and Thumper getting to their feet. Tasha's rotting corpse looked like weeks-old roadkill with a gunbelt on top of it. Connie was nowhere to be seen.

Byron opened up. "You good, Trav?"

I nodded, both of us checking corners. "Yeah. You?"

Byron nodded. "I'm good." Like me, he was surrounded by shadows. Connie had disappeared into one, which meant she could come from anywhere by now. We both spun trying to check them all.

I caught movement out of the corner of my eye, relieved to see Thumper standing up. "Thump?"

Thumper nodded, then gave a short whistle and a thumb's up. They were trying to check every shadow too, and not happy about it.

An engine roared, from behind us. We all turned to see Connie's Jeep fire up, headlights high and bright. Instead of trying to ram my Yukon, she turned a sharp left, barreling through my front yard easily. The dry turf of my lawn was too solid for her tires to kick up much of it as she went. I could see the thousand yard stare back on her face as she drove. She only turned to look, saw she wasn't running any of us down, then turned away without meeting my eyes. Passing between a pair of oak trees and barely missing Byron's car, she sped up the instant her tires hit asphalt and vanished around the same corner Tasha's lackeys had.

I stood there and stared at the corner where Connie had vanished. After several moments, the sound of engines had disappeared, and the frogs and crickets began their chattering anew. I just stared openmouthed into the distance a chunk of my life had just drove off into. Byron slid his knife back into a scabbard I hadn't noticed, then shook his head. "I'll admit I didn't see that one coming."

I held out my hand as if begging the universe for spare change. "What the fuck?"

Byron nodded. "Girl's a necromancer, man."

I didn't move, just asked the universe. "What the fuck?"

Thumper gave a low whistle, then tapped Byron and pointed at the disintegrating stain that used to be Tasha. Byron nodded, impressed. "Powerful one, too. And she's got an e-tool kill. I don't have an e-tool kill. I'm officially jealous. And I'm kinda turned on."

My brain got back into the first comfortable groove if could find. "Byron, she's a necromancer."

Byron patted my shoulder in sympathy. "I know that sums it up, man, but you gotta have more specific questions."

I holstered my pistol and shuddered, the adrenaline dump still rampaging through my system. If my mouth had been hanging open any more, I would've drawn flies. She'd been in my warded house. I'd rummaged through hours of her memories. She'd spent all day with me. She'd spent all night with me. We'd just had dinner. And I'd had no idea. I shuddered again, shock rapidly becoming disgust. Byron and Thumper nodded in agreement. It still wasn't quite real to me. Something crossed my mind. I finally turned to the others, my eyes narrowed. "Did you two know?"

Thumper shook their head. Byron did the same. "Nope. It does make sense, though."

"She never told us, Byron."

He tilted his head. "I didn't ask. Did you?"

"No. Wait, why didn't we?"

Byron shrugged. "Can't speak for all of us. I mean, what are the odds on a full force goth chick being anything more than another stander? I wouldn't have laid money on it. Personally? I was too busy being happy for you. Not only out from under Eva's thumb, but took a nice girl home? It was about damn time."

My frown darkened at him. "What the hell is that supposed to mean?"

Byron folded his arms. "When was the last time you had more than a one-night stand or a pro?"

I could feel walls in my mind crashing down like castle portcullises. I shook my head. "No. We are not discussing this now. Not in public after shots have been fired."

Thumper looked down, embarrassed. Byron looked at me long and hard, then nodded. "Your call, man."

I nodded. "Go home and gear up. Victor's gonna know the jig is up in minutes. Use your own judgment as to when you come back. If it's tonight, use your ward stone. I'm gonna batten down the hatches, prep for a fight or a meeting tomorrow." I turned to Thumper. "Feel like crashing with me, Thump?"

Thumper nodded, then gave a quiet smile, looking none the worse for wear. Byron did another check of the area all around, then nodded himself. "Watch your ass, Trav."

We grasped hands, then brought it in to a quick bro-hug. Normally we'd just chest bump and go. Tonight we lingered, and I was grateful. How screwed up am I when an elf from the Hunt is the most stable person in my life? Then Byron was off. By the time Byron's Mustang was out of sight, Thumper had found a hanky and was holding up Tasha's gunbelt, pistol and mags. All of them were only slightly greasy with vampire corpse ichor.

I walked back towards the house, stopping to take a knee and lay one of my palms on the lawn, the other on the driveway. Thumper, fairly certain what I was doing, stood patiently. I began to concentrate on my breathing. By my third breath, I whispered, *"Kyrreh."*

Energy flowed from the core of my body out through my extremities and into the earth. Within moments, the light from the streetlamps and other houses dimmed. The sounds of distant traffic and chirping crickets grew softer.

Before I'd even had my epiphany, I used to spend summers with my Uncle Mac. Learned a lot that came in handy those summers. One time he brought a friend out to teach me the rudiments of ninjitsu. Not just the martial art, but the related skill sets, one of which was active camouflage. Real ninjas didn't look like the stunt team from an 80's action movie, unless they were impersonating stagehands. They looked like everybody else. Usually they looked like working stiffs. Janitors, delivery drivers, gardeners, people you don't really talk to that are just there. They knew that the real secret of camouflage is looking like you belong there. Humans are used to noticing what stands out. Don't stand out, and half of the job is done for you.

The trick is camouflaging everything, right down to your thoughts. It's not enough to dress like a janitor going on their rounds. You have to walk like one, talk like one, and think like one. Sounds weird, but it works. With magic, you can up the ante considerably. I'd just activated a ward that told the neighborhood my house was the most boring thing there. Even if someone called the cops because of all the screaming and the cops did decide to pay a visit, any suspicion would be diverted elsewhere. It wouldn't hold up to too much action, but since the fight was well and truly over for now, it did the job.

*　　*　　*

We came in through the garage door. I had Thumper leave Tasha's ichor and ash-caked gunbelt in an empty bin. If I lived, I'd get around to cleaning it. I did take the time to unload and clear her weapon before locking it in a spare case. I left the case on top of the garage vault. Shrapnel met the two of us at the top of the stairs, meowing indignantly that I'd been late for her supper. Thumper placated her with scritches while I filled her bowls. The spoiled little beastie left Thumper's affections in an instant and headed straight for the food, ignoring all else in her mission to devour.

"Make yourself at home, Thumper. I'm gonna grab some books for tomorrow."

Without looking at them for an answer, I went back down the stairs and into the leather and textiles room. My workbench, embroidery machine, and material bins were all set up along the wall shared with the garage. On the opposite wall, which it shared with Uncle Mac's suite, I had a thin drape with ambitions of being a curtain hanging. Taking one end in hand, I slid the entire thing from front to back to open it, revealing the bookcase set into the foundation behind it.

I called it Alexandria's Revenge.

All but the most nomadic of mages have one bookcase reserved for the important stuff. Spellbooks and grimoires have existed since portable writings were a thing. And that fact has kept us from reinventing the wheel even more times than humanity already has. Magic takes almost as big a leap as the rest of technology does when some real genius comes along and invents movable type, or mimeographs, or wikis.

Given what can be done to other storage types, paper is still king in the Otherworld. For the books I know I can't replace, I made Alexandria's Revenge. As safes go, she's off the charts for both fire and entry. There's also a small faraday cage in there surrounding a separate compartment, if you must include electronics. You could dip it in a volcano like the devil's caramel apple and the books would be fine. It would take a week to cool down, be covered in igneous rock and smell like farm fresh ass, but the books would be fine. The exterior is covered in stickers, showing off everything from gun show swag to movies I liked to local bands I'd done roadie work for. The unadorned surface has my surname spray-painted through stencils on one door, the case's name on the other.

It wasn't foolproof, but it was as foolproof as I could make it. Just above the lock and door handle was my personal sigil. It was hand-engraved into the door, then inlaid with steel. Steel made from bomb fragments dug out of my own body. Ironworking is some old magic too. Old magic still in our blood. If anyone did breach Alexandria's Revenge, by force or magic, I would know.

The few guests I have think it's another gun safe. Not a bad conclusion to jump to, given my resume, but still inaccurate.

On the top shelf were paperback editions of what I considered the classics: Marcus Aurelius, Sun Tzu, Musashi, Shakespeare, Scheherazade,

Aesop and more. Literature, philosophy, history. Both for easy access and rebuilding humanity in case of apocalypse. You never knew when you were gonna have to go back to the unwatered-down editions. Books are like wine. Watering them down may make them easier to handle, but you lose a lot in the process.

As the shelves went down, the contents got more exclusive. Half of the second shelf was stuff you might be able to find secondhand if you looked a long time and got lucky. Beyond that were the genuine works. Spellbooks from around the world over the last four centuries. A few were elaborate jokes like The Cronesfoil. Others were very much the real deal. Some were in languages I didn't read. I kept them around anyway. Good spellbooks made great barter material if you needed it. The bottom shelf held the faraday cage and my own notebooks from over the years. I still have the marbled composition books from seventh grade through high school. Someday when I sit down and give the definitive version of what went on at Blue River, I'm going to be referencing those heavily. I also have a songbook put together by my friend Seb before we graduated. I told him about my survivalist family once. He set a lot of magical lessons down to the tune of songs we already knew. I know nothing about bardic magic, but what he said about things being easier to remember with a tune behind it made a lot of sense. So if you ever do find a copy of a songbook called *Grandson of a Siren*, you might want to pick it up.

I found my copy of *The Cronesfoil* as well as a copy of *Ethical Malice: Modern Curses, Hexes, and Jinxes*. Relocking Alexandria's Revenge, I pulled the curtain back and headed up the stairs. The adrenaline rush was still fading from earlier, and the fatigue was starting to hit me bad.

I dropped the books on the dining room table. I wanted to get from breakfast straight to research. Thumper was hunched over their phone on the sofa, playing a game of some kind. They looked up and gave me a slow wave and a tired smile when they saw me. I returned the wave and took a breath.

"Help yourself to a guest room or the sofa, Thump. I'm gonna take a shower and put up the rest of these wards before I hit the sack."

That got me a thumbs-up before they turned back to their phone. I was sweating, my headache was back with a vengeance, I was hungry yet again, I was exhausted, but so wound up I had no idea how I would sleep. I almost made it to my room before I heard Shrapnel yowl, claws skittering on the floor as she ran. Before I could look, I was hit in the back by something huge and solid, knocking me down. I landed in a roll, unfurling like a sleeping bag just pulled out of the stuff sack. I could hear approaching footsteps just before the darkness closed in.

After that, I didn't feel anything.

*   *   *

Chapter Thirteen

"Guideline Twenty-Six:

Lying is like premarital sex.

Just because it's a sin doesn't mean it's not a skill."

I was back in the woods that held Thumper's mindscape, sprawled out on the ground near the banks of the creek. The sun was nowhere in sight, clouds looking more ominous with every moment. I scrambled to my feet, reaching for my now empty pockets. I circled widdershins around the tree our packs leaned against. Finding nobody, I resorted to shouting.

"Thumper! Thumper, what the hell? You can't just drag me into your head whenever you like, man. You know that. Please and fucking thank you? Maybe?"

"Sorry, Trav."

They stepped out from behind a tree that hadn't been there a second ago, all poise and boarding school posture. They were dressed in a full tuxedo with tails, only with a deep red vest and bow tie. Their hair was slicked back tight against their skull. A black hooked cane with a white stripe just above the tip was over their shoulder like a drum major ready to step off, and a silk top hat was on their head. They looked ready to launch unsuspecting doves into the audience of southern yellow pines. But their face was downcast, the look of someone who cared but was bearing even more bad news.

I kept my distance, still annoyed. "Thumper, what the hell happened?"

They shook their head, stepping around me with a measured stride. "I couldn't let you go through with it, Travis. Divided loyalties really suck. But I just can't let you screw Master over like that."

That just cranked up my confusion. "Since when do you have a Master? You're vanilla as…" A stone of realization hit me right in the soul and started to sink. "You're Victor's renfield."

They smiled sadly. "You got it in one, old friend."

Even out of my own body, I wanted to throw up. "Why? What the hell for?"

They shrugged and blushed a little, having the decency to be embarrassed. "You'd have to ask Master. My guess is, he saw mommy have her own pet wizard and wanted one for his very own. And there I was." They spun around, arms out as if finishing a trick with a flourish. They sighed in thrilled memory. I could damn near see the shiver going down their spine. "And what a rush it's been. I haven't felt this alive in years, Trav." They smiled at me knowingly, as if we were sharing a risque secret. "There's a reason you did this too."

I frowned. "Yeah, I had a reason! I swore an Oath! That big ass debt I took on that saved our lives? Do you remember that? I owed a year and a day of my life! What the hell were you thinking that made you give it up for free? Sweet daddy Vulcan and a ten-mil socket, Thump! Didn't anyone try to stop you? Didn't anyone try to bring you back?"

Even as the words left me, I felt sick. An awful realization came to the back of my mind, and I became more convinced in every moment that I already knew the answer. Thumper blushed a little, and their voice got very quiet. "Who would try, Travis? Who would've been there? My parents? Were they gonna stop me being more of an embarrassment? The docs that gave up on me? The Daedeli, who poked and prodded and shook their heads and shrugged? The Nimuen, who only gave a shit about me so they could have a token enby disabled witch in their corner? How about the rest of us with barn owl tattoos? Do we have Blue River reunions, Travis? Have we ever? Do we ever talk? I'm happier with Master. You looked happier too. You looked so much happier serving your Mistress."

"What the hell are you talking about?"

Thumper kept their voice soft, nothing but compassion in their eyes. "A part of you died at the river, Travis. I lost a bit of my brain. But you lost a bit of your heart. You haven't loved a woman since Heather was killed. I don't think you've even tried. After the funerals, you ran away to study. When that didn't bring you peace, you ran away into the Marines. Then the Marines didn't give you the home you were looking for, so you ran away into your debt. Then this last year? I wish you could remember it. I saw you. You were around people, you smiled. You had a life."

They were half right, and that pissed me off. "I didn't have a life, Thumper. I had an indenture I was paying off full time. With another one hanging over my head for when I survive this one. And that's what it was. I was just surviving. I was around people, but I'd left friends all behind. There was just her and the blood. Her blood. Her needs. Her wants. I was just a means to an end to her and a face in the crowd to anyone else."

Thumper smiled gently, their eyes shining in the soft light, and with the most delicate tone in their voice, I heard them speak. "That's more than I had."

Their arms opened, cane in one hand with all the swagger of an inspecting officer. I followed their gaze, looking into this brush and that scrap of trail. Looking into the gently babbling creek, the wind beginning to rustle the branches, the clouds darkening overhead. They turned back to me and cracked a tiny smile, hiding back tears. "So yeah. I drank his blood. I call him Master. You know how wonderful that feels, don't you? Every time Heather called you that in the dark.."

I held up a hand. "Leave Heather out of this. She's got nothing to do with this."

Thumper's gaze took on a look of almost tangible pity. They barely stopped a sob from escaping. "Oh, Trav. You have no idea, do you?"

I didn't. Thumper had gotten that right. And now I was scared. "What are you doing, Thumper?"

They smiled, tears finally falling. "Taking care of old man Chittenden. That virgin sacrifice in the Cronesfoil may be bullshit. But there's a blood curse you discovered during your research, and that's very real. There's enough of Chittenden's blood in that tube to leave him weak as a kitten. Just in time for Tasha's heartbroken renfields to take him down. Master brings the renfields to justice, and reluctantly takes the lordship."

I shook my head. "Chittenden knows Eva and her children were plotting against him. That's got to be why he sent me to Eva in the first place. He's expecting my report tomorrow night."

Tears shone on their cheeks. "That's why I'll have to make my move now. It's another busy night."

If I'd been in the physical world, I'd have grabbed them and shook some damn sense into them. Not that I had a chance at catching them. Even if Thumper wasn't a master cognimancer, we were in their mind. They had the homefield advantage. I was ready to beg. I couldn't believe this was happening. "Even if you could, that blood curse requires an incantation. You can't speak in the real world! You haven't been able to since Blue River!"

They gave me a quiet little smile. One that said they had a secret. "You'd be amazed what you can do with Master's blood in you."

If anything could heal Thumper's brain paths through sheer magical power, it was vampire blood. If that was what happened, and they'd healed themselves, then Thumper was right. I dropped to a knee. "Thumper, please, don't do this..."

They put a finger to my lips, shushing me gently. "It's OK, Travis. This time tomorrow, Chittenden will be dead, your Oath will be marked fulfilled, and my Master will rule Atlanta. If you're lucky, he may even take you on too."

With me down on my knee, they still had to stand on tiptoe to kiss my forehead. Their lips felt cool, like they'd just come in from the cold. "Now get some rest, Trav. You've had a long day."

I lunged after them. I know, not in a physical body, futile gesture. Break your brain and heart in the same ten minutes and see if everything you do still makes sense. "Thumper, no, wait!"

Thumper thrust out their cane like a rapier after the heart of a foe, the tip disappearing into the waters of the creek. The world around me disappeared into darkness and silence.

*   *   *

In the void, something moved. Not enough to orient me or let me do more than float there, but it still moved. The scent of old books and mint tea went past my nose. I heard the ankle bells in what I now recognized as someone walking towards me, the bells chiming with every step.

The voice spoke. "*Follow yellow to know.*"

I answered. "Yeah, been trying that and haven't gotten far. Care to focus me a little?"

The blue scarf brushed past my arm, although now that I knew it was coming I could see it was more of a veil. I looked up from it right into those sapphire eyes.

The voice spoke again. "*At the right house, you can still be at the wrong door.*"

I tried not to blink in the hopes the eyes wouldn't vanish. They were maddeningly familiar. A part of me already trusted those eyes with my life.

The rest of me was getting ready to hold that part down before all of me did something stupid.

"Thanks. I guess. Who are you?"

The voice laughed. It was a gentle laugh. The kind a loved one makes when you've said something silly.

I blinked and the eyes were gone, along with everything else. A spike of pain shot through my head and I groaned.

"Travis! Travis, wake up!"

Byron slapped me. I managed to twitch, stir, and mutter a syllable or two. He'd woken up enough drunk Marines to know that wasn't going to get the job done. He curled his hand into a fist and rubbed his knuckles vigorously into my sternum. My eyes shot open. I was on the floor of my hallway again. It was still pitch black outside.

"Stop! Stop! I'm up, dammit!" I batted his arm away, seeing him sigh in relief. Grabbing the frame of my bedroom door, I pulled myself up into a sitting position. I almost saw stars as pain shot through my joints. Another breath and I could mostly see everything clearly. Shrapnel had trotted up and was looking curiously at both of us. Remembering her scream before I passed out, I abandoned all other priorities in the quest to diagnose and if necessary heal the cat. I grabbed her in mid-trill, picking her up and checking for any wounds. "You OK girl? You scared me something fierce. Doesn't look like anything drew blood."

Shrapnel put up with my fussing until I was satisfied. I sighed in relief, then looked up.

Byron had come dressed for a fight. By which I mean he looked like a postmodern Robin Hood. Handmade boots that would give him an incredible grip on any surface. Dark green yoga pants tucked into the boots. A matching leather vest I knew could stop bullets. Holstered inside was a custom-built pistol along Glock lines I'd made for him a few years back. Most elves didn't like guns. They appreciated the firepower, but too much steel made them uncomfortable, and they liked comfort in their violence. So I had custom made Byron's pistol, holsters, and magazines, all without any ferrous metals. Most elves didn't have an alchemist gunsmith for a friend.

"Shrapnel was fine when I came in. What happened, Trav? Where's Thumper?"

I shook my head, letting Shrapnel go. "Thumper's a renfield. Victor's renfield." Another thought came into my head and I patted myself down. One of my pockets was empty enough to confirm my worst guess. "And they got Chittenden's blood."

Byron sat back against the wall. "Shit."

"What time is it?"

Byron shrugged. "About two? I geared up quick, figured coming back and relaxing here would be safer. I came in wondering why you only had the basic wards up and found you on the floor."

I pulled out my phone. "If we're lucky, we're not too late." I looked up a number fast, then dialed it. It picked up on the second ring.

"*Yes?*" I'd never been so happy to hear Oswald's smug voice.

"Oswald? Travis. Got a heads up for you."

"*I'm listening.*"

"I just played chess with both of Eva's kids. They play rough. I've never seen anyone use their pawn to take down a king like that. Just in case they ask to play with you later."

A long pause, then, "*Understood.*"

"Good. I'll have that report ready tomorrow night as promised."

I hung up without waiting for him. Byron stood up, then helped me to my feet.

"So what now?"

I held up one finger, then slowly lurched my way down the hall. Once I could see the kitchen table, I sighed. "Thumper took the books too. About all we can do is check the defenses and get some sleep. In the morning I see if there's anything I can do to get my memories back. If Victor makes his move tonight, I already warned Chittenden and there's nothing more I can do. If all else fails, I'll make my report and see if I'm still alive to worry about anything else."

We checked. Thumper hadn't taken anything else or messed with any of the wards on their way out. We staged weapons and ammo at different spots around the house. What little energy I had, I set to activating more of the wards. Fortunately, those were all long-ago made and regularly re-inforced. It would take something designed to crack open bunkers to do so much as wake me up before sunrise. I microwaved my takeout. After a moment's thought, I microwaved Connie and Thumper's takeout too. Practice necromancy on my lawn and betray me to a vampiric master, will they? My pancakes and pie now. I washed it down with about half of the water in my bottle, then topped it off.

I took a stupidly long shower. Long after scrubbing away the day's dirt and sweat, I stood and let the water pound away at my bruises. I embraced the pain, the heat, the running water. Focusing on the sensations meant that I didn't have to think. Every time I thought about the shithole my life had devolved into, the glorious water washed it away. It was almost peaceful until Byron banged his fist against the door.

"Are you done beating off in there?"

Tears welled up in my eyes and I barked a laugh all at once. Once a Marine, always a Marine even applied to elves like Byron. "So what if I am? It's my house."

"Just sleep in your bed instead of your bathtub, bro."

Stepping out and toweling off wasn't nearly as cleansing as high pressure water. It was readying me to go back into the world, one I didn't want. But it kept Byron from fussing over me as I heard the door to the spare room close. I was exhausted and too jacked up to sleep all at once. An hour of unconsciousness on my floor did not a good night's sleep make. I finally staggered into my bed.

Lights out, phone charging, and once again horizontal, I stared at my ceiling as the exhaustion clashed with the anxiety of the last night and day. I tried an old trick of tensing and then relaxing every muscle group one at a time from toes to head, but I had to stop. I'm fairly sure cartilage isn't supposed to make noises like that. Even doing nothing but breathing failed to relax me. I sensed movement, and began to tense reflexively before the familiar form of Shrapnel jumped onto the bed. Taking her time, she padded her way across the bed to her customary spot next to my waist. Territory duly claimed, she gently headbutted my hand to remind me of my duty. I scritched her behind the ears gently. I could hear the short, soft rumbling of her purring. A breath later, I finally began letting tears fall.

Being good in a crisis doesn't mean you hurt less than anyone. It just means you can put that hurt in a box until you can let it out. You can't let it out when you're still in the fight. If the fight lasts for days, weeks, longer? It stays in the box then. Usually getting company with more hurt you pick up along the way. Until somewhere, somehow, you find the solace you can. And if you can't let it out when you're alone in the dark? Surrounded with the best home defense a pair of paranoid bastard wizards can come up with? With the only witness being a small, furry companion that'll show you all the love you can take so long as the open cans of tuna keep coming? Well then, when can you let it out?

Only humans can come up with the concept of pets. Only humans need it, because humans are too screwed up to help each other like pets do. We can't show anything to our fellow humans. Not our minds, not our bodies, certainly not our true emotions. But pets? They know how you smell and how you feel and what you do. And that's all that matters to them. And, gods love them, they want us to feel good. In the light of day, Shrapnel would judge me or anyone else at the drop of a hat. Particularly in regards to my lacking in providing the chow. But here, in the dark, at my worst, worried I was either going to die, Oathbreak, be rebound to a vampire, or all of the above, she just wanted me to feel better.

Shrapnel stretched, curled back up at my side, and stayed there. I let the tears keep falling. Eventually, exhaustion won.

*   *   *

I was on my third cup of coffee when I closed the last book. The table was covered with the remnants of a working breakfast, not to mention three trips back to Alexandria's Revenge. While Thumper had taken the books I'd left on the table, they hadn't taken my personal notebook, my phone, or my laptop. Breakfast had been spent reconstructing whatever Eva had been planning to take down Chittenden, whatever Victor and Tasha had been planning to take down Eva, and whatever I'd been planning to double-cross and deliver them to Chittenden. It was the kind of thing that made me want a big whiteboard I could scribble everything across.

"Well, I found that virgin sacrifice Tasha wanted to use. It's as much hogwash as everything else in the book, but it makes a compelling argument if you're not in the know."

Byron looked up from the book he was flipping through. "So what was she trying to do?"

"Same thing Thumper's trying to do to Chittenden. Only Thump has a clue what they're doing. They're both revolving on the concept of taking down someone powerful so you can take their place. The Cronesfoil spell takes the potential theory and applies it to sympathetic magic. The potential of the powerful dies with the sacrifice, and the potential of the sacrifice is taken on by the benefactor. The heir presumptive blood curse uses the blood to establish a sympathetic link, weakening the target."

"No wonder Victor and Tasha moved in so quickly. They were planning on taking out Eva themselves before you did it for them."

I nodded. "Makes sense. Eva has me look up the spells. I look up a couple, giving the Cronesfoil as the best option. The kids discover the heir presumptive and plan accordingly. I don't mention nexttext, so I never tell them having a virgin is unnecessary. I weaken Chittenden for Eva, the kids use Thumper and presumably Connie to weaken Eva. And my Oath ends after midnight tonight, so their go-date had to be scheduled before then."

Byron pointed in my direction. "Then Eva found out, but you screwed it up."

That derailed my train of thought. "Wait, what?"

Byron waved his finger like a lecturer pointing out something that would be on the test. "The only reason Eva had to kidnap Connie was to get her away from Tasha. She must have planned to take her kids down before they could find another virgin. Eva thought you'd take Connie off the table."

The light over my head flickered back on. "But I killed Eva instead. So Victor sends Thumper to spy for him."

Byron frowned. "Which doesn't make sense. If he already had the heir presumptive curse, why not have Thumper do it?"

"Because Thumper can't. The spell's simple, but it still requires an incantation. Thumper can't talk. Unless..."

Byron raised an eyebrow. "Don't leave me hanging like that."

"Eva's blood healed weeks of hurting in a night. Thumper insinuated that enough vampire blood would let them talk again."

Byron frowned. "Vampire blood curing aphasia?"

I shook my head. "You have no idea how magically powerful that stuff is, man! I'm getting twitchy just talking about it. It's definitely at least possible. If it did, Thump could cast that spell at any moment. If it didn't, we'll hear from Victor soon enough." I sighed. I was sweating again, and my headache was back. It had even brought friends to make themselves comfortable in the rest of me. "At least we know what Chittenden's in for. And so does Chittenden. But I haven't seen any more about following yellow in here."

Byron closed the book he'd been searching, leaving it on the dining room table. "Me neither."

I put my phone and notebook away before shutting down my laptop. "I've almost figured everything out. But I don't have my memories back and I don't know how to restore them. And that's big. I'm still missing a few pieces. But I've been all over the house and I don't see anything that looks out of the ordinary or that would make me think of following yellow. Unless Connie knew what it was and swiped it, in which case I'm screwed."

"I don't think so. Girl's a necromancer, not a thief. That said, yeah, I don't think you'd leave a clue like that at the Cotillion. And you don't have any other safe houses in Georgia."

"Well it's not here. I got no yellow to follow."

Byron nodded, then paused. "I mean, unless you left something at Warwell's range the last time we went shooting or something."

I thought. Then thought again. Then I tapped the table with my knuckles.

"At the right house, you can still be at the wrong door."

Byron raised an eyebrow. "And that's where you lost me."

I looked him in the eyes. "The Warwells still have those safeboxes at the range, right?"

*   *   *

The small tortoiseshell cat padded through the grassy border of the parking lot, and the porchmen watched it approach. Normally I'd be subjected to at least a few volleys of handcrafted sass by the time I came this close to the porch. Instead, I was upstaged by the determination of the feline guest going about their undetermined business. All four porchmen followed the tortie's progress as it jumped up onto the porch itself with expected grace.

It was more than a little humbling. After all, Byron and I were obviously loaded for bear yet coming forward to give our usual tribute of audience time. I'm a moderately infamous mage in my own right, and Byron is, if not a prince, then minor royalty of the hunt. Even if the porchmen were ordinary mortals, they had a good two centuries of Otherworld experience between them. Yet the pair of us played second fiddle to a feline on a slow Wednesday afternoon. No wonder cats are all rampant egomaniacs.

The tortie took a single bound to land in the lap of Keith. The slender old man clicked his tongue between his teeth, scritching the purring stray behind the ears. "Hey, little lady," he greeted, in a voice happier than any I'd seen him use on a human.

The old wizard's expression didn't change as he continued petting the cat, but he caught me staring and nodded in the tortie's direction. "She reminds me of someone I used to roll with in college."

Lars paused, ketchup-drenched chicken finger halfway to his face. "Was that the brunette that left the circus to shack up with you?"

Matt shook his head before gesturing with a toothpick. "Nah, this was the blonde who dumped him to run off to Vegas."

Keith kept his train of thought on the rails as the cat kneaded away at his jeans. "Cat reminds me of her. If she ever got any real power, all the kindness I've shown her won't mean shit. She'd maul me to death without hesitation and devour my corpse for funsies. But since we're both pretty sure that ain't gonna happen, she's cute and affectionate and I can enjoy that for a while."

The old men chuckled at the thought before Jim squinted harder. "So which one was it?"

Keith gave the purring cat a few more strokes before simply answering, "The brunette."

Sometimes I worry that I'm becoming a crotchety, uncouth, bad-tempered old man before my time, and I'm not even forty. But so long as the porchmen live, I think I'm relatively safe.

Lars acknowledged our presence by leaning over in our direction. I could hear wood creak under his shifting weight. "Come for some food before getting your ass kicked again, Grunt?"

Jim wiggled one of his hands. "Thought you'd still be walking funny after what Eva put you through."

Keith huffed. "Or the way Connie handed you your ass last night."

I raised a finger. "Hey, she did a lot of things last night. Hand me my ass wasn't one of them."

The porchmen all chuckled in schadenfreude. Byron shrugged. "Funny as it would've been to watch, my man's right. Connie turned Tasha into the wicked grease stain of the West, then hoofed it. Didn't so much as take a swing at him."

I didn't even bother asking how they were that caught up on current events. Out of the corner of my eye, I caught something. To the east of the parking lot was a berm that prevented people from trying to park on the range. East of the restaurant proper was the rangemaster's hut. It was only a single story, and about the size of a double-wide trailer. Near the door of the hut, a weathered white sign the size of a coffin lid listed range operation hours and admonished visitors to check in with the rangemaster before shooting.

Hanging beneath the sign on two lengths of chain was a yellow wooden arrow pointing towards the door of the range hut.

I tapped Byron on the arm, then turned back to the porchmen. "Much as I'd love to continue defending my reputation, gents, I actually came by to pick up some of my stuff. Have a good one."

We gave separate farewells to the cat, who accepted them graciously as you'd expect. She ignored us completely, purring away in the old man's lap.

*   *   *

The rangemaster's hut was set up like some shops in overseas bases I'd seen in my day. There was a sense of impermanence to it, as if the entire structure could be hooked up to a big rig and hauled away in the night. The gray linoleum of the floor reflected the dull fluorescent overhead lights, punctuated by the sunlight streaming in from the long picture windows on the north side. Through the north window, a rangemaster behind the counter could see into the firing lanes. The south wall behind the counter was covered in target samples, each marked with a price. They shared space with signs declaring the four firearms safety rules, a notice outlawing tannerite without the rangemaster's express permission, and other useful information. Security monitors near the cash register showed other views of the range. Under the glass counters were stacks of ammunition boxes, ear protection, and other range miscellany. A magazine rack held pamphlets advertising classes, competition clubs, and political action groups. On the far end, near the door to the back room, was an alcove displaying a modest collection of rental guns.

Behind the counter was a woman in her early 20's, wearing a short-sleeved peasant blouse over dark blue jeans. A mane of blonde curls was held back by an elastic band working overtime, and a radio earpiece was in her left ear. A 1911 was holstered at her right hip in a custom-made holster. I'd met Camilla Warwell before, but I couldn't place her on the family tree if you'd asked. A smile grew out of her bored face as we walked in. I tucked my thumbs into my trouser pockets again.

"Hey y'all. Come to shoot today?"

I shook my head. "Maybe later, Millie. Got some business going on."

"That's what I heard. Got half the city gunning for you after that fire. Got a couple flavors of special rounds if you need to load up. Just lemme know what your next target is and I can hook you right up. Still shooting 9-mil?"

I tried to smile. "Don't have an immediate target, Millie, but that's very sweet of you. Yes, I'm still shooting nine."

Byron's flirty smile unfolded. "Still single, Millie?"

Millie matched his smile with her own, but tsked playfully at him. "Now, Byron, you know Aunt Elaine's rules: no elves before I turn twenty-five."

He sighed dramatically. "What a birthday of hers that was."

I stepped back into the conversation. "Have I been keeping anything in the back room?"

I explained earlier that the Warwells were a big enough family to be a magical faction all on their own. That didn't mean that they didn't diversify. And one of their side hustles was a secure storage facility. A very secure storage facility. I was actually brought in to help build the latest iteration a few years back. The rangemaster hut might look like a double-wide trailer, but the back room vault was more solid than those in most banks. An Abrams tank couldn't tow the thing away. And that's without getting into the multiple mundane and magical defenses. The Warwells were arbitrarily picky about who they did business with, but they were more obsessed about upholding their end of the bargain than fae were.

Millie waved her finger at me like a teacher at a naughty student. "I knew I saw your name on the records, Travis. I was due to call you tomorrow or the next day if you hadn't come in for it yet." A red light above the register glowed. Millie held up a hand. "Hold on." She touched a radio at her hip. "Cease fire, Cease fire, shooters setting up targets, cease fire." There was an odd echo from the range loudspeakers.

Satisfied, she turned and headed for the back room. Less than a minute later, she emerged with a Marine issue ditty bag. It was an older design, OD green instead of digital camouflage and about the size of a reusable shopping bag, but a bit wider and shallower, with a zipper. It wasn't very full. She also came out with a thick leather-bound ledger, opening it to the appropriate page. Sure enough, I'd signed it in a year ago Monday. I took the pen and signed it back out. The names and dates glowed on the page for a second, just before Millie closed the book. I blinked, glancing at the ordinary looking ballpoint in her hand and stopped myself from redesigning the ledger in my head.

"Thanks, Millie. What do I owe you?"

"Ya paid in advance and picked it up on time, Travis. Your slate is clean. Pleasure doing business with you." A green light above the register glowed. She held up a finger, looked past us for a moment, then keyed her radio. "Shooters, you are cleared to fire. I say again, Shooters, you are cleared to fire." Sporadic shots began to ring out from the range again. She smiled at me, "Oh, Travis: Aunt Elaine's in the restaurant. She says to come say hi to her before you go."

Confused, I traded looks with Byron, who was no less confused. I shrugged. "Will do, Millie. Take care of yourself."

"You do the same. I don't wanna hear any nonsense about you being taken down after turning down my loads."

I elbowed Byron in the ribs before he could make a comment.

*　*　*

Elaine Warwell was the current clan matriarch of the Warwells. A grandmother more times than I knew, she had the presence of a grande dame who hadn't let the loss of a spotlight get her down. Given how good she was at turning heads now, I could only imagine what she'd been like at my own age. While day to day management of the restaurant was currently done by her eldest son, Henry Warwell IV, Elaine thrilled in the role of hostess whenever she got the chance.

She was also quite possibly the scariest old woman I have ever met. Not mean, mind you. Not vicious or crabby or bitter, she was scary. And little old ladies in general scare me. Part of this was by association. Imagine the most determined hunter, ruthless fighter or manipulative power broker, then pause and realize somebody out there changed their diapers and remembers their birthday.

Part of it was simply the nature of magic as a Eurocentric cultural power source. A lot of magic practiced by men was lost over the centuries. Being practiced by crotchety, antisocial old bastards in obscure towers lent itself to that. If they got caught by an angry mob or making the wrong king without passing on what they knew to an apprentice, all of their knowledge was lost on their death. Which meant everything they'd discovered had to be discovered again. Magic practiced by women, more often than not, took place behind a home's threshold. Which made it a lot easier to hide even in plain sight, then pass on to a daughter or niece with a flair for it.

But the biggest part of it was the simple fact that if you pissed off a little old lady way outside of your reach, you'll never know it until it's too late and you're screwed. With few exceptions, men have the ego invested in having their power witnessed and acknowledged. Everything from sports cars to Viagra takes their cues for showing off male power.

Little old ladies treat their power like the good china. They keep it safe, maintain as needed, and bring it out on special occasions, which can and do include handing some troublesome jerk his ass on a polished silver platter that she inherited from her grandmother.

Being nice to old ladies is cheaper life insurance than any deal on ammo you'll ever find.

Today, her wavy hair with much more salt than pepper was bound up in a pair of ornamental iron sticks. She wore a long but light burgundy robe with lines of intricate bronze embroidery running along the shoulders and down the front. A collection of mild percussive sounds as she moved sounded almost but not quite like the ankle bells in my dream. She flashed us both a winning smile as we came through the double doors of the restaurant. "Hello, boys."

We both nodded to her slightly. No salute or bow would have shown more reverence. "Ma'am."

"Y'all look halfway through a wild weekend, and it's only Wednesday. Come on upstairs."

Disobeying would have been unthinkable.

The entrance hall of the restaurant was two stories high. Two extended stories, as we could see into the main dining room. The high ceilings were a mark of southern architecture pre-air conditioning. The expansive walls of the hall were painted in a deep teal color that complimented the haint blue of the porch ceiling. They also gave ample room for decades worth of art. On the left as one entered was the gift shop, while the right gave access to the grand staircase to the second floor. Further forward and one could enter two of the dining rooms or the kitchen behind the hostess podium. All of the doorways were painted in an eggshell white. The floors were made of solid oak and polished in a way that showed off the years of dents and blemishes like well worn leather. In one or two spots where repairs had been made you could notice the difference in lumber sizes from different eras. The staircase was made of the same oak as the floor, and was wide enough for two to walk up it side by side, or one society lady in a hoop skirt to make a grand entrance down without catching on anything. Elaine made her way up the staircase casually, giving her hips a sway that distracted me for a moment before remembering where I was.

The second floor was one long hallway between the stair sets, which had been bedrooms once upon a time and now served as private dining rooms. The paint scheme and floors were just the same as downstairs, though the artworks were smaller. The ceiling was as high as the ones on the ground floor. Elaine led us to the last door on the right. Just before she opened it to let us in, I recalled that this room in particular had a reputation for being haunted.

There was nothing particular about the room that declared it haunted. The walls were painted in a velvet burgundy instead of teal, while the eggshell white still decorated the door, frame, and fireplace that occupied the west side of the room. The window that would have overlooked the parking lot was blocked by a tasteful curtain that matched the walls. An oak dining room table set in the center of the room could have easily seated eight in comfort. Only a water glass and teacup occupied the table, both set out before the only occupied chair at the far end of the room.

Connie looked more put together than I'd seen her last: A black and purple tank top over a fishnet shirt that came down to her elbows, jewelry more prominent without being excessive, and her eyeliner was in a perfect upward swoop. Her lips were black with a purple sheen to them. Her hair was done up in a bun, held together with a pair of sticks very similar to Elaine's. The burgundy velvet curtain blocking the window hung behind her like the banner of an invading army.

I stuck out my arm and tapped Byron in the chest, stopping him from going for a knife. My other hand I slowly opened and kept in plain view at the level of my waist. Keeping my eyes on Connie and swallowing to steady my voice, I asked quietly. "Elaine?"

Her smile, which already scared me, never wavered. "Yes, dear?"

"Not to be crude, but have I done anything to piss you off in, oh, the past year or so?"

She shook her head nonchalantly. "Not as I'm aware, darlin."

I nodded politely. "That's all I wanted to know, thank you."

Chapter Fourteen

The Warwell's reputation for a lack of violence on the premises was nearly as prominent as WaCross's. The parking lot and the woods behind the restaurant were fair game. But inside the buildings and on the range, nobody attacked anyone without Warwell approval. Satisfied in the knowledge that we weren't to be killed out of hand, Byron and I gave synchronized sighs of relief. Elaine patted my shoulder, smiling knowingly, as if one of her grandchildren had finally brought someone nice home for dinner. "I'll leave you young folks to it, then."

Elaine jingled and swayed past us. I caught a hint of her vanilla perfume as she closed the door behind her. Connie gave a little wave as if she was greeting school friends at lunch, her black and purple nails reflecting the light. "Hi, guys."

I barely moved. "Hi."

Byron nodded. "Afternoon."

Figuring I might as well be comfortable through whatever she had in mind for us, we sat down. The both of us took some time to adjust, patting various hidden weapons to assure ourselves they were still there. Connie watched us placidly.

After a minute of thickening tension I finally dismissed it with a wave of my hand. "OK, seriously, what the fuck?"

She glanced into her teacup for a moment. "You mean why?"

I didn't hesitate. "Yes, please."

She held up her hand in appeasement. "Telling the minimal truth and letting you draw your own conclusions was the best I could come up with."

"While letting me think you were a stander?"

She counted off on her fingers. "I was ambushed, I was kidnapped, and I had no idea what for or who was responsible for it. Playing dumb led me to the one responsible eventually."

"So, what, you just waited along until you could kill Tasha?"

She nodded. "Once I'd convinced myself not to kill you."

I sighed and rolled my eyes. "I'm getting really tired of asking people why they want me dead, but here we are. Again, I say, what the fuck?"

She sipped her tea. "I've wanted you dead since Blue River."

This was starting to piss me off. "Blue River? Lady, I only met you yesterday! And the entire time, I've done nothing, nothing but try and help you. I broke a damned renfield bond for you. I killed three vampires for you. I somehow got my memory wiped helping you. Who in the nine circles of hell ARE you?"

"My father's name was McKay."

In an instant, I looked at Connie, and the unflappable goth at the other end of the tables changed across the years. In her place I saw a ten year-old girl in jeans and a blouse, doing grade school homework on a kitchen table. Her auburn hair was done up in pigtails that stuck out to the sides. Her green eyes rolled in disgust the moment I walked in the room. She was an annoying distraction I had no time for, and the feeling was entirely mutual.

Time skipped again and that girl was twelve now. All knees and elbows in a plain black dress that didn't fit because she was two inches shorter last week. Stray hairs escaped her tight ponytail as tears streamed down her face. Her eyes were sunken, as if she'd barely slept for days.

Then I was back in the present and that girl was now the extremely powerful witch sitting across the table from me. Another piece of the puzzle fell into place.

"McKay. You're Heather's little sister."

She nodded, not dropping her gaze this time. "I had my Epiphany the night of Blue River."

Byron whispered. "Holy shit."

She somehow kept her voice level. "I felt her die. I felt them all die. The sun rose before I finished screaming."

My own mind cracked a little from the implications. The first kind of magic you experience during the Epiphany is usually, but not always, the kind of magic you find yourself more talented with. The thought of a natural necromancer having the Epiphany during a bloodbath like that was mindblowing.

She sipped her tea gently. "Less than an hour after I'd lost my voice, a cop knocked on our door and told us about Heather. The Warwells helped us all summer, not that it did my parents much good. Dad couldn't hack it and took off. Drank himself to death sometime before my senior year. Mom stuck around, and I stayed in Blue River for middle and high school." She quirked a look I could see the sarcasm through. "Take a wild guess what study hall was like for a natural necromancer in those days. Six years of eating Monitor shit. Crusty old Daedeli dudes wanting into my mind every time I had a lousy day. I told my Secundus to fuck off so hard I gave him a nosebleed from across the room. After that I had a deputy or some Iron Council rep ready to put me down if they ever saw 'active necromancy' coming from me. Which did wonders for my social life, too. You try having your first kiss with a dozen ghosts offering tips and cheering you on. Every study hall kid has a moment or two of being a freak to the rest of the school. Being a freak to the study hall kids from day one? Good luck finding a flavor of therapy that'll take on that. Elaine and the others here are the only reason I didn't completely lose it."

I frowned. "I've known the Warwells since you were in kindergarten. I've never seen you here."

She shrugged. "Heather took belly dance lessons from Elaine on the third floor ballroom. I did the same thing, but I never saw you there." I flushed a bit as she continued. "Elaine's the one who found me a mentor after Sextus year. You were right, by the way. There's still a good number of Nimuen out there who believe that afterlives matter. Fuck the Iron Council."

Byron tilted his head. "Wait, I thought you were a PhD candidate in Psychology?"

"I am." She left the teacup alone and sipped the water, leaving a black lip print on the glass. "I've had dead people telling me all about their problems since I started growing tits. Might as well get paid when the living ones do it."

I took all of that in, then nodded. "So why am I still alive? You had the drop on me."

"I was preoccupied with killing Tasha at the time."

I nodded grimly. "With active necromancy, no less."

She just raised an eyebrow. Byron gave a low whistle and thumped the table. "No, she didn't."

I frowned. "Byron, I was there. Tasha rotted on contact with her."

Byron shook his head and raised a finger. "She disarmed her with Necromancy. She killed her with the e-tool."

I blinked. "Huh. You're right. That still doesn't explain why I'm still alive."

For the first time, she dropped her gaze. Then she picked up the teacup, sipped, and looked back into my eyes. "You were a weirdo my sister brought home who almost never smiled and always smelled like a hardware store. Then she was dead, and you were alive, and nothing in the world was more unfair. I could barely look at you at the funeral. After that? Even after my study hall teachers told me how she really died, and they called you all heroes? Out of all of the survivors, you never came to see my parents. You never visited my class. But you didn't kill yourself either. All I ever heard was how you rigged a shotgun and killed hellhounds with it from start to finish. Just a trail of blood and gunsmoke from one end of that park to the other. That's the only image I've ever had of you from the night Heather died. This giant, ugly boogeyman with a smoking gun ready to blow apart anything in your way. And if I got too good with the dead, you were going to come for me and kill me too."

She took another sip. "I was too scared to think about going after you myself. Too many years with some Iron Council asshole looking for an excuse to put me down. I figured if I even thought too hard about hunting another mage I'd wake up in a cell under the mounds."

She put down her teacup and shook her head. "Then I woke up in that damn box. Wearing nothing but a gag and those damned cuffs of yours. And there you were. You, looking at me like a piece of meat. You, touching my hair. You. And then our eyes met and I still don't know what happened."

She took a long, deep breath, trying not to shudder, then shrugged and made a little wave. "You know the rest."

I frowned. "But the fight at the Cotillion didn't convince you. What did?"

She tapped the table once before looking me in the eye. "Thumper."

I cocked my head. "What?"

She almost smiled. "You're not the only one who can play with memories, Trav. They showed me what losing Heather did to you."

I closed my eyes, and memories hit like punches. Heather's last moments alive. Our last day together. The explosion that threw Thumper into a tree.

I want to be remembered like this for a thousand years.

I let out a breath I didn't know I had, blinking away tears. "Well, good to know you're not wanting me dead anymore."

Byron raised an eyebrow. "Oh, you might get yourself killed soon enough, Trav. Girl just won't have to wait in line, is all."

Connie nodded an encouragement at Byron before her eyes returned to me. "The more time I had to think about it, the more convinced I was. The boogeyman I thought you were wouldn't have risked what you did. He wouldn't have opened up his home when mine was compromised. He wouldn't have asked permission before reading my mind. He wouldn't have done a lot of things. Thumper just showed me more of what was in your heart. I'm convinced you're not the boogeyman."

"Trying not to be. That guy sounds like an asshole."

"You got a lot of people after your head, Travis. Some of em accusing you of Goetia, which I both think is bullshit and understand how it feels. Figured it'd be polite to let you know I'm not one of them."

"Appreciated."

She tilted her head. "Where is Thumper? They get tired of hanging around you?"

Byron gave a smirk with absolutely no humor in it. "You could say that."

I didn't bother with a smile. "Thumper's a renfield. For Victor."

I could almost see her mask fall into place. "Shit."

I nodded. "Yeah. Knocked me out right after you left and stole Chittenden's blood. Which was the only evidence we had on Victor's plot."

She slowly nodded. "So what's your plan now?"

I held up the ditty bag. "If I'm right, the key to my memories is in here. So I'm gonna take it home, batten down the hatches, and see what I've been missing. We'll see what happens after that, I guess."

She looked the bag up and down. "I kinda wonder what you'll be like. You know? When you finally remember everything?"

Byron quirked an eyebrow. "That was unexpectedly deep."

I let out a long breath. "Yeah. Unfortunately, that's a question for Cyrus and his ilk for the moment. I'll have time to introspect when I have all my death threats in a row."

Connie finally cracked a smile before raising her water glass. "Good luck."

We rose to leave, then I thought of something and raised a finger. "Connie, if I asked you something, could I rely on an honest answer?"

She paused to think, then nodded. "If it's not my secret or not your business, I'll say so. But in general, yes."

I nodded. "The memories you showed me. Were they all real?"

"I didn't alter them. You saw what I remembered."

I nodded again. "Thank you."

We left without another word.

*   *   *

We were barely off the front porch before a familiar sedan with peeling paint drifted into the parking lot. I could feel the interest of the four porchmen grow decidedly more intense. I kept walking until I made sure my feet were on the gravel of the parking lot. Then I turned back, held up a hand and pointed to the car, just to make sure the porchmen knew what was going on. In the corner of my eye I saw the cat padding away around the corner of the porch, sensing conflict and wanting nothing to do with it. Point made, I looked back at the sedan and let the pack come to me.

I could sense the porchmen backing away, not relaxed but not waiting to pounce either. The old farts knew incoming trouble when they sensed it. But they'd let me handle it until they thought I couldn't.

Doors opened, and the pack emerged. They were all in human form, dressed like the kid, in tough clothes that had seen more stains than fabric softener. The driver, who hadn't gotten any prettier, was bigger than I remembered from Connie's memory, and more defined. Since I put linebackers to shame, that was saying a lot.

The giant and the kid were followed by a middle-aged woman with harsh eyes. She looked like the type of girl who started bartending in dives at 18, and had been ridden hard and put away wet often enough that she'd looked the same for decades. She could have been a hard-ridden 30 or a fresh-faced 60 for all I could tell. Behind her was the skinny long-haired guy I recognized from Connie's house.

Now that I knew they were werewolves, I could tell they were in lousier shape than they looked. Werewolf packs were normally extended families: an alpha pair, their kids, their kids from previous pairings, assorted siblings and occasional adopted cousins. They also consisted of at least six adults to somewhere in the twenties if you counted every head. This pack had only four, and they all looked run down. This pack had gotten their asses kicked at sometime in the last few years, and this was all that was left. Which meant I had some leverage to work with.

They came in a wedge, with the giant at the point. I turned my look to him.

"I'm willing to talk."

His voice had more growl than diction. "I'm done talking." He took a step forward.

I shot him in the face.

His body collapsed like several bags of potatoes that smelled like gym shoes. The muzzle of my holdout pistol was still smoking. I slowly pulled my elbow back, ready to shoot any of the remaining three, who had frozen stiff when their point man fell over.

"Anybody else wanna talk while he regenerates? Or are we gonna play a rousing game of how fast can the alchemist turn lead into silver?"

I'll admit I was technically bluffing there. Transmutation's easy enough, but I'm way too much of a perfectionist to try and do it with any level of chemical purity on the fly. But they didn't know that. What I had done was given them a level of comfort. I was capable of killing any of them. But I'd refrained from doing so. I'd merely kept the big one from breaking down negotiations along with my face, then offered to talk again. If I could give them what they wanted without humiliating them, I could get away without painting more of the gravel red.

I didn't turn to look, but I could feel the porchmen watching the entire affair with professional detachment. They would probably argue the minutiae of the encounter for over an hour after the rest of us left. Byron was casually hanging out on my right, throwing knife in hand. I doubt anyone inside the restaurant even noticed me, given the steady background noise of shooters on the range.

The woman stepped forward. "Talk."

I kept the muzzle just above her belt buckle. "What do you want?"

She met my gaze, pride in her voice. "Our jobs back. The leech lover Oswald and the Russian pansy Victor said we attacked Chittenden. We had nothing to do with it, but Chitty wouldn't hear it. Eva tells us to do a job for her and she'd get Chittenden to listen."

I nodded. "Kidnapping Connie."

The thin guy raised a hand. "The goth chick? Yeah. Eva said we were rescuing her but we didn't need to explain. So we stripped her down and bagged her clothes so nobody'd catch her scent. Had us use these fancy cuffs make sure she wouldn't hurt herself neither."

The woman's frown creased her face deeper. "And when we delivered her, Eva paid and accepted, then handed us off to you. You hustled us out of the Cotillion and told us to wait at the goth chick's house. We waited all night, only for you to give us the runaround again. When my beta.." she indicated the giant one, "objected, you beat the shit out of him and kicked us to the curb."

I nodded. That matched what I'd pieced together. "So you started coming after me half-assed? The drive-by, the chase in the park?"

She spit on the gravel, then nodded. "Probes. Seeing what you'd do. We can't take on you and the vampires at the same time. But word got around you killed Eva. If you're on the outs with the vampires?" She gave a shrug.

I took a breath, let it out, then nodded slowly. "It's a long story. Short version: your jobs don't exist anymore. Eva and Tasha are both dead. Victor's surrounded with renfields and country vamps."

The woman spit on the ground. "Sheeit."

"I'll be honest, they were going to go anyway."

The giant started to twitch. The kid stepped in and started helping him up.

The woman met my gaze again. "What are we supposed to do?"

I shrugged. "If I was you, I'd find a stretch of wilderness and start recruiting."

"Can't." She spit on the ground again. "Death packs all around the city. No matter where you go."

I frowned. "Never heard of death packs. They have anything to do with hellhounds? I've killed a lot of those."

She shrugged. "They hunt in packs, and they smell like death. If you got the numbers, you fight em off. If you don't, you run."

I read between the lines and took a wild guess what had happened to her pack.

Byron chimed in. "Sounds like the messy eater Babs was talking about."

I glanced at the giant still recumbent in the gravel. "Am I going to have to shoot him again?"

She shook her head. "He won't be kissy face with you, but he won't start nothin."

I nodded. "Tell you what. I've been a spy for Chittenden this entire time. Victor's going to attempt a coup tonight. If Victor wins, I'm a dead man, and you're on your own. If Chittenden wins, and I live to see sunrise, I'll be in a position to do some favors. Tell your pack to back off of me and mine, and I'll see what I can do for you." I holstered my holdout. "You got a business card or something?"

*　*　*

Chapter Fifteen

"You want me to give you some privacy?"

"Hell, no. I want to know what you've been hiding from me."

Byron raised an eyebrow. "Excuse me?"

We were sitting down at my dining room table. The ditty bag lay on the old wood between us. Neither of us had bothered pouring a drink yet. I looked at the bag, feeling somewhere between a kid at Christmas and an engineer looking at an IED. My headache was back. All of my other aches had come back with it, having a party somewhere near my temple.

"You know more than you're letting on, Byron."

Shrapnel had hopped up onto Byron's lap and started headbutting him for scritches. He smirked as he obliged her. "Trav, not sure if you've noticed, but I'm an elf. Pointy ears, seven times your age, not a fan of the ferrous, the whole shebang. I always know more than I'm letting on."

"I mean about me."

"What about you?"

"I've been thinking. Ever since Babs showed up yesterday. Saying I'm too good. So too good that goetia sound like a reasonable explanation. Then Cyrus said it too. There's been a lot going on, but when I've had the chance,

I started thinking about this project and that. And I remember applying solutions, but I don't remember searching for them or finding them. I can remember old stuff, like making the Spartan Shotguns in high school. And I remember refining the Strap Ball that Heather designed, a few months after Blue River. But I can't think of anything I've done since, oh, enlisting, that I remember from start to finish."

Byron nodded, but didn't add anything. I shook my head. "I had help. Help I got while we were on active duty. Help I don't remember. And what's in this bag is the answer."

Byron let out a long breath, still petting Shrapnel. Then he nodded at the bag. "You know, you'd have figured all this out yesterday if you'd trusted me with that."

"Why didn't I trust you with it?"

He shrugged. "You never told me. If I had to guess, I'd say you couldn't."

I looked down at my hands, closed my eyes, then took a breath. "Byron?"

"Yeah, man?"

"Please tell me there's not a demon in this ditty bag?"

He paused in thought for a second. "I didn't see you do it, so I'm not completely sure. But for what it's worth, I don't think there is."

"If you know, how come you never brought it up?"

He sighed. "Look, bro. I've done my best to let you set the pace in our relationship. At the end of the day, I'm here to keep you alive so you can serve my father. You know, the other Oath hanging over your head. I've been as much of a friend as you've let me be. So yeah, I'm close enough to you to guess at this. But remember, you deliberately locked away your memories. And then your memory block malfunctioned and locked the last year. Who knows what would've happened if I'd filled in the blanks on the memory you made sure to hide? You're still alive, you're not an Oathbreaker, and you got the key. Using it now is up to you."

I let out another long breath, then shrugged. "Screw it. I've followed yellow this far."

Shrapnel fled when I unzipped and dumped open the ditty bag on the table between us. Byron watched impassively. The only object to emerge from the bag was a simple pistol case. It was your typical black plastic generic, with enough scuff marks to have gone on a couple of range trips. It was also padlocked. I held open the bag, shuffled it, turned it inside out and inspected it. Finding nothing, I set the bag aside to concentrate on the case. Taking up my flashlight, I switched to UV, illuminating the mark I'd left on the padlock. Putting the light aside, I flipped through my keyring, opening the padlock with the appropriate key and setting both aside. Popping open the tabs, I gently lifted the lid.

Inside was a plain Taurus pistol in 9mm. The slide was brushed steel and the receiver was matte black polymer. Typical ergonomics for these days. I took a breath, then whispered a charm that let me look deeper into the materials. I saw nothing but polymers and metals, springs and pins. There were no prepared enchantments in the weapon itself, the way I'd put the Hollywood Silencer on my holdout. After a moment, I gently slid my hand under the pistol and picked it up, finger off the trigger and grip resting in my palm, the muzzle facing my kitchen wall. Nothing in the weight or feel was out of the ordinary. I pressed the mag release button, catching the visibly empty magazine with my free hand and putting it on the table. Lifting the pistol towards the kitchen wall, I racked the slide, looking into an empty chamber. Thumbing the slide lever in place, I stuck my pinky into the chamber, which felt as empty as it looked. My pinky emerged without a grain of carbon or a drop of oil. Satisfied there, I removed my hand and let the slide go forward, aiming at the floor and pulling the trigger. Clicking and clacking occupied the next few moments as I confirmed to myself that trigger and safety both worked. I broke the pistol down, looking at the receiver, slide, guide spring rod, and barrel each in turn. None of the pieces revealed any secret that I could tell.

Putting the pistol aside, I picked up the empty case. I pulled out the foam padding from each side, running my fingertips along the corners. I crushed the foam in my hands, looking for hidden pockets. There was nothing in the box and nothing in the foam. I put the foam and the box down.

Follow yellow. I picked up the OD green ditty bag and rummaged around. It was still empty. No patches or other embellishment decorated the plain bag. The only personalization was my faded last name and first initial from boot camp. It was neatly written near the top between the handles, in faded black marker. Waste not, want not.

Follow yellow. That's what I'd told myself. It might have just meant the arrow outside the rangemaster's hut, but that just brought me to this. I was starting to sweat. Gods, my head hurt.

Follow yellow to know. I knew that a year ago, I'd taken this pistol, in this case, in this bag, to the Warwell vault. Something about it was the key to my memory. I sniffed the barrel and smelled nothing but steel and old oil.

Follow yellow to know. I spread out every piece on the table. The bag, the case, the foam, the pieces of the pistol, with the magazine sitting on the end. I froze, trying not to let my hands move. My eyes slowly tracked across the table, returning to the magazine.

Most magazines follow a pretty simple design: a metal box, open at both ends. Inside is a metal spring that pushes the rounds up under tension. A plate at one end to secure the spring. And at the other end, a piece of plastic molded to push the rounds up, called a follower. Most followers were black, gray, or OD green in color. This one, on the other hand, was bright safety yellow.

Very carefully, I picked up the magazine with my off hand. It didn't feel unnaturally heavy. I tilted it upside down. The magazine clinked as if metal knocked against metal. I tilted it back, and it clinked again. With my left hand, I opened my multitool, selecting a blade one-handed. Gently as I could manage, I popped off the spring plate with my knife, then gently slid the plate off of the box. The spring and follower fell onto the table.

So did a tarnished silver signet ring. One that, surprisingly, looked like it would fit even my thick finger.

"Byron? Is that what I think it is?"

He gave me a look that I'd dubbed his dealing-with-stupid-human-stuff face. "I don't know what you think it is. I do know that you're the war-weary child of man, I'm the elf that doesn't want to deal with your shit for the next age, and if that was the kind of ring you're supposed to throw into a volcano, I'd say pack your shit because we're going to Hawaii. But I can tell you now, this ain't that kind of ring."

My eyebrows furrowed. "You're so helpful."

"Gotten you this far, haven't I?"

I shrugged in acknowledgment of that, picking up the ring. It felt surprisingly warm between my fingertips. I rotated my flashlight from visible to red lens to UV, seeing nothing change. I breathed in and breathed out, relaxing a bit.

"Well, I don't think it will turn me invisible, rot my hand, make me obsessive, or otherwise curse me. That said, still not wearing it. Even if it does look like it would fit. There's some sort of faint sigil on the signet."

I licked my thumb absentmindedly and gently rubbed the face of the ring. Within three passes of my thumb over the surface, tendrils of bright blue smoke curled from the ring. I dropped it like a live snake on the table and stood, backing up. One hand opened my knife. My chair crashed to the floor, then slid into the wall as I backed up further.

"Byron! Is this something I'm going to have to shoot?"

He sat back in his chair, arms crossed. "If I had to guess, you're more likely to stand there with a dumb look on your face."

The smoke was coalescing into a humanoid figure in the middle of my kitchen. A female figure. An abundantly female figure. The last of the smoke dissipated, revealing a curvaceous woman with bright blue skin, soulful sapphire eyes lined with kohl, and a warm smile. I remembered those eyes. They were the same ones I'd been seeing in bits of dreams for over a day now. Her deep black hair was tied back in a high ponytail, and simple silver jewelry shone at her fingers, toes, ears, and navel. A heavier and louder collection of bangles and bells hung from her wrists and ankles. A knotwork array of translucent veils in navy blue silk did the work of a bra, and billowing trousers of the same material hung low on her hips. In her right hand was a brass scroll case covered in intricate etching. She spoke in a cheerful alto, as if she'd just thrown a friend a surprise birthday party.

"Hello, Master! Is your mission over?"

I blinked, standing there with what I'm sure was a stupid look on my face. "Byron, you're a prophet."

"Told ya."

I licked my lips, looking the lady in the eyes. You'd think after dealing with attractive vampires and a fairly hot necromancer I'd be used to some fear with my arousal. But no, this was coming in heavy on both ends. Everything I'd ever read about djinn told me they were the nuclear weapons of the Otherworld. Any still on this plane of reality were insanely powerful and hated mages with a fiery passion. If the Iron Council knew one was in my kitchen, the response would be somewhere along the lines of the response to letting velociraptors guard a day care. And yet here one was, her bangles jingling quietly as she smiled at me. It was like being greeted by an affectionate belly dancer holding a suitcase nuke.

I held up a polite finger, trying not to shake in fear. "Byron?"

"Yeah?"

I tried not to move in case she exploded. "Why is there a djinn in my house?"

He shrugged casually. "Because you're her Master."

The djinn nodded in agreement, setting off another chain reaction in her jewelry.

I blinked, a surge of anger crested the fear, riding the headache. "I think I'd remember owning a djinn! Especially one dressed like something out of the spank bank!"

It was the wrong thing to say. A part of me realized that the moment the moment the words left my mouth to strike every offended ear in the room. Those sapphire eyes welled with tears as the look on her face went from a welcoming smile to the picture of a breaking heart. The djinn slowly turned her eyes away from me, looking resolutely at the floor. Her voice was scarcely above a whisper.

"You sound like my last Master. The one who only spoke of my appearance when he called me names."

Behind her, Byron had me caught in his gaze, shaking his head slowly. And that gaze reminded me that my longtime friend was from a species that were predators long before humans showed up.

"You fucking monster," he said, "If you say such things again, I will slap the memory block out of your head myself."

I was bright enough to know Byron wasn't the one I should be apologizing too. Not much brighter, obviously, but bright enough. When I turned to look at the djinn, her shoulders were slouched and her head was down in long-accustomed submission. But her eyes were up, their look blazing like some of the hottest flames. Her voice was scarcely above a whisper.

"My Master before him, Professor Ryan, showed me paintings of what he thought I would dress like when he realized who I was. I thought they were silly. But then I thought they were comfortable. And I thought they were pretty."

I couldn't speak. Confusion and then shame poured into the fear and anger that kept me from moving. This was the softest ass-chewing I had ever received. It was like having a puppy tell me how disappointing my life choices were. And I deserved every excruciating moment.

"You seemed to like seeing me like this, Master. You never objected. And you seemed to smile when you thought I didn't notice." I don't know how someone with blue skin managed to blush, but, somehow, she did. "If you thought I looked shameful, you should have told me."

Another spike of pain went through my head as I tried to pull my foot out of my mouth. "No, not at all. I'm sorry. You look.." I got another eyeful and my brain tossed out an entire box of adjectives, none of which were good enough. Beautiful was only a beginning. Exotic was just a tangent of perspective. My mind grabbed the first one that probably wouldn't embarrass me further. "Amazing. You look amazing. Your outfit looks amazing. More amazing with you in it."

Byron piped up. "You've got him babbling already, Jazz. Forgive your knucklehead Master, he's had a rough couple of days."

I gave what was probably a goofy, worried smile. "I'm so sorry. I shouldn't have said that. I've been.. a lot."

She looked back up, the smile growing on her face as warm as the sun coming from behind a cloud. "Tis forgiven, Master."

Byron leaned against the wall. "Jazz here is your research assistant."

I almost went cross-eyed. "My what now?"

Byron opened his hands. "Research assistant. How did you think you got this good? How did you think you knew about the Cronesfoil? You're a good handyman, bro, but you don't speak medieval German. You're not even forty and you still one of the better alchemists this side of the Mississippi. How did you think that happened? Jazz has been hooking you up since we left active duty, man. You killed her last Master and took her ring when we were in Iraq. This is why the Iron Council has Babs watching you. They think you have a demon on speed dial. Fortunately, nobody's suspecting a djinn."

Jazz frowned at the mention of a demon, then spat on the floor, swearing in a language I didn't recognize.

I grabbed an old argument for lack of anything else to hold onto. "I think I would've remembered owning a djinn, Byron!"

Byron shook his head in teasing disappointment. "No shit. That's why you hid your memories of her, dumbass. You knew working for Chittenden would mean some bloodsucker rummaging around in your brainpan sooner or later, so you took steps to hide her from them."

It made sense. Unfortunately, too much that made sense had bitten me in the ass lately. I was still suspicious, but Byron's answer seemed more right by the moment.

"That's why the Warwells had a note to call me if I hadn't picked her up in a year and a day. If I paid off my debt and was still alive, I'd be able to handle it."

He opened his arms to indicate the entire world. "See?"

I frowned. "But why aren't my memories back yet?"

Jazz held up the scroll case. "You haven't unlocked them yet. I was trying to tell you, Master. The key is in here."

I mentally twitched at hearing myself called that title and gently took it from her. The case opened easily, but instead of a scroll, there was an ordinary headband of wide stretchy material, colored a deep kelly green. My eyes narrowed.

"What do I do with it?"

"All you have to do is smell it, Master." She nodded. "And then thank me." She swiftly held up a finger. "Oh, in that order, Master. Smell, then thank, that is."

It was the least bizarre request made of me this week. I lifted the headband to my nose, breathing deep. The scent of leather, rose oil, and sandalwood incense crossed my nose, instantly bringing a wave of emotions:

longing, sorrow, a rush of hot anger and a deep, cold grief. I realized in an instant who the headband once belonged to.

I want to be remembered like this for a thousand years.

I looked Jazz in those sapphire eyes I only remembered from dreams and gently whispered. "Thank you." Then I stood still, my breathing the only sound in the room. I couldn't do anything else. The part of my mind that initiated movement was overwhelmed with memories opening up in a relentless flood. All I could do was breathe.

Byron broke the silence. "You starting to remember, Travis? That unlock the compartment?"

I slowly nodded, the pain beginning to fade. "Yes. Both of them."

I was unconscious before I hit the floor. Turns out, being hit with a few years worth of memory all at once is a touch overwhelming.

*　　*　　*

Chapter Sixteen

"Guideline Twenty-Five:

Make Apologies at a sprint.

Make Amends at a marathon pace."

Her proper name is Jasmine bint Rashid Abdul Bayt al-Hikmah and a dozen other titles I can't remember. I call her Jazz. She's a brunette, about five foot seven, and one of the most persistently cheerful people I've ever met. She's also brilliant, and I say that having regularly hung out with multiple levels of genius. Girl speaks more languages than I have toes, among other things. She's doe-eyed, with bright blue skin and a figure best described as an hourglass for two and a half hours. As far as her taste in clothing goes, a comic book artist from the nineties who couldn't spell 'odalisque' at gunpoint yet was convinced he knew what Ottoman era harem girls dressed like would be deeply impressed.

Before you ask, I'm only partially responsible for her wardrobe. Two Masters ago, she was serving a British historian in post-Ottoman Baghdad. From what I could tell, the guy had seen too many Gerome and Ingres paintings. Jazz herself is impervious to weather and most internalized shame, so she's rolled with it ever since. I never complained because, I'll be honest, I enjoyed the view. If the picture of Heather I kept didn't clue you in, ample curves and bare midriffs are guaranteed distractions for me.

If you've read this far, you got plenty of things to judge me on, leave my lascivious aesthetics alone, please and thank you.

To mention the other elephant in the room, yes, I'm her Master. Capital M. That took some working my brain around the concept. I'd had an excellent postgraduate education in this flavor of ethics, but I doubt even Lady Sina could've seen this one coming. Jazz was born sometime after the Demon War to a pair of bound djinn. She was trained to be a librarian like her parents, and she excelled at it.

I'd killed her last Master during the Iraq war. It was clear she didn't enjoy her time serving him and I asked as few questions as I could manage. Near as I could tell, he'd looted Jazz's ring from a museum. Not being the brightest glowstick in the rave, he seemed content to unimaginatively use her as a weapon. He was in my unit's area for about a week, during which we'd been hit with IED's that had myself and the engineers stumped as to how they were being placed. Then one night her Master decided to stick around after using her to set off a bomb. In the subsequent fight, Byron and I kicked in the door, killing her Master and his teammates. While clearing the room I'd noticed the shine and pocketed her ring. I didn't technically loot his corpse, as the ring had gotten separated from him before I was in the room. The weird bombings stopped. Just another thing to deal with in Iraq. I smuggled her ring back to the U.S. in a mix of cheap souk jewelry, just another souvenir. It wasn't until I went home on leave that I realized exactly what and who I'd gotten my hands on.

I was worried about boring her at first. She reminded me of service submissives and working dogs I'd known. And by that I mean if not regularly given tasks to do, she'd find something to do. With the considerable powers of djinn at her disposal. As it turned out, given enough loaded bookshelves, she was perfectly happy to explore pages to her heart's content. I could relate. Over time, she became a boon companion. No wonder the Iron

Council thought I had a demonic hookup. I had a centuries-old research assistant reducing my R&D time to fractions of what it could be.

What I refused to let myself do was think at all in romantic or sexual terms about her. Under normal circumstances, I'd probably turn more monosyllabic and start drooling in her very presence. Smart, subby, bibliophilic, sweet, curvy, dressed like a *Heavy Metal* cover model, and confident in all of the above? What's not to like? But given the nature of our relationship, I'd established some fairly severe mental blocks for the sake of my personal ethics. The end result being that I usually managed to not think about the kind-hearted and dangerously curvaceous librarian that called me 'Master' in ways that got my libido involved. Usually.

Unfortunately, the Iron Council worried about the existence of people like Jazz for some understandable reasons. Mages like me can adjust reality in unexpected ways, because humanity hasn't read all the fine print in the laws of physics. But there's some serious limits into how much damage a single mage can do. A djinn fulfilling the wish of a human Master can pull reality apart and rearrange it like a kid's playset, with time, space, and sanity sold separately. I could make a sand castle with a pail and a shovel. A djinn working on their Master's orders could turn the beach into a floating city of glass before lunch.

When I met Jazz, I had a vague concept of how dangerous she could be. Careful questioning only made the big picture nastier. I didn't have the ruthlessness to drop her ring in the ocean. And even if I did, she'd just be bored and lonely for a few thousand years until someone found her again. And someone, somehow, would find her again.

Nor could I start making wishes. I read the damned stories. I have my moments, but I'm not stupid. Adjusting reality bit by tiny bit to get the job done, that I could manage. Unraveling and reweaving the fabric of reality on even the most well-thought-out desire was a recipe for unmitigated disaster with extra screaming.

Setting her free wasn't an option either. She'd seen the movie and pointed out the flaws too. I'm a good craftsman as enchantments go, but I'm no Suleiman. And even if I was crazy enough to crack open reality by using a wish to set her free, she'd still be a djinn. Which meant any yahoo with half my mojo and a decent understanding of Solomanic mysticism could bind her into something else: another ring, a lamp, whatever.

Theoretically, I could take her to the djinn realm in the Otherworld. But she'd never been there herself. She had no idea what sort of reception either of us would get. She knew it was accessed through a specific portal, but that portal could be anywhere between Istanbul and Tehran. Even if I could find the portal and take her to the djinn realm, I'd still be a mage with a djinn bound to me. Convincing the local djinn not to rip me apart on general principle would be a tall order even for a charmer like Jazz.

Which left being her Master, in the painfully platonic sense. On the plus side, she was a rock star of a research assistant. Especially when I kept her regularly supplied with used paperbacks. But keeping her true nature a secret was one of my more stressful duties. A duty in need of fulfillment, to be sure. Even in the Otherworld, the kind of raw power controlled by djinn was both rare and highly sought after. At best, it was sought by people with good intentions but no clue at the potential consequences. At worse, people with plenty of ill intentions who knew damned well about the consequences, but didn't give a tin shit. Hence, my hiding her from everyone.

*   *   *

One of the blocks in my memory covered the existence of Jazz and her time in my life.

The other covered the past year, from the night I began fulfilling my Oath to Chittenden until I woke up to find Connie in my kitchen.

The first block was much more pleasant.

Life as both a Mage and a renfield at once means a life of power and blood.

I went to Chittenden dressed and equipped, like I was checking into a new unit. I relied on the nature of the Otherworld Oath keeping Chittenden from making me do anything I couldn't live with.

It was the last night I had any naïveté about the nature of vampires.

Within nights, I was passed off to Eva like a prize horse, repaying some vampiric debt owed to Chittenden. She was old enough and predatory enough to have entirely different concepts of human resources. Not to mention old enough to have ancient views on consorting with one's servants.

At first, she was just enough of a temptation that I could play the role. By the time I'd tasted enough of her blood, the role had taken control.

Every single piece of gear in that boudoir cabinet had been used more than once.

Our shared lust far overpowered the cries from the part of me that was still myself. The part of me that wasn't fooled by blood, by lust, or by loneliness. The part of me in the depths of my mind, somehow free from the renfield condition.

The part of me that drowned in the rich energy of Eva's blood while begging her to stop.

The part of me that watched Eva and I lounge in postcoital, not bliss, not contentment, but sensory burnout.

The rest of me, the part that stretched out on that enormous bed, was too focused on coming down from the blood-surged orgasm high to notice that faraway part of me. But maybe, just maybe, someone heard that tiny part that was still me and me alone. The part of me that huddled against a wall in a faraway corner of the mindscape, gently beginning to cry.

*　　*　　*

Chapter Seventeen

"Guideline Twenty-Nine:

Students, Servants, or Pets,

If you've accepted them, they are yours.

Fight for them accordingly."

"Travis!"

"Master?"

The blood hangover was back with a vengeance. And it had brought friends. I felt like a pack of trolls had strung me up by the ankles and used my carcass to play a rousing game of tetherball. On top of that, I was pissed. If I hadn't felt so weak I probably would have snarled something profane at one of my best friends and my loyal servant.

I remembered everything now. But over everything I remembered the blood. I remembered the rush of that first taste. I remembered the power radiating through my body, like the warm tingle from a shot of moonshine multiplied tenfold. I remembered every craving. How much work it took to hide even a piece of my mind from Eva. I remembered two nights ago, firing the wolfpack on orders from Eva I was too addled to question. Less than an hour after they'd kidnapped Connie on Eva's orders, I turned them out. I remember beating the snot out of the giant one, their beta, on Connie's front porch.

I remembered through my own eyes now, opening that box and seeing Connie lying inside it. Taking her hair in my hand, her own scent mixed with leather and sandalwood incense and rose oil. The keys to unlock my memory taken under the blood. The spell backlashing, blocking everything up to the moment I cast it the year before.

Somehow, the past finally faded away. In the present, I waved a hand in surrender. "I'm here."

Byron and Jazz gently helped me sit up, leaning me back against my kitchen cabinets. I wound up breathing hard from the exertion. When they were convinced I wasn't going to die right there, Byron visibly breathed in relief.

"You look like hammered shit, man."

"I feel like it. It's a side effect."

"Side effect of what?"

"The spell. And the blood. Oswald warned me. I thought he was just full of shit."

Byron frowned. "What about the?... Oh, shit."

"Yeah. I just remembered a year's worth of getting my fix. I must have used up all I had to heal when I drank that tube of Eva's. Now I've been off it for a day and a half. And now my mind remembered all of that in... how long have I been out?"

"Maybe two minutes."

"Fuck." Eloquent, I know. But it's all I had. It took me three tries, and the last time I leaned on Byron more than I was comfortable with, but I managed to stagger to my feet. "I need a shower. And caffeine. And red meat. There's a bigger list, but that'll get me to make my report."

Byron looked dubious. "What about Thumper?"

I shook my head, then winced as a spike of pain driving through my head convinced me that was a bad idea. "If they're still alive, Victor will call to gloat about it and make me some kind of sadistic offer after sundown. He's that kind of asshole. If not, I can turn in my report and see if I can get Victor's head on a plate as a performance bonus."

"No way is it gonna be that easy."

"I don't think so either, but the thought makes me warm and fuzzy."

*   *   *

"This coffee is amazing, Jazz. I feel moderately human again."

She smiled big enough for her eyes to shine. "It's called Smite the Infidel, Master. It's the kind of coffee you really only want to use in an emergency."

"Gearing up for our third vampire fight in as many nights probably qualifies, Jazz. Thank you."

I'd used all the hot water in the house taking that shower, then had started on the cold before Jazz marched in, dragged me out, and started throwing towels at me while yelling. I understood enough Arabic to know what she was insinuating I did with my downtime. I managed to escape the shouting djinn, towel off, and get into an old shirt and some track pants. I have no idea why people consider sweatpants comfortable. I live in the South. Wanting to sweat more is somewhere between stupidity and sacrilege. Sweat-wicking track pants in unnatural fibers, on the other hand, are a comfort.

Sometimes, I managed to get a whole two minutes without thinking about the tube of blood in my nightstand. It was still sitting there, among the spare magazines and a box of condoms that had to have expired by now and everything else I might want to have at hand in the middle of the night. After all, Eva was dead. It's not like drinking her blood could put me under her control. Before I knew it, I'd been sitting on my bed, looking at my nightstand for I'm not sure how long.

I picked up a knife, flashlight, and pen from the nightstand and wandered back to the kitchen. The smells damn near had me swooning in ecstasy before I passed the front door. Byron had gone on a grocery run, and Jazz had started making various kebabs from whatever meats Byron had brought home. Shrapnel was diligently stalking them both, pouncing on any tidbits dropped in the process.

The moment I entered the kitchen, Jazz filled a mug labeled 'blood of my enemies' with her fresh coffee, and I sat down to sip it as my brain defragmented. I was used to Navy coffee. Jazz's blend had tones of that mind-hardening elixir, but stronger, more agile. Jazz had found some sort of Barbary Coast pirate coffee and named it appropriately. Shrapnel abandoned her foraging to climb onto the table and demand scritches. I checked my message-free phone while obliging my feline overlady.

Byron, having stayed out of Jazz's way playing a game on his own phone, holstered it and sat back across from me. "How you doing, man?"

It was a big enough question I had to put my mug down and start counting on my fingers of my nonscritching hand. "Well, the werewolf pack doesn't quite want me dead anymore. Neither does Connie. I've got all my memories back, including the last year and everything to do with Jazz. I gave Chittenden a fair heads-up and I'm ready to write up my report for tonight. Once I do that, my Oath is fulfilled, and I'm that much more free."

"That's a respectable win column."

I let out a deflated sigh. "On the other hand, Thumper is either dead or being tortured. Getting them back will mean facing whatever Victor can bring to bear. And I'm having trouble concentrating because I keep thinking about that blood. Which is going to be hilarious given that I have to survive a pack of vampires, then give a report to another vampire so the former can piss off and the latter can clear my debt to him."

"Formidable."

"Sorry I'm dragging you into this, man."

He opened his hands. "Hey, just means I get more camp stories to tell when I go back home, man. I knew what I was getting into."

"Did you really?"

He shrugged. "No, but it's been a fun ride so far."

I kept forgetting how old Byron actually was. Probably because he still had the looks, stamina, and libido of a college athlete. He probably regarded his time watching over me as a summer vacation. Or at best an extended deployment. I wondered if that made me like his third dog. The blood hangover had my mind going into some very weird places. I tried to clear away more of it with another swig of Jazz's coffee.

Jazz slid plates of fresh kebabs in front of both of us. With all the newly-restored memories swirling around in my head, I couldn't remember the last time I'd eaten properly. I hadn't sat down for a meal since last night at Waffle Crossing. The steam was still rising from the hunks of grilled beef on bamboo skewers and the chopped vegetables they laid on. I looked up to see Jazz smiling at me.

"Jazz, what are you waiting for? Grab yourself a plate and let's eat."

She blushed, which is impressive for someone with a blue complexion. "Yes, Master."

*   *   *

I hit Save, letting the final draft of my report load itself onto the thumb drive. I'd discovered a brand I liked with a rubberized casing. Not much in the way of shockproofing, but better than most. One drive already had the report loaded, which I was going to lock in Alexandria's Revenge. The other was going into my pocket to be taken to Lord Chittenden. As it turns out, I had plenty of photos and transcripts I'd made over the year to back it up. Now that I had the whole thing put together, putting all the pieces into place had been relatively easy. I even had a hard copy printed out in a big envelope and tucked into my pack, in case the man wanted paper.

I could faintly hear Byron playing a video game down the hall in my living room. I pushed myself back from the computer, stretching and rolling everything above the waist that needed it. Even after years of being used to hurrying up and waiting, there was always a tension in your body when you knew a fight was coming. Even if it was coming hours out.

A small set of bells jingled somewhere just out of reach of my tinnitus. I smiled without looking behind me. "Hi, Jazz."

"Hello, Master."

I swung my chair around to find her standing in the doorway with her smile. It was her way of checking on me without bothering me by asking if I needed anything. She had centuries of experience at being an attentive servant, and wasn't about to stop just because I had silly ideas. I offered her the bed with a silent hand, and she accepted, sitting quietly.

"You were right last year, Jazz. That puzzle I put in my own head was drastic."

She smirked a bit. "I'm not one to say I told you so, Master."

"I'll do it for you. You told me so. Unfortunately, now I'm going back in the vampire nest and the problem of keeping you safe is proving difficult. I can't set you free, even though I want to. And I can't get rid of you even if I did want to. Which, for the record, I don't. So if I die tonight, what happens to you?"

Jazz had grown somber. This wasn't a topic she liked. "Whoever takes up my ring becomes my next Master."

I nodded. "Which means Byron or Uncle Mac if we're lucky. Victor if we're not."

She shook her head violently. "No vampire or ghul can command a djinn. Nor can an elf. Only a human, mage or otherwise."

I tried to look sympathetic. "Renfields are human too, hon. But it's good to know." I blinked. "What happens if a nonhuman tries?"

She gave a more wicked smile than I thought she was capable of. "I am not bound to obedience to them and may do as I like until a Master arrives."

I nodded. "Which will be fun and games until someone thinks of having a renfield grab your ring. Or just lets word out that you're on this continent at all. I'm not planning on dying tonight, Jazz. But I'm worried about your future. Keeping you cooped up in your ring in a safe was a bullshit move and I'm sorry I did it."

Her smile softened. "Apology accepted, Master. But you look like you've got a plan."

"I do. You know I want you free, one way or another. But what comes after that is the problem. I want you to start putting together a human identity for yourself, mundane and magical. One that mostly tells the truth. You were trained by your family, we met in Iraq, and you came over to the states to be my research assistant. The fact that you're not technically a mage and that you've forgotten more magic than I've learned is easy enough to gloss over."

She looked confused. "Master?"

"The world's gotten a lot bigger since you wound up in that ring, Jazz. And it's unfair to keep you away from so much of it. Especially since your survival may depend on it. It's time to start hiding you in plain sight. Which means you need to start passing for human on the regular. So start thinking about paperwork, a glamour, and a wardrobe. I want to start introducing you to people soon."

Her smile was almost as bright as the Georgia sun. "Thank you, Master."

*   *   *

The sun went down around nine, which was when I woke up from a catnap and made a snack. It was almost like being deployed again. Working in the late morning. Sleeping in the late afternoon when it's at the hottest. Come out at night, when it's hot and steamy but somewhat more bearable.

At half past nine, my phone rang. Apparently, I'd made Victor's ringtone "Playing with the Boys," by Kenny Loggins. Byron gave me some serious side eye as I took a breath and swiped to answer. "Yeah?"

Victor sounded his usual smug self. "Travis! My man with the pack of plans. So many good plans. And then, so many not-so-good plans. Damn shame your plan on fucking me over kinda stumbled there. Good thing for me Thumper was Jenny-on-the-spot with that one. Pity she's not quite the witch she hyped herself up to be. Did you know she can almost talk sensible?"

I slipped into my security voice. The one I use when politely asking people to leave before I have to tell them they don't have an option. "I want them back, Victor."

He sounded incredulous. And annoyed. "You want them back? Thumper was never yours in the first place, you fat backstabbing grease monkey. What could you even possibly give me for her anyway?"

"You got another mage willing to cast this curse of yours?"

There was a long silence. "I'm listening."

"You still need a mage to cast that blood curse. And that curse is now your only hope to pull off this coup, let alone survive the night with your head attached. Five bucks says you're already set up somewhere to trade me Thumper for a casting. I make my report to Chittenden tonight. But I'm willing to see you first. You give me Thumper unharmed, I'll cast the curse myself on the spot. You get Chittenden weakened and the biggest piece of evidence against you destroyed in one go."

Another long silence, then, "You fuck with me, Wayland, and I promise you, Thumper lives. She won't be very comfortable without ears, nipples, or fingers, but she'll live."

"Where?"

"Top of Stone Mountain. Midnight."

"I'll be there."

*   *   *

Chapter Eighteen

"Guideline Fourteen:

Stocking more ammo is like baking more cookies:

You want everyone to have plenty

no matter how many friends arrive."

Yesterday was for recon. Tonight was for combat. My fashion choices changed accordingly.

I started with a cast titanium cup in an otherwise ordinary jockstrap. Anything that tried taking me down with a shot to the nuts was in for a surprise. After my more comfortable shorts came a set of my fighting cargo pants. Instead of ripstop nylon or a cotton-poly blend, this pair were made of transmuted spider silk. Took a lot more effort to rip, tear, or slice. Special pockets sewn on the inside let me slip in a pair of kneepads; just to give myself a bit of comfort. No, I wasn't starting to creak in the joints as I got older. Really. Honest.

I held all that up with a leather gunbelt I tooled myself. Multitool, flashlight, and small knife in pouches on my right side, M9 holstered on my left. Holdout pistol in a pocket holster on my front left side. Wand in the same pocket. Ahead of the multitool came a pouch full of some one-ounce goodies I'd made last year: a smoke grenade, a flashbang, and a rapid soft tissue healer.

I slipped on a pair of my tactical boots, which were nicely broken in. They zipped up the sides, but for tonight I took the effort to re-tie the laces. Wooden stakes the size of drumsticks, carved in just the right way to slide between ribs and punch into hearts, slid into trouser pockets just below my knees. I'd sewn in said pockets for the purpose. A spider silk tshirt in navy blue to match my pants, extra tall to come down to mid-thigh even on me helped with concealment. Then came the sling bag. I already had a hard copy of my report put together in the frame sleeve. My kukhri slid into a pouch for it on the inside. A first aid kit, tourniquet, a few more stakes, and a couple of more one-ounce goodies filled some of the supplement compartments. But the main pouch was filled with a dozen loaded magazines for my pistol. On the outside I'd sewn a handful of my favorite morale patches. Far as I'm concerned, hook and loop are for quitters.

Now I looked like a hipster nerd, it was time to get a bit more martial. Wide leather cuffs with chrome rings and double buckles secured my wrists. After that, I pulled on leather fingerless gloves. Steel plates reinforced the ridge and palm, just in case I had to ram a stake down myself without waiting to use a hammer.

Dressed for war, I opened my nightstand drawer and looked at Heather's picture. My memories restored, I noticed that she held the green headband just under her hand. She'd left it at my house the day I took that picture, and she never came back for it. I'd kept it, remembering her. It was in my pocket during the funerals. The smell of leather, rose oil, sandalwood incense, and just plain her, guiding my memories.

I want to be remembered like this for a thousand years.

I'd kept it locked in a box all this time, until I'd needed a trigger to restore my memories. Go figure I'd chosen a bittersweet one to unlock all of the rest. In the drawer was the headband, and the scroll case I'd kept it in. I picked up the headband, smiling down at the picture into Heather's eyes.

"Ain't been nearly a thousand years yet, luv. But it's gotten me through a lot. And for what it's worth, your kid sister turned out pretty badass."

I breathed, the familiar scent of the headband now no less poignant. Tears filled my eyes, ready to fall as I put the headband and picture away in their cases. They lay naturally among the mess of knives, flashlights, pens, lighters, and pistol magazines that littered the drawer.

Sitting among the debris, something caught the light. I reached into the mess and brought out the tube of Eva's blood. My hand almost shook thinking about the raw power in that tube. Power to take on Victor and his country vamp cronies. Power to get Thumper back. Power to walk away from Chittenden free and clear.

And then what? How long could I hold out before I started begging one of those bastards for another taste? How long before I was an unquestioning flunky right alongside Oswald?

From the dining room, I heard Byron yell, "Trav! You might want to come out and see this!"

I slipped the tube into my right front pocket. Before I could leave the room, I was glomped by Jazz. This time I didn't hesitate. I held on as tight as I could. Ever the faithful, Jazz only indulged herself for a moment before whispering in my ear, "Good luck, Master." Before I could open my mouth to respond, she had vanished into her ring. I took it off, threading it into the chain that held my old dog tags together.

Meeting Byron on the stairs, I held up my free hand to stop him before he'd opened his mouth halfway to say whatever he had to explain to me. "Byron, I need you to do something for me."

"Sure, bro."

I opened my other hand, holding out the dog tag chain with Jazz's ring. "Something happens to me, take Jazz and present her to Elaine Warwell."

His frown came back stronger. "What have I told you about bullshit..."

"Just promise me, godsdamnit!" I caught myself shouting, forced myself to breathe, and damn near was begging by the time I spoke again. "It's you and me versus Victor and every country vamp and renfield he can gather. I'm a blood junkie and Thumper's worse. The only thing keeping me from outright calling this a suicide mission is the Oath I made to your dad. Worst case scenario, you get out of this alive anyway. She can't serve you or your father, you know that. And if I'm gonna hand off that sweetheart to anyone, I want it to be someone with the ethics not to abuse her and the power to not be messed with because of her. And Elaine is the only one I know who fits that description. So for once in your life, shut the fuck up and promise me you'll take care of her."

Byron looked me in the eyes for several moments, then quietly nodded. His frown faded. He barely spoke above a whisper, but I could feel the power coursing in his words. "I swear to you on my shooting eye, if you are incapacitated tonight, I will see her safe and protected."

Elves did not make promises often. When they did, the universe held them to the letter of it. I think the Otherworld Oath was tried out on them before it was applied to the rest of us. Which is why most elves are unscrupulous weasels. Byron's promise had loopholes big enough for me to drive a big rig through. But unlike most of his kind, Byron had figured out what the spirit of a promise was. And hearing him say it, I could feel a massive weight coming off my shoulders. He gently took the ring, chain, and tags, securing them in a pouch. Then he smiled. "You good?"

I nodded, exhaling from the pressure release. "Yeah."

"Good." He clapped me on the shoulder. "Now come on."

He opened the front door and we stepped out onto the porch. The sun had gone down an hour ago, and Victor's call a half hour after that. The heat had dropped a bit but the southern humidity was still thick in the air. Crickets chirped softly to each other. In the distance, amateur fireworks were being shot off every few minutes, shining lights in the sky here and there.

Next to my mailbox stood the lanky form of Cyrus. He'd traded his suit for loose jeans faded from rich black to a charcoal gray, shitkicker boots with scuffed toes, a gray undershirt tucked in and small leather pouches flanking the buckle on his belt. His open button-down collared shirt was black with purple flames rising from the hem and short sleeves. He carried a hooked cane and wore a gray porkpie hat.

Next to him was a purple compact car that had seen better days. Cyrus tapped something on his phone, gave a salute with his cane to the driver, and turned around to smile shamelessly at us. The compact drove off quietly into the night.

Before Cyrus could holster his phone or take a step, not to mention before I could question his presence, a dark blue sedan parked on the other side of the driveway. Babs stepped out of the driver's seat. She'd traded her suit for cargo pants and tactical boots. A royal blue windbreaker barely covered her Kevlar vest. It did, however, manage to at least partially conceal the heavily modified duty belt she now wore under the streetlight. As she started walking, she pulled the name tape of her agency off the vest, stuffing it in a pocket.

From the passenger side of Babs' sedan, the door opened. A pair of small feet in modern sand-colored combat boots hit the gutter at the edge of my lawn. Then the hat, somewhere between the classic black cone of a witch's hat and a sensible wool cornucopia shape rose from the shotgun seat to peek above the passenger door. Grabbing the door with one hand, Lori lifted herself up from the car and opened the door completely in the same motion. Lori had the kind of curves good for wrangling small children, carrying off dead Vikings, and being worshiped to ensure a good harvest. Her navy blue dress was covered with what at second glance appeared to be purple dinosaurs. Over her shoulder was an expansive bag of rich brown leather. If civilization consumed us all in a fiery apocalypse, she would have us back to at least the industrial revolution by the contents of the bag alone.

Reaching into the backseat, Lori pulled out a handmade broom nearly taller than she was. One of the old-school kind, with the round bundle instead of the flat kind you usually see. Her hand neatly slid into a leather loop tied just below the bristles. As likely predicted, I was standing there with my jaw hanging open.

I barely heard the lifted pickup truck come roaring around the corner. At first I thought it was patterned in flames, then realized the burgundy body had a splattered layer of Georgia red clay across the bottom half. The tires were taller than my mailbox, and the bull bar mounted on the front would have given a moose pause. The truck rumbled to a halt, and the driver stepped out. I'm a big man, but I only recognized Bubba because Sasquatch aren't known to wear overalls. He was still well over six-six and three feet across the shoulders, with a farmer's tan, beard just starting to grow gray, and a green ball cap jammed on his tousled hair.

From the passenger side, I first saw a silhouette I was more used to seeing on mudflaps. Becky Sue was almost as tall as Bubba and just as wide across the shoulders. Her mane of platinum hair had calmed down to a more sedate dishwater blonde in a high ponytail. But while the years had brought her wrinkles and pounds just like the rest of us, no mere turn of the season could make Becky Sue give half a shit about that. She still wore her daisy dukes, tied off her shirt under her breasts, and would most likely punch the first person to sneer anything about muffin tops in her direction. She took one last drag off her cigarette and dropped the butt, grinding it out with the toe of her boot.

I turned to Byron in shock. "What did you do?"

He shrugged. "Figured you were going to try some kind of atonement kamikaze bullshit, and figured rather than listen to you bitch about it, I'd just arrange for some force augmentation. Made some calls while you were in the shower earlier." He shrugged. "If you can't get your shit together, getting the old gang together is usually the next best thing."

An odd grinding sound came from a pair of oak trees in the yard, like sliding a boulder across a stone floor. I squinted, eventually realizing that the light from the street lamp didn't match between the trees the way they did in front of them. And the tire marks Connie's jeep had made on the lawn the night before didn't continue past the gap in the trees. Instead, a shadow as tangible as a velvet curtain hung between the trees. From the shadow stepped a man with an unruly mane of sandy brown hair. He had a medium build and the start of a paunch but defined forearms. He wore a pair of custom moccasins, well-worn blue jeans, and an old band t-shirt. A small leather pouch or two adorned his belt, and a guitar, short bow, and quiver of arrows was slung across his back.

I was dumbstruck. After blinking twice, I finally managed to crack an incredulous smile. "Seb?"

He smiled back. "In the flesh. Fortunately that low road running parallel to I-75 is still there." He tossed an acorn to Byron, who caught it. "Your cousin Thorn says hi, by the way."

Byron tucked the acorn into a vest pocket. "Good to hear from her."

I looked out at the assembled pack of mages that stood before me, feeling my face flushing. With the exception of Thumper, every survivor of the Blue River massacre was standing on my front lawn. I had to breathe two times before managing to let out a, "Hi, guys."

Cyrus took the lead. "We're here to help, Trav. You and Thumper."

I started shaking my head almost before he finished. "I can't. Guys, this isn't your..."

"Fuck. You. Trav." That was Babs, thumbs hooked into her front pockets. "It's our fight now."

Seb nodded. "We didn't just survive because of the shady deals we all made. We survived because we worked together."

Becky Sue smirked. "Besides which, letting him get away with taking Thumper would set a bad precedent."

Bubba nodded. "We probably should've started helping a year ago. But we're here now."

Lori unbuttoned the top three buttons on her dress, shoving it aside to show the barn owl tattooed on her left breast. "You're still a jackass, Travis. But we all crossed the river together. Time to do it again."

Becky Sue shoved her shirt aside to show her own Barn owl tattoo. Seb and Cyrus moved their own shirts to do the same. Bubba popped an overall tab and shoved his undershirt aside. I finally tugged the v-neck of my own shirt. Six barn owls inked in the skin of six people shone in the streetlight.

Babs shook her head. "I ain't dropping my flak or flashing my titty in Travis' front yard. Y'all know I got one too."

That finally broke the tension as we all busted into mild laughter. We all adjusted our clothes as an engine rumbled in the distance. I looked to see Connie's Jeep drive up, parking in front of Babs. We all watched as Connie stepped out. She'd tied her hair back in a single, simple braid. The only other place simple could be described was the black fishnets that sheathed her from wrists to ankles. On her feet were scuffed surplus jungle boots. Not the platformed buckle collections that would put her at eye level with me, but ones I'd use in a different size to run through the woods any day. Hard shell knee pads were strapped on over the fishnets. A pair of black cargo shorts with purple trim was held on with a belt more tricked out than Bubba's truck. Over that was a leather vest that, under all the patches and studding, looked like it would give Kevlar a run for its money. Decorating everything else was enough silver jewelry to beat a werewolf unconscious. Her makeup was a perfect mask that could shift from comedy to tragedy in an instant. She stopped a double arm's length from the rest of us and quirked an eyebrow. "Am I late to the party?"

Byron's teeth flashed in his best flirtation. "On the contrary. Your timing is excellent."

I shook my head, still in shock. "I didn't think I'd be seeing you again."

She shrugged a little. "Victor's gonna go after me sooner or later. Might as well help take him down with a lot of backup before he takes the city. Besides, nobody deserves what's happening to Thumper."

I nodded in gratitude, almost whispering. "Thank you." I remembered the others were there and waved a hand in Connie's direction. "Guys, this is Connie. Probably the best necromancer I've ever seen in action. She's also Heather's little sister, so make her feel welcome."

Nobody spoke. Babs raised an eyebrow at me. I looked around and noticed the others trading odd looks with each other. After a few moments, Connie smirked. I threw up my hands. "I'm the only one who didn't know? Seriously? What kind of asshole have I been all this time?"

Byron put his hand at his heart and rolled his eyes skyward. "Let me count the ways..."

"Shut up, Byron." I managed to laugh, mostly at myself. Which made me wince. The headache was starting to return. I checked my watch, took a breath, then nodded at the assembled mages. The gathered old friends. "Thank you. All of you. And welcome to my home. Victor's got Thumper on top of Stone Mountain. And he's got country vampires and renfields backing him up. He's expecting me at midnight. He notices anyone besides myself, Byron, and Connie, he mutilates Thumper without hesitating." I checked my phone. "It's just before ten now. It's a twenty minute drive to the base of the mountain, and about a thirty minute walk up the side in the dark. Come on inside, help yourselves to whatever you need. We roll out in forty-five minutes."

I turned and led everyone else into the house. But instead of leading everyone upstairs to the kitchen, I went downstairs and turned left into the garage. There I set about unlocking the garage vault. First with a padlock that looked ordinary, but the key would be entirely different if turned left than it did when turned right. Following that was a sixteen-digit combination on a keypad.

It was somewhat crowded in the garage. Lori, shaking her head, spoke up first. "Fun as it sounds, I don't think we have time to ooh and ah over your gun collection, Travis."

Becky Sue snorted. "Or for all them leather toys you made over the years."

I smirked, entering the last few digits. "You're both wrong."

I lifted the bar up and out, opening both doors to the vault. Reaching to the ceiling, I turned on the lights. The vault was half the size of a shipping container. Both walls were lined to the ceiling with racks and cases of ammo. I stepped back and waved at the collection.

"Pistol calibers are on the left wall, rifle and shotgun along the right. Arrows, crossbow bolts, grenades, smoke, and pyro are in the back. If you want anything really special, there's a manifest taped up inside the door. Help yourselves."

My friends took a moment to stare. With the exception of Byron and possibly Bubba, it was more ammo than any of them had ever seen in one place.

Lori broke the silence. "Well then. Blessed be and pass the ammunition."

* * *

"Byron, where does Travis keep the gun oil?"

"Liquor cabinet. Bottom shelf. Next to the cheap vodka."

Everyone had grabbed a cup of what they liked and got to work. Byron and Cyrus were plotting at the dining room table over a map. Seb was changing out the heads on all his arrows. I didn't have thermite arrowheads for him and no time to machine any, so he was replacing his broadheads with bodkins. With vampires, penetration in the hopes of finding a heart was going to be more effective than widespread soft tissue damage on the way in. Seb was a musician by trade on the Renaissance festival circuit, but archery was one of his loves, and he could possibly give Byron a run for his money. Given we were dealing with vampires, his ballistic stakes would come in handy. As would his knowledge of the low roads, which would help us gain the advantage when we got to the mountain.

Lori had press-ganged Connie and taken over my kitchen to brew potions. Bubba and Becky Sue were cleaning weapons and loading magazines on my sofa, laying completed projects out on the coffee table. Shrapnel was sitting on one of her favorite perches on the back of the sofa, watching the sudden mob of guests with interest. As I came in, I could hear Lori and Connie's conversation first.

"I don't know how you could sleep after that!"

"I didn't, really. After he went to bed, I stayed up for an hour or two reading."

"What does Travis keep on the shelves these days?"

"In the guest room? The Anarchist's Cookbook."

"That piece of trash? He really hasn't changed."

"His personal copy was actually pretty entertaining. He'd gone through the entire thing with a red pen. Corrected all the recipes and some of the grammar. Went on a lot of rants in the margins. When he wasn't doodling in them, that is."

I shook my head, smiling, then wiped my brow as I headed down the stairs. I could tell myself it was just the usual swamp of Georgia summer making me sweat already. Shame I'm lousy at lying to myself.

Stepping past Alexandria's Revenge, I noticed the door to the garage was open. And a faint, moving green glow was inside. I'm not sure what kept me from yelling, but I slid out my wand and crept to the door. Years of experience kept my feet off the floorboards that creaked. My free hand gently brushed the door open as I crouched by the inside wall.

It was Babs. She was walking the perimeter of the room as best she could, swinging what looked like an ordinary green glowstick on a string. She never stopped swinging it in a circle, just paused to swing it in front of one project or another. As she swung it in front of my drill press I stood up.

"What color does it turn if I'm evil?"

She didn't stop swinging or even turn in my direction. "Red."

I stood there with my arms folded until she made it back to the doorway. Then I raised my hands in the standard detainee pose. I cut Babs off before she finished opening her mouth. "Shut the fuck up and do it before I slug you."

She shut up and kept swinging the stick, miming a raver's idea of a wanding, before letting the stick slow and stop. She grabbed it, then snapped it, which cut the light immediately, before tucking it into a pouch. Her eyes met mine defiantly.

I put my arms down. "Satisfied?"

She pondered this for a second before nodding. "Actually? Yeah. I don't want to think about what would happen if it had gone the other way."

"Yeah, well, make sure word gets out. I'm branding a devil on the ass of the next clown that pulls something like that."

"Sucks when you don't trust anyone, doesn't it?"

I waved my hand around to indicate the state of my world. "Yeah, well, look what happens when I do. What was I supposed to say at the funerals, Babs? My best friend killed half our class, but he also killed my girlfriend and punched his own ticket so we're all square now? I'm amazed I got through the funerals without having to fight a duel."

"And we're all amazed the next funeral wasn't yours."

My train of thought fell off the unfinished bridge and plunged into the gorge. "You what?"

When I turned to look at her, I saw Babs' eyes begin to glisten with tears. "We thought you were next, Travis. Andy blamed himself even though that was bullshit. Lily, we could blame on the trial. We got no justice there and Lily didn't want to live in a world without it. But the rest of us all came together afterwards. Except you. You kept pushing away. Heather was dead, Ethan was dead, and Thumper was in a coma. The rest of us were terrified we were going to bury you next. So you kept going away, and we kept letting you. Now look at us. Only reason we came was an elf stole your phone and you kept our numbers. We should have finished this years ago."

I wondered how many more ways I was going to feel like a jackass before the sun came up. I opened my arms, and Babs fell into them. We clutched each other tight for half a second before my body caught up with our emotions.

"Ow! Shit!"

"What?"

"Bruised ribs on that side. Still ain't healed from the other night."

She stared at me incredulously before we both busted out laughing. Laughing hurt just as much as the hug did and I so didn't care. I recovered first and held up a hand. "But you're here now. Now if I lose another friend tonight, it's not going to be for lack of trying or not bringing out the big guns. And If I live, then I can start working on being a better friend."

She smiled, her eyes glistening with tears still threatening to fall. "I can live with that."

"Good. Now get out. The others are gonna think we're having we're-all-gonna-die sex in here."

She grinned. "Ooh. You mean we're not?"

"Out."

"Damn. Your workbench was on my bucket list."

"Out!"

*   *   *

Bubba finished setting a new barrel into a well-used Mossberg 12ga shotgun, screwing the magazine knob back onto the tube. He lifted the polished wood stock to his broad shoulder and racked the slide. The action moved in a satisfying Ka-CHUNK sound that brought a smile to my face. I could see the kitchen lamps reflecting off the single word engraved into the receiver: PRIVILEGE.

I went to the end of the dining room table that wasn't being used and upended a cardboard box over it. A deluge of leather collars and cuffs in assorted colors dominated by basic black landed in a heap. Leather straps decorated with everything from spikes to rings to locking buckles fell on the table before I tossed the empty box into a corner.

"Anyone who wants to, armor up."

Becky Sue tilted her head, amused. "I thought we didn't have time for your kinky games, Travis."

I nodded. "We don't. I just don't have time to make these for everyone." I held up my arm, showing the wide, ring-decorated cuff on my wrist.

Seb cocked his head. "Those are supposed to be effective?"

I shrugged, waving my hand in the universal sign of possibility. "I know, I know, they look like metalhead accessories. But it makes sense, fighting vampires. Vampires are resource predators. I overheard Eva and Chittenden discussing it once."

Byron nodded, "Right, you got all your memory back."

"All at once. I still have a headache." I opened a cold soda and took a long swallow before continuing. "Anyway, I picked Eva's brain for how vamps fought in person. She was using me as a bodyguard as much as a boytoy, so she gave me a lotta intel. Vamps are used to taking humans one-on-one to feed. If they're fighting groups of humans, it's a torch and pitchfork mob. So they usually eat one fast as they can, then use the blood they gorged on for whatever their next step is: run, fight, whatever. Armor on your pulse points won't stop that, but it'll buy you a few seconds. And everyone in this room can do a lot with a few seconds."

Becky Sue grinned like a kid with a new toy. "Shit, I'll take some."

Becky Sue finished the magazine she was loading, then wandered over to paw through the leather. Byron didn't take his eyes off me, just raised an eyebrow. "How you holding up?"

I shrugged, then winced. "Dunno. Is there a gnome using my skull for an anvil at the moment?"

He didn't laugh. "Not that I can see."

"Oh good, it's just my throbbing migraine." I shrugged again. "I'm upright, speaking clearly and walking under my own power. Unless Lori's got a recipe for organic methadone that works for renfields in her handbag of doom, this is as good as I'm gonna get."

From the sink, Lori spoke up. "I wish I did. But that's a tall order even for me."

"No worries, Lori. I'll have to be satisfied going in with four times as many hitters as I thought I would." I sat down at the dining room table, my back to the front door. "Anyone else need anything?"

Babs shook her head. "Looks like we got this set up. Seb knows a low road he can take that will get him almost to the summit. Connie and Lori have a potion that will hide our body heat and heartbeats, should keep the country vamps from sensing us. You take your team up the long way and we'll meet in the middle."

I nodded. "Sounds good." I tossed a Strap Ball to Connie, who caught it easily. "I only have one of those, and you'll probably put it to good use. I don't need Victor in one piece, but it might make my life easier. I'll tell you the safeword on the way up there." Connie nodded, hooked it to her belt, and went back to helping Lori without a word. Nobody else bothered to comment.

Becky Sue had selected a wide collar of thick black leather with spikes and was posing for selfies in the hallway. Lori dried her hands on the towel hanging from my stove before wandering over to the sofa. "Bubba, you load those mags with Travis' thermite rounds for me?"

Bubba didn't miss a beat from the work he was doing, just pointed with his head to one of the stacks laid out on the coffee table. "Right over there, hon. I'll admit, I didn't have you pegged for a Glock girl."

"We all have stereotypes to overcome, dear."

I pulled a handful of IR chemlights from a cargo pocket and dropped them on the table near Seb, then checked my watch and got up. I resisted the urge to groan as my joints protested. "Five minutes before Team High Road rolls out. Babs, can we get a final briefing?"

Everyone finished up what they had and turned to look at Babs. She nodded, then pointed at the map. "Team High Road is who Victor's expecting: Travis, Connie, and Byron. They enter the park through the western entrance, then go up the hiking trail to the summit. They're expected at midnight, so we'll try and have them there at fifteen prior." Everyone nodded in turn as Babs met their eyes, then continued. "Team Low Road is everyone else. The potions Lori and Connie made should keep us hidden, but the longer we're there, the greater chance we'll be caught and Thumper will be fucked. So we'll time it to step out of the portal near the summit at five till. The portal's in this last copse of evergreens on the south side of the walking trail, just before the summit. Which is one of the last areas of cover even in darkness. Try not to get in a chase. Falling off the mountain's a lot easier than it looks, especially at night."

She took a breath, then kept going. "First and foremost, we're here to get Thumper. We grab them and we take them home. Seb will be closing the Low Road portal the moment we come through, so we'll be heading home down the mountain with team High Road's vehicles. Travis, adversaries?"

I held up my phone with a picture of Victor on it. "This walking jock itch is Victor. He's a city vampire, about two centuries old. Plotting to take over Atlanta's vampire community by having me put the current lord under a blood curse. He's got an unknown number of country vampires and renfields on the mountain with him. He also has Thumper in a renfield bond. I don't think Thumper wants to hurt us, but they're bound and determined to serve and defend Victor. Thumper knows how we've all operated in the past, so if you've learned new tricks they don't know about yet, keeping them handy would be a good idea."

Becky Sue nodded, her new spiked collar clashing loudly with her teased hair. "Thumper, Victor, and a peanut gallery of country vamps and renfields. Sounds easy enough."

I put my phone back in my pocket. "Killing or capturing Victor would be helpful, but unnecessary. Grabbing the vial of Lord Chittenden's blood he's carrying would also be helpful. But like Babs said, our main goal is Thumper and each other. We meet in the middle, but we'll all leave together. Connie and Byron are driving. If either of them are too injured, take their keys. Good to go?"

Nods all around.

"One more thing. My biggest screwup this entire time was allowing myself to be used as a renfield in the first place. We all know why and I'm not going to apologize. But I also can't let that happen to another mage ever again." I took a thumb drive out of my pocket and left it on the table. "If I go down, that drive has my full report of the plot against Lord Chittenden. Getting it to him will fulfill the terms of my Oath posthumously. It will also point out that I broke the renfield bond without explaining how. No matter what happens tonight, the Otherworld needs to know that can happen."

I tried not to tear up again. Instead of a suicide mission, I had a halfway decent chance of getting everyone home alive. And I was doing it with people I hadn't seen or been around in far too long. If I survived the night, I promised myself, I was going to change that.

I looked at each and every one of them in turn, then cracked a smile. "Let's go climb the mountain together."

*   *   *

Chapter Nineteen

"Guideline Twenty-eight:

Make plans, but have priorities.

When plans fall apart, you'll still know where to improvise."

Connie pulled up into the Confederate hall lot at Stone Mountain, just before the walkup trail. Byron in my SUV followed close behind. By unspoken agreement, we both parked facing outbound in case we had to leave in a hurry.

Stone Mountain is an enormous hunk of exposed granite that rises up out of the woods more or less east of Atlanta. The mountain and the surrounding park is a relatively popular tourist attraction. Although Atlanta being Atlanta, much of the attraction is due to the arguments around it. The north face has a gigantic bas-relief of Jefferson Davis, Robert E. Lee, and Stonewall Jackson, all of them on horseback. It's bigger than Mount Rushmore. It was also both paid for and used as a rally location for at least two different generations of the KKK. Even now, their successors hold more discreet meetings there.

Magically, Stone Mountain is a mystery collection. It sits on a junction of several ley lines, including one that merges to the southeast with the Blue River, less than two miles from the battle. Another big one follows an old hunting path straight through Atlanta, running parallel to I-20 but about five miles north. At the summit there once was a rock wall about four feet high. The local Creek and Cherokee claimed the wall was built before their ancestors came to the area. By the 20th century, the wall was broken up and gone. The spot is a lousy site for a fort, but a great one for ritual purposes. A handful of practitioners to this day go there to enact some of their more discreet workings.

Discretion wasn't on our minds that night. It was the 4th of July holiday, and a crowd was on the big lawn north of the mountain, packing up after the end of the first laser show or inbound for the second. The last of the fireworks were still going off as we came in from one of the western side entrances, which weren't even supposed to be open. I could almost smell Victor's influence as we stepped out into the warm summer night.

I stepped out of the car, my head giving an extra throb as my boots hit the pavement. Free of the comforting embrace of the air conditioning, I started sweating almost instantly. Rolling my neck and shoulders to work out the kinks from riding shotgun only made my aches more prominent. I thought again about the tube of blood in my pocket. The plan was solid. If I could just take the edge off. I forced myself to stop thinking in that direction. It was time to go to work.

I popped open the back of the Yukon and pulled out my staff. I'd made it myself: five feet of hand carved and stained oak. One end capped with a rubber walking tip, the other ending in a solid bulge the size of a normal man's fist. Twisting the bulge opened up a slot that fit my wand perfectly. I loaded my wand and locked the bulge in place. The staff was strengthened with several of my more intricate spells, and was a focus for several others. Plus, I could use it to walk up a mountain in the middle of the night. I glanced over to see Byron take out his own staff, which I knew was a glamoured boar spear. The elf knew his hunting tools. Connie had only her shoulder bag visible, though I could only imagine what her actual arsenal consisted of. I took another walking stick, this one completely unmagical, out of the Yukon, holding it up.

"Want a stick?"

She smirked, taking it. "Our third date and I already get presents? Cool."

I blushed and tried to wave it off. Then an old memory hit me and I was lost in thought for a moment. Connie must have noticed, given her reaction.

"If you're worried I'm expecting you to put out tonight, relax."

I shook my head and managed a smile. "Never mind."

"No, what?"

"It'll sound weird."

She raised an eyebrow. "Weird? To us?"

I managed a breath, my head still throbbing, then let myself actually smile. "Heather used to joke like that. Tease people into saying what they really thought. Made people comfortable like that."

I looked up off the ground to see she was smiling too. "That was kind of weird. I'm glad you told me, though."

The moment passed as I threw the sling bag over one side, A gym bag just long enough to carry a few baseball bats went over the other. She tilted her head. "What's in that one?"

I grinned like a kid who'd just gotten away with breaking the rules. "Homemade rocket launchers."

That got me a wry smile. "Really?"

I nodded, my inner weapons nerd coming forth. "Fifty millimeter HEDP warhead, saltwater countermass to keep the backblast to a minimum. Won't do much to a real tank. But anything up to an armored car will look like a beer can full of spaghetti with an M-80 in it."

"You do come prepared."

"The werewolves didn't attack Chittenden last year. But something big and hairy enough to be mistaken for one did. Probably whatever's been leaving carcasses lying around the Appalachians. If Victor still has it around, I want something handy to take care of it."

"And that'll do the job?"

I shrugged. "Spent a summer testing it a few years back. A distant cousin has over a hundred acres in the back end of Louisiana, no neighbors, and a wild hog problem. The final version turned a two hundred pound porker into instant barbecue spread out over half a football field. It'll do for bloodsuckers easy enough."

Byron raised an eyebrow. "Babs would have a fit if she knew you were bringing that."

I smiled. "Good thing she doesn't know I'm bringing two then."

*   *   *

If you ever get the feeling that you're being watched, you probably are. That's not paranoia. It's just the multitude of people and critters out there in the world that can make themselves undetectable by basic human senses. A lot of em take the excuse to be complete voyeurs and run with it. The paranoia is assuming that what's watching you has a particular interest in who you are and what you're doing. Unless you're like me, in which case you've annoyed enough people to be sure they're interested. The distance between paranoia and preparation is only a couple inches of dictionary page.

That said, the feeling that you're being watched is one of the magical senses being alerted. The same way magic is a collection of sciences not understood enough, the magical senses alert us in ways we don't have the common vocabulary to express.

We knew there were eyes on us before we were halfway up the mountain. All three of us mentally noted and ignored said eyes while keeping up the pace. A few strides later, a figure stepped out from the shadows between the trees to the north. By the time he stepped out far enough to block our way, I could see he was a young black man in a sleeveless hoodie. His arms had enough muscle definition to be visual aids in an anatomy class. I didn't recognize him, but figured he was here on Victor's behalf. We stopped outside of spear range, just to be polite.

After an awkward moment, I decided to break the silence. Memories of being Eva's security lead came to the fore in my head and I settled on a casual tone. "Hey, I'm Travis. You new? I ain't seen you around."

A nod from Muscles. "A job's a job."

Connie bit her lip mischievously. "Nice definition."

Muscles nodded politely. "Thank you." His eyes flickered, then hardened. "Where's the other one?"

A quick glance around revealed that Byron had disappeared. Muscles was getting more nervous by the second, and I was moderately surprised he hadn't drawn a weapon yet. I rolled my eyes. "Byron, we're here on business. Stop screwing around."

"What?"

We all turned to look further up the path, where Byron stood in plain sight a few paces away from Muscles. I sighed the sigh of the world-weary. "Knock it off, Byron." I turned back to Muscles. "Lead on."

Muscles recovered well, I'll give him that. "Walk with me please."

Muscles walked past Byron without any petty shoving. Byron, for his point, took a moment to check out Muscles' butt before joining us in our walk. I tried not to roll my eyes again, then looked back at our guide. Polite, professional, hardworking, responded to flirtation on the clock with professionalism, I kinda liked Muscles already. Byron and I didn't need to trade glances as we sensed two more people following us as we went.

When we got to the small pavilion and walkway with guide rails that were near the summit, I could see a small light reflecting off of moving bodies in the distance. Far beyond was the horizon from the mountain into the stars. To the north I could see the lights from the crowd far below us, gathered to watch the laser show.

As we kept coming, Byron and Connie flanking me, our walking sticks punctuating our footfalls, I could make out individuals slowly walking in and out of the shadows. I couldn't tell the difference between renfields and country vampires, except the former were more likely to have clean and untorn clothes. The small light turned out to be a battery powered camping lantern set on the ground, throwing up light at the nearer figures. Opposite us with his back to the closed and dark restaurant at the summit was Victor. For once he was dressed to the nines, wearing a tailored suit that looked more expensive than my truck. Crumpled in a barely upright heap at Victor's feet was Thumper. They looked starved and gang beaten all at once. Their eyes had sunken back into their head. What skin they had was either fishbelly pale or covered in bruises. My heart sank at seeing them put together like that. Thumper finally looked away from us and up at Victor, like a whipped dog looking for any sign of approval. I mentally shoved my rage back into a quiet room. I could bring it back when it was time for me to let Victor suffer.

The renfields and country vamps were constantly moving, making it hard for me to tell how many there were. I counted perhaps a dozen before Victor waved like he was greeting old fraternity brothers at a summer cookout.

"Travis! My man with the plans! Almost fifteen minutes prior, just like I thought. What's that old Marine Corps saying you told mom that one time? If you're early, you're on time. If you're on time, you're late..."

I nodded, "... and if you're late, you're fucked."

He snapped his fingers. "That's what I'm talking about! And rolling deep with that squad of yours. Grunt, Ranger, and Necromancer. If I played D&D I'd be aroused. Y'all can stay where you are."

We stopped maybe twenty yards from him. I didn't have to look to know we were surrounded. I recognized some of Eva's human security guards, as well as at least one of Tasha's renfields.

"You upped your entourage, Vic. Moving up in the world."

"That's what happens when you keep on inheriting, man. My mother and sister left some folks at liberty."

"Mighty big of you to take them on. And a few more besides, looks like."

He shrugged. "I got a lot of things to do. Gonna need a lot of hands on deck. If nothing else, figuring out what to do with all the furniture is gonna be a stone bitch."

I made eye contact with a handful of them. Some were still human, as renfields still counted. Some even looked like they were questioning their life choices. I try not to kill humans if I can possibly avoid it. I try not to kill anyone, for that matter. It's like unclogging a toilet. Sometimes life gets nasty enough that it's a job that needs doing, but anyone who goes around bragging at how good they are at it deserves the dirty looks they get.

Thus, I had to try to avoid it. So I spoke up. "Gentlemen, ladies, if there are any among you, I'd guess that the ink on some of your contracts is still drying, so let me be honest. I'm here to settle accounts with your headman there. Violence may indeed ensue. Walk away, right now, and you have my word I won't follow you with it. Beyond that, I can't make guarantees. Just an assurance that my conscience will be clear no matter what."

Victor stood there grinning like an idiot. Not one of his followers; human, renfield, or vampire, had moved. Thumper shivered at Victor's feet. Even Muscles seemed to harden in their resolve more than anything. Victor held out his hands.

"Nice offer. Pity I didn't keep anyone who would've taken you up on it."

Byron held out his hand to me, nodding. "I tried telling him that."

I sighed, pulled a five-dollar bill from my pocket, and handed it over to Byron. "It was worth a shot."

"It's a damn shame you couldn't see the writing on the wall, Travis." Victor sneered down at Thumper. "Thumper was telling you the truth, I would have held your Oath paid in full. But you just couldn't hold up your end of the deal, could you?"

I smirked. "You haven't even kicked off your little coup and your co-conspirators are both dead. I made a deal with you, but I swore an Oath to Chittenden. Risk my magic on the off chance you succeed where they failed? No way. The Otherworld enforces that shit, Vic. It's why we're not all long dead. I'm not surprised Eva never filled you in there. I am surprised you didn't take me up on my offer. It's already over, Vic. Chittenden knows. You're not going to see the end of the week."

His stupid smile never dropped. "Really? Tell him yourself, did you?"

"Called Oswald."

Victor snorted. "And you think he dutifully reports to his master? The way you did? The way Thumper here did?"

He had a point there. Renfield loyalty was deep, but it wasn't absolute. I was a prime example of that. But it was equally likely he was bluffing. And I wasn't about to give him the satisfaction of seeing me in doubt. "Oswald's done exactly that for a long time. And he's not a mage."

Victor waved a dismissive hand. "His days are numbered. Half the renfields in this city follow me now. I might even be able to take him down without the blood curse. I'm going to have it done anyway, of course. But now it's more insurance than linchpin."

I nodded, "The country vamps."

Victor waved at one I hadn't even noticed yet. "These guys? Hell yeah! Chittenden and his old school assholes kick these guys out of civilization any chance they get. And what's the damn point? So they eat messy sometimes. That's what it's like out in the country. And country is what Atlanta is. Shit, turn around if you don't believe me! You can barely see the skyscrapers for all the trees!"

"So you'll take over Chittenden's court and let these guys feed on Atlanta?"

He shrugged. "Who needs a court when you have a horde? Sometimes the older ways are even better."

Behind Victor, what I'd thought was a boulder started to move. As it kept moving, I realized it was a humanoid of some sort that had been squatting down watching me. It began to stand up and kept on going. Making it all the more eerie was the fact that it didn't make a sound in the process.

I'm a big guy. This guy was ridiculous. Easily had a head and shoulders on me, and at least eighty pounds. He was built like a weightlifter, a thick barrel torso and limbs that were all muscle. But I'd never seen a bodybuilder with claws before. He was covered in what had long ago crossed the line from body hair to fur.

Victor glanced at it, then smiled. "Oh yeah, here's the country vamps' head honco. No fancy titles or anything. They just call him Moose. Apparently it's his favorite food."

The last piece of the puzzle fell into place. "The so-called werewolf attack on Chittenden."

Victor snapped his fingers and pointed at me. "You are a sharp one, Trav." He turned back. "Hey Moose, do me a favor and cover our escape, if you would be so kind."

Moose paused for a second, then nodded, turning past us. Something that damn big moving that damn quietly gave me the creeps.

I shook my head, then winced as my headache flared. "Screw it. Gimme the blood so I can cast this curse and take Thumper with me."

Thumper croaked. It was the first time I'd heard their voice in the real world over a decade. They had been a redneck alto. Now they were barely human. "Sorry Travis. I shouldn't have gotten you-"

Victor kicked Thumper in the ribs, bringing a cry of pain followed by several hacking coughs from them. I managed not to clench my jaw seeing that. Victor shook his head as if disappointed by a misbehaving puppy. "You hear that? How's an incantation for that blood curse supposed to make it through vocal chords like that? Must have lost her goddamned mind. Still, she's been useful enough in her time. Even warned me about that low road over there."

Victor waved a hand south of us. Near the last copse of trees, about fifty yards away, I could see what I'd thought at first was a shadow and some rocks. Instead it was a hasty machine gun nest. The gunner was laid out in the prone on the smooth rock of the mountain. I recognized the model of his gun as an FN M240, a Belgian machine gun I'd used in the Marines. Not sure what it was about Belgium, but finding better waffles, chocolate, or machine guns was not easy. They'd laid down sandbags, giving the bipod of the gun something to dig into rather than the slippery, unyielding granite. The muzzle was aimed directly between a familiar-looking pair of trees. Next to the gunner, an ammo bearer was sitting down, watching us. They'd daisy-chained several cans of ammo into one long belt, laid out neatly to feed the gun hundreds of rounds.

And my friends were going to walk right into those rounds in a few minutes.

Time to bluff harder. I kept my poker face on even as my heart heated up. "Let's get on with this. I don't have all night."

Victor shook his head, waving his finger at me like a teacher at a naughty student. "Slow down there, Trav. See, you cast this curse for me, I'll let Thumper go. But I've gotten used to having a mage for a renfield. And I'm not leaving here without one."

Byron almost growled. "That wasn't part of the..." He stopped when I held up my hand. A bead of sweat ran down my cheek. Byron stepped back. I stared at Victor a long time, then nodded. I was about to take a step forward when Victor's hand shot up in a halting gesture. I froze.

Victor gave that smirk I wanted to punch clean off his face. "Not so fast, magic man. I haven't forgotten what little miss grave rot here did to Tasha. I'm gonna have some insurance, if you know what I mean. Besides, you look like you could use a little pick me up."

Victor threw a slender object at me, which my dialed-up reflexes let me catch instantly. I could smell it almost as soon as I touched it. It was a tube full of vampire blood. I shuddered. I nearly drooled. I held it up in the moonlight, feeling the craving run through my body. I could barely keep myself from taking a sniff as if it was a fine cigar.

Victor quipped, "Fascinating, isn't it?" I caught myself staring at the tube and finally lowered it, looking Vic in the eye as I tucked the tube into my pocket.

Victor held up a finger. "Now, now, Trav. That's my blood. And I know you must be hurting for a dose. I want you nice and focused when I give you Chittenden's and get this curse going. Wouldn't want you drinking a component before setting it in motion, yes?"

I looked over my shoulder. "Byron?"

He looked warily, still holding his spear ready as he could without directly aiming it at anyone present. "Yeah?"

"Do me a favor and settle my affairs."

Byron's face grew stoic, the way elves in the middle of serious business would be expected to look. "You sure about this, Travis?"

I nodded gravely, trying both to speed it up and not looking like I was trying to speed it up. "Yeah. Yeah, I'm sure. Make the arrangements." I looked Vic in the eye, pulling the tube out of my pocket and grabbing the stopper. "You're right. Lemme get my fix and give me Chittenden's blood, I'll fire off that curse hard enough to take him down. My Oath said I just had to serve the old bastard for a year and a day. And it's almost midnight."

Vic chuckled outright. "You? I was reborn at night, Travis. But not last night. I know all about Otherworld Oaths. I know what you owe to the Wild Hunt. And I'm not about to risk insulting the Hunt by taking you away to be my own personal plaything." Vic pointed straight at Connie. "This one, on the other hand? Now, she'd be all manner of useful."

Connie kept most of her poker face, but her eyes grew wide. I almost growled. "What?"

"You heard me, Travis. She's been nothing but trouble since the day I picked her out for Tasha's ritual. If there's a witch among you that needs to be on a leash, it's this one. I'm not sure how you managed to break the bond with mom, but I'll make sure this one never does that with me. I'll even give her the fun of putting the blood curse on old Chitty, once she's got her mind in the right place. You're right, it looks like a simple enough spell."

My hand was clenching my staff hard enough to nearly dent the wood. "Not going to happen, Vic."

That damned smirk just wouldn't go away, "When is it gonna get through your ironmongering skull that it ain't your call, Travis?"

Connie held out her hand. "Give me the blood, Travis."

I turned to her, "What?"

Byron gripped his spear tighter. "What?"

"You're not the only one who owes a debt. You saved me when you didn't have to. I'll be all right." Connie stepped closer to me and smiled. Her voice softened and dropped, as if she was almost sharing a secret. "I saw how you looked at her, Travis. When her blood was in you. I've never looked at anyone like that in my life. There's far worse I could do than feel like that for a good cause."

She took my face in her hands, took one step closer, and kissed me. I was frozen to the spot, stunned beyond measure. I closed my eyes and disappeared into that kiss. I was somewhere I knew nothing about. I knew the far reaches science had never approached, but what was happening between my own heart and the one beating so close to mine was an undiscovered country. There was only the feel of her soft hands, fingerless fishnet gloves, and the well worn leather of her wrist cuffs against my skin. Only her lips against my own. Only the scent of leather and sandalwood and rose oil.

It was compassion.

It was forgiveness.

It was goodbye.

She took the tube from my unresisting hand, wrapping her fingers gently around the smooth tempered glass. I opened my eyes. Through falling tears, I could almost see her shiver a bit in the lantern light.

She whispered. "So much power in such a little tube. No wonder the stories get told this way."

She twisted off the stopper easily. The scent of the blood hammered at my enhanced senses, almost making me stagger. My mouth was dry from hunger, and I was hard as a rock. My shirt was soaked with sweat. Connie smiled as the raised the tube in an obscene toast, throwing her head back and pouring the contents down. It went down slow but smooth, the consistency of maple syrup. I could see the shudder as the first rush of power slammed through her body. She gave a tiny ecstatic moan, and I could see her tongue flick around the edges of the tube for the last few dregs of the blood.

In one long exhale, she nearly swooned, dropping the tube to let it clink on the rocks. Her staff fell from her other hand, clattering. Every muscle in her body flexed, and she breathed again in what was nearly an orgasmic sigh.

"No wonder you kept this up for a year, Trav. Oooh..."

I clenched my jaw, finally finding my voice. "She drank it, now let Thumper go."

Vic gave a smirk so triumphant I wanted to punch him on general principle. "What's the rush? Come on over, darling."

Connie smiled languidly as she began to saunter towards him, unsteady on her feet. "Yes, Master."

"Now that's what I liked to hear. Thumper here never could get that one straight."

Connie's walk was becoming more of a strut by the moment, even as she looked back at me. "It's OK, Travis," she purred, "I was worried for a second about my doctorate and everything. But y'know, if I get to feel like this on the regular? Fair trade. Besides, lotta powerful women took a path like this. Bowing to a king-" just inside arm's reach of Victor, she took one knee, then another, sitting back on her boot heels- "and kneeling for a man."

Vic shoved Thumper away, letting them stumble. "It's going to be good, being both."

Byron caught the staggering Thumper, gently helping them up.

Vic opened his arms. "Stick around, ladies and gents. Catch the show. No point in unwary phone calls happening, no?"

I nearly growled. "We had a deal, Vic."

"And I stuck to it. You have your companion. But I don't yet have my curse."

Vic drew another blood tube and a scrap of paper from his pocket. "Chittenden's blood and the curse. Requires nothing more than a candle and an invocation. Simple enough, yes? Now put down those staves, gents. We wouldn't want anything sudden to kick in."

I knew there were minions with pistols aimed at my back and Byron's. Both of us were wearing charms that could allay that, but Vic was too focused on us. I dropped my staff, letting it come to a stop on my instep, and Byron let go of his spear. Connie rummaged through her purse, finding a small pillar candle and a bronze plate, setting it up as prim and proper as an impromptu tea party.

"Thank you, gents. Feel free to watch the show. I'm sure a little ritual magic is nothing you haven't seen before. But watching a lord who reigned for over a century fall from grace? That's a once-in-a-lifetime."

At Victor's feet, Connie nuzzled his leg like a cat, then lit the candle by passing her fingers over the wick wordlessly. The faint scent of honey in the air told me that she'd come prepared with beeswax. Victor turned away at the sight of the flame, an age-old fear clamped down with practiced willpower.

Byron stumbled, taking a knee with Thumper in his arms.

I folded my arms, trying to keep a snarl out of my voice. "This was a bad idea from start to finish, Vic. And Chittenden will see you in ashes for it."

He sneered, shaking his head. "You young wizards have no idea what progress really means."

"And you old vampires have no clue how much the world left you behind. You're not a vampire lord, you're a gas station knife. You're dull, you're tacky, and you're destined to hurt some poor bastard that didn't know any better. You belong in a dusty plastic case between the bootleg CD's and the hooker thong incense. But I'll settle for dropping off your staked ass at Chittenden's office with my next invoice."

Victor's sneer became a snarl. "You miserable shit. You think running to tattle at that fat old fuck would stop me?" He took a page torn out of a book, handing it triumphantly to Connie while keeping his eyes on me. "I have the allegiance of the country vampires! I have years of planning and no rivals left! And now I have a peerless necromancer bound to serve by the power of my blood!"

I shrugged. As my hands rose to the level of my shoulders, Victor's eyes widened in realization. I didn't need a wand or a staff to open up any number of ass-kicking spells. I just needed a clear line of fire. And he'd just given me one.

*   *   *

Chapter Twenty

"Guideline Seventeen:

Don't bury the bodies in your own yard.

If feasible, bury them in the yard of someone you don't like."

Victor saw it coming, but not in time to warn his cronies as I opened my arms, shoving them outward to the side. Magic surged in my body as I called, *"HAMRAR!"*

A expanding circular wave of kinetic energy burst from my body at the height of my shoulders. Connie, Thumper, and Byron were all crouched down below it. Everyone else took a hit to the head from the dodgeball of the ancient gods. Every renfield, country vampire, and hanger-on went down, one behind me getting a shot off in the air. Victor almost landed headfirst into the ritual candle Connie had lit. He scrambled away from the flame, just shy of panic.

I was already in motion, having kicked my staff back into my hand and headed straight for the machine gun. Team Low Road was inbound any second and I had to get that gun down now. I could hear screaming, growling, and the impact of bodies hitting rock behind me as Byron tried not to be overwhelmed.

The ammo bearer saw me coming, drew a pistol and started dumping the mag in my general direction. I didn't slow down. Sounds suicidal, but I was counting on him not being much in the way of trained. If he had a clue, he was aiming for my armored torso. It was also the middle of the night and he suddenly had a pissed off wizard the size of a hairy sofa heading for him at full speed. Things like that will throw off someone's aim if they're not used to it.

Running into the gunfire, I gripped my staff just a touch harder, whispered, "*Geirr,*" and hurled it knob-first like a javelin. My staff shot out in a tight arc, the knob morphing into a hardened spike in midair. It flew just under the ammo bearer's shooting arm, impaling him just under the rib cage. He collapsed on the rock, his pistol clattering into the darkness.

The gunner heard her partner go down, and turned away from the gun just as I caught her in a flying tackle. She went down fighting, getting one arm free. She flailed at my head before I grabbed her shoulders, slamming her head against the ammo cans. She yelled in pain and kept swinging for me, her gloved fists barely missing my face. I caught movement out of the corner of my eye, grabbed the gunner by the shirt and rolled, pulling her on top of me. The ammo bearer, his face and side covered in blood, put five bullets into the gunner's back, where I'd been an instant before. Two of the rounds went through her body, hitting my spidersilk shirt and cracking my ribs behind it. The wind was knocked out of me even as the gunner spit blood in my face. I got a hand free, drew my Beretta, and put two rounds in the ammo bearer's chest, with a third into his throat. He slumped over, the thermite rounds sizzling in his flesh.

I shoved the gunner's body off me, gasping for breath. Looking back, I saw a handful of Victor's people heading my way, the rest in confusion. Byron was probably throwing illusions around and spreading panic. I couldn't see Moose, who was next on my mental threat list. A half second let me see Thumper and Connie weren't in my line of fire. I lined up my pistol and started shooting. The rearmost stumbled and fell after two rounds. The next in line fell three shots later. Third up kept moving after three more rounds went in him, then howled eerily as his chest ignited. The wail distracted most of the crowd, including the last one running to me, who turned to look.

I bent my elbows, lifting my pistol closer to me and whispered, "*Molon Labe.*" A stylized Greek helmet on the magazine plate glowed and faded in an instant. I extended the pistol again and fired five more rounds into the back of my last attacker, who burst into flames as swiftly as his companion did. The two writhed on the ground, trying to beat out the flames themselves.

Now that reloading my pistol wasn't an issue, I went for the machine gun. I could hear Victor swearing loudly, trying to assume something resembling command. I didn't do much more than slew the gun to the Northwest, keeping the portal on my left. A sandbag let me set the bipod up and with a little give, and shoving the other sandbags out of the way let me drop to the ground and sight in. Old memories let me do a quick function check: feed tray, bolt, safety, charging handle, everything up. The growing crowd was only getting bigger, and sooner or later they'd either swarm Byron or use Thumper and Connie as hostages, so I made a choice.

Taking a breath, I bellowed, "Byron, down!"

I gave him a single beat to get clear, then opened up with the longest burst I'd shot in years. The ammo was a helpful mix of ball and tracer rounds, so I was able to walk my shots a little, tearing through vampire and renfield alike. The mob looking for Byron scattered, so I let go of the trigger and slewed the muzzle of the gun over towards Connie. She was on her knees, holding open a folded sheet of paper and chanting something I couldn't hear from the gunfire. I screamed on the off-chance the reverse wasn't true.

"Connie, down!"

From her kneepads she hit the prone easily, and I could see the faint glow of a kinetic shield. She didn't even stop her chant. The group surrounding her had a half second to try and run. It didn't do them much good, as a stream of lead flew across them, punching holes in living and dead flesh. A falling vampire corpse came within inches of disturbing her candle.

A massive pain bloomed in my right side as if I'd been hit in the ribs with a hot hammer, knocking me off the gun and onto my left side. One of the renfields I'd recognized earlier was holding a smoking pistol aimed right at me. Behind him was a squad's worth of dark shapes, all of them country vampires by the look of them. The preview lights for the laser show gave the horizon of the mountain a soft glow, backlighting them all. I could barely breathe without screaming from the pain in my ribs. I didn't move. If I went for my pistol, holstered on my left side and currently under my body, he'd finish me off.

Through the pain I could hear Victor screaming. "I want the wizard alive! Take him alive! So I can kill him slow!"

I laughed, then winced, then spit blood. Then I regretted it, feeling the wave of hungry anger coming from the country vampires. I managed to shake my head a little, meeting the eyes of the renfield who'd shot me. Orders or no, if I moved wrong, this guy was going to shoot me again and worry about Victor's wrath later.

I groaned. "Typical asshole boss, huh? Top shelf for him, cash bar for you."

Not the best last words in history.

*   *   *

Chapter Twenty-One

"Guideline Thirty:

When the cavalry arrives, try not to spook the horses."

From behind me came a slow grinding sound, like an old oak door moving against a worn stone floor. I couldn't take my eyes off of the renfield holding me at gunpoint. What I could do, once I realized what was going on, was slowly smile bigger and bigger until he started getting nervous about what I knew and he didn't.

There was a whisper of movement, and an arrow sprouted from the renfield's eyeball. As his body collapsed, gunshots began to ring out again. Overhead, Lori flew past on her broomstick, hat held in place with a strap under her chin and flight goggles shielding her eyes. One of her boots was using the leather loop near the bristles as a stirrup. She was holding onto the broom with one hand while strafing the gathered country vamps with her Glock. Two of the vampires burst into flames, howling in pain and rage. Lori cackled a gleeful war cry as she came around for another pass.

I rolled over, gasping at the pain. One of my ribs was definitely broken. But I had to smile at the sight of team Low Road charging through the portal. Seb took three steps before going down on one knee and loosing his next arrow. Babs passed him with her pistol at the low ready, Cyrus on her heels with his cane and Bowie knife in hand. Bubba lifted Privilege to his shoulder and let her roar, chambering another shell as a vampire I couldn't see shrieked in pain. A full grown mountain lion wearing Becky Sue's collar charged the crowd, knocking a screaming renfield down in a tackle. Blood flew as they both hit the solid rock of the mountain.

Bubba saw me down and ran, slinging Privilege across his broad back as he went.

"Trav! You good?"

"Got hit. Dunno if it penetrated."

Babs covered us while Bubba manhandled me. I winced as he got to certain spots, which made him nod stoically in response. Bubba was a veterinarian who lived out in the sticks. Which meant he was used to healing big, dumb animals. I held that comforting thought close. He pulled a one-ounce vial out of his overalls and handed it to me. "Drink this. If you live, I'll tell you what else to do."

I popped the cork. "You should've been a corpsman, Bubba." I swallowed it in one hit. It tasted powerful and foul, like a bad moonshine. But it worked. The pain in my chest turned to heat inside a few breaths. I was already soaked with sweat and was only going to be stickier, but it was summer in Atlanta, who'd notice?

Bubba helped me up. I slapped his shoulder in thanks. "Have fun. I gotta destroy this gun and I'll meet you over by Connie." He nodded and shouldered Privilege again, letting the shotgun roar.

Cyrus ran full out towards a waiting vampire with a stocky build, only to turn at the last moment, vanishing into a shadow. The stocky vampire turned, then bared his fangs and hissed, seeing Cyrus emerge from behind a tree, knife and cane at hand. The stocky vampire took a single step, then froze, the pointed tip of Cyrus' cane bursting from between his ribs. The illusion of Cyrus that had stepped out from behind the tree tipped his hat gallantly and vanished into shadows. The real Cyrus, standing behind the staked vampire, brought his Bowie knife down in an arc that decapitated his opponent in one blow. Cyrus kicked the rapidly decomposing vampire corpse off his cane before ducking back into another shadow.

We were in the thick of it now, and the machine gun had become more of a problem than a solution. I popped the cover and cleared the ammo belt off the tray. From my belt pouch I grabbed a thermite grenade. The military uses ones the size of a soup can. My homemade ones were closer to the size of an energy shot bottle, but it would do the job. I let the bolt close on it, wedging the grenade between the bolt and the receiver. A pull of the pin and letting go of the handle later, and I had a tiny welding torch destroying the machine gun from the inside out.

I got to my feet as the gun began to weld itself useless, checking to make sure my pistol was still there. The crowd was ignoring me for the moment, so I spent a handful of awkward seconds with my boot on the ammo bearer's corpse, pulling my staff from their torso. The wet sound it made was more disgusting than the look. I left the machine gun nest at a limp. Then Bubba's potion kicked in further, the warmth radiating from my body. I chugged another swallow of water as sweat made my clothes stick.

Mercifully, none of the bodies on the rock were ours. Byron was blood-ied but holding his own, jumping in and out of shadows easily as Cyrus was. Babs had tagged Byron out and was guarding the recumbent form of Thumper, shooting anyone not us that came near. Seb and Bubba fought back to back, bow and shotgun in accord. Becky Sue, her muzzle covered in blood, was terrifying the remaining renfields. Here and there were small, smoking heaps where vampires had once been. It looked like Cyrus' theory about flammable vampire blood was on the money.

Victor was crouched behind a chanting Connie, letting his people do the fighting. None of us managed to get within twenty feet of him, and I didn't look to see if any of us had even tried.

The renfields seemed to be mostly dead or gone, but the vampires were fighting hard. Those I'd suppressed with the machine gun had shaken it off and come back with a vengeance. I couldn't see Moose, and that worried me. A vampire tried to catch Cyrus, who sidestepped and lopped off one of the vampire's hands with his Bowie knife, lashing the screaming bloodsucker across the face before turning to the next problem.

A vampire, a big male, caught me in a flying tackle. I went down, screaming in pain as my torso hit solid rock. What felt like flames of liquid pain shot up and down both sides of my rib cage. I spun, trying to bring my pistol to bear, but the bloodsucker caught my wrist and pinned it to the ground. If I hadn't kept my finger off the trigger I'd have fired off a wasted shot into the darkness.

He hissed into my face, fangs bared completely. The feeling put a bolt of primal fear down my spine solid enough to compete with the pain in my sides. Vampires creep people out because they do all the right things but they still feel all wrong. City vamps can easily blow enough pheremones under your nose that leave you too distracted to notice that you're prey. Country vamps are apex predators and they know it, chasing and attacking like anything else their size. Humans have lost the apex predator sweepstakes enough to understand when an angry beast is ready to eat them. Muzzle in the face, fangs out, drool on your clothes. It's no fun, but it's normal.

It's when the breath of the beast is ice cold that human nature wants to hit the time out button with a hammer. Everything in your body tells you it's not just death, but wrong death. I can see where a lot of victims would be paralyzed until the inevitable came.

Personally, I'm more of a practical sort.

I drew a knife with my right hand and started punching holes up and down the vampire's side. Long-dead meat and tattered clothes gave way under sharpened steel with a wet squelching sound, like punching cantaloupes. He shrieked in fury, more slaver splattering my face, then he froze as something hit him from the side. The vampire collapsed, fletches of Seb's arrow sprouting from his armpit.

The falling vampire knocked the wind out of me, sending fresh bolts of pain up my sides. My gun hand free, I got the vamp in a hug and rolled him off me. The bleeding, paralyzed body fell stiffly onto its back, and the overwhelming smell of vampire blood passed my nose again.

The pain began to fade into a dull heat, overshadowed by the hunger and arousal that kept growing by the moment. Time slowed down for me. My friends, my enemies, the battle itself, all faded into the background. All I could see was the knife. Slathered with that thick blood like the knife that spread syrup on my waffles. Just a taste was all I needed.

Just a taste.

Yeah, I don't need telepathy to read your thoughts about now. I'd truly hit rock bottom and decided to start coal mining while I was down there. Which, if I'm gonna be honest, happens. Magic doesn't make you any less of a fallible human. We may be the guides and guardians of humanity itself, but that doesn't let us stand apart from what makes us human. Including the potential to fuck up completely. I could've wound up in a flophouse with a needle. I could've wound up in an alley with a bottle. Instead I wound up on top of Stone Mountain, drooling at my own knife, slathered with a couple tonguefuls of vampire blood.

If you're looking for inspiration, I don't have much. What I do have is the knowledge that, as long as you're still alive, you still got options. So even though I was ignoring my loved ones, my Oaths, and everything that truly mattered to me, I still had hope.

In my case, hope came in the form of Babs and her size nine boot upside my head.

"Travis!"

My knife clattered away, taking my heart with it. A screaming whistle came from the north, and fireworks began going off overhead. The midnight laser show had begun. I was mildly grateful to realize that. It meant not everything was going off inside my head. I was on my hands and knees on the rock, feeling the pain coming back everywhere. I could see Victor crouched behind Connie a few yards away. Connie was still chanting, her recital growing faster and louder. Finally, her candle burst into a tongue of purple flame three feet high before sputtering out, consuming what was left of the wax and leaving a scorchmark on the rock. Connie exhaled, seemingly exhausted.

"Travis!"

I winced. Babs was close. Almost on top of me, though covering me from Victor and his remaining vampires with her pistol. I licked my lips in a vain attempt at moisture before looking at her closer.

"Babs?"

"Get up, Travis. Time to go."

She hauled me to my feet. I had the presence of mind to holster my pistol and hold onto my staff to keep from falling. A whistle at my side caused me to look, seeing Byron emerge from the trees behind us. Babs looked over at him. "You give them the keys?"

Byron frowned. "No, why?"

"They're headed down the mountain. If they can be there with the engine running-."

"-Wait. They're already heading down?" Byron's face looked more concerned by the moment.

"Going already?"

Victor was back on his feet, with a shit-eating grin plastered across his smug face and Connie on his arm like a drunken prom date. My brain was putting everything back together at speed. At the same time, my heart sank as I noticed the missing variables.

"Where are the others?" I muttered to Babs.

"They grabbed Thumper and headed down the mountain."

Victor was close enough for his ugly smile to grow even wider as Babs told me. I didn't even try to hide the incoming despair. "Oh, shit."

Victor snapped his fingers, pointing one at me. "And Travis figures it out! Close, but no cigar, my man with the plan. Here they come now."

Coming up the path were the others. Bubba was carrying Thumper in his arms, Privilege slung over one thick shoulder. Behind them all, I could make out the huge form of Moose slowly herding them up the mountain.

Victor laughed and shook his head. "Got to hand it to you, Trav. You almost made it. Almost triple-crossed me for that fat confederate bastard. But that whole leave nobody behind mentality just ain't doing wonders for your survival instincts, I must say. Now, Connie here?" His hand came down in an arc, catching Connie right on the ass. She squeaked and giggled. He copped a feel and laughed before moving on. "Connie worked like a little gothic charm! I bet old Chitty's feeling under the weather as we speak."

The others were gently herded in our direction. Lori dismounted, helping Thumper slide off into a sitting position on the ground. We all still had our weapons, and Victor was down to a handful each of vampires and renfields. His mission done, Moose started back down the mountain, disappearing into the trees. Connie, softly giggling, slid down Victor's side until she curled up against his leg.

Babs scowled. "What do you want?"

Victor laughed. "Hell, I got what I want! Chitty's weakened and ready for me to step up, take Atlanta. Get some places together for these fine folks. Unfortunately, I got no further use for-."

Victor managed to stagger for the half-second it took Connie to hit him in the crotch with the Strap Ball. The Strap Ball pulled itself apart, sounding like four whip cracks fractions of a second apart. The enchanted restraints flailed like an angry octopus, seeking wrists and ankles with disturbing speed. Victor went down under a mass of leather and chain.

Connie straightened up, stretching as if she'd just woken from a relaxing nap. Her leathers creaked with her movement. When she opened her eyes, they glowed an unearthly green.

"Sit down and shut up, Vic."

Chapter Twenty-Two

"Guideline Sixteen:
If you can't call down fresh lightning
on your opponent,
store-bought explosives will do."

When Victor went down, his people panicked. Some fought and some fled. Moose, somehow, had disappeared entirely. It became a claws, fangs, and blades fight swiftly. One particularly feral-looking vampire wound up in a rolling ball of slashing claws with Becky Sue. Another stalked Connie, then bolted when green flames ignited in her palms and she started giggling. The fireworks show kept going, with bursting rockets punctuating the fight as it went.

It also illuminated a huge form moving through the trees to the northwest. Using my staff to keep me stable, I wove my way through the gunfire, arrows, and magic to pace it. It was Moose. And it was trying to sneak up on Connie.

The moment he stepped through the treeline I shot him in the face. He stopped moving to turn and look at me. His eyes were solid black, like no human's eyes I'd ever seen. No vampire's eyes, for that matter. I could see the flesh on his cheek sizzle, char, and then nothing.

Victor chuckled from the ground, straining against his bonds. "You think yours is the only magic? Moose! Let him die stupid."

Moose stepped forward. I started to run, firing as I went, heading east towards the summit. Spikes of pain shot through my body with every step. Round after round impacted his torso, but the thermite never seemed to ignite. From behind me I saw a slug from Bubba fly past and catch Moose clear in the torso. We both kept shooting, the cracks from my pistol accentuating the blasts of his shotgun as we led the enormous vampire ever further east.

I had to think fast and shoot at the same time. Fortunately, I'm good at that. First point: Moose, presumably a vampire, was shrugging off thermite rounds. Second: Victor just claimed he has access to magic. Third: Victor himself didn't know a tarot card from a Christmas card. Therefore, Fourth: Thumper had to have hooked Victor up. Fifth: The simplest way to magic someone else is to magic an object they can carry. Looking at the charred rags hanging off of his shoulders that might have once been a shirt, I found what I was looking for. In the middle of Moose's chest was an amulet the size of a challenge coin, hanging around his neck with a leather thong. I kept shooting, then started yelling.

"Lori!"

She flew just above my line of fire, calling as she went past. "Yeah?"

I fired one-handed, pointing right at Moose with my free hand. "Magpie on my go!"

She frowned, then came about for another pass as Bubba and I kept shooting. I saw her give a thumbs-up out of the corner of my eye. That was one position set up.

"Bubba!"

"Yeah?" The big veterinarian was holding his own, the muzzle of Privilege smoking.

"How are you on ammo?"

"Spartan!" Privilege roared again, an empty shell flying past me as he worked the slide.

"Awesome, keep shooting!"

"What are you gonna do?"

I had no time to explain, just hope he'd figure it out. "Transition!"

"To what?"

I didn't answer. I had already turned and started running south. My legs screamed, but I was the only one who could hear them and I wasn't about to let them dominate the conversation. Almost to the copse of trees where the portal still was. I don't know how far I had to sprint, but I headed right for it. Behind me I could hear Victor scream, "Travis, you coward!"

I went down in a baseball slide past the portal. Somewhere beyond the magic and willpower that flooded my senses, my leg screamed in protest that I wasn't a schoolkid anymore and that further suffering was already scheduled for the near future. Bubba was racking and shooting like a machine, keeping time with every blast. The rest of Moose's raggedy clothing had all fallen off in charred tatters and his fur was singed in several places, but his skin looked undamaged.

I unslung the gym bag, somehow still with me the entire time, and pulled the zipper open. The rocket launchers were innocuous gray cylinders. Well, innocuous except for the bright red spray paint stencil that read BACON-MAKER. Twisting open the ends like an old-fashioned LAW armed it. I'd had the foresight to have an arrow pointing in the muzzle direction labeled: *this end towards bacon source.* I pulled the safety pin, racked the charging handle, rolled it onto my shoulder and flipped open the sight. A cleansing breath in and out focused me, just like magic. I focused the sight on Moose's slowly approaching chest, then bellowed with all the force I had in my voice.

"Magpie go!"

Lori came about one more time, silhouetted against the bursting fireworks and blaring music from the laser show. Her pistol holstered, hat and dress pressed against her by the wind, I saw her come in like a dive bomber. Her jaw was clenched and her eyes narrowed in determination behind her goggles.

Lori and I don't get along very well, for a lot of the same reasons I don't get along with Babs. But I knew her strengths, and knew I needed them. She had the targeting instincts of a crow finding discarded sequins on a beach. Snatching the pebble from the master's hand was nothing to her after snatching scores of lethal objects from her grabby-handed children before they managed to swallow them. Along with that was a grip strength that would give an industrial vise a run for its money. Among the Blue River survivors, she was second only to Bubba and myself when it came to arm wrestling. Which would come in handy when she started dealing with teenagers, but at the moment made for a handy weapon coming in at full speed.

Thumper and I, on the other hand, were more alike than either of us wanted to admit right now. At heart we were still just a couple of kids blowing stuff up in the woods. But where Thumper still just loved explosions for their own sake, I'd taken that love and turned it around to focus on making things that would last. So, while I could easily see Thumper making amulets that rendered the wearer immune to fire, an overengineering bastard like me would have reinforced the leather thong it was hanging from. Thumper didn't think about things like that.

Moose had an instant to turn before being buzzed by a ballistic mother of three. Lori's hand clamped down on the amulet like the claws of a bird of prey. The leather thong hanging it from Moose's excuse for a neck showed no resistance, snapping instantly. The unarmored Moose remained in my sights, not yet registering what had happened. Out of the corner of my eye, I could see Lori was already several yards away and climbing, holding the amulet aloft like a trophy. I let out one more breath before pressing the firing stud.

The rocket flew from the launcher, ramming into Moose's torso without slowing down, flying ever faster with his helpless body draped over it. In the light of the rocket wash, I could see Moose's eyes grow wide as his feet were dragged into the air, off the mountain and over the crowd watching the laser show. The rocket exploded in the brightest firework the sky had yet seen. The echo reverberated so loud it drowned out the music for a few moments. The biggest piece I saw in the afterimage of the blast was a clawed hand, engulfed in flames, falling claws over stump until it disappeared over the horizon and out of sight.

I turned to look at the fight. It had stopped, mage and vampire and renfield alike frozen in shock.

I dropped the spent launcher, reached into the bag, and pulled out the second one with an industrious air.

A vampire that had been just outside of Cyrus' reach turned and ran, vanishing into the woods. One near Connie did the same. One by one, the remaining country vampires and renfields all fled. Bubba and I walked fast to get close to the others. Amazingly, everyone on both teams were all still alive and still in the fight. Lori came in for a landing, dismounting her broomstick with a smile. The amulet was absently tucked into her bra. She removed her flight goggles, letting them rest on the brim of her hat.

The fireworks kept bursting as we all smiled. Everyone was filthy, most were bloody, but all were whole. I felt miserable and wonderful all at once. We'd done it.

Out of the corner of my eye, I saw something move. It took me half a second to realize it was one of Thumper's exploding disks. I turned to see Thumper coming to their feet, their hands moving fast and lunging straight for Connie. Before I even realized I was doing it, I closed my eyes, dropped my staff, and was off and running. I heard the flash-bang go off, my vision red as I kept my eyes tightly shut. I opened my arms as I heard the screams of the others.

I slammed into Thumper like a linebacker blindsiding a running back. The moment my shoulder hit them in the chest, the world vanished.

*   *   *

Chapter Twenty-Three

"Guideline Eleven:

The best part of going to hell

is going back to lead loved ones out."

I was alone the moment I hit the ground.

Turning away with my shoulder, I rolled, coming to my feet quickly. I was back in Thumper's woods. In the far distance, I could see angry reds and oranges through a faraway haze. The smell of smoke was everywhere. My weapons and gear were gone.

"It's over, Thumper!" I bellowed, "Your Master's toast!"

Their voice echoed from the haze. "Not yet."

I glanced over at the leaning tree. Thumper's pack was gone. Next to my pack was a familiar looking shotgun. A Remington 870 with a wood stock. I tossed the pack over my shoulders, picked up the shotgun, and opened the action just enough to see it was loaded. The clouds overhead were darkening, just as the light from beyond the haze was getting brighter. I kept my shotgun at the alert, my senses as open as they could be.

Thumper emerged from the haze, kicking aside a fallen branch before gliding towards me in a rustle of pinestraw and dead leaves. They were stripped down and barefoot, wearing only a sports bra and a sarong girded around their waist like an elaborately draped pair of shorts. They looked like hell. Their muscles had withered under taut skin, letting them look as gaunt as a zombie. They were already sweating, their eyes wide and bloodshot. Their hair was matted against their skull like a wig left in the gutter. Their pack was worn backwards, the main compartment zippered open. They breathed heavy, "Not yet, Trav."

"Thump, it's over. Victor's caught and his people are dead or on the run."

They took a battered plastic flying disc from their pack and began tossing it from hand to hand. "I can't let you take him."

I backed up in a crouch, resisting the urge to sight in on Thumper. At Blue River, Thumper had packed old flying discs with explosives and clay, making crude but effective grenades. I did not want to be on the receiving end of them. Even in a mindscape like this. "Thump, seriously. Listen to yourself. Hell, look at yourself! Victor's done. He's going into a box in Chittenden's game room, and we're going to get you some help."

They shook their head, wailing. "Help me? Help me?!"

I didn't even see them light the fuse. But with a flick of their wrist, the disk was headed towards me. I dropped to one knee, sighted in without thinking and pulled the trigger. The disc exploded in a shower of flames, clay, and plastic shards.

I didn't want to hurt them, but in their mind, I was in trouble. Thumper threw two more. I ducked to the side, pumping and firing as fast as I could aim. Both discs exploded, shards from one caught me behind the knee, knocking me off my feet. The back of my knee burned in pain as I went down hard, barely able to hear Thumper's screaming.

"All I needed was a little more time! A little more blood! You heard me! I could talk again! I could've made the incantation! I could've cast that curse!"

I'd just staggered upright when one of their discs came through. I knocked it away with the butt of my shotgun just before it exploded, tearing open a series of nasty gashes on my arm. I was driven back towards the creek, away from the flames I could feel now. It took me a moment to catch my breath in the thickening smoke.

"You could barely say you were sorry! Victor didn't even let you try! He beat you senseless for suggesting it! You never would've held it together long enough to incantate. You know it, I know it, and he knows it. He used you to get me. And the second he had me, he used me to try and get Connie! And he would've had her if we hadn't tricked him!"

Thumper lit and threw two more discs, one after the other. I managed to shoot and destroy both, the fragments missing me by inches. "You're damaged goods and cheap insurance to him, Thump. He cashed you out the moment I showed up. Even if he escapes, he'd never keep you alive."

A disk came spinning straight for my chest. I missed, and the disk exploded right in front of my chest. The explosion knocked me on my mental ass. Pain shot through my consciousness as Thumper stalked closer. "Not if I take you for him, Travis."

Rivulets of blood opened up across my chest, face, and hands. I got back to one knee and faced them again. Another disk came spinning at me. I blew that one apart with the shotgun, but missed the next, which smashed into my kidney and exploded, ripping open flesh and nearly making me drop the shotgun.   I staggered against a tree, trying not to slip on my own blood while I pulled myself up. Thumper's eyes looked like a hungry animal's, and I was getting scared fast. "Take me for him? What the hell is that supposed to mean?"

I knocked away the next disc like a baseball, which exploded over the creek. I could hear the crackling of flames now, seeing individual trees on fire in the distance.

"It means you take a nap. I take your body. Nobody would question poor little Thumper being lost in another coma. They wouldn't question big bad Travis being all quiet and stoic, either. You've got Master all nice and tied. And that hunky voice of yours can do the incantation easy enough. That would be a lovely gift for Master, taking Chittenden down and handing him to Master in one nice package. Especially when Chittenden's expecting you. When Master's taken over, I can even give you your big ol body back."

Now I was terrified. Ever since their injury, Thumper had studied cognimancy. They'd worked on it every day since out of sheer need to communicate. They had built everything I could sense: from the sight of each other down to the feel of twigs and leaves under my feet and the faint smell of mud and smoke. None of it was really there. It was a construct in Thumper's mind that they'd dragged me into when I touched them. If Thumper felt the need, they didn't even have to fight me as themselves. The trees, the ground, the creek itself could attack me. If they hadn't been so messed in the head from Victor, they might have started doing so already.

All of our fighting here was a translation of our minds fighting each other in a way that made sense to our brains. Attacks, wounds, even exertion was all about our minds instead of our bodies. Whoever lost consciousness or died in here would be helpless against whatever the other wanted to do to them mentally. What they were proposing was at best murder. At worst, it was destroying my soul to make way for theirs. Either way, they were more than capable of what they'd threatened.

"Thumper, please. I'm your friend."

The sound that came from Thumper was barely human, but I could just make out the three words they used. "You left me."

A disc spun towards my head. I barely managed to shoot it in time.

"What are you talking about?"

They kept coming. I was too confused to even try to attack. Thinking and destroying inbound grenades at the same time was keeping me occupied. They growled. "My friends killed and died and left."

"I was the one who saw you were still alive! I carried you across that river!"

Thumper slowed down only so they could attack and yell at the same time. "And then you left! When I woke, you were gone! Everyone was gone!"

"Thump, you were in a coma. Ethan was dead. Heather was dead. Half of us were dead! What was I supposed to do?"

I barely missed losing a hand, knocking one of the discs away. It disappeared into the creek and exploded, sending a spout of water everywhere. "Get it right, Travis. Ethan killed Heather. He killed my best friend. My only real friend."

I missed the next disc, which flew past and exploded, tearing another collection of gashes into my forearm. I kept backing up. "Thump, I might suck at it, but I'm still your friend."

"Only as long as I showed you what you liked. You and Ethan liked the weird little tomboy who liked blowing shit up with you. Some of the girls didn't pick on me because a butch little runt like me would never be competition for them. But real friends? Ones who liked you for who you were? Only one of those I ever had was Heather. Even Lori thought I was just coming on to her. Not Heather. She never judged. She just-"

"-listened to you. The way you were."

Thumper slowly nodded. "I watched her die too. And then I faded away. I thought I was right behind her. And that maybe death wouldn't be so bad if she was already there. Then I woke up and you were gone. You were my best friends. She was dead, and you were gone and I couldn't even say it."

I blinked away tears. The only thing I could think to say was lame, but I still said it. "Thump, I came to visit you."

They almost growled. "But you went on without me. And you held onto memories of Heather like she was still around. I've seen how much of your head she took up. Until you found a Mistress to serve."

I almost growled. "You mean Eva? She wasn't my mistress, Thumper. She was my rapist. That's why I killed her the second I made her let go of my mind."

Thumper came back with a screaming vengeance. Disc after disc flew from their hands. I couldn't destroy them all. One exploded and tore into my shin. Another tore into my thigh, fragments burning my trousers like a dozen cigarettes being stubbed out at once. One went past my head just as it exploded. Fragments ripped into the right side of my face. I suddenly couldn't see out of that eye. When Thumper closed the distance and lashed out with a foot, it caught me in the ribs hard enough to send me airborne. My bloody spit flew, splattering against the needles on the pine.

If it had been my real body, I'd barely be awake from the blood loss. I had dozens of openly bleeding cuts and burns on every limb. Three of my teeth were missing. I couldn't feel two fingers on my right hand. Amazingly, I still had a firm grip on my shotgun.

"You're still bleeding, Trav. That's a good sign. Means you're still living. That's what it all boils down to, Trav. One more beat of the heart. Makes you know you're alive."

I'd been thrown into the tree we used to lean against on hot days. The one we'd left our packs lying against to go mess around in the creek. My own pack had burst open when I'd fallen. Scattered along the ground was the familiar detritus of school: pens and lighters and paper scraps and old snack wrappers.

Lying among them in the pine straw and sand was the picture frame from my nightstand, with the picture of Heather lying on the sofa.

I want to be remembered like this for a thousand years.

I focused on that picture as I sat up against the tree. With the creek to my back, Thumper was outlined by the flames now, tossing another disc back and forth between their hands. My one good eye found theirs bloodshot and twitchy, in as much pain as I was. I took a breath, trying not to either succumb to weariness or let Thumper know what I'd realized. With trembling hands, I curled my remaining fingers around the shotgun. Pressing the slide release with my trigger finger, I racked the slide back. Thumper's smile began to return.

Then I racked the slide forward, and thunder rolled as the bolt locked into place.

I raised the muzzle to the sky and pulled the trigger.

A lightning bolt shot out of the muzzle into the clouds, knocking Thumper over and sending every loose leaf and crumb of dirt scattering. The lightning reverberated among the clouds, cracking them open. Rain began to fall, building from drizzle to downpour in moments.

With every drop that landed, one of my wounds healed. Rain washed away blood and soot to leave behind healthy flesh. After a few moments of blinking, I could see out of both eyes again. I stood up, needing to lean against the tree less and less with every passing second. The rain was thick enough that I could actually drink by opening my mouth to the sky. Swishing around a bit and spitting out the blood from my last few wounds. I could speak again. And instead of my old shotgun, I held my staff again.

"You fucked up, Thumper."

Behind me, the creek rose and swelled, becoming the Blue River itself. The beach collapsed into the rocky and rising banks of the river. The rains pushed the fire back, the angry red receding further beyond the horizon with every moment. I could feel all my fingers again. Even the old pains in my ribs and the ache in my head I'd had for days washed away as the water came down.

Thumper began staggering to their feet as I continued. "See, cognimancy was never really my big thing. I was so used to just coming in your mind whenever you needed me to. But I've learned a few things along the way, this last year."

I swept my staff across the ground, knocking Thumper's foot away. They went back down, breathing hard.

"You never saw that picture of Heather. Because I never showed it to anyone. You had no idea that picture even existed. Which means you didn't pull me into your mind. You invaded mine instead."

Thumper sneered. "You hang onto her memory like a crutch."

"What, because I never dated seriously again? She was my lover and I watched her die."

Thumper didn't try to get up again. They just spit out a bloody tooth. "She was the only one I could talk to."

I took my staff and threw it like a javelin into the river. Behind us, the fires faded into nothingness. The rain began to slowly clear. Across the river, we could start to see the flashing blue and red lights of emergency vehicles. I looked back down at Thumper. "Like I said, MY mind."

Thumper's lip curled back in an inhuman snarl as they crouched. "Mine soon."

Thumper charged. I sidestepped their blow, following it up by sending my fist like a hammer into their temple. Thumper collapsed, fuse hissing on a disc. I kicked it into the river, where it exploded, sending a splash of water across the banks.

"When I knew I had to lock my memories away from vampire bullshit, I doubled down on how mind magic works. And I got a really awesome assistant these days. I don't know if I'm a better cognimancer than you. But I know I've held my own. I know I have all my memories back. I know you're strung out, exhausted, and desperate. And most of all? I know about homefield advantage. And you're on my turf."

Thumper sprang from the floor and caught me in a tackle. Thumper was bleeding from the nose and ears. But looking into their eyes, I could see they were still determined to come take me down. They flailed at me again and again, knuckles bleeding freely. I ducked under one punch and snaked my arms around them in a wrestling hold. Thumper roared incoherently, trying to break free still.

For the second time in my life, I waded into the waters of the Blue River with Thumper in my arms. Even here, I was twice Thumper's size, and I could feel them beginning to wear out. I had my head tucked in close to theirs to keep from being headbutted. For a moment, I was grateful. Thumper couldn't see the pity in my eyes. They would have hated that.

"I'm sorry, Thumper. I should've realized all we really had was each other. But I'm gonna help you. I got out from under Eva, and I'm gonna get you out from under Victor."

I kissed them on the temple.

"I love you. And I'm taking you home. Now get out of my head."

I turned, tucked my leg over theirs, and fell backward into the river. The rushing waters closed over us in seconds, and the woods faded away into darkness.

*   *   *

"Travis! Trav!"

Bubba was gently slapping me, which felt like an old boxing glove being knocked into my face by storm winds. I lifted a hand in surrender. "I'm here. I'm here and I'm me."

Bubba sat back and let me stand up. Fireworks were going off in the skies above, and I could faintly hear the music from the laser show playing on the front lawn, eight hundred feet and change below us. Thumper was out cold. Lori was painting some kind of salve over a nasty cut on Cyrus' forearm. The others were gathered more or less where I'd last seen them.

I got to my feet, wincing at newfound layers of pain. My shirt was soaked in grimy, bloody sweat, and Gods know what I'd be feeling without whatever Bubba had dosed me with. I held up my hands, talking down the police style. "Thumper tried to body swap me. Victor's really got them hooked."

There was a sound of igniting flames, and Connie stepped closer to me. Her palm was full of green fire and she had it aimed right at my face. Babs started to talk, but Connie held up her other hand in a gesture that said she had this, whether Babs liked it or not. The others watched with varying degrees of too old for this shit.

Connie gently said. "Three of the werewolves were waiting at my house for me. Which ones?"

I frowned. "Three? What the hell? There were only two. The big guy I shot in the face at Warwell's and the skinny one that drove the car."

Connie clenched her fist, snuffing out the flames before nodding in satisfaction. "It's him."

Babs gave me a look. "You shot a werewolf at Warwell's?"

I shrugged, then winced. "It was in the parking lot. Besides, we kissed and made up afterwards."

There was a metallic click. I could hear Byron, out of my view, command, "Don't even try it."

I slowly turned around, coming face to face with Muscles. He had a pistol in a textbook-perfect isosceles stance, aimed right at my center of mass. The ribs on my right side started to burn with every breath. I held out my right hand and whistled. My staff jumped up from the ground. I caught it with one hand and planted it on the rock, resisting the urge to put my weight on it. I nodded to Muscles.

"Definition, technique, and assessment. I'm impressed. You a renfield, Muscles?"

His gaze didn't waver. "Dunno what that means."

Victor growled from somewhere near my kneecaps. "It means shoot him now."

I glanced to my right. Victor was sitting upright, his ankles manacled to each other and his wrists manacled to his ankles behind his back by the Strap Ball. Connie was holding him by the hair, smiling cheerfully and giving a little wave, her eyes still glowing green.

I nodded to her. "Renfield means you drank that Russian asshole's blood."

His aim didn't waver, but his lip curled in a sneer. "Hell naw."

"Did he tell you you'd be facing wizards when he hired you?"

He snorted. "Shit, like I'd have believed him."

I nodded, slowly opening my belt pouch and taking out a soft tissue healer. I passed it over to Bubba and raised a questioning eyebrow. He took it, opened the cap, sniffed it, and nodded. Nothing in my healing potion was going to react badly to his. Taking it back, I downed the entire shot in one go and grimaced. The healer tasted like an unholy blend of chalk, fruit, and bile that never sat right with me. Dropping the empty in my pocket, I looked back at Muscles. "Well, Muscles, like I said earlier, I don't like killing humans I don't have to, and my dance card for the evening is pretty full. Connie, Victor got a wad?"

Connie rummaged in Victor's pockets, taking out a fat roll of cash bound with a rubber band. She tossed it to Seb, who held it up. I nodded at it. "Not sure what your usual fees are, Muscles. But given as you weren't informed proper, I think you can take the money and walk away with your reputation intact."

He didn't even look at the furious Victor. "And if I feel the need to see the job through?"

I shrugged, then winced. "Ow, shit. Then you don't get paid, we kill you, and the green-eyed goth chick turns you into a zombie plaything."

He didn't ponder that long before nodding. "I gotchu." Muscles slowly holstered his weapon, then held out his hand, accepting the wad from Seb.

I nodded in return. "Appreciated, Muscles. If you would be so kind as to help your surviving former companions after we leave? Cleanup crews should be a few hours at most." I unbuckled my belt, taking off my knife sheath and buckling it back. I tossed the sheath underhand at Muscles, who caught it. I pointed at it. "The knife that goes in that is lying around here somewhere. Anyone tries biting you, cutting their heads off will make them stop."

He nodded and stepped away. I breathed deep. The healer was taking effect fast. I felt really light headed and thirsty. I turned over to where Connie had Victor strapped up. He grimaced in cold fury. "Clever magics. But they won't last forever. The blood will. It always does. The curse is already cast, and she'll be bent to my will again."

I shrugged. "You know, you might have been right. Damn shame she didn't drink your blood then."

He snarled. "What?"

I took a full tube of blood from my pocket. "This is the blood you gave me. I took a tube from your mom after I staked her, then I brought it with me tonight. Connie knew I'd made the switch. So she made a big production out of kissing me goodbye. While everyone was watching that, I slipped the tube of Victor's blood into her pocket. That's the tube she spilled during the curse."

Victor stared in shock as Connie took another full tube from her pocket, handing it to me. "This one's Chittenden's, sealed and decidedly un-cursed."

Connie held up the curse in her other hand. "I didn't cast the curse either. This is the right curse, but it's not what I was chanting. Turns out it's got the same meter as an old erotic poem about the virtues of older women. But it really sounds spooky if you chant it in Latin, y'know?"

I pocketed the tube then handed Connie a stake. Victor was still staring when she tried to ram it into his chest. The stake broke into splinters on impact. Connie swore and gingerly pulled out a splinter from her hand.

We all looked confused at Victor. Connie rapped her knuckles against his chest, frowned, then ripped open his shirt. His chest was wrapped in a low profile plate carrier.

Bubba shook his head in disappointment. "Vampires wearing body armor? Now that's just cheating."

Lori shrugged. "We're mages with guns, dear. I don't think we have room to talk."

Connie opened up the straps, letting the plate carrier hit the rock. Shaking her head in annoyance, she took another of my stakes and rammed it through Victor's chest. I watched the vampire stiffen with paralysis, then clutched my staff, leaning on it hard.

Lori had wandered up gently, taking a bottle of water with a screwtop lid from her bag. Shaking her head, she offered it to me. "Goddess love you, Travis, you're red as a lobster. Get some water in your system, you..." Her eyes narrowed and she held the bottle back.

"Travis?"

I tilted my head, then winced again. "Yeah, Lori?"

"Why are your lips black?"

Connie blushed.

*　*　*

Chapter Twenty-Four

"Guideline Ten:
Wars begin in the field
But they end at a table."

We didn't get halfway down the mountain before Babs and I started bickering again.

"You know I'm getting a serious ass-chew because of all that."

"Would it help if I sent a satisfaction card to your supervisor?"

"You were shooting a machine gun off the top of Stone Mountain!"

Byron spoke up. "In Trav's defense, the other guy brought it."

I nodded in thanks. "And it was during the laser show. Nobody noticed."

"Then you followed it up with, and I cannot stress this enough, a home-made rocket launcher!"

I shrugged. "You saw how big that Moose guy was. Besides, it was during the fireworks. Nobody noticed that either."

Connie opened up, possibly trying to derail our train of rant. "Vampires have actual centuries to spend learning. Why do so many of them so stubbornly don't?"

Byron shrugged. "Not to cast aspersions on mortal maturity, but when's the last time you saw one who was older than twenty-five when they were turned?"

I rolled my eyes. "Big words coming from an elf sent to spend his terrible two hundreds among mortals and out of your dad's hair."

Byron laid his free hand on his heart, looking appalled. "Where did you learn that term?"

The others chuckled as I smirked. "Not telling."

We'd policed up our brass, mags, arrows, and assorted trash as best we could. There was still a hell of a mess near the summit. We counted nine dead humans, probably renfields, and seventeen of the smoldering heaps that spoke of dead vampires, not including Moose. I don't believe Atlanta had half that many city vampires calling her home. Babs had gotten her boss on the phone, and a cleanup crew from the Iron Council would be along within hours. Thankfully we'd be gone by the time they showed up and started acting like they owned the place. Assuming they didn't pull her badge for aiding and abetting us, the SiS deputy they'd send to interrogate us about it would be Babs herself. Fortunately, she could at least testify that I was no longer an active renfield. I was still mildly annoyed that I'd had to destroy a perfectly good machine gun.

Becky Sue, back in human form and wearing her collar and a bloodstain collection, kicked a pebble out of her way. Byron raised an eyebrow. "Hon, one of the other mortals could've carried something for you to wear if you'd asked."

She shrugged. "What's it to you, elf?"

"Curiosity, mostly. The local authorities might object, assuming they ever show up."

"Eh, not the first time I've been caught at Stone Mountain like this, ain't gonna be the last."

As the parking lot came into view I marveled at how we hadn't seen a single authority figure. No cops, no park staff, no nothing. I'd have thought for sure the racket we made on the summit would've bothered somebody even if it was drowned out by all the fireworks in the laser show. Victor's handiwork, I guessed. Those of us with sticks, canes, spears, or brooms were all using them to help us down the mountain. Bubba carried Thumper in his arms, as gently as he could manage. Byron and Seb had Victor trussed to a pole like a deer and were carrying him between them. Seb, setting the pace, was sweating like a hog but refusing to complain. Byron contentedly shouldered his half as if he was on a pleasant evening stroll. The Strap Ball was hanging from Connie's belt once more. We'd replaced it with heavy-duty zip-ties keeping his wrists behind him and ankles together. Some would call that and a stake overkill, but I considered it all the kill I needed and leftovers to boot. I'd retrieved my rocket tubes and was carrying the pack. Beyond that, I was hoping my painkillers didn't give out before I'd gotten home.

I turned back towards Bubba as I opened the tailgate, drawing my wand from my staff and tucking it into a pocket. My staff went into the truck. The others took turns dropping our long weapons in the truck as I pointed to the rest of the cargo space. "We'll put Thumper in the back of my Yukon. I'll figure out what we can do for them when I get us home."

Babs spoke up. "I can take them. SiS has a rehab center near Warm Springs, maybe three hours' drive from here. The healers there can at least get started working on Thumper."

Becky Sue accepted a scrunchie from Bubba, then spoke up as she corralled her hair. "You hooked that up with one phone call? Shit, I should try being a fed."

Babs shook her head. "I set up a slot a month ago. Thought I'd need it for Travis."

That silenced us all for a moment. I broke it up by quietly saying, "Every day, in every way, I find out I'm another kind of asshole."

While the others chuckled, I got the tube of Victor's blood out of my pocket and offered it to Babs. "This is Vic's. Maybe the healers can use it to help Thumper. But whatever you do, don't let anyone drink it." Babs hesitated. She could feel the power radiating from that tube two feet away, and a part of her that probably kept her alive was telling her she wanted none of it. I tried not to let my hand shake. It had taken so much out of me to not lick the blood off the knife, and I wanted more. I wanted more so badly. I regretted even making the offer. Before I could stop myself, I whispered, "For the Gods' sake, Babs, get this away from me before I do something stupid with it."

She took an evidence bag from a pouch, then took the tube between two fingers of a gloved hand, sliding it into the bag. I've never seen a plastic bag glow, but something shone in the night when she sealed the bag and tucked it into a cargo pocket. We all let out a breath we didn't know we were holding in relief.

I caught a glimpse of headlights in the distance, heading south on Robert E Lee. Connie and I watched the lights approach while everyone else helped get Thumper somewhere comfortable. Byron and Seb casually dropped Victor, each checking idly to make sure the stake hadn't gotten loose on impact. Stepping out, I took a swig from my water bottle. Then thinking of something, I looked back. "Hey, Becky Sue: I have a case of baby wipes in the truck. Help yourself."

She gave me a thumbs-up. "Appreciated."

Bubba and Byron snickered at the innuendo as she went rummaging through my backseat. The headlights turned east on mountain road heading straight for us. Those of us in view tried to look casual. Just a handful of hikers with a bound and impaled corpse coming from the top of Stone Mountain in the middle of the night. Bloodstained, reeking of gunpowder, and occasionally singed. The car came closer to the circle of light provided by the nearby streetlamp, revealing itself to be a white stretch limo. The limo came to a smooth halt just below the streetlight, almost shining. We watched the limo sit there, the chorus of crickets and frogs joining in the far-off traffic as the laser show audience headed home for the night.

Connie murmured, "Is that who I think it is?"

Byron, Babs, Cyrus, and myself answered in stereo surround, "Yeah."

The driver, in full white-gloved uniform, wordlessly walked around the back before opening the middle door. A familiar, slender figure emerged, the deep purple of his suit reflecting the streetlight as he approached. Cyrus gritted his teeth.

"Mr. Wayland," Oswald nodded politely, "I trust that your report is prepared?"

I strolled up to him. "Your trust is well kept," I replied, cocking my thumb. "You'll find Victor's body near my tailgate."

His poker face held. "Very well." He turned and walked over to the trunk, which the driver opened remotely for him.

Connie looked up at me. "So what do we do?"

The others looked just as expectant. I shrugged, then pulled the bag containing my last Baconmaker out of the backseat, passing it to Connie. "Hang here, watch Oswald stuff Vic into the trunk of the limo, play on your phones, whatever. If I don't come out in fifteen minutes, aim for the gas cap and make some bacon."

Connie nodded solemnly. With some adjustment of jewelry, she managed to sling the rocket launcher over her shoulder without catching anything on anything else. Everyone else looked different levels of nervous. Babs had only gotten more annoyed. "Are you high or trying to kickstart a war?"

I shook my head. "I don't have nearly enough endorphins left. I'm trying to end one before it starts. Chittenden can't be allowed to kill me and leave here alive. Once word gets out, the Iron Council will be fighting city vamps all over the country."

A lot of shocked faces made to speak their peace when Seb beat them to it. "He's right."

Babs frowned. "How?"

Seb opened his hands in storyteller's gestures. "How many mages become renfields? We have three here tonight. By using one, Chittenden wiped out three rivals to his throne in two nights without getting out of his chair. Chittenden kills Travis and gets away with it, that's the story that gets told. Any city near a study hall will have vampires coming out to make deals to sextus year students. It'll be an arms race."

I nodded. "I made a bad deal when I was a scared kid. We all did, to one degree or another. I don't regret it. It kept us all alive. But we can't let this happen again. You all felt the power coming from those blood tubes. I'm giving Chittenden an ultimatum. No mage drinks vampire blood again. He knows I broke the bond. He just doesn't know how. With time, we can find out a way to make even normal humans immune from the renfield bond."

Becky Sue cocked her head. "How would that even work?"

Seb shrugged. "Connie and Thumper know enough for the rest of us to find out. If Travis goes free tonight, then Eva, her brood, and the country vampires on the mountain are just collateral damage from Travis fulfilling his oath. Mages and vampires both claim mage renfields are too uncontrollably dangerous to use."

Cyrus nodded, figuring it out. "And if Travis and Chittenden both die here, then four city vampires died trying to control mage renfields. And a pack of country vampires on the mountain were killed easily by a mage cabal with less than half their numbers."

I smiled through the exhaustion and shrugged. "Either way, we win."

Babs stared at me for a long moment, then hid her eyes with her fingers, shook her head, and let out a weary sigh. "Please don't make it necessary to shoot another one of those things in my jurisdiction tonight."

Becky Sue looked up from her wipedown, frowning in annoyance at Connie. "Hey, how come she gets the rocket launcher?"

Byron, his arms folded and pouting, shook his head in disappointment. "I wonder."

Before the proper bickering could start, Lori planted her fists on her ample hips, and with a shake of her head and a tone which had settled a thousand playground battles said, "Well, since Travis didn't think to bring enough for everyone, you're just going to have to share."

I threw up my hands in defeat, sighed, and went off to do my exit interview with the vampire. At least everyone was in good spirits, or the remnants of an adrenaline high. Even money either way. If I survived, I was gonna hold the fact that she'd complained about me not bringing enough explosives over her head for the rest of our lives.

Oswald reached into the trunk and pulled out a folded square of flexible plastic, which he unfolded with a practiced hand into a familiar shape. I can't say I was surprised to see that Oswald kept body bags handy. In his own way, he believed in being prepared as much as I did.

I walked up to the limo, looking the driver in the eye. He nodded politely, "Evening sir. If you will please remove your weapons?"

I stopped before him. "No."

That threw his train of thought off the track. "Beg pardon?"

Two kinds of people demand you surrender your weapons before speaking to them. The first are the kind of power-hungry authoritarian despots who think all weapons everywhere should be controlled by them and only them, but they'll oh-so generously settle for controlling every weapon that could possibly be used on them. The second was usually less dangerous but more pathetic: the kind of entitled weakling that regarded violence as something you paid other people to do. Even if they lowered themselves to speak with a filthy peasant like yourself, they weren't about to let you have the tools of such a trade on hand when you did. You might get ideas above your station.

Both types are strictly modern humans. No supernatural being ever bothered with such nonsense. Any serious mover and shaker in the Otherworld was just as dangerous butt naked as they were buttoned up in a loaded Abrams with all the trimmings and a few extras from the Janes Christmas catalog. Weapons were personal preferences. You either talked to such a person, or you got on with it and tried to kill them. Trying to disarm one was both rude and a complete waste of time. Not even Victor, dumb as he was, tried that kind of crap.

Chittenden damn well knew better. Which meant he was probably messing with his driver and wondering what I'd do. If he expected someone to be turned into a frog, he was destined to be disappointed. I just shook my head slowly.

"I've had a long night, man. Besides which, not sure if Oswald clued you in, but I'm a wizard. Yes, I'm packing. A lot. But my brain is far more dangerous. If you think Lord Chittenden can spend time twiddling his thumbs while you set up a Mongolian striptease and a follow-up lobotomy before I give my report, then by all means, bring on the probe. Otherwise, just save us all the hassle and open the damn door."

He paused only a second before nodding. "As you will, sir."

That got a smile out of me. "I thought it was, 'as you wish?'"

"Not since that movie, sir."

I made a mental note to tip this guy later if I got a chance. He had solid brass ones and a sense of humor. The driver opened the door and stepped aside.

*　*　*

Chapter Twenty-Five

"Guideline Thirteen:

Working for a monster is a common hazard.

It's still something to remember during contract renewal time."

There's a trick to getting in and out of limos without looking goofy. Instead of stepping in sideways like a normal car, you have to turn your back on it, sit down backwards, and then slide inside. I'd seen Eva do it in a tight evening gown and look like a million bucks without flashing anyone. I, on the other hand, had to fold my massive, aching, sweaty, bloodstained carcass like an amateur hour yogi in order to do it without kicking the doorframe or banging my head against the roof. But I managed, with a certain amount of dignity, to slide into the back-facing middle seats and finally see my host.

Chittenden gave me a welcoming politician's smile. "Mister Wayland! Long time no see!"

I nodded politely. "Lord Chittenden."

Lounging across the power seats in the back was Samuel Chittenden, vampire lord of Atlanta. He was almost as tall as me, and quite a bit wider. He'd been turned well into his forties, and like a lot of big men who spent their early lives very physically, working their way up to the big chair led to filling it further before they'd realized what happened. He wore an immaculately tailored white three-piece suit. His modern tie and spread collar his only real concessions to modern fashion. His salt and pepper hair was held back with old-fashioned pomade, and his goatee of the same colors was waxed into just a bit more flair than is typical for today. His right hand, with the mild calluses of those who worked manually for a living and now didn't have to, rested on the brass knob of a polished hardwood cane.

The polite lack of ostentation extended to the inside of the limo. My returned memories reminded me that I'd ridden in Eva's limo escorting VIP's from the Cotillion to their hotels or the airport. That limo had been tarted up with so much neon and flash it looked like a cross between a strip club and an alien spaceship. It also smelled like a bad college party. Chittenden's limo looked more like a politician's. Black leather seats and matching short-pile carpet made for easy cleaning and easy bloodstain hiding at inconvenient moments. The bar was tidy and closed up, appropriate for a guest that didn't trust offered drinks and a host that no longer drank juleps. Whatever the staff used to clean it had mild and pleasant scents that didn't overpower anything.

"Word is, you've had a busy few days, boy. And if you'll forgive my saying so, you look like hammered shit fresh off the anvil."

A part of me wanted to relax. He gave off that kind of aura. He looked like he should be peddling fried chicken and sounded like he wanted to go chase some bootleggers in a Dodge Charger. The man's entire persona gave off the vibe of a dixiefied Santa. But one didn't become a vampire lord of a major city by collecting special edition soda cans. If anything, the man was more ruthless and calculating than Eva had been.

I could feel the slight movement as the trunk slammed. The door near me opened and Oswald sat gracefully beside me. I nodded to him before giving my host my attention.

"The days have been busy, sir. Excuse my appearance, I took a round in the chest half an hour ago and haven't had time to freshen up."

He waved the apology off. "Hard work's a reason, not an excuse, son. Care to enlighten me as to your investigation?"

I nodded. "Your suspicions were true on multiple levels, sir. Eva and both of her children were plotting to overthrow you and assume the throne. Linear is probably the best way to explain it."

He nodded, folding his hands atop his cane to listen. I unzipped my pack and handed over a hard copy of my report along with a thumb drive. Amazingly, nothing had splattered on either of them during the night. I took a swig from my water bottle and faced Chittenden again.

"Eva planned on ruling Atlanta for years, possibly since she arrived. But learning about my debt to you gave her an idea as to a probable method. Blood is central to the supernatural power of any vampire. Magic concerning blood is uncommon in this day and age but not unknown to mortal mages. Eva figured that was her way to taking you down, using me to do it.

Eva already had a base of operations in the Cotillion and a trusted subordinate in her daughter Tasha. But she needed a reason to expand her power base without arousing too much in the way of suspicion. So she arranged for Victor's visit last year, and had the false werewolf attack you at the same time, murdering your son."

A bushy eyebrow arched in suspicion. "False werewolf you say?"

"Yes sir. The local werewolf pack had nothing to do with it. You were attacked by a giant country vampire going by the name of Moose."

"I see. And this Moose is currently...?"

I nodded to my left. "In crispy chunks northwest of the mountain. Most of him probably landed in the woods south of that small tourist railroad."

"I see." He motioned for me to continue.

"Victor was put in a position to rescue you from that attack, which also put him in a position to take your blood." From my pocket, I took the tube of Chittenden's blood. I was surprised my hands didn't shake. "According to Victor, he used a small blood drawing device concealed in a pen. Some sort of KGB spy toy re-engineered to take blood instead of inject poison."

He took the tube gently, his face hardening. "He did have a fancy pen that night. I teased him about it."

"After that attack, Eva had your blood, and Victor could claim the boon of remaining in Atlanta. Victor had also made deals with a large group of country vampires. Some of them came all the way down the Appalachians. Now they needed magic. By this time you'd grown suspicious. You'd heard of Eva making magical inquiries, and called on me. You offered to let me pay off my debt by serving Eva, operating as your mole. We both knew Eva would make me a renfield, so we arranged to compartmentalize my memories. As far as Eva knew, you were granting my services to her for her part in your rescue. And the moment I'd tasted vampire blood, that's all I would know about it as well."

I took a swig from my water bottle and continued. "Eva herself had me research a blood curse going back to the sixteenth century. It's a sympathetic ritual, where the blood is treated in a way that will weaken the subject. Most likely, she was preparing for a night where other agents were in play.

At the same time, both of her children were plotting against her. Victor found a down-on-their-luck mage named Thumper and took them as a renfield of their own. Meanwhile, Tasha stole a copy of a spell I'd considered and then rejected using on you. That spell was specifically tuned for cursing a member of one's immediate family. It suited their needs in that they didn't need a sample of Eva's blood to use it. That said, it was particularly ugly in that it required a virgin sacrifice."

His brow furrowed. "We talking throwing the chief's daughter in a volcano or upside down crosses and black mass?"

"From the context, the latter. My guess is, Tasha was rushed. My service was due to end soon, and everyone planning on using magic that needed me had to do it while I was still serving Eva."

I took another swig of water. "Which takes me to two nights ago. Eva discovered what Tasha was up to, and had the werewolves kidnap the virgin in question, intending to give her to me as a going away present."

Chittenden frowned. "They did what now?"

"Kidnapped her off her front door, stripped her naked, tied her up with my own cuffs and put her in a velvet box. Said she'd gotten her for me special. She'd gone to the werewolves offering cash and her influence to clear their name with you. Then when they came with the young lady, Eva had me kick them out. She'd planned for me to violate the young lady, then cast the curse on you. With you weakened magically, your entourage would be overwhelmed. The country vampires would move in and ensure you didn't survive the night. They'd also be able to wipe out the remaining werewolves in short order. Which would leave Eva and her children as the largest power base standing."

"If memory serves, Miss Marazzi did not survive the evening."

"No sir, she did not."

"Go on, son."

"Eva stumbled into something that I believe is rarely encountered in renfields. But non-magical forms of mental conditioning have long held it as a truth. It's effectively impossible to mind control someone into doing something that they refuse to do. On some level, they have to want it. With enough time and effort and enough lack of care as to what's left of the mind in question, you can change what they want. But outright convincing them to do something they refuse? Doesn't happen."

His expression didn't change. "And I gather that ravishing unwilling young ladies is not something you particularly want?"

"Damn skippy. Don't get me wrong, I'll ravish the willing all day. But I'd see myself dead before I'd cross that particular line. A line tight enough that it broke the renfield hold on me. And when it broke, I knew the only way I was leaving the room alive was to ensure that hold never got me again.

So I killed Eva. Once you get rid of the renfield control, vampire blood is just concentrated magic. And since Eva planned on taking you down that night, she'd topped me off, just in case. Not going to speculate how I'd have done normally, and I did take an ass-kicking in the process, but I did stake her."

"But she wasn't the only one you killed that night."

"Nope. I think that once her sacrifice was taken, Tasha knew the jig was up, so she called on two of the country vampires and went to take out Eva when the Cotillion was closed and we'd be alone in the building. Instead, they walked in on me staking her. Tasha ran off when I shot her in the belly with a flare gun. The country vamps I killed not long afterwards."

"That explains why nobody I knew was missing. You don't do anything by half measures, son. Accounts for the three bodies in the Cotillion, and the conditions in which we found them."

"I'm a student of duct tape, sir. I can improvise a lot when I need to." I thought of something and frowned. "By the way, am I still a suspect in that? As far as mortal authorities are concerned?"

"Not if you don't need to be."

I nodded a thank you before continuing. "Ordinarily, I would have come to you and reported in as usual. But the sun was already coming up by then, so I'd have to wait anyway. I took the ex-sacrifice home and patched myself up. Which was when the spells I had on myself started backfiring."

"How did that happen?"

"I had two different memory compartments. One we arranged before I worked for Eva, and one I put on myself before working for you."

I'm not sure why I expected a visible reaction. Old vampires have incredible poker faces. So I took an educated guess. "Don't take it personally, sir. We all got our secrets, our own and other people's, and I had to take steps."

He waved it off. "No offense taken, son. Would've been mighty dense of you not to."

I love working for professionals. They really do understand. "Thank you, sir. Anyways, when I'd learned something actionable and had recently been fed by Eva, I would remember my service to you, report in, cover my tracks, and my memory would relock itself after I'd slept. The key to permanently unlock the compartment we arranged was set for when I had no vampire blood left in my system, and if I'm guessing right, the key was kept with you."

"You guessed right there, son." Chittenden motioned to Oswald, who handed me an envelope. It was sealed with my personal sigil impressed in red wax. I nodded and tucked it away in my pocket.

"The compartment I locked before beginning my service with you, I left the key with a friend. In that case, the key was a scent and a phrase. When Eva opened the box with the young lady, it released the same scent, and my very next words were the same phrase. That would have unlocked the older compartment. But the younger compartment was set to open only when my body was free of vampire blood."

"And Eva had topped you off, as you put it."

"Yes, sir. Instead of unlocking the memories I stored before serving you, it locked up all of my memories since I entered your service. Like a lock with a key broken off inside it. So, it locked away my memories of the entire past year. From my point of view, I left my house the evening of July first last year and woke up the morning of July second this year."

He nodded in thought. "Well that explains that. Oswald claims you called him that night saying my suspicions were confirmed. Then the next morning when he called on you, you were evasive and full of shit."

I opened my hands. "Not proud of it, but crises do things to our principles. Anyways, while I was figuring out what the hell was going on, the siblings were trying to discover how much you knew and how they could respond. Vic sent his mage renfield, who turned out to be an old friend, to spy on me. Last night, Victor offered me your blood to perform the curse in exchange for freeing me from my Oath once he took the throne in your stead. When I got home, Tasha confronted us. As it turned out, the virginal young lady is also a rather powerful necromancer. She took Tasha's head last night, for understandable reasons."

"That young lady outside?"

"Brunette with the fishnets and the rocket launcher? That's her. Anyways, I was recovering from that one when Thumper got the drop on me and stole your blood. When I came to, I warned Oswald."

He nodded without adding anything, which I took as a cue to go on.

"Earlier today, I managed to unlock my memories completely. All of them. In the process, purged the last of the vampire blood from my system. Not pleasant, but doable. Called in some friends. Victor bade me come here tonight, offering me Thumper in exchange for casting the curse on you. We got the drop on him, killed or drove off his minions, and Oswald just put him in your trunk."

Chittenden looked off at nothing in particular. He had that statuary look vampires get when they really think hard. They don't fidget. They stop pretending to breathe. He just looked like a southern fried gargoyle overlooking a church before finally turning back to look at me.

"Well, that's one mighty winding road you took on that there adventure, son. Mighty winding indeed. But you have in fact served me honorably for a year and a night. I'd even venture to say you went above and beyond in my service. I consider your Oath fulfilled."

I didn't know what to say. I didn't know what to think. An ax that hung over me my entire adult life had just been lifted. A part of me insanely missed it. Another part of me tensed against a trick, convinced it was still there. Most of me told the rest to shut up and let me do the talking, and managed a polite nod. "Thank you, sir."

"Been a right pleasure doing business with you, son."

"At heart, I'm a craftsman, sir. Satisfying customers is the hallmark of a good day."

"Indeed it is. I don't suppose you'd consider serving me on a more regular basis? You've proven true to your word, good in a fight, and skilled a wizard as any I've heard of."

I honestly considered it. Weyland's forge and a ten-mil socket help me, I considered it. I could remember with perfect clarity the sheer power in that blood. Wizards never rule, but they've been the powers behind almost every throne in human history, why not a modern one full of vampires? With enough blood and instinctual magic alone I killed three vampires in a few minutes and woke up with some bruises and a hangover. I'd never find a power source that flowed like that again. A part of me wanted, yearned, screamed to have that back.

But I remembered everything else too. I remembered what the blood made me forget. What the blood made me not care about. I remembered what the blood had done to Thumper. I remembered my time with Eva. From the outside, she'd become the closest thing to a relationship I'd had in years. But at the end of the night, I was her toy with delusions of importance. Allowed to fool myself into thinking I had a will of my own. If push had come to shove I would have wound up like Thumper, somewhere between a slave and a pet, and eventually even worse.

And what would've happened if I hadn't broken the bond and killed Eva? My next report to Chittenden would have put my Oath up against the blood. If I had sold Chittenden out to Eva and broken my Oath, the Otherworld would have started by shattering my ability to do magic, and kept going from there. If I had upheld my Oath, the blood would have fought me at every turn. And I had no illusions about how little of a damn Chittenden would have cared about me. The fact that he even offered confirmed that.

I thought about Jazz. If she was human, her state would be considered a curse. She was bound to serve the human who held her ring. Whether the binding was done by a deity, by Solomon, or some other old jackass depends on which story you read. Jazz didn't know for sure and I've never met another djinn. I did the best I could at being an ethical master for her, but at the end of the day, she was compelled to do as I said. Pulling the stunt with my memory of her worked once, at a cost I wasn't willing to pay again. Even if I was willing to bend my own will to a predator like Chittenden, I had no right to bring Jazz along with me.

No. I was a mage, godsdammit. I was supposed to be a guide and guardian of humanity, not a power junkie behind a throne that could only steal from humanity instead of champion it. The hell with Chittenden and every other smooth-talking leech in the damned swamp.

But being an asshole about it wouldn't be helpful to me or anyone else. I held up a hand gently. "This whole mess happened because of a magical arms race between vampires. Now it's been shown that magic can break the renfield bond. I think it would behoove all concerned not to risk anything of the sort happening again. Let the fate of Eva Marazzi and her brood stand as a warning to those who would risk another such disruption. That said, I would be amiable to a cash retainer for consulting services relating to my trade."

Chittenden, for his part, let out a hearty laugh. "Keep our respective people from stirring each other's pudding anytime soon. I like it, son, I do like it. I'll have Oswald put it together, and we'll meet quarterly absent my need to call on you."

I broke an honest smile for the first time. "Done."

We both leaned forward to shake on it. His hand felt like a steel vise padded in old leather. He may have gone to fat, but he'd gone to blood harder.

Oswald had taken from his portfolio a piece of high quality paper, faded only slightly with age. On the bottom of one side was the chicken scratch of a signature I'd written in my blood. Oaths didn't strictly require written records. But writing was a kind of magic almost as old as the Oaths themselves. It was oddly comforting knowing that if you'd pawned your very soul you'd at least get a receipt. I hadn't laid eyes on the marker for over a decade, but I remembered the terms completely. A year and a day of service for a night of aid. So much that little slip of paper cost me. And so much it let me keep.

Chittenden took an expensive-looking nib pen from his jacket pocket. Curling his lip, he sliced open a wound in the back of his left hand with a single fang. Using his left hand as an inkwell, Chittenden wrote out what he'd told me, ending in his flourishing signature. Oswald handed me the marker as Chittenden put his pen away, the wound already healed. I held the parchment in my hand, my mind working away.

"You look like you've got a question on your mind, son."

I honestly did. But I wasn't going to ask Chittenden. The old bastard's charm was working overtime to make me forget that he'd handed me over to a rapist for a year, just to gain a political edge on a rival. Now that I wasn't beholden to him, he had nothing to say that I wanted to hear.

"Had a lot to think about lately, sir. Nothing I should be troubling you with. Take care of yourself."

"Oh, I do, son. Get yourself some rest. You've earned it."

I nodded. "I will. Oh, I almost forgot." I dug in my pocket and came up with the card the werewolf alpha had given me, passing it to Oswald. "That werewolf pack aren't the sharpest knives in the drawer. But they work well as a team and they were busting their asses to get back into your good graces. They might come in handy. Also, there's a young man with some impressive triceps on top of the mountain who used to work for Victor. He doesn't look interested in blood, but he's got ambition, judgment, and a pair of solid brass ones. If you have interest in having the scene perused before SiS shows up, I'd keep an eye out for him."

The old vampire nodded in acknowledgment. "I'll remember that."

Chittenden nodded to Oswald. Oswald knocked on the door. The driver opened the door and I followed Oswald out. As we walked the short distance to my companions, Oswald spoke without looking at me.

"I will have the terms of your retainer written up and delivered by the end of the week."

"Appreciated. You know Victor in there questioned your integrity."

His head tilted. "Is that so?"

"When he brought us out here, I mentioned I'd called you and warned you about him. He intimated that you aren't as diligent in keeping your Master informed as you look."

His expression didn't waver. "Is that a fact?"

"Sadly it is. Had too much else to do instead of defend your honor at the time, but if you get a few good licks in yourself, I figured you'd like to know."

"That's very thoughtful of you, Mr. Wayland. Alas, I do believe the gentleman in question will be answering to my betters for some time."

"Fair enough."

We came up to my waiting friends. Oswald glanced at Thumper's reclined form in the back of my truck. "Regrettably, your friend's Master will be unable to attend to them for the foreseeable future."

I shook my head. "We'll take care of Thumper's needs, Oswald. Kind of you to think about them, though."

"Are you sure about this? Remember what I told you."

I smiled at that one. "No substitute for the blood? I hate to break it to you, Ozzy, but I'm a wizard. Magic may not be a substitute itself, but it comes in handy when substitutes are what you need to find."

I offered him my hand. He politely ignored it, nodded to us and walked back. We all watched as the driver let him back into the limo, then took his own seat and drove off into the night. We all watched it vanish in silence. None of us had words, and everyone else had questioning looks.

I took the marker from my pocket, already dog-eared from minutes in my presence. My face finally cracked in years of relief. Tears shone down my face as I saw the smiles on everyone else's. I tossed the parchment into the air, where it broke apart as noiselessly as a dandelion in the wind into hundreds of tiny lights. A swarm of lightning bugs dispersed into the hot summer night. Word of an Oath fulfilled, a marker no longer held, would spread quickly as anything in a rumor mill does.

The moment passed. Byron smirked. "Don't humans call this Independence Day?"

Groans all around.

Babs shook her head. "I'm hungry."

Connie nodded. "Waffles. Definitely waffles."

Cyrus waved a finger in agreement. "And coffee."

Lori adjusted her collar. "Is it OK if I keep this, Trav? The husband could use some ideas."

Becky Sue nodded. "Oh, same here."

I waved a hand at both of them. "Help yourselves."

Seb secured his quiver in the truck. "Waffles, then a shower."

Bubba pointed at Seb. "Seconded."

Babs smirked. "All in favor?"

The ayes had it.

*　*　*

Chapter Twenty-Six

"Guideline One:

Thou. Art. Mortal."

"Hey all of you out there putting the super in supernatural, it's Bob the nite owl here on the Otherworld Overlook, the mouth of the Southeast, bringing you the word of the Otherworld.

Werewolf attacks along the Appalachian trail dropped sharply in the second half of the summer. My source in fish & game tells me that a trail of dismembered corpses from central Pennsylvania down to the Raburn Gap abruptly ended in early July. So for all you hunters out there, congratulations! You've got a little less competition. For now."

I shut off the radio as I pulled into the parking space, glancing with a smile at my date riding shotgun. The cool breeze welcomed me as I stepped out of the Yukon into the overcast false autumn day. It was late September, on the equinox. Georgia was finally starting to drop hints that maybe, just maybe, Summer wouldn't last forever. The existence of a cool breeze that didn't come from an air conditioner was, for now, a novelty enough to be worth savoring.

The time had gone by fast. We'd called ahead to Loretta's Waffle Crossing, picking up a massive takeout order for the nine of us before retiring to my place for a low-key victory party. We let the energy burn off while we devoured Grover's cooking, taking turns watching over Thumper, hosing off in the showers, and tending each other's wounds. Jazz, bless the woman, had done several loads of laundry while I'd taken my enforced nap, and I had more than enough fresh towels to be a decent host.

Marshal Sims arrived soon after we started eating. I gave him and Babs a room for privacy to work. I got the impression that if Babs hadn't been with us, he'd have brought in a team of hitters in to take turns grilling the pack of us. As it was, he just took Babs' report and volunteered to help get Thumper to safety. I kinda like him. Babs still wonders why I have no interest taking up a badge.

I promised everyone I'd keep in touch, and we started to go our separate ways. Most left before the sun rose: fed, washed, bandaged, and not quite too tired to drive. Seb stayed the longest, getting a good night's sleep and breakfast the next morning before taking the low road back to the Midwest. After he left, I locked the doors, activated the wards a little heavier than usual, let Jazz out of her ring long enough to tell her what had happened, and went back to bed.

I spent most of the next week in that bed. Proving to Jazz that I ate, slept, and bathed kept her from worrying too much. To be honest, it probably did me some good too. Otherwise I wouldn't have moved for much beyond using the facilities and feeding Shrapnel. Another week and I was a functional human again. I was still more bruise than skin for a while, but healing naturally was better for me than any of the alternatives available. I was grateful Bubba had knit my broken ribs back together before heading home.

Babs had told me Thumper was adjusting to treatment about as well as could be expected, but it looked like their addiction would be as permanent as mine was. I still thought about the blood more often than I was comfortable with. But I was also convinced Oswald was full of shit. At the end of the day, the blood was nothing but a passion and a power source. And I had plenty of each to choose from.

On a hunch, I called Connie. Turns out, she'd been having similar issues. One thing led to another quickly. When Thumper was released, I offered them one of my spare rooms. The three of us figured we were the only mages in the country who really understood each other. If that wasn't a good reason to coven up, what was? We've been watching each other's backs and looking for substitutes that worked for us ever since.

The Cotillion had been repaired, and was going to be reopened under an owner I'd never heard of. The wolfpack told me they'd been hired as a team for security purposes. Chittenden may be a ruthless, plantation-loving bastard, but he was good to his word.

I'd called everyone else who'd fought at Stone Mountain and had at least a good long conversation out of each call. One evening I dropped by at the tail end of office hours to say hi to Cyrus. Things ain't exactly warm between us, but at least we'd started talking to each other on occasion.

I'd started up my online business again. All I really had to do was get the website back up and running and sew some stock. It was slow going, but money thankfully wasn't an issue. Oswald had come by with retainer terms, and it turns out I was making more quarterly being an on-call magical expert than I had annually as a grunt. A part of me was still waiting for another shoe to drop. But instead I had the occasional direct deposit and was more or less left alone. Thank goodness for huge favors.

My date smiled brightly as she climbed out of the truck, paying more attention to the technical details of seat belt and shotgun side door than most. She'd only ridden in an SUV a dozen or so times before. She did look incredible in a pair of cutoff shorts and a crop top that complimented her sapphire blue eyes. Jazz was officially staying in my other spare room. Jazz told Connie and Thumper that we'd met overseas. The simple leather collar

Jazz wore around her neck and her habit of calling me Master convinced them they knew all the details they needed to. For now, they were right.

Connie and Thumper stepped out of the backseat. Connie was in the rougher side of her Goth finery, while Thumper had just broken in some jeans and a shirt since they'd moved in with me. All three of us sported a new patch on our gear bags: A bright red capital R followed by a shining white capital A, with a slash of both colors between them. All on a black field. Simple, as sigils go. But it worked for us.

We strolled across the parking lot together, Jazz and her strappy sandals keeping up with the scuffed boots worn by the rest of us. Our strides were occasionally punctuated by the cracking of shooting over at the range.

The four porchmen noted our approach. The tortie, in her feline wisdom, had chosen to again grace Keith's presence, curled up in the old man's lap as he scritched her ears idly. Lars, with his usual taste and discretion, was the first to greet us.

"Hey Grunt. What Goddess of mercy to sad sacks did you impress?"

I smirked. "Not sure, Lars. Just hope I never manage to piss her off. This is my friend Jazz, gentlemen. She'll be staying with me for a while."

Keith barely looked up from the attentions he was giving the cat. "My condolences, Ma'am."

The others snickered at that before nodding their own greetings. Matt took the toothpick out of his mouth in an impressive display of courtesy. "Where did our young friend find you, young lady?"

Jim snorted. "Five bucks says Antarctica."

I smiled, mostly at getting the reference, before shaking my head. Jazz gave one that was far more dazzling. "We met during the war, gentlemen. It's just taken me a while to get here. You can't even imagine the enhanced pat-downs."

I'd turned a bubbly bibliophile like Jazz loose in a world where double entendres were considered an art form. I might have created a monster.

Keith looked up once more. "I like this one. Keep her."

The old man had no idea. Most likely.

We made our way inside and caught the eye of Elaine, who directed us up the stairs with a nod and a wave of her hand. The couple before us didn't even notice that her attention had been split for a second. Up the grand staircase and to the first door on the right led us to the largest private dining room in the building.

All of the other Blue River survivors were gathered in the dining room that could easily seat three times their number. All were in their finest comfort wear and chatting up a storm. Several had brought family. I recognized Bubba's wife chatting away in a corner with Becky Sue. Seb and Cyrus were arguing about something at one of the windows. Byron was flirting with Lori's husband and Lori's wife simultaneously, which was par for the course for him. Two middle school aged kids played chess at another table. I couldn't have said whose they were if I was being interrogated.

Byron saw us first and raised his wineglass. "And now we are met! Renfields Anonymous and company are among us!"

Heads turned, not quite in unison but enough to put us on the spot. I decided to roll with it.

"Hi folks. This is my friend Jazz."

The silence was palpable as it was sudden. I looked both ways, wondering what the silent treatment was about before finally shrugging. "Don't everyone say hi at once."

Cyrus opened up his hand. Seb rolled his eyes, dug a dollar out of his pocket, and handed it over.

I raised my eyebrow at that one. "You have got to be kidding me!"

Bubba nodded. "Yeah. Now Babs owes me five."

Lori stepped forward and shook Jazz's hand, which Jazz remembered her practice and returned easily. Lori smiled and shook her head. "Pay no attention to them. We've just wondered when Travis was going to wander out of his workshop and actually socialize for once."

Jazz blushed and turned to me. "I didn't mean to make things awkward."

I shrugged and gave her a confident smile. "I don't mind the awkward if you don't."

Our loved ones surged forward. Hands shook and embraces were traded. Some took their turns in welcoming Thumper home. Others welcomed Connie, Byron, and Jazz to the first gathering of its kind.

At sunset, pictures of our fallen were produced and leaned against a mantlepiece along the back wall. From my cargo pocket, I took the picture of Heather I'd kept in a pocket for so long and put it on display next to the others. I stepped back from it to find Thumper, Connie, and Jazz were all by my side. Thumper stepped up to get a closer look, turned back to smile at me, then gently blew a kiss in Heather's direction.

I want to be remembered like this for a thousand years.

"You really did love her, didn't you?" said Connie. She was her usual stoic self, but I noticed a bit of softness in her eyes that told me she was getting sentimental.

I looked down and hugged Thumper, who clung as tight to me as I did to them and showed no intention of letting go. "Yeah. Yeah, we did."

Candles were lit and toasts were given. Stories were told and gossip was exchanged. Jazz, who had heard very little of them before, swiftly became a popular listener. As we feasted and laughed in our chosen haven, Summer quietly gave way to Autumn. We were too busy with each other to pay much attention to watching the one leave or the other arrive.

None of our problems were solved that night. But for the first time in a long time, a lot of us believed doing so was possible. That made all the difference.

*   *   *

EPILOGUE

Babs sat in the Wacross booth with her back to the rest of the clientele, a position that normally would professionally annoy her. The diner sat, as all of its kind did, on an old crossroads that happened to be off a highway exit between Nashville and Chattanooga. Far from my senses both magical and mundane.

Sitting opposite Babs was Marshal Jimbo Sims. Babs didn't mind at all that Jimbo had the seat with his back to the wall. For one, rank hath its privileges. For another, if anyone had been stupid enough to violently interrupt a pair of marshals in the middle of a Wacross, Jimbo would be faster on the draw than anyone else.

Finishing the last bite of his pancakes, Jimbo took a small brass cat from his pocket, laying it on the table between them. With a single finger, Jimbo began stroking the cat's back. Without moving, the brass cat started to quietly purr. The purring was a white noise charm, keeping their conversation from mundane or magical observation.

Jimbo held his hands together for a beat, then opened them. "How are they?"

Babs shrugged a little. "Too soon to tell. But Thumper's a month out from treatment and seems to have recovered well. Travis, Thumper, and

Connie meet once a week. Renfields Anonymous isn't the fanciest name for a coven, but it works for them. Chittenden and his subjects seem to have gotten the word that trying to turn a mage into a renfield is a bad idea."

Jimbo nodded, processing that. "And the rest of your investigation into Wayland?"

Babs shook her head negatively. "Still no evidence whatsoever of demonic influence. That's from observation of his home and sanctum as well as himself both in and out of combat. From what I can tell, he knew fulfilling this Oath was going to be a harsh duty to face alone. But he faced it, he survived it, and he's recovering as well as can be expected. He's even dating someone that seems to be good for him."

Jimbo nodded. "Thanks, Babs. I know that wasn't easy."

"You didn't offer me this job telling me it was easy."

He waved the thought off with a few fingers, like swatting a mental fly. "Fair enough. With any luck, that much time on it will let the Council be satisfied and back off. You and yours have suffered too much to keep dealing with this crap. Besides, we're going to need him sooner rather than later."

She nodded. "I appreciate it, sir. But let's be honest. As long as Neary's in charge, anyone says boo around any of us and we're going to be facing this crap again."

Jimbo steepled his fingertips, then opened his hands in concession. "I hear ya. And it is crap. Hopefully we'll be rid of it in the long run." He took a long breath, then looked in her eyes. "This next I got to ask too."

Babs barely opened her mouth before Jimbo held up a hand to silence her. The look in his eyes hardened. "I know we normally don't operate like this. I am not questioning your loyalty, or your judgment. I never would have brought you aboard if I did. But I need to know. And it'll save us a lot of screwing around if you're open and to the point about it. You already know what's at stake here."

Babs held her jaw tight, waiting for Jimbo to ask what she'd worried he would.

He asked.

She looked him in the eyes, and slowly breathed out. A long moment later, she began to slowly shake her head.

"No. None of them suspect a thing."

*   *   *

About the author

Jay Peterson has a resume that would let him take over the world, but he's seen the paperwork and wants none of it.

When not writing, Jay is a film and TV actor, best known (at the moment) for his appearance in *The Conjuring: the devil made me do it.*

He lives with his family outside of Atlanta, GA.

You can follow his exploits at Jaythebarbarian.com.

www.ingramcontent.com/pod-product-compliance
Lightning Source LLC
Chambersburg PA
CBHW070620300726

48975CB00006B/1877